L.A. Dead

Books by Stuart Woods

FICTION

L.A. Dead*
The Run
Worst Fears Realized*
Orchid Beach
Swimming to Catalina*
Dead in the Water*
Dirt*
Choke
Imperfect Strangers
Heat
Dead Eyes
L.A. Times
Santa Fe Rules
New York Dead*
Palindrome
Grass Roots
White Cargo
Under the Lake
Deep Lie
Run Before the Wind
Chiefs

TRAVEL

A Romantic's Guide to the Country Inns of Britain and Ireland (1978)

MEMOIR

Blue Water, Green Skipper

*A Stone Barrington Book

L.A. Dead

Stuart Woods

G. P. PUTNAM'S SONS

NEW YORK

This is a work of fiction. Names, characters, places, and incidents either are the product of the author's imagination or are used fictitiously, and any resemblance to actual persons, living or dead, business establishments, events, or locales is entirely coincidental.

G. P. Putnam's Sons
Publishers Since 1838
a member of
Penguin Putnam Inc.
375 Hudson Street
New York, NY 10014

Published simultaneously in Canada

Library of Congress Cataloging-in-Publication Data

Woods, Stuart.
L.A. dead / Stuart Woods.
p. cm.
ISBN 0-399-14664-4
1. Barrington, Stone (Fictitious character)—Fiction.
2. Private investigators—New York (State)—New York—Fiction.
3. New York (N.Y.)—Fiction. 4. Venice (Italy)—Fiction.
I. Title: L.A. dead. II. Title.
PS3573.O642 L15 2000 00-028059
813'.54—dc21

Printed in the United States of America

1 3 5 7 9 10 8 6 4 2

This book is printed on acid-free paper. ♾

BOOK DESIGN BY LYNNE AMFT

This book is for Barbara Danielson and Lewis Moore.

L.A. Dead

Chapter 1

ELAINE'S, LATE. Stone Barrington and Dino Bacchetti sat at table number four, looking grim. Elaine joined them.

"So, what's happening here? You two look like you're going to start shooting any minute."

"I'm getting married," Stone said. "Congratulate me."

"Congratulations," Elaine said. "Anybody you know?"

"Hilarious," Stone said.

"It would be, if it weren't so insane," Dino added.

"You and Dolce are really going to do this?" Elaine asked, incredulous.

"Now don't *you* start," Stone growled.

"He won't listen to me," Dino said. "I've been telling him for a year to stay away from her."

"What've you got against your sister-in-law?" Elaine asked him.

"First of all, she's my sister-in-law," Dino replied. "Second, she's evil. Her old man is the devil, and Dolce is his handmaiden."

"Don't start that again, Dino," Stone said. "I don't want to hear it anymore. We're in love, we're getting married, and that's it. What's wrong with that?"

Elaine shrugged. "You're still in love with Arrington," she said. "Everybody knows that."

"What do you mean, 'everybody'?" Stone demanded.

"Me and Dino," Elaine replied.

"Right," Dino chimed in.

"She's married; she has a child," Stone said.

"So?" Elaine queried. "So, she's married to a movie star; nobody ever took a girl away from a movie star? Happens all the time."

"I'm not breaking up anybody's marriage," Stone said, "and Arrington knows it. I've told her so. Anyway, there's the boy."

"Wouldn't be the first kid raised by a stepfather," Elaine said.

"I think it's Stone's kid, anyway," Dino said.

"Dino, I told you, the blood test was done; I saw the lab report. The boy is Vance Calder's, and that's all there is to it. I'm not taking a kid away from his father. Besides, I like Vance."

"What's not to like?" Elaine asked. "He's handsome; he's the biggest star in Hollywood; he's the most charming man I ever met." She sipped her drink. "Present company included," she added.

"Thanks," Stone said. "I needed that."

"So, when's the happy day?" Elaine asked. "You going to be a June bride?"

"Monday," Stone replied. "In Venice."

"This is Thursday," Elaine pointed out. "What the hell are you doing here?"

"We're leaving tonight," Stone said.

"I got news for you. It's after midnight, all the flights have departed."

"We're taking a private jet, belongs to some friend of Eduardo."

"Not bad," Elaine said, looking impressed. "That way, you get to your hotel late enough tomorrow, so you don't have to wait for the people in your room to check out."

"Eduardo has a palazzo," Dino said. "We're being forced to stay there."

"You're going, too?" Elaine asked, incredulous again.

"He's my best man," Stone said glumly.

"If I don't go, my wife will divorce me," Dino said.

"She's Italian," Elaine pointed out. "She won't divorce you."

"The Bianchi family has found a way around that," Dino said. "Remember how Dolce got divorced?"

"I didn't know she was married," Elaine said.

"A youthful indiscretion. She married a capo in the Bonnano family when she was nineteen. It lasted less than three weeks, until she caught him in her bed with her maid of honor."

"So she got a divorce?"

"Not for some years. When it was inconvenient for her to still be married, the guy turned up in New York dead. Took two in the back of the head, a classic hit."

"Let me get this straight," Elaine said, turning toward Stone. "The girl you're marrying on Monday in Venice had her ex popped?"

"Of course not," Stone said hotly. "That's Dino's theory. In the guy's line of work, it was an occupational hazard. Anybody could have had it done."

"Yeah, sure," Dino said. "Funny, it didn't get done until Dolce decided to throw a bag over Stone's head and lead him to the altar."

Stone glanced at his watch. "Dolce and Mary Ann are going to be here any minute. I want you to decide what you're going to do, Dino; are you going to stand up for me, or not? And if you are, I don't want to hear another word about Eduardo and his connections. You married into the family, too, remember?"

"Yeah, with a bun in the oven and a gun to my head. If I hadn't married her, I'd be at the bottom of Sheepshead Bay right now, with a concrete block up my ass."

"You love that girl, Dino," Elaine said, "and the boy, too. You know goddamned well you do."

Dino looked into his drink and said nothing.

"Make up your mind, Dino," Stone said. He looked up to see Dolce and Mary Ann walk into the restaurant. "They're here." He stood up to greet them.

"All right, all right," Dino said. "I guess I can't let you go over there by yourself."

Stone kissed the gorgeous Dolce. She was wearing a cashmere track suit and a huge smile.

"Everybody ready?" she asked. "The car's at the curb, all the bags are in the trunk."

"Everybody's ready," Stone said, shooting a warning glance at Dino.

Elaine stood up and kissed everybody. "Mazeltov," she said. "Send me a postcard."

"Come with us," Stone said. "There's room."

"And who'd mind the store?" she asked.

"You've got plenty of help here."

"They'd steal me blind. Go on, get going; send me a postcard from Venice."

"You bet," Stone said, hugging her.

The foursome left the restaurant. At the curb a spectacular car was waiting.

"What is this?" Stone asked, running a finger along the glossy paintwork.

"It's a Mercedes Maybach," Dolce replied. "The first one in the country. Papa knows somebody in Stuttgart."

"Papa knows somebody *everywhere*," Dino muttered, collecting a sharp elbow in the ribs from Mary Ann.

They piled into the spacious rear seats, facing each other, Pullman style.

"Not bad," Dino admitted, looking around. "I don't suppose there's a phone? I've gotta check in with the cop shop." Dino ran the detective squad at the nineteenth precinct.

"Oh, leave it, Dino," Stone said. "They can get along without you for a week."

Dolce handed Dino a phone, and he began dialing. "Did you pack all my stuff?" Dino asked Mary Ann.

"Everything's in the trunk," she replied. "I ironed your boxer shorts, too." She winked at Dolce. "They love it when you iron their underwear."

"I'll remember that," Dolce laughed.

"Gladys," Dino said into the phone, "I'm off. You've got the number in Venice if anything really important comes up, otherwise I don't want to know, got that? Good. Take care." He hung up. "Okay, I'm cut loose," he said to the others. "What kind of jet we going in, Dolce? I hate those little ones; this better be a G-Four or better."

"Wait and see," Dolce said smugly.

4

They drove onto the tarmac at Atlantic Aviation at Teterboro Airport, across the Hudson in New Jersey, and up to an airplane that dwarfed everything on the ramp.

"Holy shit!" Dino said as they got out of the limousine. "What the fuck is this?"

"It's a BBJ," Dolce replied, grabbing her jewelry box and cosmetics case from the backseat. The others took their hand luggage from the trunk.

"Sounds like a sandwich."

"A Boeing Business Jet, the biggest thing in the corporate skies."

Hank Esposito, who ran Atlantic Aviation, was at the airplane's stair door to greet them. "You're fueled for maximum range," he said. "You could make it to Tokyo, if you wanted."

"Not a bad idea," Dino said, boarding the airplane.

"*Dino . . .*" Stone warned.

Esposito helped the chauffeur stow the luggage into a forward area of the interior.

The party stepped into a cabin that looked like the living room of a New York City town house.

Stone was flabbergasted. "Where's the fireplace and the grand piano?" he asked.

An Armani-clad stewardess took their hand luggage and showed them through the airplane. Besides the big cabin, there was a conference room and, behind that, two sleeping cabins, each with its own bathroom.

Dino shook his head. "The wages of sin," he said under his breath, avoiding Stone's glance.

As if from a great distance, there was the sound of jet engines revving, and almost imperceptibly, the big airplane began to move.

Chapter 2

SOMEWHERE OVER THE ATLANTIC, Stone stirred in his sleep and turned over, bringing his chest against Dolce's naked back. He reached over her and cupped a breast in his hand, resting his cheek on the back of her neck. With thumb and forefinger, he lightly caressed the nipple.

At that moment, a chime sounded and the soft voice of the stewardess spoke. "Ms. Bianchi, we're two hours from our destination. If you and your party would like breakfast, it will be ready in half an hour."

"I think we're going to be late for breakfast," Stone breathed into Dolce's ear.

She turned over, put her feet on the floor, and stood up. "No, we're not," she said.

"You mean you're spurning your intended?"

"I mean I've decided to be a virgin until we're married."

"Isn't it a little late for that?"

"I can start over whenever I like," she said, "and I've just started over."

Shortly, they joined Dino and Mary Ann at the breakfast table. Scrambled eggs and smoked Italian bacon were set before them.

"That was the best night's sleep I've ever had on an airplane," Dino admitted.

"We didn't sleep all *that* much," Mary Anne rejoined, poking him in the ribs.

Stone indicated the large moving map at the front of the cabin. "We're just crossing the Portuguese coast," he said. "Nice tailwind; we're doing over six hundred miles an hour."

The moving map dissolved, and CNN International appeared on the screen.

"Turn that off," Dolce said to the stewardess. "I don't need news for a while."

The stewardess pressed a button, and Vivaldi came softly over hidden speakers. "Better?" she asked.

"Perfect," Dolce said. She turned to Stone and the others. "I have a little announcement," she said.

"Shoot," Stone replied.

"Papa is giving us the Manhattan town house for a wedding present."

Stone stopped eating. His fiancée was referring to a double-width brick-and-granite mansion in the East Sixties that Eduardo Bianchi had built. He took Dolce's hand. "I'm sorry, my dear, but I can't accept that. It's very generous of Eduardo, but I already have a house, and we'll be living there."

"Don't I have any say in where we live?" Dolce asked.

"You've never asked me very much about my background," Stone said, "so it's time I told you about my family."

"I know all about that," Dolce replied.

"Only what you read in the report Eduardo had done on me. It doesn't tell you everything."

"So, tell me everything," she said.

"My parents were both from wealthy textile manufacturing families in western Massachusetts, the Stones and the Barringtons; they knew each other from childhood. Neither of them liked the plans their families had made for them. When the crash came in 'twenty-nine, both families were hit hard, and both had lost their businesses and most of their fortunes by the early thirties.

"My parents used this upheaval as an opportunity to get out from under their parents' thumbs. My mother left Mount Holyoke, where she was studying art, and my father left Yale, where he was meant to study law, although the only thing he had ever wanted to do was carpentry and woodworking; they married and moved to New York City. My father's family disowned him, because he had joined the Communist party; my mother's family disowned her, because she had married my father.

"They found themselves very broke and living in a Greenwich Village garret. My mother was doing charcoal drawings of tourists in Washington Square for fifty cents a shot, and my father was carrying his toolbox door to door, doing whatever handyman's work he could find, for whatever people would pay him. He was about to go off and join the Civilian Conservation Corps, just to stay alive, when a wonderful thing happened.

"My mother's aunt—her mother's sister—and her new husband bought a house in Turtle Bay, and my aunt hired my father to build her husband a library. That job saved their lives, and when it was done, Aunt Mildred and her husband were so pleased with it that they also comissioned my father to design furniture for the house and my mother to paint pictures for some of the rooms. When their friends saw the house, they immediately began offering him other commissions, and before too many years had passed, both my parents had won reputations for their work. I didn't come along for quite a long time, but by the time that accident had occurred, they could afford me."

Dolce started to speak, but Stone stilled her with a raised hand.

"There's more. Many years later, when Aunt Matilda died, having been preceded by her husband, she left the house to me. I was still a cop then, working with your brother-in-law, and I poured what savings I had into renovating the house, doing a great deal of the work myself, using skills learned in my father's shop. Finally, after leaving the NYPD—by popular request—I was able to earn a good enough living as a lawyer to finish the house. So, you see, the house is not only a part of my family history, it is all I have left of my parents and the work they devoted their lives to. I have no intention of moving out of it, ever. I hope you understand, Dolce."

Nobody moved. Stone and Dolce stared expressionlessly at each other for a very long moment, then Dolce smiled and kissed him. "I understand," she said, "and I won't bring it up again. I'll be proud to live in your house."

"I'll be happy to explain things to Eduardo," Stone said.

"That won't be necessary," Dolce replied. "I'll explain it to him, and, I promise, he'll understand completely."

"Thank you, my dear," Stone said.

"So," Mary Ann said, changing the subject, "what's the plan for Venice?"

"We'll go directly from the airport to Papa's house," Dolce said. "We'll have dinner with him tonight; tomorrow, Saturday, the civil ceremony will be held at the town hall, where we'll be married by the mayor of Venice. Then, on Monday morning, a friend of Papa's from the Vatican, a cardinal, will marry us at St. Mark's, on the square of the same name. After that, Stone and I will go on a honeymoon, the itinerary of which I've kept secret even from him, and the rest of you can go to hell."

"Sounds good," Mary Ann said.

"Who's the cardinal?" Dino asked.

"Bellini," Dolce replied.

"Doesn't he run the Vatican bank?"

"Yes, he does."

"How like Eduardo," Dino said, "to have his daughter married by a priest, a prince of the Church, and an international banker, all wrapped up in one."

"Why two ceremonies?" Stone asked.

Mary Ann spoke up. "To nail you, coming and going," she said, laughing, "so you can never be free of her. The two marriages are codependent; the civil ceremony won't be official until the religious ceremony has taken place, and the priest—pardon me, the cardinal—has signed the marriage certificate."

"It's the Italian equivalent of a royal wedding," Dino said. "It's done these days only for the *very* important, and, as we all know, Eduardo . . ." He trailed off when he caught Stone's look.

"Eat your eggs, Dino," Mary Ann sighed.

Chapter 3

THE GLEAMING MAHOGANY MOTOR LAUNCH, the Venetian equivalent of a limousine, glided up the Grand Canal in the bright, spring sunshine. Stone looked about him, trying to keep his mouth from dropping open. It was his first visit to the city. The four of them sat in a leather banquette at the stern of the boat, keeping quiet. Nothing they could say could burnish the glories of Venice.

The boat slowed and turned into a smaller canal, and shortly, came to a stop before a flight of stone steps, worn from centuries of footsteps. Two men dressed as gondoliers held the craft still with long boat hooks and helped the women ashore. As they reached the stone jetty, a pair of double doors ahead of them swung open, as if by magic, and Eduardo Bianchi came toward them, his arms outstretched, a smile on his handsome face. He embraced his daughters, shook hands fairly warmly with his son-in-law, then turned to Stone and placed both hands on his shoulders. "And my new son," he said, embracing him.

"Very nearly," Stone said. "It's good to see you, Eduardo, and it's very kind of you to arrange all this for us. Dolce and I are very grateful."

"Come into the house," Eduardo said, walking them toward the open doors. "You must be exhausted after your flight."

"Not really; it's hard to know how we could have been made more comfortable in the air," Stone said. "Once again, our gratitude."

Eduardo shrugged. "A friend insisted," he said. "Your luggage will be taken to your rooms. Would you like to freshen up, girls?"

The girls, dismissed, followed a maid down a hallway.

"Come into the garden," Eduardo said. "We will have lunch in a little while, but in the meantime, would you like some refreshment?"

"Perhaps some iced tea," Stone said. Dino remained silent. Eduardo ushered them through French doors into a large, enclosed courtyard, which had been beautifully planted, and showed them to comfortable chairs. Unbidden, a servant appeared with pitchers of iced drinks, and they were served.

"First of all, I must clear the air," Eduardo said. "I quite understand that you may be very attached to your own house; I would not impose mine on you."

Stone was once again astonished at Eduardo's apparently extrasensory intuition. "Thank you, Eduardo. It was a magnificent offer, but you are quite right—I am very attached to my own house. It is much caught up with my family's history in New York. Fortunately, Dolce has consented to live there."

"She is a smart girl," Eduardo said, smiling slightly. "I would have been disappointed in her, if she had begun her marriage by attempting to move her husband from a home he loves."

"I expect she will find my taste in interior decoration inadequate, and I have steeled myself for the upheaval."

"You are smart, too," Eduardo said. He turned to his son-in-law. "Dino, how goes it among New York's finest?"

"Still the finest," Dino replied.

"Are you arresting many innocent Italian-American businessmen these days?" Eduardo asked impishly.

"There aren't many left," Dino said. "We've already rehoused most of them upstate."

Eduardo turned back to Stone. "Dino disapproves of my family's former colleagues," he said. "But he is an honest policeman, and there are not many of those. Many of his other colleagues have also been 'rehoused upstate,' as he so gracefully puts it. Dino has my respect, even if he will not accept my affection."

"Eduardo," Dino said, spreading his hands, "when I have retired, I will be yours to corrupt."

Eduardo laughed aloud, something Stone had never heard him do. "Dino will always be incorruptible," Eduardo said. "But I still have hopes of his friendship." Eduardo glanced toward the French doors and stood up.

Stone and Dino stood with him. A tall, thin man with wavy salt-and-pepper hair was approaching. He wore a black blazer with gold buttons, grey silk trousers, and a striped shirt, open at the neck, where an ascot had been tied.

"Carmen," Eduardo said, "may I present my son-in-law, Dino Bacchetti."

To Stone's astonishment, Dino bowed his head and kissed the heavy ring on the man's right hand.

"And this is my son-in-law-to-be, Stone Barrington."

The man extended his hand, and Stone shook it. "Your Eminence," he said, "how do you do?"

"Quite well, thank you, Stone." Bellini held onto Stone's hand and stared into his face. "He has good eyes, Eduardo," he said to Bianchi.

Stone was surprised that the cardinal spoke with an American accent.

"My son," Bellini said to Stone, "it is my understanding that you are not a Roman Catholic."

"I am a believer, Your Eminence," Stone said, "but not a registered one."

Bellini laughed and waved them to their seats. He accepted a fruit juice from the servant, then reached into an inside pocket and took out a thick, white envelope sealed with red wax, and handed it to Eduardo. "Here is the necessary dispensation," he said. "The Holy Father sends his greetings and his blessing."

"Thank you, Carmen," Eduardo said, accepting the envelope.

If Stone understood this transaction correctly, he now had papal approval to marry Dolce. He was embarrassed that the necessity had never occurred to him. "Your Eminence, I am surprised that your accent is American. Did you attend university there?"

"Yes, and preparatory school and elementary school before that. I was born and raised in Brooklyn. Eduardo and I used to steal fruit together, before the Jesuits got hold of me." He said something to Eduardo in what seemed to Stone flawless Italian, raising a chuckle. He turned back to Stone. "I understand that you are engaged in the practice of law."

"That's correct."

"If I may torture the scriptures a little, it is probably easier for a camel to pass through the eye of a needle than for a lawyer to enter the Kingdom of Heaven."

"I tread as narrow a path as my feet will follow," Stone replied.

Bellini smiled. "I should hate to oppose this young man in court," he said to Eduardo.

"Are you a lawyer, as well?" Stone asked.

"I was trained as such at Harvard," Bellini replied, "and my work requires me still to employ those skills from time to time—after which I immediately visit my confessor. I should hate to die with the practice of law on my soul."

"I understand you also dabble in banking."

"Yes, but there is nothing so pure as money, used properly. I am required to ask you, Stone, if you have ever been married."

"No, Your Eminence; I've come close, but I've never been in serious trouble."

"And do you willingly consent to your wife's devout practice of her religion?"

"Willingly, Your Eminence. To deny Dolce anything could be dangerous to my health."

Bellini seemed to try not to laugh, but Dino couldn't help himself.

The women arrived, and they all moved to a table set in the center of the garden, where they feasted on antipasti, a pasta with lobster sauce, and a glittering white wine, served from frosted pitchers. During most of lunch, Eduardo and the cardinal conversed seriously in Italian.

When they got up from the table, Stone sidled over to Dino. "What were Eduardo and Bellini talking about at lunch?" he asked.

"Not you, pal," Dino said. "They were doing business." He glanced at his father-in-law to be sure he would not be overheard. "Eduardo still doesn't know how much Italian I understand."

Stone and Dolce took a walk together through the narrow streets of Venice, becoming hopelessly lost. They did a little window shopping and talked happily. Stone tried to find out where they were honeymooning, but Dolce would reveal nothing.

They returned to the palazzo in the late afternoon, ready for a nap. Stone was shown to a suite—sitting room and bedroom—that overlooked the Grand Canal. He dozed off to the sounds of motorboats and of water lapping against stone.

He dreamed something that disturbed him, but when he awoke, he couldn't remember what it was. He joined the others for cocktails with a strange sense of foreboding.

At cocktails, Eduardo's sister, Rosaria, was present; she was a large woman who perpetually wore the black dresses of a widow. Stone had met her at Eduardo's home in New York, where she had kept house for her brother since his wife's death. Her younger niece was named for her, but the family had always called her Dolce.

The cardinal was now dressed in a beautifully cut black suit.

Half an hour later they were all shown aboard Eduardo's motor launch and transported to dinner at the world-famous Harry's Bar. Stone suspected that Eduardo's presence alone would be cause for considerable deference from the restaurant's staff, but the presence of a cardinal sent them into paroxysms of service. Stone had never seen so many waiters move so fast and from so crouched a position.

They dined on a variety of antipasti and thinly sliced calf's liver with a sherry sauce, with a saffron risotto on the side. The wines were superlative, and by the time they had been returned to the Bianchi palazzo, Stone was a little drunk, more than a little jet-lagged, and ready for bed. Dolce left him at his door with a kiss and vanished down the hallway.

Stone died for ten hours.

Chapter 4

AT NINE O'CLOCK the following morning, Stone was resurrected by a servant bearing a tray of blood-red orange juice, toast, prosciutto, sliced figs, small pastries, and coffee. A corner of the huge tray held that day's *International Herald Tribune* and the previous day's *New York Times.* By the time he had breakfasted and done the crossword puzzle, it was after ten.

The servant knocked and entered. "Mister Bianchi requests that you be downstairs at eleven o'clock," he said. "The civil ceremony is to be at noon." He disappeared.

Stone shaved and showered then went to the huge cupboard where his clothes hung, all freshly pressed. He dressed in a white linen suit he had bought for the occasion, a pale yellow, Sea Island cotton shirt, a tie with muted stripes, and tan alligator oxfords. Finally, he tucked a yellow silk square into his breast pocket, stuffed his trouser pockets with the usual contents, including some lire, and consulted the mirror. It occurred to him that he might never look so good again.

The group gathered in the central hall of the palazzo. Dolce wore a dazzling white silk dress that showed a becoming amount of very fine leg and wore only a single strand of pearls for jewelry, along with the five-carat, emerald-cut diamond engagement ring supplied by a man of Stone's acquaintance in the diamond district of New York.

"You are very beautiful," Stone said to Dolce, kissing her.

"Funny, that's what I was going to say about you," Dolce replied. "I love the suit."

"It's my wedding dress," Stone explained.

Dino and Mary Ann were well turned out, and to Stone's astonishment, Aunt Rosaria wore a dress of white lace. She was, apparently, out of mourning, at least for the day.

"Is the cardinal coming?" Stone asked Dino.

"No," Dino replied. "Cardinals don't attend civil marriage ceremonies."

"I suppose not," Stone said.

They were escorted to the palazzo's jetty where a small fleet of gondolas, garlanded with flowers, awaited, and they were rowed down a bewildering series of canals to the town hall, where the mayor awaited on the jetty.

Moments later, the party was arranged before an impossibly ornate desk in the mayor's office. Much Italian was spoken. At one point, the mayor turned to Stone, his eyebrows lifted high.

"Say '*sì*,'" Dino whispered.

"*Sì*," Stone said.

Dolce also said, "*Sì*," then an ornate document was produced and signed by Stone and Dolce, then by the mayor and the witnesses. The mayor said something else, delivered sternly.

Dino translated. "He says, 'Remember, you are not yet entitled to the pleasures of the marriage chamber.'"

Back on the jetty outside the town hall, Stone discovered that the gondolas had been replaced by Eduardo's motor launch, and shortly, they were moving fast over open water, toward an island.

Dolce, who held fast to Stone's arm, explained. "Papa has taken the Cipriani Hotel for lunch."

"You mean the dining room?"

"I mean the entire hotel; Papa has many guests. There will be many people at lunch, but don't worry about remembering their names; they don't matter."

Stone nodded.

The hotel occupied the entire island, and lunch was held in its garden.

"Not much chance of party crashers," Dino commented as they walked into the garden. "Unless they swim well." He looked around at the huge crowd of guests who were applauding their entrance—middle-aged and elderly Italians, dressed for Sunday, who were demonstratively affectionate with Dolce and who behaved toward Eduardo pretty much as if he were the Pope. Stone was introduced to each of them, but the flood of Italian names passed him by.

"Who are these people?" he asked Dolce.

"Distant relatives and business acquaintances," she replied tersely.

Stone could not see any family resemblance. "Who are these people?" he asked Dino, when he had a chance.

"I can't prove it," Dino said, "but my guess is you'd have a real problem placing a bet, buying a whore, or getting a fix anywhere in Italy right now."

"Come on, Dino."

"You'll notice that, although there's a band and lots of food, there's no photographer?"

Stone looked around and couldn't see a camera in anybody's hands.

"My guess is, the wedding pictures will be taken Monday, at the church, and that none of these people will be there, which is okay with me. I certainly don't want to be photographed with any of them."

It was late afternoon before they returned to the palazzo. Stone was told to be downstairs at eight for cocktails, then he was allowed to stagger to his room, strip, and fall facedown on the bed, until he was shaken awake by a servant and told to dress. He'd had the bad dream again, but he still couldn't remember it.

Aunt Rosaria had prepared what Stone assumed was their wedding dinner. They ate sumptuously, then adjourned early, everyone being tired from the day's festivities.

"Sleep as late as you like," Eduardo said to the group. "Mass is at eleven tomorrow morning."

Each retired to his own room. Stone, having had a three-hour nap, was not yet sleepy; he changed into a sweater and decided to go for a walk.

He was almost immediately lost. There was a dearth of signs pointing to anywhere, except St. Mark's Square, and he didn't want to go there. Instead, he just wandered.

An hour later, he found himself approaching what he recognized from photographs as the Rialto Bridge. As he climbed its arc, a woman's head appeared from the opposite direction, rising as she walked backward toward him, apparently talking to someone following her. Immediately, Stone knew her.

The shining hair, the slim figure, the elegant clothes, the shape of her calves. It was Arrington. His heart did strange things in his chest, and he was suddenly overcome with the unexpected thrill of seeing her. Then he remembered that she was now Mrs. Vance Calder, of Los Angeles, Malibu, and Palm Springs, that she had borne Vance's child, and that he had sworn off her for life.

Stone was struck heavily by the fact that his reaction to seeing her was not appropriate for a man who would be married on the morrow, and he was suddenly flooded with what had been pent-up doubts about marrying Dolce. In a second, every reservation he had ever had about marriage, in general, and Dolce, in particular, swept over him, filling him with a sickening panic.

On Arrington came, still walking backward, talking and laughing with someone who was still climbing the other side of the bridge, probably Vance Calder. Stone recovered quickly enough to place himself in her path, so that she would bump into him. She would be surprised, they would laugh, Vance would greet him warmly, and they would congratulate him, on hearing of his plans.

She ran into him harder than he had anticipated, jarring them both. Then she turned, and she wasn't Arrington. She was American, younger, not as beautiful; the man following her up the bridge was young, too, and beefy.

"I'm awfully sorry," Stone said to her.

Her young man arrived. "You did that on purpose."

"I apologize," Stone said. "I thought the lady was someone I knew."

"Yeah, sure," the young man said, advancing toward Stone.

"Don't," the girl said, grabbing at his arm. "He apologized; let it go."

The man hesitated, then turned and followed the woman down the bridge.

Stone was embarrassed, but more important, he found himself depressed that the woman had not been Arrington. He stood at the top of the bridge, leaning against the stone railing, looking down the canal, wondering if the universe had just sent him a message.

Chapter 5

STONE WAS HAVING the unpleasant dream again, and in it, someone was knocking loudly on a door. Then someone was shaking him, and he woke up this time, remembering that Arrington had been in the dream.

A servant was bending over him. "Signore Bianchi asks that you come to the library at once," the man said. "Is not nessary to dress."

"All right," Stone replied sleepily. He looked at his bedside clock and saw that it was shortly before eight A.M. He found a large, terry robe in the wardrobe, put it on over his bedclothes, found his slippers, and, smoothing down his hair, hurried to the central hall, where the servant directed him to the library, a room he had not yet seen.

It was a large room, the walls of which were lined from top to bottom with leather-bound volumes, leaving room for only a few pictures. Stone thought he recognized a Turner oil of the Grand Canal. Eduardo, the cardinal, and Dino, all in dressing gowns or robes, stood before the fireplace.

"Good morning," Stone said. "Is something wrong?"

None of the men seemed to want to speak first. Finally, Eduardo spoke. "We have had some bad news from the States." He turned to his son-in-law. "Dino?"

Dino flinched as if he had been struck, then he began. "My office called a few minutes ago: Rick Grant from the LAPD called and left a message."

Stone knew Rick Grant; he was a detective assigned to the office of the chief of police of Los Angeles, who had been helpful to him on an earlier visit to California. "What is it?"

Dino took a deep breath. "Vance Calder is dead."

"I am very upset about this," Eduardo said. "Vance was my friend, too."

Stone knew that Eduardo was a stockholder, with Vance, in Centurion Studios and had been an investor in some of Vance's films. "How?" he asked Dino.

"He was shot. Last night, in his home."

"Murdered?"

"Yes; shot once in the head."

"Is Arrington all right?" He steeled himself for the answer.

"Yes; she's in a local hospital."

"Was she hurt?"

"No."

"Who shot Vance?"

"That's undetermined," Dino said. "But when I got back to Rick, he told me he thinks Arrington might be a suspect."

Stone found a sofa and sat down. "Jesus Christ," he said, then remembered in whose company he was. "Forgive me, Your Eminence."

The cardinal nodded soberly.

"I wouldn't put too much stock in that theory," Dino said. "You and I both know that, in cases like this, the spouse is always a suspect until cleared."

Stone nodded. He was trying to think what to do next but not getting anywhere.

The cardinal came and sat down beside him. "Stone," he said, putting a fatherly hand on his shoulder, "I am aware of your previous relationship with Arrington. Eduardo and I have discussed this at some length, and we agree that it would be extremely unwise to go forward with the wedding, until . . . this situation has been, in some way, resolved."

Stone looked at the man but said nothing.

Eduardo came and stood next to Stone. "This is very complicated," he said. "Both Dolce and I are friends of Vance's, and you, of course, were very close to Arrington. There will be many emotions at work for a while, so many and so confused that to proceed with the marriage at this time would be folly."

"Does Dolce know about this?"

Eduardo shook his head. "I am going to go and wake her now and tell her; this is my duty, not yours."

"I will come, too," the cardinal said. "She may need me."

Stone nodded. "All right. Tell her we'll talk the minute she's ready."

Eduardo and the cardinal left the room.

"What haven't you told me?" Stone asked Dino.

"Rick says Arrington hasn't made any kind of statement yet. She apparently can't remember what happened. They've put her under sedation in a private clinic, but . . ."

"But what?"

"Before she went under, she was asking for you; she said she wouldn't talk to anybody but you."

"I'll have to call her," Stone said.

"I told you, she's under sedation, and Rick didn't know the name of the place where they'd taken her."

"How about Peter? Where is he?"

"The servants are taking care of him; he has a nanny. Rick said his people had spoken to Arrington's mother, and she's on her way out there from Virginia."

"That's good."

"Did Rick say anything else at all?"

"No. He was going to make some calls, and he said he'd get back to me the minute he found out anything more."

Stone walked to the windows and looked out into the lovely garden. "Dino," he said, "did Arrington know that Dolce and I were being married this weekend?"

"I have no idea. Did you tell her?"

Stone shook his head. "I haven't talked with her since last summer; Dolce and I had dinner with them in Connecticut, at their place in Roxbury. It's only a few miles from my new place in Washington."

"And how did that go?"

"Not well. Dolce was very catty, obviously jealous. The next morning, Arrington showed up at my cottage and, well, sort of threw herself at me."

"And how did you handle that?" Dino asked.

"I managed to keep her pretty much at arm's length—though, God knows, that wasn't what I wanted. I told her I wouldn't do anything to harm her marriage, and that was pretty much that. A couple of minutes after she left, Vance showed up—I think he must have been following her. He asked if he had anything to worry about from me, and I told him he didn't. He thanked me and left. That was the last time I saw either of them."

"Sounds as though you handled the situation about as well as it could be handled."

"God, I hope so; I hope none of this has anything to do with Arrington and me."

"I hope so, too," Dino said, "but I'm not going to count on it."

"Come on, Dino, you don't really think she . . ."

"I don't know what to think," Dino said.

Eduardo and the cardinal returned, and Dolce was with them, her face streaked with tears. She came and put her arms around Stone.

Stone had never seen her cry, and it hurt him. "I'm sorry about all this, Dolce," he said to her.

"It's not your fault," she said. "You didn't have any control over her."

"Now, let's not jump to conclusions," he said. "We don't know what happened yet."

"All right, I'll give her the benefit of the doubt."

"You'd better get ready to go, Stone," Eduardo said.

"Go?"

"You're going to Los Angeles, of course," Eduardo said. "She asked for you, and she may not have anyone else."

"Her mother is on the way."

"Her mother can take care of the child, of course, but this is going to be a very difficult situation, given Vance's fame and position in the film community."

"Go, Stone," Dolce said. "We can't have this hanging over us; go and do what you can, then come back to me."

"Come with me," Stone said, wanting her protection from Arrington as much as her company.

"No, that wouldn't do. You're going to have to deal with Arrington on your own."

"My friend's jet is not available today," Eduardo said, "but there's a train at nine-thirty for Milano, and a one o'clock flight from there to Los Angeles. If you miss that, the trip will become much more complicated."

Stone held Dolce away from him and looked into her face. "You're sure about this?"

"I'm sure," Dolce said. "I hate it, but it's the only thing to be done; I know that."

He hugged her again, then left and went to his room, where he found that a servant had already packed most of this things. Half an hour later, he stood on the palazzo's jetty with Dino, Eduardo, the cardinal, and Dolce. He shook hands with Eduardo and Bellini. The cardinal gave him a card. "If I can ever be of service to you, please call me. Of course, I'll make myself available for a service when this situation has been sorted out."

"Thank you, Your Eminence," Stone said. He turned to Dolce and kissed her silently, then motioned Dino into the launch. "Ride with me," he said.

"Have you heard any more from Rick?" Stone asked as the launch pulled away from the jetty.

"No, but it's the middle of the night in L.A. Where will you be staying?"

"At the Bel-Air Hotel. Oh, will you call and book me a room?"

"I'll let Eduardo handle it; you'll get a better room."

A few minutes later they docked at the steps to the Venice train station. Eduardo's butler met them there with Stone's train and airplane tickets and took his bags. Dino walked him to the train.

"I wish you could come with me and help make some sense of this."

Dino shook his head. "I'm due back in the office first thing Wednesday. Call me when you've got your feet on the ground, and I'll help, if I can."

The train was beginning to move, and Stone jumped on. He and Dino managed a handshake before the train pulled out of the station.

Stone found his compartment and sat down. Stress often made him drowsy, and he dozed off almost immediately.

Chapter 6

EVEN A FIRST-CLASS transatlantic airline seat seemed oddly spartan after the pleasures of the Boeing Business Jet, but Stone managed to make himself comfortable. A flight attendant came around with papers; none of the English-language papers had the story yet, but he caught Vance's name in the headlines of an Italian journal.

He managed to sleep some more and had a decent dinner, which, for him, was lunch, then the lights dimmed, and Vance Calder's face appeared on the cabin's movie screen. It was a report from CNN International and mentioned no more than the bare bones of the story, which Stone already knew. He'd have to wait unti LAX for more news.

He thought about another flight, how if Arrington hadn't missed it, things would have been very different. They had planned a winter sailing holiday on the island of St. Mark's, in the Caribbean, and he had planned, once at sea, to ask her to marry him. She had called him at the airport as the flight was boarding and said she had just gotten out of an editorial meeting at the *The New Yorker,* for which she sometimes wrote pieces. There was no way for her to make the plane, but she would be on the same flight the following day. The airplane had taken off in the first flurries of what would become a major blizzard in New York, and there was no flight the next day, or the day after that.

Then he had a fax from her, saying the *The New Yorker* wanted a pro-file of Vance Calder, who hadn't given a magazine interview in twenty years. It was a huge opportunity for her, and she had begged to be allowed to miss their holiday. He had grudgingly agreed and had put the newly purchased engagement ring back into his suitcase, to await a return to New York.

Then he had been caught up in an extraordinary situation in St. Mark's, had become involved in a murder trial, and by the time he was ready to return to the city, there was a fax from Arrington saying that, after a whirlwind romance, she had married Vance Calder.

After that had come news of her pregnancy and her uncertainty about the identity of the father. The paternity test had come back in Vance's favor, and that was that. Now Vance was dead, and Arrington had turned Stone's life upside down once again.

Stone looked up at the cabin screen again. A film was starting, and it was Vance Calder's latest and last. Stone watched it through, once again amazed at how the actor's presence on screen held an audience, even himself, even now.

The time change was in Stone's favor, and they reached LAX in the early evening. Stone stepped off the airplane and found Rick Grant waiting for him. The LAPD detective was in his fifties, graying, but trim-looking. They greeted each other warmly.

"Give me your baggage claim checks," Rick said, and Stone complied. He handed them to another man. "The Bel-Air?" he asked Stone.

"Yes."

Rick guided Stone through a doorway, down a flight of stairs, and out onto the tarmac, where an unmarked police car was waiting. Rick drove. "You all right?" he asked.

"Well, it's three o'clock in the morning where I just came from, but after some sleep I'll be okay. How about you? How's the job?"

"I made captain; that's about it."

"How's Barbara?" Stone had introduced Rick to Barbara Tierney, who was now his wife.

"Extremely well; in fact, she's pregnant."

"At your age? You dog."

"How about that? I thought I was all through with child rearing."

"Bring me up to date on what happened, Rick, and don't leave anything out."

"The Brentwood station caught the case on Satuday evening, about seven P.M. Calder's Filipino butler called it in. There was a patrol car there in three minutes, and the detectives were there two minutes after that. Calder's body was lying in the central hallway of the house, face down. He'd taken one bullet here," he tapped his own head at the right rear, "from about three feet. He was still breathing when the patrol car got there, but dead when the detectives arrived."

"The gun?"

"Nine millimeter automatic; Calder owned one, and it hasn't turned up, in spite of a *very* thorough search."

"Where was Arrington when it happened?"

"In the bathtub, apparently. They were going out to dinner later. The butler heard the shot and sent the maid to find her. She was still in a robe when the detectives arrived. They noted the strong smell of perfume; there was a large bottle of Chanel No. 5 on her dressing table."

"And that made them suspicious, I guess."

"Yeah."

"But how would Arrington know that perfume can remove the residue from the hands of someone who's fired a gun?"

Rick shrugged. "It's the sort of thing that pops up on the news or in a television movie. Anybody could know it."

"Did Arrington say anything to the detectives?"

"She was distraught, of course, but she seemed willing to talk; then she fainted. By this time, an ambulance had arrived, and the EMTs revived her. When she came to, she seemed disoriented—gave her name as Arrington Carter and didn't recognize the maid or her surroundings. The maid called her doctor, and he arrived pretty quickly. He had the EMTs load her up and take her to a toney private hospital, the Judson Clinic, in Beverly Hills. After the crime scene team arrived, they went to the clinic to question Arrington but were told she'd been sedated and would be out for at least twenty-four hours."

"Anything missing from the house?"

"Calder's jewelry box, which, the butler said, had half a dozen watches and some diamond jewelry in it, and the gun. None of Arrington's stuff had been taken, according to the maid."

"So, Calder could have interrupted a burglary and gotten shot with his own gun for his trouble."

"That's one scenario," Rick said.

"And I guess another is that Arrington shot Vance during a quarrel, hid the gun and the jewelry box, scrubbed her shooting hand and arm with Chanel No. 5 and jumped into a tub, just in time to be found by the maid."

"That's about it."

"Any other scenarios?"

"Nope, just the two."

"How's the voting going?"

Rick shrugged. "I'd say the burglar is losing, at the moment."

"Are you serious?"

"I think the detectives would have felt better about her, if she'd kept her head and told them a convincing story. They weren't too keen on the hysterics and fainting."

"They think she was acting?"

"They think it's a good possibility. I'd find her a shrink, if I were you, and a lawyer, too. A good one."

The two men rode along in silence for a few minutes. Shortly, Rick turned off the freeway and onto Sunset Boulevard. A couple of minutes later he turned left onto Stone Canyon, toward the Bel-Air Hotel.

"Is there anything else you want to ask me, Stone?" Rick said. "Next time we meet, we might not be able to talk to each other so freely."

"I can't think of anything else right now. Any advice?"

"Yeah, get Centurion Studios involved; they're equipped to handle something like this, and I understand that Calder was a major stockholder, as well as their biggest star."

"I'll call Lou Regenstein tomorrow morning," Stone replied.

Rick turned into the hotel parking lot and stopped at the front entrance. "Good luck with this, Stone," he said. "Don't hesitate to call, but don't be surprised if I clam up or can't help. I'll do what I can."

"Thanks for all you've done, Rick, and thanks for meeting my flight, too."

"Your luggage will be here soon."

Stone shook his hand and got out of the car. He walked over the bridge to the front entrance of the hotel and into the lobby. "My name is Barrington," he said to the young woman at the desk. "I believe I have a reservation."

"Oh, yes, Mr. Barrington," she replied. "We've been expecting you." She picked up a phone and dialed a number. "Mr. Barrington is here."

A moment later a young man arrived at the desk. "Good evening, Mr. Barrington, and welcome back. My name is Robert Goodwood; I'm the duty manager. Did you have any luggage?"

"It's being delivered from the airport," Stone said.

"Then I'll show you to your suite."

The young man led the way outdoors and briskly up a walkway, asking about Stone's flight and making chitchat. He turned down another walkway and arrived at a doorway hidden behind dense plantings, unlocked it and showed Stone in.

Stone was impressed with the size and beauty of the suite, but concerned about the cost.

As if anticipating him, Goodwood said, "Mr. Bianchi has insisted that your stay here is for his account."

"Thank you," Stone said.

"I'll send your luggage along as soon as it arrives. Can I do anything else for you?"

"Please send me the New York and L.A. papers."

"Of course." Goodwood gave Stone the key and left.

Stone left the suite's door open for the bellman, shucked off his coat, loosened his tie, sat down on a sofa, and picked up the phone.

"Yes, Mr. Barrington?" the operator said.

"Would you find the number of the Judson Clinic, which is in Beverly Hills, and ring it?" he asked.

"Of course; I'll ring it now."

Apparently the hotel knew of the hospital.

"The Judson Clinic," a woman's voice breathed into the phone.

"My name is Stone Barrington," he said. "I'm a friend of Mrs. Arrington Calder. Can you connect me with her room, please?"

"I'm afraid we have no guest by that name or anything like it," the woman said.

"In that case, please take my name—Stone Barrington—and tell Mrs. Calder that I'm at the Bel-Air Hotel, when she feels like calling."

"Good night," the woman said, and hung up.

The bellman arrived with the luggage and the papers. "Shall I unpack anything, Mr. Barrington?" he asked.

"You can hang up the suits in the large case," Stone said. The man did as he was asked, Stone tipped him, and he left.

Stone picked up the papers. Vance had made the lower-right-hand corner of *The New York Times* front page and the upper-right-hand corner of the *Los Angeles Times*. The obituary in the L.A. paper took up a whole page. There was nothing in the news report he didn't already know.

Stone ordered an omelet from room service and ate it slowly, trying to stay awake, hoping Arrington would call. At eleven o'clock, he gave up and went to bed.

Tomorrow was going to be a busy day.

Chapter 7

THE TELEPHONE WOKE STONE. He checked the bedside clock: just after nine A.M. He swung his legs over the side of the bed and picked up the phone. "Hello?"

"Is this Stone Barrington?"

"Yes."

"This is Dr. James Judson, of the Judson Clinic."

"Good morning. How is Arrington?"

"She's been asking for you. I'm sorry the woman who answered the telephone last night didn't know that."

"When can I see her?"

"She's still sleeping at the moment, but why don't you come over here around noon? If she isn't awake by then, I'll wake her, and the two of you can talk."

"What is her condition?"

"Surprisingly good, but there are complications; we can talk about that when you arrive." He gave Stone the address.

"I'll see you at noon," Stone said. He hung up, then pressed the button for the concierge and ordered a rental car for eleven-thirty, then he called room service and ordered a large breakfast. While he was waiting for it to arrive, he called Centurion Studios and asked for Lou Regenstein, its chairman.

"Good morning, executive offices," a woman's voice said.

"Lou Regenstein, please; this is Stone Barrington."

"May I ask what this is about?"

"He'll know." Stone had met Regenstein the year before, when he was in Los Angeles on another matter involving Vance and Arrington.

A moment later, Regenstein was on the line. "Stone, I'm so glad to hear from you; you've heard what's happened, I'm sure."

"That's why I'm here; I got in last evening."

"I've been going nuts; the police won't tell me where Arrington is, and the coroner won't release Vance's body to a funeral home without her permission."

"Arrington is in a hospital; I'm going to see her at noon today."

"Is she all right? Was she hurt in the shooting?"

"She's fine, from all accounts. I'll be talking to her doctor, too."

"What can I do to help?"

"Lou, who is the best criminal lawyer in L.A.?"

"Marc Blumberg, hands down; does Arrington need him?"

"Yes, if only to contain the situation."

"He's a personal friend of mine; I'll call him right now. Where can he see Arrington?"

"I want to see her before she talks to another lawyer," Stone said. "Tell Blumberg to expect a call from me at some point, and to deny that he's representing Arrington, if the press should call in the meantime."

"All right." Regenstein gave him Blumberg's number. "Remember, Stone, Centurion is at Arrington's disposal—anything she needs; you, too. Look, I've had an idea: You're going to need some place to get things done while you're here. I'll make Vance's bungalow available to you for as long as you need it."

"Thank you, Lou; it would be good to have some office facilities."

"You remember Vance's secretary, Betty Southard?"

Indeed he did; Stone and Betty had spent considerable time together during his last visit to town, much of it in bed. "Of course."

"She's there, holding down the fort; I'll let her know you're coming, and I'll leave a pass for you at the main gate."

"Thank you, Lou, I'll be in touch later." Stone hung up and called his own office, in New York.

"Stone Barrington's office," Joan Robertson said.

"Hi, it's Stone."

"Oh, Stone, I'm so glad you called. Have you heard about Vance Calder?"

"Yes, I'm in L.A. now, at the Bel-Air Hotel."

"What's going on?"

"I haven't had time to find out, but I want you to go into our computer boilerplate, print out some documents and fax them to me soonest."

"What do you want?"

Stone dictated a list of the documents, then hung up. Breakfast arrived and he turned on the TV news while he ate. The local channels were going nuts; the biggest star in Hollywood had been murdered, and they couldn't find out *anything*. They were treading water as fast as they could, recycling what little information they had. They couldn't find Arrington, the police wouldn't issue anything but the most basic statement, Centurion had no comment, except to express deep loss and regret, and no friend of either Vance's or Arrington's would talk to the press, even off the record, not that any of them knew anything. That was good, he thought.

The phone rang. "Hello?"

"Mr. Barrington?"

"Yes."

"This is Hillary Carter, Arrington's mother."

"How are you, Mrs. Carter?"

"Terrible, of course, but I'm glad you're here. Arrington badly needs someone to take charge of things."

"Have you seen her?"

"Only for a few minutes, yesterday, and she was semiconscious. She was asking for you, though."

"I'm seeing her at noon today."

"Oh, good. The doctor doesn't want her to see Peter, yet; I don't know why."

"I'll see if I can find out."

"I'm at Vance's house, now, and the situation here is nearly out of hand. I've had to call the police to keep people from climbing over the fence."

"I'll see if I can arrange some private security."

"That would be a very good idea, I think."

"Is Peter all right?"

"Yes, but he wants his mother and father, and I'm having to stall him. What I'd like to do is to get him out of this zoo and take him home to Virginia with me. Arrington is quite happy for him to come with me."

"That might be a good idea. Can I call you after I've seen Arrington?"

"Yes, please; I'll give you Vance's most secret number. The press hasn't learned about it, yet."

Stone wrote down the number.

"I'm so sorry we've never met face to face," Mrs. Carter said. "Arrington has always spoken so well of you."

"Mrs. Carter, do you have any objection to my taking over all of Arrington's legal decisions and contacts with . . . everyone outside the family?"

"I'd be very grateful if you would, but of course, I'd like to be consulted about any medical treatment beyond what she's getting now."

"Of course. I'll talk to you later today." He said good-bye and hung up. There was a knock on the door, and an envelope was slid under it. Stone checked the contents and found the documents Joan had faxed to him.

He telephoned Lou Regenstein.

"Yes, Stone?"

"I've just spoken with Arrington's mother, who is at Vance's house with her grandson. She says the press there is out of hand, and she's had to call the police. Can you arrange for some private security to take over that?"

"Of course; how many men do you want?"

"She says they're coming over the fence, and my recollection is that they've got a large piece of property there."

"Something like eight acres," Regenstein said.

"I should think half a dozen men inside the fence, two in the house and a car patroling the perimeter of the place, twenty-four hours a day, for the time being."

"Consider it done; anything else?"

"Mrs. Carter wants to take Peter back to Virginia with her. Do you think you could arrange transportation?"

"The Centurion jet is at her disposal," Regenstein said. "I'll have a crew standing by in an hour."

"I shouldn't think she'd need it until later today. Is it at Burbank?"

"Yes, but the press would know that. I'll have it moved to Santa Monica and hangared at the Supermarine terminal, until she's ready to leave."

"Thank you, Lou. I'll call you later."

There was nothing else to do, Stone reflected. Dino would be in the air, now, on his way back to New York. He checked his notebook, dialed the palazzo number in Venice and asked for Eduardo.

"Stone?"

"Yes, Eduardo?"

"This is Carmen Bellini. Eduardo and Dolce are on their way back to New York. I'm spending a couple of more days here to rest, at his suggestion. Are you in Los Angeles?"

"Yes." Stone told him most of what he knew so far. "If Eduardo contacts you before I reach him, please pass on that information."

"Certainly. Is there anything I can do for you?"

"Pray for Arrington," Stone said.

He hung up, and it suddenly occured to him that, since he had left Venice, he had not thought of Dolce once.

Chapter 8

STONE COLLECTED HIS RENTAL CAR, a Mercedes E430, and drove to the Judson Clinic, arriving at noon. The place was housed in what had been a residence, a very large one, on a quiet Beverly Hills street, set well back from the road. The reception desk was in the marble foyer, and Stone asked for Dr. Judson.

A moment later, a man appeared on the upstairs landing, waving him up. Stone climbed the floating staircase and was greeted by a distinguished-looking man in his sixties, wearing a well-cut suit. Stone thought he would make an impressive witness, if it came to that.

"Mr. Barrington? I'm Jim Judson."

"Please call me Stone."

"Thanks. Come into my office, and let's talk for a moment, before we see Arrington."

Stone followed him into a large, sunny office and took a seat on a sofa, while Judson sat across from him in a comfortable chair.

"I want to tell you what I know, thus far, so that you'll be prepared when you see Arrington," he said.

"Please do."

"Arrington was brought here by an ambulance on Saturday evening, at the request of her personal physician, Dr. Lansing Drake, a well-known Beverly Hills doctor. She was alternately hysterical, disoriented, and lethargic. Dr. Drake explained briefly what had occurred at her residence, and he and I agreed that she should be sedated. I injected her with twenty milligrams of Valium, and she slept peacefully through the night.

"When she awoke on Sunday morning she seemed quite calm and normal, and she immediately asked that you be contacted. She said that you were on an island in the Caribbean called St. Mark's, and that she was supposed to meet you there. My staff made repeated attempts to contact you there, without success. I reassured her that we would find you, and she seemed to accept that. She slept much of the morning, had a good lunch. When she questioned why she was here I said that she had collapsed at home, and that I thought it a good idea for her to remain here for observation for a day or two. She accepted that.

"Late in the afternoon, her mother arrived, having flown in from Virginia. I was in the room when they met, and it became immediately apparent that Arrington was very disoriented. She seemed not to understand that she was married to Vance Calder, saying that she was supposed to interview him, but that she had changed her mind and had decided to meet you in St. Mark's instead. When her mother mentioned Peter, her son, she became disturbed again, but after a few moments seemed to understand that she had a son and that Calder was the father. Her mother, quite wisely, turned the conversation to trivial things, and after a few minutes she left. Arrington immediately went to sleep again."

"And what do you make of all this?" Stone asked.

"It seems clear that Arrington is undergoing periods of anterograde amnesia, brought on by the shock of her husband's murder. Anterograde amnesia is a condition during which the great mass of old memories, prior to a certain point, remain intact, while the subject does not have access to more recent memories, or those memories are intermittent or scrambled—this, as opposed to retrograde amnesia, during which the subject may lose memory of all prior events, even her identity."

"Forgive me, Jim, are you a psychologist?"

"A psychiatrist. This is, primarily, a psychiactric clinic, although we do some work with patients who have substance abuse problems."

"Is Arrington likely to recover all her memory?"

"Yes, if the basis for her amnesia is emotional, not physical, and that seems the case. Her mother had spoken with her on the previous Sunday and said that at that time she seemed perfectly normal. If she should show signs of not recovering her memory, then I think a brain scan would be in order, to rule out a physical basis for her problem."

"Does she know that Vance is dead?"

"That's hard to say; I haven't asked her that, directly, and when the police came here, I refused to allow her to be questioned."

"You did the right thing," Stone said.

"Arrington seems to have an idea that something may be wrong, but she tends to divert the conversation if it heads in a direction she doesn't want it to go. She may very well be, unconsciously, protecting herself emotionally from a situation which she is not yet ready to confront."

"I see. Perhaps it's time to explain to her what has happened?"

"Perhaps it is. She'll have to be told sooner or later, and since she seems to have an emotional attachment to you, it might be best that she hear it from you."

"All right. Jim, I should tell you that, for the moment, I am acting as Arrington's attorney, as well as her friend, and that, given the circumstances, you may be asked questions by the police. Should that occur, I advise you to rest on doctor-patient confidentiality and decline to answer. At a later date, with Arrington's concurrence, I may ask you to give a statement to the police or the district attorney."

"I understand completely."

"Shall we go and see Arrington, then?"

"Please follow me." Judson led the way from his office, down a hallway to the last door on the right-hand side. He knocked softly.

"Come in," a woman's voice replied.

Judson opened the door. "Arrington, I've brought someone to see you," he said. He stepped aside and ushered Stone into the room.

The room appeared much like a guest room in a sumptuous home, except for the elevated hospital bed. On the far side of the room, a cabinet had, apparently, once held a television set, which had been removed. Sunlight streamed through the windows, which were open above a garden at the rear of the house. Arrington sat up in bed and held out her arms. "Stone!" she cried.

Stone went to her and took her in his arms, kissing her on the cheek. To his surprise, she turned his head and gave him a wet kiss on the mouth. Stone glanced at the doctor, who evinced surprise.

"How are you feeling?" he asked.

"Much better. For a while, all I was doing was sleeping. What took you so long to get here?"

"I had to come a great distance," he replied. "Do you feel well enough to talk for a while?"

"Yes, I do; I feel very well, actually. I'm not quite sure why Dr. Judson is keeping me here."

"Your mother came to see you yesterday, remember?"

"Of course. We had a very nice visit. I'm sorry to have alarmed her; it was a long way for her to come, to find me perfectly well."

"She wanted to be sure Peter was all right without you."

Arrington's face clouded slightly. "Yes, she told me. I'm a little confused about that."

"How so?"

"Well, apparently—this is very embarrassing—I had forgotten that I'm his mother."

"That's all right," the doctor interjected. "Don't worry about that."

"Did you remember who Peter's father is?"

"Yes, after I was prompted, I'm ashamed to say. Stone, I'm so sorry; I wanted a chance to explain to you about Vance and me. I wrote to you in St. Mark's, but I suppose you must have already left there by the time the letter arrived. Can I explain?"

"Yes, go ahead," Stone said, sitting on the side of the bed.

She took his hand in both of hers. "Stone, I think I knew that you were going to ask me to marry you when I arrived in St. Mark's. Am I right, or am I being presumptuous?"

"You're right; I was going to ask you. I had a ring, even."

"I think I felt . . . a little panic about that, as if I weren't really ready to be your wife. I think that may be why I missed the first flight. The snowstorm was something of a relief, I'm afraid."

"You were a free woman," Stone said. "You didn't have to marry me."

"Then Vance arrived in town, and although we'd known each other before, something was different this time."

Stone recalled that Arrington had been with Vance, at a dinner party, when they had first been introduced.

"We spent all our time together, working on the interview, which turned into a *very* long conversation about everything in the world, and before I knew it, we were in love. I can't explain it; it just happened."

"It's like that, sometimes," Stone said.

"Do you hate me for it?"

"I could never hate you."

"Oh, I'm so relieved," she said, squeezing his hand. "I don't think I could be happy without you in my life—as a friend, I mean." She blushed a little.

"I feel the same way," Stone said. "And it's because I'm your friend that I have to tell you some things, now." Stone took a deep breath, looked directly into her large eyes, and told her.

Chapter 9

ARRINGTON STARED AT STONE as he spoke, her eyes wide and unblinking. Gradually, tears rimmed her eyes, then spilled down her cheeks. She seemed unable to speak.

Stone stopped talking for a moment. "Do you remember any of this?" he asked.

She shook her head, spilling more tears.

"What's the last thing you remember before Saturday?" Dr. Judson asked.

She closed her eyes tightly. "Someone cutting the grass," she said.

"And what day was that?"

"I'm not sure. I had a brief conversation with . . . Geraldo, his name is. I asked him not to cut the grass quite so closely. We agreed on two inches; I remember that."

"Do you remember what plans you and Vance had for Saturday night?" Judson asked.

She shook her head. "I'd have to look at the book."

"What book is that?"

"The book that Vance and I keep our schedules together in. I have my own book, too, for things I don't do with him, and he has his own book that Betty keeps."

"And who is Betty?"

"Betty Southard, his personal assistant; she works in his office at the studio."

"What were you doing immediately before you spoke to Geraldo?" the doctor asked.

"I was cutting flowers in the garden," she said.

"And what did you do after you finished cutting the flowers and speaking to Geraldo?"

Her shoulders sagged. "I don't remember. I suppose I must have gone back into the house, but I can't remember doing it."

"What jewelry had you planned to wear Saturday night?" Stone asked.

"Diamonds," she replied. "It was black tie."

"Who was the host?"

"What?"

"The host of the dinner party?"

"What dinner party?"

"The one on Saturday night."

She looked lost. "I don't remember."

"Did you take your jewelry out of the safe?"

"I don't know."

"What is the last thing you remember Vance saying to you?" Judson asked.

"He said I should wear the diamonds. He was taking his jewelry box out of the safe; I remember that."

"What else was in the safe?"

"I remember who was having the dinner party," she said. "It was Lou Regenstein."

"Did you enjoy the party?" Judson asked.

"I don't remember the party," she said.

"Arrington," Stone said, "does Vance own a gun?"

"I think so," she replied. "At least, he said he did. I've never seen a gun in the house."

"Do you know how to fire a gun?" Stone asked.

"My father taught me to fire a rifle, a twenty-two, when I was sixteen."

"Did he teach you to fire a pistol, too?"

She shook her head. "I don't think I've ever even held a pistol."

"Well," Dr. Judson said, "I think we've covered about enough for now."

"Is Peter all right?" Arrington asked.

"Your mother wants to take him back to Virginia with her for a visit."

"I think that's a good idea," Arrington said, nodding. "I want to say good-bye to him."

"Suppose you telephone him," the doctor said.

"Yes, I could do that." She turned to Stone. "Tell me the truth. I'm not crazy, and I want to know. Is Vance dead?"

"Yes," Stone replied. "I'm afraid he is."

She was silent, seeming to think hard. "Who's taking care of everything?" she asked finally.

"You mean the house? The servants are there."

"No, I mean, there has to be a funeral; things have to be done; decisions made. I don't know if I can do this."

"I'll help in any way I can," Stone said. He had intended to bring this up, himself.

"Oh, would you handle things, Stone? There are legal matters, too, I'm sure."

"Who is your lawyer?" Stone asked.

"You are, I guess; I don't have another one. Vance has one, but I can't think of his name."

"Would you like me to represent you both legally and personally?" Stone asked.

"Oh, yes, please, Stone. I'd feel so much better, if I knew you were handling everything."

"What about medical decisions?"

"I'll make those myself," she said. "Unless I'm not able to, then I'd like you to make those decisions, too."

Stone opened a hotel envelope and took out a sheaf of papers. "Dr. Judson, do you believe that Arrington is capable of making decisions about her affairs?"

"I don't see any reason why she shouldn't," the doctor replied.

"Do you have a notary public here?"

"My secretary," he said, picking up a phone.

The woman arrived shortly with her stamp.

Stone explained each of the documents to Arrington—a general power of attorney, a medical authorization, an agreement appointing him as her attorney, and a letter addressed, "To whom it may concern," stating that Stone had authority to act on her behalf in all matters, business and personal. When everything had been signed, notarized, and witnessed by the doctor, Stone kissed Arrington good-bye.

"I'll be back to see you tomorrow and bring you up to date on events," he said. "Why don't you call your mother now, and say good-bye to Peter?"

"All right. Stone, I'd like it very much if you would stay in our . . . my home; it would be comforting to know you are there. Manolo and the staff will make you comfortable in the guest house, and use the phones, the cars, anything you need."

"Thank you, I may do that," Stone said. "I'm going to go over there now and drive your mother and Peter to the airport. Will you tell her I'm on my way?"

"Yes, of course."

"Is there another way to the house besides through the front gate?"

"Yes, there's a service entrance about a hundred yards down the road, and there's a utility service road into the back of the property; you enter it from the street behind. I'll tell Manolo to open it for you."

"Thanks, that would be good." He kissed her again and left with the doctor. "What did you think, Jim?" Stone asked as they walked down the corridor.

"My diagnosis hasn't changed. She seems to remember something about that night, the thing about the jewelry; I'd like to know exactly when the conversation with the lawn man took place."

"So would I," Stone said. He thanked the doctor, then drove to Vance's house, entering through the utility road, where a servant stood waiting to close the gate behind him. He parked in a graveled area near the back door and went inside, where he was greeted by Manolo, the Filipino butler.

"It's good to see you again," Mr. Barrington.

"Thank you, Manolo," Stone replied. "I wish the circumstances were different. Mrs. Calder has suggested I move into the guest house."

"Yes, Mrs. Calder's mother passed on that message," Manolo said. "The guest house is all ready for you."

"I'm going to take Arrington's mother and Peter to the airport now, and after that I'll go back to the Bel-Air, return my rental car, and take a cab back here. Mrs. Barrington suggested I use one of her cars."

"Of course, and I'll give you a remote that will open the back gate, too," Manolo said. "I'm afraid the media have the front gate staked out—permanently, it seems."

A man approached Stone. "Are you Mr. Barrington?"

"Yes."

"My name is Wilson; I'm commanding the security detail here."

"Good; what kind of vehicles do you have available?"

"I've got a Chrysler van with blacked-out windows, and two unmarked patrol cars."

"I'd like you to drive Mrs. Carter and the boy to Supermarine, at Santa Monica Airport. The Centurion Studios jet is waiting there to fly them to Virginia."

Mrs. Carter appeared in the hallway, a handsome little boy of two holding her hand. "Hello, Stone," she said. "Have you met Peter?"

Stone knelt and took the boy's small hand. "Not since he was a baby," he said. "Peter, you're getting to be a big boy."

"Yes, I am," the boy said gravely.

There was something familiar in the child's face, Stone thought—some characteristic of Vance or Arrington, he wasn't sure just what. "You're going to get to ride on a jet airplane this afternoon," he said.

"I know," Peter replied. "My bags are all packed."

Two maids appeared, carrying the luggage, and everyone was bundled into the van.

"I'll lead the way out the back," Stone said, "and I'd like a patrol car to follow us. If necessary, I'd like that car to block the road."

"I understand," Wilson replied. He spoke softly into a handheld radio. "My people are assembling out back, now. Shall we go?"

"Manolo," Stone said, "I'd like to talk with you when I get back."

"Of course, Mr. Barrington," Manolo replied. "I thought you might wish to." He handed Stone a small remote control for the rear gate.

"By the way," Stone said, "on what days is the lawn mowed?"

"The man is here today," the butler replied. "Ordinarily, it's on Fridays, but he was ill last Friday."

"When was the last time he was here?"

"A week ago Friday."

"Do you recall Mrs. Calder having a conversation with him on that day?"

"Yes, she asked him not to cut the lawn so closely. She asked me to see that it was done."

"A week ago Friday?"

"Yes, sir."

"Thank you, Manolo. And do you recall if Mr. and Mrs. Calder went out that evening?"

Manolo looked thoughtful. "Yes, they went to Mr. Regenstein's home for dinner. I drove them; the chauffeur was on vacation."

"Was it a black tie dinner?"

"Yes, sir; Mr. Calder was dressed in a dinner suit."

"And do you remember what jewelry Mrs. Calder wore?"

"She wore diamonds," he said. "She usually does, when it's a black tie event."

"Thank you, Manolo; I should be back in a couple of hours."

"Will you be dining here, then?"

"Yes, I think I will," Stone said.

"I'll tell cook."

"Something simple, please; a steak will be fine."

"Of course."

Stone helped Mrs. Carter and Peter into the van, then got into his own car. They made it out the back way undetected.

Chapter 10

STONE SAW MRS. CARTER and Peter off on the Centurion jet, then returned to the Bel-Air, checked out, left his rent-a-car with the parking attendant, and took a cab back to the Calder residence. He had thought of returning through the rear entrance, but he didn't want a cab driver to know about that, so he called Manolo and asked him to be ready to open the front gate. There was only a single television van at the gate when he arrived, and the occupants took an immediate interest in him, but before they could reach the cab with a camera, he was safely inside. Before he got out of the cab, he handed the driver a hundred-dollar bill. "That's for not talking to the TV people about who you delivered here," he said.

"Thank you, sir," the man said, "but I don't know who you are, anyway."

"Just don't stop when you go out the gate."

Manolo and a maid took Stone's bags through the central hallway of the house, out the back, and around the pool to the guest house. Stone thought the little house was even nicer than the suite at the Bel-Air. While the maid unpacked for him and pressed his clothes, Stone walked back into the house with Manolo.

"You said you wished to speak with me, Mr. Barrington?"

"Yes, Manolo; it's important that I know everything that happened here on Saturday night. Please tell me what you saw and heard."

"I was in my quarters, a little cottage out behind the kitchen entrance, when I heard a noise."

"How would you characterize the noise?"

"A bang. I didn't react at first, but I was curious, so I left my quarters, entered the house through the kitchen door and walked into the central hall." He led the way into the house.

"Which door did you come through?" Stone asked.

"That one," Manolo replied, pointing to a door down the hall.

"And what did you see and hear?"

"I saw Mr. Calder lying right there," he said. "He was lying . . . he . . ."

"Can you show me?"

"Yessir." Manolo walked to the spot and lay down on his side, then rolled partly on to his belly. "Like this," he said. "Can I get up, now?"

"Yes, of course."

Manolo stood up. "He had a hole in his head here," he said, pointing to the right rear of his own head. It was bleeding."

"Did you think he was alive?"

"Yessir, he was. I felt his pulse in his neck."

"What did you do then?"

"I went to the phone there," he pointed to a table, "and called nine-one-one and asked for the police and an ambulance quick."

"What next?"

"The maid, Isabel, came into the hall from the kitchen; I told her to go and see if Mrs. Calder was all right, and she went toward the master suite, there, through the living room, and through that door."

"How much time elapsed between the time you heard the shot and the time you found Mr. Calder?"

"I didn't go right away; I kept listening and wondering if I had heard what I heard. I expect it may have been two or three minutes."

"Which—two or three?"

"Closer to three, I guess. I wasn't running."

"Were those doors open?" Stone asked, pointing to the French doors that led to the pool, guest house, and gardens.

"One of them was," Manolo said. "It was wide open, in a way it wouldn't ordinarily be. Normally, it would either be closed, or both doors would be latched open."

"What happened next?"

"Mrs. Calder came running into the hall with the maid; she was wearing a robe and dripping water."

"What did she do or say?"

"She yelled out, 'Vance!' and then she got closer and saw the wound, and she backed away from him. She was making this noise, sort of like a scream, but not as loud, and she said, 'No, no!' a couple of times. I told Isabel to take her into the bedroom, that I would see to Mr. Calder and that an ambulance was on the way."

"Manolo, when Mrs. Calder came in, did you smell anything?"

"Well, yessir, I guess she smelled real sweet, having just got out of the tub."

Stone looked at the Saltillo tiles that formed the floor and saw a dark stain on the grout between the tiles.

"I couldn't get that out," Manolo said. "I tried, but I couldn't."

"What happened next, Manolo?"

"Two uniformed police officers arrived—they rang the bell, and I let them in the gate. They looked at Mr. Calder and felt his pulse, but they didn't move him. One of them talked to somebody on a walkie-talkie. Not long after that, another police car arrived, this time, plain-clothesmen. They went and talked to Mrs. Calder, and I followed them, but she wasn't making any sense; she was hysterical and didn't seem to know where she was or what had happened."

"Show me where the master suite is, please."

Manolo led him through the living room and through a set of double doors, then through a small foyer and into a large bedroom, which contained a king-size bed, a fireplace, and a sofa and chairs in front of a hearth. "Mrs. Calder's dressing room and bath are through here," he said, leading the way through a door to one side of the bed. There was another foyer, and to the left, a very large room, filled with hanging clothes, cubicles for sweaters and blouses, shoe racks, and a three-way mirror. To the right was a large bathroom with a big tub and a dressing table. On top of the dressing table was a large perfume bottle, emblazoned with the name "Chanel," and next to that a bottle of bath oil with the same brand name. Stone smelled them both.

"Now, can I see Mr. Calder's dressing room?" Stone asked.

"Right this way, sir."

They walked back into the bedroom, around the bed, and through another door. The arrangement was the same but both the dressing room and bath were smaller and decorated in a more masculine style. "Where is Mr. Calder's safe?" Stone asked.

Manolo went to a mirror over a chest of drawers, pressed it, and it swung open to reveal a steel safe door, approximately fifteen by twenty inches, a size that would fit between the structural studs. An electronic keypad, not a combination lock, was imbedded in the door.

"Do you know the combination?" Stone asked.

"Yessir, it's one-five-three-eight. You press the star key first, then the numbers, then the pound key, then turn that knob."

Stone opened the safe, which was empty. "What did Mr. Calder keep in here?" he asked.

"He kept his jewelry box and a gun," Manolo said.

"Do you know what kind of gun it was?"

"I don't know the brand of it, but it was an automatic pistol. There was a box of ammunition, too, that said nine millimeter, but the police took that."

"What was in the jewelry box?"

"Watches and other jewelry. Mr. Calder liked watches, and he had six or seven. There were some cuff links and studs, too, a nice selection."

"What did the box look like?"

"It was about a foot long by, I guess, eight inches wide, and mabe three or four inches deep. Deep enough to have the watches on mounts that displayed them when you opened the box. It was made out of brown alligator skin."

"The safe is pretty shallow," Stone said.

"The box would just fit into it, lying flat on the shelf, there. The pistol was at the bottom, along with the box of bullets."

Stone took one more look around. "Thank you, Manolo, that's all I need. Where is Mr. Calder's study? I'd like to make some phone calls."

"The main door is off the living room," Manolo said, "but you can get there this way, too." He walked to a double rack of suits, took hold of the wooden frame, and pulled. The rack swung outward. Then he pressed on the wall, and a door swung open, offering entry to the study.

Stone followed the butler into the study, then watched as he swung the door shut. Closed, it was a bookcase like the others in the room.

"Mr. Calder liked little secret things like that," Manolo said, smiling. "What time would you like dinner, Mr. Barrington?"

"Seven o'clock would be fine."

"And how do you like your beef cooked?"

"Medium, please."

"Would you like it served in the dining room or in the guest house?"

"In the guest house, I think."

"We'll see you at seven, then," Manolo said, and left the room.

Stone turned to examine Vance Calder's study.

Chapter 11

THREE ACADEMY AWARDS gazed at Stone from the mantel of the small fireplace in the room. Stone knew that Vance had been nominated seven times and had won three. The room was paneled in antique pine that radiated a soft glow where the light struck it; there were some good pictures and many books. The room was extremely neat, as if it were about to photographed for *Architectural Digest*.

Stone sat down at Calder's desk, and as he did, the phone rang. He checked the line buttons and saw that it was the third line, the most secret number. He picked it up. "Hello?"

There was a brief silence. "Who is this?" a woman's voice asked.

"Who's calling?"

"Stone?"

"Dolce?"

"I've been trying to reach you; the Bel-Air said you had checked out."

"I did, an hour ago. I'm staying in the Calders' guest house."

"With Arrington?"

"In the guest house. Arrington is in a hospital."

"What's wrong with her?"

"I don't think I should go into that on the phone; the press, as you can imagine, is taking an intense interest in all this. I wouldn't put it past some of the yellower journals to tap the phones."

"So you can't give me any information?"

"Not about Vance and Arrington, but *I'm* fine; I'm sure you wanted to know that."

"I don't like any of this, Stone."

"Neither do I; I'd much rather be in Venice with you."

"Sicily."

"What?"

"I was going to take you to Sicily, to show you where my family came from. I'm there now, on our honeymoon."

"I'm sorry to miss it; can I have a raincheck?"

"We'll see," she said, and there was petulance in her voice.

"Dolce, in Venice, you encouraged me to come here and help; that's what I'm doing."

"I had Papa and the cardinal to deal with. And exactly how are you helping?"

"I can't go into that, for the reasons I've just explained. Perhaps I can call you tomorrow from another number."

"Yes, do that." She gave him her number and the dialing codes for Sicily.

"How are you feeling?" he asked.

"Randy, actually. There's a rather interesting looking goatherd on the property; I was thinking of inviting him in for a drink."

"I can sympathize with your feelings," he replied. "I'd rather not be sleeping alone, myself."

"Then don't," she said. "I don't plan to."

"I meant that I'd rather be sleeping with you."

"You'd be my first choice, too," she said, "but you're not here, are you?"

Stone hardly knew what to say to that. Dolce had been mildly difficult, at times, but she had never behaved like this. He was shocked.

"No answer?"

"What can I say?"

"Say good night," she said, then hung up.

"Well," Stone said aloud, "that was very peculiar." He turned his attention back to the desk and began opening drawers. The contents were pretty much the same as in his own desk, but they were much more neatly arranged. He had never seen anything quite like it, in fact; it was as if a servant had come in and arranged the contents of the desk every day. He looked around for filing cabinets, but there were none. Apparently, all business was done from Vance's studio office.

Stone opened the center drawer, and, to his surprise, it pulled right out of the desk, into his lap. The drawer was lacking at least eight inches in what he had expected to be its depth. But why? He examined the bottom and sides of the drawer, which seemed perfectly normal, then he looked at the back. At the bottom of the rear of the drawer were two small brass hooks. Then he noticed that the drawer was slightly shallower than it might have been expected to be. He set the drawer on the desktop and looked at it for a minute. There was no apparent reason for the drawer to have hooks at its back. Unless . . . He took hold of the two drawer pulls and twisted, first to the left, then to the right. They moved clockwise for, perhaps, thirty degrees. He looked at the hooks on the back of the drawer; instead of lying flat, they were now positioned vertically.

He turned the knobs counterclockwise, and the hooks returned to their horizontal position. He reinserted the drawer all the way into the desk, turned the drawer pulls clockwise again, then opened the drawer all the way. The hooks had engaged another, smaller drawer that accounted for the missing depth, and in that drawer were some sealed envelopes, which he began opening.

The envelopes contained a copy of Vance's will, a note to Arrington, with instructions in the event of his death, and two insurance policies, with a value of five million dollars each, payable to Vance's estate.

He placed the will on the desk and read it. There was a long list of bequests, most of them for a hundred thousand dollars or more. Two, to universities, were for a million dollars, for the establishment of chairs in the theatrical arts, and one was personal, in the same amount, to his secretary, Betty Southard. Arrington and Lou Regenstein had been appointed executors. The will was dated less than a month before. If everything else in Vance's estate was as well organized as his will, Stone reflected, then his affairs were as neatly arranged as his desk drawers. Stone made a note of the law firm that had drawn the will, then he replaced the documents in the secret compartment, closed the drawer, turned the pulls counterclockwise, and opened it again, just to check. Everything was as before.

Stone then went to the bedroom and searched it thoroughly; he assumed that the police had done the same thing and that the maid had tidied the place after them. Maybe that was why Vance's desk drawers were so neat. He found nothing but the ordinary detritus of wealthy married couples' lives—keys, address books, family photographs, bedside books, remote controls. Stone realized that the room did not appear to have a television set. He pressed the power button, and the lid of an old trunk at the foot of the bed opened, and a very large TV set rose from its depths and switched on.

The local news was on, and it was about Vance. A handsome young woman gazed into the teleprompter and read: "Vance Calder's widow has still not been questioned by the police. Greg Harrow has this report."

The scene shifted to the Calders' front gate, where a young man in an Italian suit spoke gravely. "Amanda, police department sources tell us that, as yet, there are no suspects in the murder of Vance Calder, and that his widow is still hospitalized, with no sign of emerging to speak. The investigating detectives want very much to talk to her, but her doctor refuses to allow her to be interviewed. Some of my colleagues in the media have been to every private hospital in the L.A./Beverly Hills area, without finding out where she is a patient. It had been suggested that she may have been taken to the Calder Palm Springs home, or to their Malibu Beach house, but both those residences are dark, and during the past twenty-four hours, only one vehicle, a taxicab, has arrived here at the Calder Bel-Air home, and the driver refused to talk to the media. There was one man in the taxi, and he, apparently, remained at the house. Centurion Studios has issued a press release expressing the sorrow of everyone there at the news of Calder's death and asking that the media leave Arrington Calder alone and allow her to rebuild her shattered life. The Calders' only child, Peter, may still be at the Bel-Air house, cared for by the servants, but he has not been spotted here. All we have seen here is security, and plenty of it. A private service has the house and grounds completely sealed off, and no one, except the taxi, has arrived or departed today. We'll keep you posted as details come in."

Stone switched off the TV set, pleased with the news. He could hardly have written it better, himself, but he knew the lid could not be kept on for much longer. He picked up the phone and called Rick Grant's home number.

"Hi, Stone, how's it going?"

"As well as can be expected," Stone said. "Let me give you a number where you, and only you, can reach me." He dictated the number. "You can also reach me at Vance Calder's offices at Centurion, as of tomorrow. I'm going to work out of there."

"Anything new?"

"Not much. Arrington is still under a doctor's care."

"How much longer?"

"You can tell your people that I'll make her available at the earliest possible moment."

"Tell them yourself," he said. "That would be better. The lead detectives on the investigation are Sam Durkee and Ted Bryant, out of Brentwood." He gave Stone the number.

"I'll call them tomorrow morning."

"These are decent guys, Stone, and Durkee, in particular, is a very good detective, but unless they start getting cooperation from Arrington, they're going to begin leaking stuff to the media, and that would not be good for her."

"We're not hiding anything; Arrington really hasn't been up to questioning, but she's getting better."

"I'm glad to hear it. Anything else I can do for you?"

"Not a thing, Rick; I'll call Durkee tomorrow."

"Good night, then; Barbara sends her best."

"My best to her, too." Stone hung up and felt a hunger pang. He walked back out to the guest house, where he found Manolo setting a small table and the maid hanging his clothes in the closet, having pressed them.

He sat down to his steak and half a bottle of good Cabernet and tried to forget both Arrington and Dolce as he watched a movie on television. He was unable to forget either of them.

Chapter 12

IT WAS A PERFECT SOUTHERN CALIFORNIA MORNING, cool and sunny. Stone swam a few laps in the pool, then put on a guest's terry robe and breakfasted by the pool, looking over the *Los Angeles Times* and *The New York Times,* which had arrived with his breakfast. The Vance Calder story had been relegated to the inside pages of the New York newspaper, and was struggling to cling to the front page of the L.A. journal, but it wasn't going to go away, he knew. The moment a fragment of new information surfaced, there would be headlines again.

He showered, shaved, and dressed and walked into the house, carrying his briefcase. He retrieved the documents from the secret compartment of Vance's desk and put them into his briefcase, then he rang for Manolo. "I'd like to use one of the Calders' cars," he told the butler.

"Of course, Mr. Barrington, right this way." He led Stone to a door that opened into the garage, which had enough room for six cars, but held only four: a Bentley Arnage; two Mercedes SL600s, one black and one white; and a Mercedes station wagon. "The nanny and I use the station wagon for household errands, unless you'd like it," Manolo said.

The Bentley was too much, Stone thought. "No, I'll take one of the other Mercedes—the black one, I suppose. That was Mr. Calder's wasn't it?"

"Yes, sir. The white one is Mrs. Calder's. You'll find the keys in the car."

Stone had used the black convertible once before, when in L.A., and he recalled that it did not have vanity plates, so it would not be immediately recognized by the media. In fact, he reckoned, a black Mercedes convertible would, in Beverly Hills and Bel-Air, be a practically anonymous car. He backed out of the garage, drove around the house and, using his remote, let himself out of the utility gate and onto the street beyond. He checked to be sure that he was not followed, then drove to Centurion Studios.

The guard was momentarily confused to see Vance Calder's car arrive with a different driver, but when Stone gave his name, he was immediately issued with a studio pass.

"The one on the windshield will get this car in," the guard said. "Use the other pass, if you drive a different car."

"Can you direct me to Mr. Calder's bungalow, please?" The guard gave him directions, and five minutes later, he had parked in Vance's reserved parking spot. The bungalow was just that; it looked like one of the older, smaller Beverly Hills houses below Wilshire. Stone walked through the front door into a living room.

A panel in the wall slid open, and Betty Southard stuck her head through the opening. "I knew you'd turn up," she said. She left her office, walked into the living room and gave him a big hug and a kiss. "I'm glad to see you again," she said.

"I'm glad to see you, too; I'm going to need a lot of your help."

"Lou Regenstein called and said you'd be using Vance's office. She waved him into a panelled study, much the same as the one at the house, but larger, with a conference table at one end. "Make yourself at home," she said. "The phones are straightforward; you can make your own calls, or I'll place them for you, depending on whether you want to impress somebody."

"Thank you, Betty," Stone said, placing his briefcase on the desk. "I have some personal news for you; have you seen Vance's will?"

"Not the new one; he made that recently, and he hadn't brought a copy to the office."

"You're a beneficiary," Stone said. "He left you a million dollars."

Betty's jaw dropped, and a hand went to her mouth. "I think I'd better sit down," she said, and she did, taking a chair by the desk. Stone sat down behind it. "You didn't know?"

"I hadn't a clue," she said. "I mean, I suppose I would have expected something after fifteen years with him—I joined him at twelve, you know," she said archly.

Stone laughed. "Now you're a rich woman; what are you going to do?"

Betty sighed. "I haven't the foggiest idea," she said. "Lou has told me I could have my pick of jobs at the studio, but I don't know, I might just retire. I've saved some money, and I've done well in the bull market, and there's a studio pension, too; Vance got me fully vested in that last year, as a Christmas present."

"Then you can be a woman of leisure."

"A lady who lunches? I'm not sure I could handle that. Certainly, I'll stay on long enough to help you settle Vance's affairs—and Arrington's, too," she said darkly. "I'm sure she'll have a lot to settle."

"And what does that mean?" Stone asked.

"Oh, I don't know. I guess you know that Arrington and I have never gotten along too well—yes, you can call it jealousy, if you like, but there were other reasons."

"Tell me about them."

"Stone, tell me straight: Did Arrington shoot Vance?"

"I haven't the slightest reason to think so," Stone replied. "And I don't know why it even occurred to you to ask the question."

"As I understand it, the police have not cleared her."

"They haven't even talked to her, but I expect them to clear her when they do. She's at the Judson Clinic."

"Is she ill?"

"Not exactly, but she's been better. When she saw Vance on the floor of their home with a bullet in his head she pretty much went to pieces."

"Yes, she would, wouldn't she?" Betty said with a hint of sarcasm.

Stone ignored that. "I hope she can get the police interview out of the way soon, maybe even today. It will depend on what her doctor says."

"Look, I certainly don't have any evidence, but—call it woman's intuition, if you like—I think Arrington is perfectly capable of having killed Vance, then pretending to break down, just to keep from having to talk to the police."

"Tell me why you think that."

"Just for starters, I think Vance was miserable in the marriage. Oh, he never said so, in so many words, but I knew him as well as anybody, and I think that, in spite of his constant good humor, he was unhappy."

"Give me some example of his unhappiness."

"I can't. It was just the odd comment, the raised eyebrow when Arrington was mentioned. He did love Peter, though; I've never seen a man love a child so much."

"Anything more specific?"

"No, certainly nothing I could testify to under oath."

Stone relaxed a little inside; he hadn't realized he had become so tense. "Well, I hope you'll keep your feelings to yourself. If you think of anything specific you can tell me, I want to hear about it, though."

"Of course."

Stone glanced at his watch. "Let's get started. Will you get me Dr. James Judson at the Judson Clinic?"

Betty placed the call from the conference table phone, then left the room and closed the door.

"Good morning, Jim, it's Stone Barrington."

"Good morning, Stone."

"How's your patient this morning?"

"She's very well, I think. I believe she's about ready to go home."

"Not just yet," Stone said. "She's going to have to talk to the police, and I'd like her to do it from a hospital bed."

"I understand. When do you want them to see her?"

"Today, if you think it's all right."

"I think it should be. She's mentioned that she expects them to come, so we may as well get it over with. I'd like to be with her when they question her, though."

"Of course, and I will be, too. How about early afternoon?"

"All right; I'll prepare her."

"I'll do some preparation, too, before they arrive. I'll let you know the exact time, after I've talked to them."

"I'll wait to hear from you, before I tell Arrington."

"I'm working from Mr. Calder's office at the studio, should you need to reach me." Stone gave him the number, then hung up. He found the intercom and buzzed Betty.

"Yes, Stone?"

"Now get me Detective Sam Durkee at the Brentwood LAPD station."

After a short wait, Betty buzzed him, and he picked up the phone. "Detective Durkee?"

"That's right."

"My name is Stone Barrington; I'm handling the affairs of Mrs. Vance Calder."

"I know your name from Rick Grant," Durkee said. "Rick says you're an ex–homicide detective."

"That's right; NYPD."

"Then you'll understand what we have to do."

"Of course. I've just spoken to Mrs. Calder's doctor, and he says you can interview her this afternoon. How about two o'clock at the Judson Clinic?"

"That's good for me; I'll bring my partner, Ted Bryant."

"You have to understand her condition," Stone said. "She's been very badly shaken up, and there are some big gaps in her memory."

"Oh? How big?"

"When I spoke with her yesterday, the last thing she could remember was a conversation with her gardener eight days before the homicide. I've confirmed the date with her butler."

"So, basically, when we question her, she's going to say she remembers nothing?"

"Her doctor says she may recover some of her memories, but I can't promise you anything. For a while, she didn't remember being married to Calder, but she's gotten past that, so she may remember even more.

I can tell you that she has no hesitation about talking to you; she wants her husband's murderer caught and prosecuted."

"Well, we'll certainly try to make that wish come true," Durkee said.

"There have to be some ground rules: Both her doctor and I will be present at the interview, and if either of us, for any reason, feels she shouldn't continue, we'll stop it."

"Understood," Durkee said dryly. "See you at two o'clock."

Stone hung up and began to think about this interview. It was crucial, he knew, for Arrington to convince them she was innocent. If she couldn't do that, her life was going to change even more dramatically than it already had.

Chapter 13

STONE COULD HAVE SPOTTED the two men as detectives in any city in the United States. They were both middle-aged, dressed in middling suits that revealed bulges under the left arm to anyone looking for them. Sam Durkee was at least six-four and beefy in build; Stone made him as an ex-athlete. Ted Bryant was shorter, bald and pudgy. He didn't expect either of them to be stupid, and his plan was to be as cooperative as humanly possible, without handing them his client on a platter.

He shook their hands, then led them upstairs to Arrington's room. She was sitting up in bed wearing cotton pajamas; Dr. Judson was at her bedside. Stone made the introductions, and everybody pulled up a chair.

Durkee took the lead. "Mrs. Calder," he said, "first, I want to offer the department's condolences on your loss."

"Thank you," Arrington said, managing a wan smile.

"I hope you understand that there are questions we must ask, if we're to apprehend your husband's killer; I know this won't be pleasant, but we'll keep it as short as we can, and we'd like the fullest answers you can give us."

"I'll do my best," Arrington replied.

"What do you recall about the evening your husband was shot?"

"Absolutely nothing, I'm afraid. I remember going to the hairdresser's the day before, the Friday, but I don't remember driving home, or anything after that, until I woke up here."

A Friday memory was progress, Stone thought.

"Are you beginning to pick up pieces of your memory?" Bryant asked.

"It seems so," she said. "Every day, I remember a little more."

"Are you aware that your husband owned a gun?"

"He told me so, but I never saw it."

"Was he the sort of man who would have used a gun to defend his home?"

"He certainly was; I'm sure that's why he owned it."

"Do you know where he kept the gun?"

"No."

Stone spoke up. "The butler told me that Mr. Calder kept a nine millimeter pistol in the same safe where he kept his jewelry."

"Thank you," Durkee replied. "Mrs. Calder, how would you characterize your marriage?"

"As a very happy one," Arrington replied.

"Did you and your husband ever quarrel?"

"Of course." She smiled a little. "But our quarrels were almost always good-humored. You might call them mock quarrels. We argued about lots of things, but always with respect and affection."

"You say your quarrels were 'almost' always good-humored. Did they ever become violent?"

"You mean, did Vance ever hit me? Certainly not."

"Did you ever hit him?"

She looked down. "I can remember slapping him, once and only once. He'd said something that offended me."

"What did he do when you slapped him?"

"He apologized, and it never happened again. My husband was a gentleman in every possible sense of the word."

"When you argued, what did you argue about?"

"He would give me a hard time, sometimes, about how much shopping I did. Vance had a tailor, a shirtmaker, and a bootmaker; he ordered his clothes from swatches, so shopping was very simple for him. I think it both amused and horrified him how to learn how women shop. He could never understand why I would buy things, then take them back the next day."

"Any other subjects you argued about?"

"Sometimes we'd disagree on child rearing. Vance believed strongly in corporal punishment, and I didn't. He'd been brought up that way by his parents, and in English schools, and he thought if it was good enough for him, it was good enough for his son."

"Did he use corporal punishment often with your child?"

"Rarely, and then only a palm applied to the bottom."

"And you disagreed with that?"

"Yes. I was never struck, as a child, and I didn't want Peter to be."

"What else did you disagree about?"

She shrugged. "I can't think of anything else specifically."

"What about women?"

"There were one or two of my friends he didn't like much, but he tolerated them for my sake."

"That's not what I mean," Durkee said. "Are you aware that your husband had a reputation for sleeping with his leading ladies?"

Arrington smiled. "That was before we were married. My husband walked the straight and narrow."

"And if you had learned that he didn't, might that have provoked a quarrel?"

"It might have provoked a divorce," Arrington replied. "When we married, I let him know in no uncertain terms what I expected of him in that regard."

"And what did you expect?"

"Fidelity."

"Were you always faithful to him?"

"Always," she replied.

"Was there any man in your past for whom you still felt . . . affection?"

Stone was a little uncomfortable with this, but he kept a straight face and waited for her answer.

"I feel affection for a number of friends," Arrington replied, "but I was as faithful to my husband as he was to me."

Stone didn't like this answer, and he saw the two detectives exchange a glance.

Arrington saw it, too. "What I mean is, I was faithful to him, and he was faithful to me."

"Mrs. Calder, are you acquainted with a woman named Charlene Joiner?"

"Of course; she costarred with my husband in a film."

"Were you and Ms. Joiner friends?"

"No; we met a few times, and our relationship was cordial, but I wouldn't call us friends. The last time I saw her was when she and Vance cohosted a political fund-raiser at our house."

"Would it surprise you to learn that your husband, while he was filming with Ms. Joiner, was spending considerable periods of time in her trailer?"

"No; I suppose they had lines to read together."

Bryant spoke up. "Mrs. Calder, when did you become aware that your husband was having sex with Ms. Joiner?"

"I was not and am not aware of that," she replied icily.

"Come on, Mrs. Calder," Bryant said impatiently, "while they were filming together, your husband stopped having sex with you, didn't he?"

They were good cop/bad copping her, and Stone hoped Arrington had the sense to realize it. He made no move to stop them.

"My husband and I had a very satisfactory sex life, and I can't remember any period of our marriage when that wasn't the case," Arrington replied firmly.

"Do you not recall ever telling another woman that your husband had stopped making love to you?"

Arrington frowned. "Ah," she said, "I think I know what you're getting at. A friend of mine once complained to me that *her* husband had stopped sleeping with her, and I believe I tried to commiserate by telling her that all couples went through periods like that. I think you must have spoken with Beverly Walters."

"Do you deny telling Mrs. Walters that your husband had stopped fucking you?" Bryant demanded.

Stone began to speak, but Arrington held up a hand and stopped him. "I think Mrs. Walters may have inferred a bit more than I meant to imply," she said, and her color was rising.

"Mrs. Calder," Durkee said, breaking in, "if you had learned that your husband was having sex once, sometimes twice a day with Ms. Joiner in her trailer, would that have made you angry?"

"Hypothetically? Yes, I suppose it would have hurt me badly."

"When you are hurt by a man, do you respond angrily?"

"I have a temper, Detective Durkee, but on the occasions when it comes out, I have never harmed another human being."

"When was the last time you fired a handgun?" Bryant asked suddenly.

"I have never fired a pistol," she replied.

"But you know how, don't you?"

"I have never, to the best of my recollection, even held a handgun."

"Mrs. Calder," Durkee asked, "where is your husband's jewelry box?"

"I'd like very much to know, detective; I had hoped that, by now, you might be able to tell me."

"Where did you hide the jewelry box and the pistol?"

"I didn't hide either of them anywhere," she replied.

"But you say you don't remember anything about the shooting. How could you remember not hiding them?"

"To the very best of my recollection, I have not handled either my husband's jewelry box or his gun."

"Mrs. Calder, do you recall hearing or reading somewhere that perfume applied to the hands and arms removes any trace of having fired a weapon?"

"No, I don't."

"What kind of perfume do you use?"

"I use several, but my favorite is Chanel No. 5."

"Did you use that the night your husband was shot?"

"I don't remember the night my husband was shot."

"Would you use perfume before taking a bath?"

Arrington looked at him as if he were mad. "No."

"Then why would you reek of perfume on getting out of a bath?"

"I use bath oil, detective, of the same scent as my perfume, but generally speaking, I never reek."

Stone supressed a smile. He sensed that the two detectives were running out of questions, but he didn't rush them.

"Mrs. Calder," Durkee said, "I have to tell you that, after investigating your husband's murder very thoroughly, we have concluded that the two of you were alone in the house when he was shot."

"That hardly seems possible," Arrington replied. "Otherwise, where are the jewelry box and the gun?"

"We believe you hid them after shooting your husband."

"Where? Have you searched our house?"

"We haven't found them—yet," Bryant said.

"Let me know when you do," Arrington said. "Otherwise, I'll have to file an insurance claim."

Durkee stood up. "I believe that's all for now," he said, turning to Stone. "I want to be notified when she leaves the hospital, and I want to know where she goes."

"I'll give you a call," Stone said, walking both men toward the door.

When they were outside, Bryant turned to Stone. "She killed him," he said.

"Nonsense," Stone said. "It's obvious that someone got into the house. Haven't you found any evidence of anyone else?"

The two detectives exchanged a glance.

"I want disclosure," Stone said.

"Are you licensed to practice law in the state of California?" Bryant asked.

"No."

"My advice is to get her a lawyer who is. I'm sure the D.A. will disclose to him."

Stone watched as the two detectives walked to their car. He didn't like the way this was going.

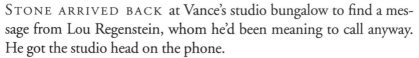

Chapter 1 4

STONE ARRIVED BACK at Vance's studio bungalow to find a message from Lou Regenstein, whom he'd been meaning to call anyway. He got the studio head on the phone.

"How is Arrington?" Lou asked.

"Much better. Her doctor says she can go home tomorrow."

"Have you given any thought to funeral arrangements?"

"I was going to ask you the same thing. I'm sure the studio can do a much better job of this than I can."

"I have a suggestion," Lou said.

"Go ahead."

"We have a cathedral set on our biggest sound stage right now. I'd like to hold a memorial service for Vance there and, in addition to his friends, invite many of the studio employees who have worked with Vance over the years."

"That sounds good to me," Stone said.

"I'd like to invite a small media pool and allow them to tape the service. I think that will go a long way toward keeping them off Arrington's back right now."

"Why don't you give Arrington a call at the Judson Clinic and discuss it with her? I think she's up to it now; she saw the police this afternoon."

73

"Is Arrington facing any legal difficulties?" Lou asked.

"It's too soon to tell, Lou; the police, not having a suspect, quite naturally look at the spouse. I think we'll just have to wait for them to get past that."

"Have you called Marc Blumberg, my lawyer friend, yet?"

"Not yet; I hope we won't need him. Also, there's a downside to calling him; if somebody in his firm leaked the call to the press, it would make it look as though we expected Arrington to be charged."

"I understand," Lou said. "I'll call Arrington now."

Stone hung up and glanced at his watch. It would be midnight in Sicily, now, and he hadn't called Dolce yet. He knew she liked to stay up late, so he dialed the number.

It rang once, before being picked up by a machine. "I'm entertaining a guest right now," Dolce's voice said, "so go away."

Stone hung up, angry, and tried to think of something else. He thought of Marc Blumberg and dialed his number.

"Mr. Blumberg's office," a woman said.

"My name is Stone Barrington; I'm calling Mr. Blumberg at the suggestion of Lou Regenstein."

"And how can Mr. Blumberg help you, Mr. Barrington?"

He obviously wasn't going to get past this woman without telling her the purpose of his call, and he had no intention of doing that. "Please ask Mr. Blumberg to call me at Centurion Studios." He gave her the number and hung up.

Betty Southard came into the office. "I was passing and heard you mention a Blumberg. Marc Blumberg?"

Stone nodded.

"Is Arrington in *that* much trouble?"

"It's just a precaution," Stone replied. "I think it's best to be ready for anything."

"I suppose so," she said. "How about some dinner tonight?"

"I'd like that," Stone said. He hadn't been looking forward to being sequestered at the Calder house, and Dolce's behavior had removed any guilt he might have felt about seeing another woman. "Book us at your favorite restaurant."

"Pick me up at seven-thirty?"

"Sure."

"You remember the address?"

"How could I forget?"

The phone rang, and Betty picked up the one on the desk. "Mr. Calder's bungalow?" She handed the phone to Stone. "Marc Blumberg."

"Thank you for returning my call, Mr. Blumberg," Stone said. "Lou Regenstein has suggested we meet to discuss something very important."

"Of course," Blumberg said. "Tomorrow morning okay?"

Stone could hear diary pages turning. "I'd rather not come to your office, for reasons I'll explain later. Would it be possible for you to meet me at Centurion Studios after office hours?"

"I'll be finished here by five-thirty," Blumberg replied. "I could be there by six, but I'll only have about forty-five minutes; I have to get home and change for dinner."

"Six will be fine," Stone said. "I'll leave instructions for you at the gate." He hung up. "Betty," he said, "will you have a pass and directions to the bungalow at the main gate? Blumberg is coming here at six."

"Consider it done," she replied.

"Do you mind if I don't change for dinner?" he asked. "I won't have time to go back to Vance's."

"No problem. When is Arrington getting out of the hospital?"

"Tomorrow, I hope."

"Do you think you should be living at the house then?"

"You have a dirty mind."

"You bet I do; I have two suggestions."

"What?"

"The first is, move in with me. I managed to make you comfortable the last time you were here."

"I think it's best that I just move back to the Bel-Air," Stone said. "What's your second suggestion?"

"Vance has . . . had a place at Malibu; I think that might be enough distance between you and Arrington, and I've got the keys."

"That's a thought," Stone said. "I'll let you know."

Marc Blumberg bustled into the bungalow promptly at six, a small, fit-looking, deeply tanned man of fifty in a perfectly cut suit and gleaming shoes.

Stone shook his hand. "Can I get you a drink?"

"I'm okay," Blumberg said, taking a seat on a leather sofa. "I believe I've heard of you, Stone. May I call you Stone?"

Stone sat down beside him. "Of course."

"And I'm Marc. I remember that business in St. Mark's a few years back, when you defended the woman on a murder charge. Saw it on *60 Minutes,* I think."

"Yes, that was a difficult one."

"Pity she was hanged."

"Yes."

"I remember from Lou that you're a friend of Mrs. . . . . the Calders. I take it I'm here to talk about another murder trial."

"Let's call this a precautionary meeting."

"It's always wise to take precautions. Has Arrington talked to the police yet?"

"Earlier this afternoon."

"I should have been there for that," Blumberg said.

"I didn't want to appear to be running scared," Stone said. "You'd have been happy with the way it went." He gave Blumberg a detailed rundown of Arrington's questioning.

"That sounds okay," Blumberg said. "You handled it well."

"Thank you."

"Sounds as though they don't have another suspect."

"That's how I read it. They went through the drill the night of the murder, and they didn't come up with anything, and that disturbs them. Cops like early indications, and when they don't find them, they look at the household."

"Anybody in the house besides Arrington?"

"No. The butler and maid were in their quarters; the butler found Vance and called the police."

"What was the scene like?"

"Vance was dressed in tuxedo trousers and a pleated shirt, no tie. They were going to a black-tie dinner at Lou's house a little later. He was found lying face down in the central hallway of the house, one bullet here." Stone pointed at the spot.

"You used to be a cop didn't you?"

"Yes."

"Have you got a scenario for this that doesn't involve Arrington shooting Vance?"

"Here's how I read it," Stone said. "Arrington was in the bathtub; Vance was getting dressed. His safe was open, containing his jewelry box, a nine-millimeter automatic, and a box of cartridges. He either walked in on a burglary, or a burglar walked in on him, probably the former. The burglar took the jewelry box and the gun, walked Vance into the central hallway and shot him."

"Any struggle?"

"Looks like an execution to me. My guess is, Vance saw it coming and turned away. That's why the wound in the back of the head." Stone stood up, held out his hands in the "no, no" position, then half turned away from his imaginary assailant.

"Makes sense," Blumberg said.

"For Arrington to have done it, she would have to have gone to the safe, taken out the gun, cocked it, flipped off the safety, then either marched her husband out into the hall, or gone looking for him and found him there. That doesn't fit a domestic quarrel."

"It fits a cold-blooded, premeditated murder," Blumberg said. "How do you figure the chances of that?"

"Unlikely in the extreme."

"I'm glad to hear it. So what we've got is an innocent woman who loved her husband, who is a suspect only because the police haven't done their job and found the real killer."

"In a nutshell," Stone said. "A couple of other things you should know: I got the impression from the detectives that they might have other evidence we don't know about. They refused to disclose it to me, said they'd talk to a California lawyer."

"We'll get it, don't worry. What's the other thing?"

"The police talked to a woman named Beverly Walters, who told them Vance was screwing an actress named Charlene Joiner; they took that as Arrington's motive for the shooting."

"I know her; she's a complete bitch, and she could give us trouble at a trial. Charlene Joiner, huh? If it's true, Vance was a lucky guy."

"Yeah, I've seen some of her pictures."

"Tell me, Stone, what's your role in all this?" Blumberg asked. "Family friend?"

"That, and for the moment, Arrington's personal representative. I have her confidence and a power of attorney."

Blumberg looked Stone in the eye. "You and Arrington ever have a thing, Stone?"

"We were living together in New York when she suddenly married Vance."

"You want me to represent her?"

"If it becomes necessary."

"I think you're right about my presence being a red flag; the media would play that big. Here's what we do. I don't so much as even speak to Arrington, unless we find out she's going to be arrested."

"I might be able to get advance notice of that, if it happens."

"Good. If you do, I surrender her to the D.A. I can arrange that. From then on, I'm her lawyer, not you; I'm running the case."

Stone shook his head. "If it comes to that I'll want to be involved every step of the way."

"That's not how I work."

"Then I can only thank you for your time," Stone said.

Blumberg thought for a moment. "What do you want?"

"Second chair; partner in decision-making; no move without my agreement."

"All right," Blumberg said. "Are you licensed in California?"

"No."

"I'll deal with that. I'll want a hundred-thousand-dollar retainer up front, against a half-million-dollar fee, the remainder payable before the trial starts."

"To include all your expenses," Stone said.

"Agreed. If I can stop it before it goes to trial, I'll bill her at a thousand dollars an hour."

"To include your associates and staff."

"Done." Blumberg held out his hand, and Stone shook it.

"I'll draft a letter appointing you and get a check drawn, immediately after any arrest."

"When is Arrington returning home?"

"Tomorrow, I think."

"Where are you living while you're here?"

"In the Calders' guest house."

"I don't want the two of you to spend so much as a single night under the same roof. Move out before she gets home."

"All right."

Blumberg looked at his watch and stood up. "I've got to run," he said.

"One thing, Marc," Stone said. "I don't want you to mention this to *anybody*—staff, wife—*anybody*."

"That goes without saying," Blumberg replied.

Stone walked him to his car. "Thanks for coming," he said.

"Don't worry about a thing," Blumberg said breezily. "I'll get her off."

Stone waved good-bye, then went to his own car. You probably will, he thought, but I hope to God it doesn't come to that.

He went back to his desk, called Dolce again and got the same message. It only made him angrier. He was glad to be having some company tonight.

Chapter 15

STONE AND BETTY sat at a good table at Spago Beverly Hills. "I remember when this was another restaurant," he said. "I had lunch here a couple of times, in the garden."

"I'll give you a little Beverly Hills gossip," Betty said. "You know why the old place failed, after many years as a success?"

"Tell me."

"The story is, a group of prominent wives were having lunch here, when they overheard the owner make an anti-Semitic remark. They told their friends, their friends told their friends, and within two weeks, the place was empty. It went out of business not long afterward."

"I'll bet you're full of Beverly Hills gossip," Stone said.

"You bet I am."

"Then tell me, was Vance sleeping with Charlene Joiner?"

Betty smiled. "What do you know about Charlene Joiner?"

"Just what I read in the papers during the presidential campaign. She had once had an affair with Will Lee, back when he was first running for the Senate, and the Republicans tried to make something of it."

"Well, let me tell you; Charlene is some piece of work. She has cut a swath through the rich and powerful in this town, and she has done

it very cleverly, choosing her partners carefully, as much for their dis-
cretion as for what they can do for her career."

"Sounds like a smart girl."

"Smart, and from what I can glean, spectacular in the sack, in a
town where outstanding is ordinary."

"But was Vance sleeping with her?"

Betty toyed with her drink.

"I don't think it would be disloyal of you to tell me."

"Yes, I know; Vance is dead, but sometimes I feel as though he's
just on location, or something, and that he might walk into the bungalow at any moment."

"If you feel you'd be betraying a confidence, I understand."

"This has something to do with Arrington, doesn't it?" she asked.

"It might, before this is all over. It's important that I know whether
this is just a rumor, or if it's true."

Stone looked up to see a lush-looking brunette in her mid-thirties
walk up to their table. She was fashionably dressed, coiffed, and made
up, and Stone thought her breasts seemed too large for the rest of her.

"Hello, Betty," the woman said, her voice dripping with sympathy.
"How are you doing, Sweetie?"

Stone stood up.

"Hi, Beverly," Betty replied. "Oh, Stone, this is Beverly Walters;
Beverly, this is Stone Barrington."

"Arrington's friend?" she held out a hand. "She's told me so much
about you."

"How do you do?" Stone said.

"How long are you in town for?"

"Not very long," Stone replied.

She fished a card from her handbag and handed it to him. "Call
me; maybe I can help."

Stone pocketed the card. "Thank you."

"Betty, I'm so sorry about Vance; I know how close you were."

"Thanks, Beverly," Betty replied, without much enthusiasm.

"Call me, if you want to bend an ear," the woman said. She gave
Stone a little wave and walked back to her table.

"Steer clear of *her*," Betty said through clenched teeth.

"She's the source of the rumor I'm trying to confirm," Stone said. "She told the police that Vance was sleeping with Charlene Joiner."

"She doesn't know anything; she's just inventing gossip."

Their dinner arrived.

"Betty, one more time: Was Vance sleeping with her?"

"All right, I'll tell you about Vance. It was his practice to sleep with *all* his leading ladies, and a lot of those in supporting roles, too."

"Even after he was married?"

"He never wavered. He'd either have them back to the bungalow for lunch or to his trailer. You haven't seen the trailer, have you? It is *very* comfortable."

"*All* his leading ladies?"

"You go back and watch *any* film that Vance starred in, and you may wonder why the love scenes are so convincing. Well, they were convincing, because they had been *very* well rehearsed."

"And how many pictures did Vance make after he was married?"

Betty counted on her fingers. "Four," she said.

"You think Arrington knew about this?"

"I don't think Vance was shortchanging her, if that's what you mean."

"This Walters woman told police that Arrington had complained to her that Vance had stopped sleeping with her, and that the reason was an affair with Charlene Joiner."

Betty shook her head. "That just doesn't ring true. Vance was a sexual athlete his whole life. He was in superb physical condition, and he *loved* sex. He could have made a very nice living doing porno movies, because he had both the equipment and the endurance for the work. It's much more likely that Arrington would have complained of *too much* sex, rather than not enough."

"How do you know about all this?"

"Because I know *everything* about Vance Calder. I worked for him for fifteen years, and I got the job while in bed with him. I was a script girl on one of his pictures, and we were fucking each other for most of the shoot. Toward the end of the picture, he offered me the job. He told me, quite frankly, that our little affair was going to end with the wrap, and I knew he was telling the truth. I took the job, because it was better than the one I had, and we didn't make love again. But he never kept secrets from me. Maybe that's why he left me the million dollars—because he knew I could make that much writing a tell-all book. I could, too."

"I'll bet you could."

"So, now you know what you want to know?"

"I do."

"Now you tell me something," she said.

"Anything."

"The last time you were in L.A., you and I had a rather delicious time together."

"We certainly did."

"Why do I get the feeling that isn't going to happen this time?"

"Things have changed," Stone said. He told her about Dolce and why he had been in Venice.

Betty nodded. "I understand," she said. "I don't like it much, but I understand."

"Thank you for not liking it," Stone replied.

Chapter 16

STONE SLIPPED INTO THE ESTATE through the utility entrance, parked his car in back and walked to the guest house. He got out of yesterday's clothes, slipped into a robe, called Manolo, and ordered breakfast. As soon as he set down the phone, it rang.

"Hello?"

"Stone?" It was Arrington, and she sounded agitated. "I've been trying to reach you since last night—where have you been?"

"Right here," he lied. "I was tired, so I unhooked the phone. I just plugged it in again so I could order breakfast. How are you feeling?"

"I'm feeling very well, thank you. The doctor says I can leave this morning. He wants to check me over once more, but I should be ready to go by ten. Will you come and get me, please?"

"Of course. I'll be there at ten sharp."

"Oh, good. Will you bring me some clothes? Ask Isabel, the maid, to put together an outfit—slacks and a blouse, shoes, stockings, and underwear. They brought me here practically naked, and I don't have anything to wear."

"Sure. I'll call Isabel, and I'll see you there at ten." He started to tell her he was moving out of the house, but he thought it might be best to wait until he saw her.

"See you then, darling," she said and hung up.

Stone called the maid and asked her to put the clothing into his car, then, as he promised he would, he called Sam Durkee at the Brentwood station.

"Durkee."

"Morning, Sam. It's Stone Barrington."

"Oh, yeah."

"You asked me to let you know when Mrs. Calder was leaving the clinic; it's this morning." He paused for a moment, native caution coming into play. "At ten-thirty."

"Hey, Ted," Durkee called out, "Vance Calder's widow is getting out at ten-thirty." His voice returned to the receiver. "Thanks for letting us know," he said.

"Do you need to speak with her again?" Stone asked.

"Not at the moment."

"If you do, call me at Centurion Studios, and I'll arrange it. The operator there will find me."

"Sure thing."

"Good-bye." Stone hung up, wishing he hadn't called Durkee; he had a funny feeling about this.

At nine-fifteen, as Stone was finishing breakfast, the phone rang.

"Hello?"

"Stone? It's Jim Judson, at the clinic."

"Morning, Jim; is Arrington still going to be ready to leave at ten?"

"I'm not sure if you'll want her to," Judson replied. "As we speak, the press is gathering outside. There are three television vans with satellite dishes, and at least a dozen reporters."

"Ah," Stone said, once again regretting his call to Durkee. "I think this calls for a change in plans."

"I thought you might think so."

"Is there another way out of the building besides the front door?"

"We have a small parking lot for staff at the west end of the building.

You enter it from near the front door, but the exit is around the corner. From my office, I can see media people staking that out, too, but only a handful of them."

Stone had a look at his street map of Beverly Hills. "All right, here's what we do," Stone said. "Can you find a nurse's uniform that will fit Arrington?"

"Yes, I suppose so."

"Get her dressed in the uniform, cap and all, and borrow a car— the older and more modest, the better—from one of your staff. Have Arrington walk out to the parking lot, get into the car, and leave by the side street exit. Have her turn left, then take her first right. I'll be waiting there. She'll leave the borrowed car there for you to pick up."

"All right. When do you want her to leave the building?"

Stone looked at his watch. "Half an hour?"

"Fine."

"How is she this morning?"

"She's all right, but you might still find her a little fragile. She still hasn't remembered anything between her hair appointment the day before the murder and waking up here the day after."

"Thanks, Jim; I'll speak to you later, if I have any questions." Stone hung up, then checked his map again. He'd have to pass a corner near the clinic to position himself where he wanted to be; he hoped his car would be anonymous enough. He called Manolo. "I'd like to take the station wagon today," he said.

"Of course, Mr. Barrington; I'll have Isabel put the clothes in that car. The keys are in it."

Stone drove out the utility exit and made his way toward the Judson Clinic. He had to stop at a traffic light on the corner half a block from the clinic, and as he waited, Sam Durkee and Ted Bryant drove past him on the cross street, toward the clinic. "You sons of bitches," Stone muttered. The light changed and he drove straight ahead, past the exit from the employees' parking lot, which a small group of

L . A . D E A D

reporters had staked out. He turned right at the next corner and pulled over, leaving the engine running.

Ten minutes passed, and, right on time, Arrington appeared, driving an elderly Honda. She parked the car, ran over to the Mercedes station wagon, and got in. "Thank you for getting me out of there, Stone," she said, planting a kiss on his cheek.

Stone pulled out of his parking space. "Your clothes are in the backseat. Did anybody recognize you?"

"Nope; they hardly gave me a glance. I wasn't what they were expecting, I guess." She began undressing.

Stone tried to keep his eyes straight ahead and failed. "I don't think we should go to the Bel-Air house," he said.

"Shall we just check into a motel, then?" she suggested.

"How about the Malibu house?"

"I don't have a key with me."

"Betty gave me one; I was going to move out there today."

"All right, let's go to Malibu; I have clothes and everything I need out there, except maybe some groceries."

Stone made his way to the freeway, then got off at Santa Monica Boulevard and drove toward the ocean. Soon, they were on the Pacific Coast Highway.

"God!" Arrington exclaimed. "It feels so good to be out of that place."

"Seemed like a very nice place," Stone said.

"Oh, it is, and they were wonderful to me, but I still felt like a prisoner. Now I feel free again!" She turned to him. "Why were you going to move to the Malibu house? Weren't you comfortable in Bel-Air?"

"Oh, yes, and Manolo was taking very good care of me. But, at the moment, it's important that you and I not be living under the same roof."

"Why not?"

"You're going to be under a lot of scrutiny for a while, and having an old boyfriend living at your house would give the press just a little too much to write about."

87

"I suppose you're right," she said. "God, but I hate living under a microscope. How long is this going to go on?"

"Weeks, maybe months. If the police find Vance's killer, that will help it go away. How is Peter?"

"He's wonderful; we talked this morning, and he's having a great time in Virginia; Mother keeps horses, and she has a pony for him. I want him to stay there until this is over."

"That's a good idea, I think."

"Drive straight through the town," she said. "The house is in the Malibu Colony, just past the little business district."

Stone followed her instructions, and turned through a gate, where they were stopped by a security guard.

"It's me, Steve," she said to the man.

"Welcome back, Mrs. Calder," he replied.

"If anybody asks, I'm not here," she said. "This is Mr. Barrington; he'll be coming and going."

"I'll put his name on the list."

Stone followed Arrington's directions to the house, a large, stone and cedar contemporary on the beach. He gave her the key, and she opened the door and punched in the security code. He made a note of the code.

Stone went to the phone and called Betty.

"Where are you?" she asked.

"I've taken Arrington to the Malibu house; there was a mob of press at the clinic."

"The police have called here twice."

"Guy named Durkee?"

"That's right."

"If he calls again, tell him you haven't heard from me today."

"All right; are you coming in at all?"

"Maybe later." He gave her his cellphone number. "You can reach me there in an emergency. If you call here, let it ring once, hang up, and call again."

"You were wonderful last night," she said. "This morning, too."

"Same here," he replied.

"Oh, she's there, huh?"

"I'll talk to you later." He hung up.

"I want to take a bath," Arrington said. "Join me?"

"Thanks, I've just showered," he replied.

"Oh, it's going to be like that, is it?"

"You're a grieving widow, and I'm an old family friend."

"We'll see." She went upstairs.

Stone found Vance's study and picked up the phone. It was time to call Marc Blumberg.

C h a p t e r   1 7

MARC BLUMBERG came on the line. "Congratulations on getting her out of the Judson place," he said. "I passed the clinic on the way to work this morning; there were a lot of disappointed TV people out on the street."

"The cops leaked it to the media," Stone said. "I made the mistake of giving them advance notice."

"I saw a cop car there this morning, with Durkee in it."

"I saw them, too; do you think they were just there to watch the fun?"

"I think they were there to arrest Arrington," Blumberg said.

"Why do you think that?"

"I heard from a source at the LAPD that they have a witness who says Arrington expressed an interest in killing Vance."

"I don't believe it," Stone said.

"I don't believe she'd say that, either," Blumberg replied, "but I do believe that someone might say she did."

"Any idea who?"

"Not yet. I think it's time for me to call the D.A. and express our desire to cooperate, offer to let them question Arrington."

"They're not going to like what she has to say. She still has a memory gap from the day before the killing until she woke up in the clinic. They're probably going to want a polygraph, too."

"I'll have the usual reasons for not cooperating on that, plus there's the memory loss; she can't lie about what she can't remember."

"They'd want to ask her if she *can* remember," Stone said. "If she says she can't, and the needle jumps, they'll be all over her."

"I think we should consider doing a polygraph of our own," Blumberg said.

"And leak it to the press?"

"Right."

"Couldn't hurt."

"Where is she now?"

"At the Malibu house; I'm with her." Stone gave him the phone number.

"Have any funeral arrangements been made yet?"

"Lou Regenstein is handling that; he plans to do it on a sound stage at the studio."

"Good idea; that'll keep the public at arm's length. Stone, I think they're going to arrest Arrington, but I think I can hold them off, until after the funeral."

"What do you think the charge will be?"

"If they have faith in their witness, it could be murder one."

"Shit," Stone said. "And that will mean no bail. I don't want to see her in jail for weeks or months, waiting for a trial."

"Neither do I," Blumberg said. "There's an outside chance that I could get house arrest, under police guard, with high bail. Can she raise it?"

"How high are we talking about?"

"At least a million; maybe as high as ten million."

"I'll have to talk to Vance's lawyer and financial people about that," Stone said. "I've been putting it off, hoping the situation would be resolved. There are two big insurance policies, but they're not going to pay, if Arrington is arrested."

"Is she the beneficiary?"

"No, the estate is, but she's the principal heir."

"If the estate is the beneficiary, the insurance company has to pay; no way around it for them. But, of course, there's a law against a murderer profiting from his crime, so probate would be another story. However, we could offer to sign over Arrington's interest in the estate to secure a high bail; a judge might go for it, because until she's convicted, she's innocent."

"Any precedent for that?"

"I'll get somebody researching; we'll do a brief."

"Good; I'll get on to the Calders' financial people and see how liquid she is."

"Okay. If the police show up there and want to arrest Arrington or take her in for questioning, tell them her doctor has ordered her to bed and to call their captain or the D.A. before proceding."

"Right." Stone said good-bye and hung up. Immediately, the phone rang. "Hello?"

"Stone, it's Betty; Manolo just called and said the police are at the Bel-Air house with a search warrant, tearing the place apart."

"Call him back and tell him not to impede them in any way," Stone replied. "I'll call him later."

"All right. Anything else?"

"Did Vance have a principal financial adviser?"

"He pretty much managed his own affairs," she replied, "but the person who would have the greatest grasp of his affairs is Marvin Kitman, his accountant. His lawyer is Bradford Crane."

Stone jotted down both numbers. "Call both of them, and tell them I'm handling Arrington's affairs. There's a power of attorney in Vance's office desk, giving me full authority; fax that to both of them."

"All right. Are you still out of touch, if the police call again?"

"I am. I'll talk to you later." Stone hung up to see Arrington coming down the stairs. She was wearing a thin, silk dressing gown, and judging from the way she was lit from behind by a large window on the stair landing, nothing else.

"Ah, that's better," she said, heading for the bar. "Can I fix you a drink?"

"It's a little early for me, and for you, too. Come and sit down, Arrington; we have to talk."

"I'm having a Virgin Mary," she said, pouring tomato cocktail over

ice, "or, as Vance used to call it when he was dieting, a 'bloody awful.'"
She came and sat down beside him on the sofa, drawing a leg under
her, exposing an expanse of inner thigh. "I'm here," she said, placing
her hand on his.

Stone took her hand. "I've got to explain your situation to you," he
said, "and you're going to have to take seriously what I tell you."

She withdrew her hand. "All right, go ahead."

"I've retained a criminal trial lawyer to represent you, a man named
Marc Blumberg."

"I know him a little," Arrington said. "His wife is in my yoga class.
But why do I need a criminal lawyer?"

"Because there's a good possibility that you may be charged with
Vance's murder."

"But that's ridiculous!" she said. "Utter nonsense!"

"I know it is, but you have to understand how the police work.
They suspect you, because you were the only one in the house when
Vance was shot."

"Except the murderer," she said.

"They think you hid the gun somewhere in the house, and they're
over there right now with a search warrant."

"Suppose they find it? What then?"

"Then they'll check it for your fingerprints."

"Complete nonsense."

"What I'm trying to tell you is that you have to be prepared to be
arrested and charged."

"You mean go to jail?"

"It's possible that, in such a case, bail could be denied by a judge,
and you'd have to remain in custody until a trial was over."

"Oh, God," she said, bringing both hands to her face, "I don't
think I could take that."

"Blumberg is exploring every possible option as to bail, and you
might have to raise a very large sum of money. Are you acquainted
enough with Vance's financial affairs to know whether that would be
readily available?"

"I only know that Vance was very well off. I mean, we lived

splendidly, as you know, but I never took an interest in his finances, and he never sat me down and explained things to me."

"I'm going to be calling his lawyer and accountant to discuss things with them. I'll know more after that, and I can explain your situation to you then." Stone thought for a moment. "Do you know if Vance had any life insurance?" He felt very sneaky asking this, but he wanted to know her answer.

"I've no idea," she replied. "My assumption is that he was rich enough not to need life insurance."

Stone breathed a little easier. "Did you have a joint bank account?"

"Yes, but I had my own account. Vance put money into it as necessary. There was a household account that Betty paid all our bills from—she signed the checks on that one—and we had the joint account, which Vance used pretty much as his own; I almost never signed checks on that one. I don't know what other accounts he had, because all that sort of mail went to his office, not to the house."

"Do you have any idea how much cash you have immediately available?"

"Vance put twenty-five thousand dollars in my account a few days before he was killed, and I probably had five or six thousand dollars in there already. So, thirty thousand, maybe? I've no idea what the joint account balance is."

"I'll check into that," Stone said. He took a deep breath. "There's something I have to ask you, Arrington, and I want the straightest answer you can give me."

"Shoot."

"Did you ever tell anyone that you were considering killing Vance?"

"Of course not!"

"Something else, and this is even more important. I have to know this: Do you think that it is within the realm of possiblity that, during the time you can't remember, you and Vance had such a serious fight that you might have killed him?"

"Absolutely not!" she cried. "How can you even ask? Don't you know me any better than that?"

"As a lawyer I sometimes have to ask unpleasant questions, even of people I know very well."

She moved across the sofa, her dressing gown falling open, and put her arms around his neck, pressing herself to him. "Oh, Stone, I'm so afraid," she said. "And I'm so glad you're here."

Stone could feel the familiar contours of her body against him. He should have pushed her away, but he couldn't bring himself to do so. "I'm here for as long as you need me," he said, stroking her hair.

They remained like that for what seemed a long time; she took his face in her hands and kissed him.

Then the doorbell began to ring repeatedly, and someone was knocking loudly.

Chapter 1·8

STONE OPENED THE DOOR. A steely-looking man in his sixties, carrying a large case stood on the doorstep.

"I'm Harold Beame," the man said. "Marc Blumberg sent me; you Stone Barrington?"

"Yes, come in."

"Marc didn't want to come himself; he figured there'd be press at the gate, and he was right."

"Might they have recognized you? Marc says you're well-known to the press."

"My car windows are heavily tinted, and they wouldn't recognize the car. Where's my subject?"

"She's upstairs; I'll get her in a minute." He led the man into the study. "Can I see your list of questions?"

"Sure." Beame handed over a sheaf of papers. "Marc faxed them to me."

Stone read through the list. They were tough questions, designed not for a milk run polygraph, but for learning the truth. Apparently, Blumberg wanted very much to know if his client was really innocent. "Fine," Stone said. "I'll get Mrs. Calder." He went upstairs and found Arrington at her dressing table. She was wearing a cotton shift over her bikini and was brushing her hair.

"Mr. Beame is downstairs in the study; he's ready for you."

"I'll be right with him." She seemed entirely serene.

"This is nothing to worry about; just give a truthful answer to each question."

"I'm not worried," she said. "I have nothing to hide."

Stone walked her downstairs to the study. "Do you mind if I sit in?" he asked Beame.

"I mind," Beame said. "It has to be just me and my subject; I don't want her to have any distractions."

Stone left the two of them alone in the study and walked out to the rear deck of the house. Beyond a carefully tended beach, the blue pacific stretched out before him. He took off his jacket and stretched out in a lounge chair. He'd had hardly any time to himself, and he was grateful for the break.

He thought of Dolce, and his thoughts were still angry. He felt some guilt about her, but he told himself he was now a free man. Dolce's behavior had made him want out of the relationship; he couldn't imagine a lifetime with a woman who behaved that way. He should have taken Dino's advice, he thought, and he'd certainly take it now. He would have to call Dolce and tell her flatly that it was over.

He thought of Arrington, and his thoughts were not pure. They had lived together for nearly a year, and during all that time, he had been happier than he had ever been with a woman. He had been crushed when she had married Vance Calder, a fact he had tried to hide from himself, without success. Now she was a free woman again—except, she might not be free for long. He had to get her out of this mess, and if he could, then they could see if they might still have some sort of life together. He thought about the money, and it annoyed him. Eduardo Bianchi's money, and his casual gift of the Manhattan house, had bothered him; he was accustomed to making his own way in the world, and the thought of a wife who was half a billionaire was, somehow, disturbing. He thought of Arrington's son, Peter. He liked the child, and he thought he could get used to being a stepfather. He might even be good at it, if he used his own father as a model. He took a deep breath and dozed off.

Arrington was shaking him, and he opened his eyes. The sun was lower in the sky, and the air was cooler.

"We're all done," she said.

"How'd it go?"

"You'll have to ask Mr. Beame."

Stone walked into the study and found Beame packing his equipment. "Want to give me a first reaction?" Stone asked.

"Marc said I could," Beame replied. "I'll send him a written report, but I can tell you now that she aced it." He frowned. "Funny, I don't think I've ever had a subject who was more relaxed, less nervous. I don't think she was tanked up on valium, or anything like that; I can still get good readings when they try that."

"I don't think she was," Stone said.

"Anyway, if she can pass with me, she can pass with anybody."

Stone realized that his pulse had increased, and now he could relax. "Thank you; I'm glad to hear it."

Beame smiled. "It's a lot easier to represent an innocent client than a guilty one, isn't it?"

"Yes, it is. When you leave, make sure that crowd at the gate doesn't see your face. I assume your windshield isn't blacked out."

"I'll wear a hat and dark glasses, and don't worry, the car is registered to a corporate name. If they run the plates, they'll come up dry."

Stone showed Beame to the door and thanked him, then he went back out to the terrace. Arrington was out of the shift, now, stretched out on a lounge in her bikini, and there was a cocktail pitcher on the table next to her.

"It's not too early for a drink now, is it?" she asked. "I made one of your favorites."

Stone poured the drinks into two martini glasses, handed her one and stretched out on the lounge next to her. He sipped the drink. "A vodka gimlet," he said. "It's been a long time."

"Poor deprived Stone," she said.

"I think I associated the drink with you."

She smiled. "I'm glad you waited until now to have one."

"You passed the polygraph with flying colors," he said.

"I know."

"You know? Arrington, you haven't been taking tranquilizers, have you?"

"Of course not. You told me just to tell the truth, didn't you?" She smiled again. "Are you relieved?"

Stone laughed. "Yes, I'm relieved."

"There was always the possibility that I'd killed Vance, wasn't there?"

"I never believed that," he said truthfully.

She reached over and took his hand. "I know you didn't; I could tell."

They sat in silence for a minute or two and sipped their drinks.

Finally, Arrington spoke. "I told you last year I'd leave Vance for you, remember?"

"I remember."

"You were terribly proper, and I was angry with you for not taking me up on it, but I must admit, I admired you for the way you behaved."

Stone said nothing.

"I'm free now, Stone; I hope that makes a difference to you."

"It does, but there's something that troubles me, and I'm not quite sure how to deal with it."

"I'm listening."

"I've spoken with Vance's accountant and lawyer, and as soon as we're past this thing with the police and the will is probated, you're going to be a very rich woman."

"Well, I suppose I assumed that," Arrington said. "How rich?"

"Half a billion dollars."

Her jaw dropped. "Half a *billion*? Is that what you said?"

"That's what I said. In fact, right now, you're a multimillionaire. You and Vance have a joint stock account that's currently worth more than fifteen million dollars."

"I suppose I thought that's what the whole estate would be worth. I guess I don't think about money, much. I don't even pay much attention to the trust Daddy left me."

"You don't have to think about this right now, but you will have to later on."

"I suppose so." She looked at him narrowly. "Are you troubled by my newfound wealth, Stone?"

"Well, yes. I guess I'll just have to get used to it."

"I was wealthy before, you know. Daddy's trust fund is a fat one, worth about twelve million, last time I checked. It never bothered you before."

"I didn't know the details," he replied. "I didn't know you were all that rich."

"Poor baby," she said, patting his cheek.

Stone took a deep breath. "Now, there's something about me you have to know."

"What's that?"

"You remember Dolce."

"Eduardo Bianchi's daughter? How could I forget that dinner party in Connecticut last summer?"

"Dolce and I were to have been married last weekend, in Venice."

Arrington sat up and looked at him, surprised. "Oh?"

He started to tell her about the preliminary, but thought better of it. What did it matter? "But before it could take place, I was on a plane to L.A."

Arrington placed a hand on her breast. "Close call," she said. "Whew!" Then she sat back. "Are you in love with her?"

"I'm . . . a little confused about that," Stone said.

She took his hand again. "Let me help clear your mind."

"I'll admit, I had misgivings, even before going to Venice, but she was pretty overwhelming."

"I can imagine," Arrington said tartly.

"Now, I think I must have been crazy. Dino has been telling me that since the moment I met her."

"Dino is a very smart man," Arrington said. "Listen to him. I know how overwhelming a moment can be; that's how I came to marry Vance. You're well out of that relationship."

"I'm not exactly out of it, yet," Stone replied. "I still have to speak to her; she's been . . . unavailable when I've called her. She's in Sicily."

"That's just about far enough away," Arrington said. "That should make it easier for you."

"I'm going to have to tell Eduardo, too."

"I can understand how facing him might be more daunting than telling Dolce."

"He's been very kind to me; he made it plain that he was very happy about my becoming his son-in-law."

"He's a nice man, but try not to make him angry. He would make a bad enemy, from what Vance has told me about him."

"Yes, I know; or, at least, that's what Dino keeps telling me. God knows, I don't want him for an enemy."

"Well, I wouldn't let too much time pass before squaring this with both Eduardo and Dolce," Arrington said. "It won't get any easier."

"I know," Stone replied.

The phone on the table between them rang, and Arrington picked it up. "Yes? Oh, hello, Manolo; yes, I'm very well, thank you. I'll be spending a couple of days out here." She listened for a moment. "Did the police make much of a mess? Well, I'm sure you and Isabel can handle it. Yes, he's right here." She handed the phone to Stone. "Manolo wants to speak to you."

Stone took the phone. "Hello, Manolo."

"Good evening, Mr. Barrington. A lady has been telephoning you here; she's called several times. A Miss Bianchi?"

"Yes, I know her; I'll call her tomorrow."

"She left a number."

Stone realized he had left Dolce's number in Sicily at the Bel-Air house. He took out a pen and notebook. "Please give it to me."

Manolo repeated the number; Stone thanked him and hung up.

"Dolce called?" Arrington asked.

"Yes." He looked at his notebook. "She seems to be at the Bel-Air Hotel."

"Why don't you call her from the study," Arrington said. "I don't want to hear this conversation."

"Good idea." Stone went into the study and dialed the hotel number.

"Bel-Air Hotel," the operator said.

"Miss Dolce Bianchi, please."

"One moment. I'm sorry, sir, but we don't have anyone by that name registered."

Stone was baffled for a moment, then he had a terrible thought. "Do you have a Mrs. Stone Barrington?"

"Yes, sir; I'll connect you."

As the phone rang, Stone gritted his teeth.

Chapter 19

THE PHONE RANG AND RANG, and for a moment, Stone thought she'd be out. He was sighing with relief when Dolce, a little breathless, picked it up.

"Hello?"

Stone couldn't quite bring himself to speak.

"Stone, don't you hang up on me," she said.

"I'm here."

"I'm sorry I took so long to answer; I was in the shower."

"We need to talk," he said.

"Come on over; I'll order dinner for us."

"I won't be able to stay for dinner; I have another commitment." This was almost true.

"I'll be waiting."

"It'll take me at least half an hour, depending on traffic. See you then," he said hurriedly, before she asked where he'd be coming from. He hung up and went back out to the deck. "I'm going to go and see her now," he said.

Arrington stood up, put her arms around him and gave him a soulful kiss. For the first time—for the first time since she'd run off with Vance—he responded the way he wanted to. Arrington stepped back and patted him on the cheek. "Poor Stone," she said. "Don't worry, you can handle it." She turned him around, pointed him toward the door, and gave him a spank on the backside, like a coach sending in a quarterback with a new play. "I'll order in some food and fix us some dinner," she called, as he reached the door.

"Don't start cooking until I call," he said. "I don't know how long this is going to take."

The mob at the Colony gate had boiled down to one TV van and a photographer, and although they stared at him as he drove through, they didn't seem to connect him with Vance Calder's widow. A few miles down the Pacific Coast Highway, there was an accident that held up traffic for half an hour, giving Stone more time than he wanted to think.

Women, he reflected, usually broke it off with him, for lack of commitment. He had never been in the position of breaking off an engagement, and he dreaded the thought. By the time he got past the accident and made it to the hotel, he was an hour late.

Dolce opened the door and threw herself into his arms. "Oh, God, I've missed you," she whispered into his ear. It did not make Stone feel any better that she was naked. It seemed that women had been flaunting nakedness all day, and he had never been very good at resisting it. He pushed her into the suite and closed the door. "Please put something on; we have to talk."

Dolce grabbed a robe and led him into the living room. Stone chose an armchair so he wouldn't have to share the sofa with her. "I'm sorry you came here," he said. "It was the wrong thing to do, in the circumstances."

"What circumstances?" she asked.

"Arrington is in trouble, and until I can get her out of it, I can't think about anything else."

"She killed Vance, didn't she? I *knew* it."

"She did not," Stone said.

"I could smell it as soon as I arrived in this town. The newspapers and TV know she's guilty, don't they?"

"They don't know anything, except the hints the cops are dropping."

"The cops know she's guilty, don't they?"

"Dolce, she passed a lie detector test this afternoon, a tough one, by a real expert."

"You need to think she's innocent, don't you, Stone? I know you; you have to believe that."

"I *do* believe that," Stone said, although Dolce was still shaking her head. "The police are trying to railroad her, because they can't find the real perpetrator, and I can't let that happen."

"Are you still in love with her, Stone?"

"Maybe; I haven't had time to think about that." In truth, he'd hardly thought of anything else. "Dolce, we very nearly made a terrible mistake. Let's both be grateful that we were spared a marriage that would never have worked."

"Why would it never have worked?"

"Because we're so different, tempermentally. We could never live with each other."

"Funny, I thought we had been living with each other for the past few months."

"Not permanently; we were playing at living together."

"*I* wasn't playing," she said.

"You know what I mean. We were . . . acting our parts, that's all. It would never have worked. I wish you hadn't come."

"Stone, I'm here, because you're my husband, and you need me."

"Dolce, I am *not* your husband, and I'd appreciate it if you'd tell the hotel that."

"Have you forgotten that we were married last Saturday, in Venice, by the mayor of the city?"

"You know as well as I do, that ceremony is not valid without a religious ceremony to follow."

"We took vows."

"I said '*si*' when prompted; I have no idea what the mayor said to me."

Dolce recited something in Italian. "'Til death us do part," she translated.

"Well, that's what happened with your previous husband, isn't it?" He shot back, then immediately regretted having said it.

"And it could happen again!" Dolce spat.

"Is that what we've come to? You're threatening me?"

Dolce stood up and came toward him. "Stone, let's not do this to each other; come to bed."

Stone stood up and backed away from her. The robe had come undone, and he fought the urge to touch her. "No, no. I have to leave, Dolce, and you should leave, too, and go back to New York or Sicily or wherever."

"Papa is going to be *very* disappointed," she said in a low voice.

That really did sound like a threat, Stone thought. "I'll call him tomorrow and explain things."

"Explain what? That you're abandoning me? Leaving me at the altar? He'll just *love* hearing that. You don't know Papa as well as you think you do. He has a terrible temper, especially when someone he loves has been wronged."

Stone was backing toward the door. "I haven't *wronged* you, Dolce; I've just explained how I feel. I'm doing you a favor by withdrawing from this situation now, instead of later, when it would hurt us both a lot more." He was reaching for the doorknob behind him.

"You're my husband, Stone," Dolce was saying, "and you always will be, for as long as you live," she added threateningly.

"Good-bye, Dolce," Stone said. He got the door open and hurried out, closing it carefully behind him.

He had gone only a few steps when he heard a large object crash against the door and shatter. On the way through the lobby, he stopped at the front desk. "I'm Stone Barrington," he said to the young woman.

"Yes, Mr. Barrington," she said. "Are you checking in again?"

"No, and please be advised that the woman in suite 336 is Miss Dolce Bianchi, not Mrs. Stone Barrington. Will you let the telephone operator know that, please?"

"Of course," the young woman said, looking nonplussed. "Whatever you say, Mr. Barrington."

Stone got the station wagon from the attendant and headed back toward Malibu. Before he had even reached Sunset, the car phone rang.

"Hello?"

"Stone," Arrington said, "I'm on my way back to Bel-Air."

"Why and how?" Stone asked.

"I caught sight of a photographer on the beach with a great big lens, and I guess it just creeped me out. Manolo came and got me; he had to smuggle me past the gate in the trunk."

"All right, I'll meet you at the house. Tell Manolo to use the utility entrance." He said good-bye and hung up. How long, he wondered, had that photographer been on the beach?

Chapter 20

STONE GOT TO THE HOUSE FIRST. He parked the car, went into the house and out to the guest house, where he started packing his clothes. He had his bags in Vance's Mercedes by the time Arrington arrived.

She came in through the front door, took a few steps, and froze, staring down the central hallway. "That's where he was, isn't it?" she asked Stone, nodding toward the spot.

"You remember?" Stone asked.

She nodded again.

He turned to the butler. "Manolo, will you fix us some dinner, please? Anything will do."

"Of course, Mr. Barrington," the butler said, and disappeared into the kitchen.

Stone took Arrington's hand and walked her to the bedroom. He sat her on the bed and sat down beside her. "What else do you remember?" he asked. "This is important."

Arrington wrinkled her brow. "Just Vance lying there, bleeding."

"Do you remember anything immediately before that?"

"I don't think so."

"Do you remember hearing the shot?"

She shook her head. "No. Just Vance lying there."

"Do you remember the police and the paramedics arriving?"

"No. Nothing until I woke up in the clinic." She laid her head on his shoulder. "When is this going to be over, Stone?"

"Not for a while," Stone replied. "We've still got the funeral on Friday, and on Saturday, we have to take you to the district attorney's office."

"Will they put me in jail?"

"I hope not; Marc Blumberg's working on that."

"I'm so glad you're here," she said. She put her hand on his cheek and drew him closer, kissing him.

Stone pulled back. "Listen to me carefully," he said. "You and I cannot be seen by *anybody* being . . . affectionate with each other."

"Only Manolo and Maria are here."

"And they'd both be shocked, if they walked in here and found us kissing. If they were called to testify in court, they'd have to tell the truth. Your husband has been dead for less than a week; you have to be seen to be the grieving widow for some time to come; I cannot tell you how important that is to your future."

She nodded. "I understand." She took his hand. "But it's important for you to know that I still love you. I never stopped."

Stone squeezed her hand but could not bring himself to respond. "Go freshen up for dinner," he said.

They dined in the smaller of the two dining rooms, on pasta and a bottle of California Chardonnay. They chatted about old times in New York, but as dinner wore on, Arrington seemed increasingly tired.

"I think you're going to have to put me to bed," she said finally.

Stone rang for Manolo. "We'll get Isabel; she'll put you to bed."

Arrington nodded sleepily. "I wish you were coming to bed with me."

"Shhh," Stone said. He turned her over to Isabel, got the keys and the alarm code for the Colony house from Manolo, then drove back to Malibu. He chose the guest room nearest the kitchen, unpacked, soaked in a tub for a while, and fell asleep.

He was awakened by the telephone. Nine-thirty, he saw by the bedside clock. He had slept like a stone.

"Hello?"

"Stone?"

"Yes."

"It's Marc Blumberg."

"Good morning, Marc."

"No, it's not."

"What's the problem?"

"The problem is, there is a very nice color photograph of you and Arrington in each other's arms, on the cover of the *National Inquisitor.* She's wearing a very tiny bikini."

"Oh, God," Stone groaned.

"Did the two of you spend the night together?"

"No, we didn't. I had to go into L.A., and while I was gone, Arrington spotted the photographer on the beach. Her butler came and drove her to the Bel-Air house. I met them there, we had dinner, then I moved out of the guest house and out here."

"Did the media outside the gates figure out that Arrington left?"

"No, I don't think so; she left in the trunk of the car."

"Did any media see you return to the house last night?"

"There was a TV truck there, but they paid little attention to me."

"So they think she's still there, and that you spent the night together."

"I suppose they could draw that conclusion."

"All right, I'm going to have to hold a press conference and try to contain this."

"I suppose that's the right thing to do."

"The upside is, you were fully clothed and were seen to leave after kissing her, while she remained on the deck. The photograph is a little ambiguous, too; I can claim that you were simply consoling her. The *Inquisitor* hasn't figured out who you are, yet; I'll describe you as a family friend who drove her home from the clinic."

"All right."

"They're going to put all this together sooner or later, probably sooner, so be prepared for some attention. Tell me, does Vance's bungalow at Centurion have a bedroom?"

"Yes, it does."

"I want you to move out of the Malibu house and into the bungalow this morning."

"All right. I'm very sorry about this, Marc. It was all very innocent."

"Don't worry about it; damage control is part of what I do. I'd just like there to be as little damage as possible to have to control."

"I understand."

"Now, listen: I don't want you to leave by the Colony gate."

"I'm afraid that's the only way out, Marc."

"Here's what you do. Pack your bags into the car and leave it in front of the house, with the key in the ignition. Then walk south along the beach about a mile, and you'll come to a restaurant. Walk through the building and be in the parking lot at, say, eleven o'clock. One of my people will pick up the car at the house and drive it to the restaurant."

"All right."

"Now, for God's sake, don't wear a business suit for your walk down the beach. Blend in."

"Will do."

"What kind of car is it?"

"A black Mercedes SL600 convertible."

"Be there at eleven. I'll call you around noon at the studio." Blumberg hung up.

Stone made himself some breakfast, then packed his bags, put them into the car, then showered and dressed in a guest bathing suit. He grabbed a towel and left the house by the front door. He walked down a couple of houses and cut through a yard and onto the beach.

It was a beautiful California morning, and Stone enjoyed the walk. He was passed by other people in bathing suits, joggers, and people walking their dogs. He got to the restaurant a little early, had a cup of coffee, then walked out into the parking lot. An attractive young woman was standing beside the Mercedes, waiting.

"Good morning, I'm Stone Barrington," he said, offering his hand.

"Hi, I'm Liz Raymond, one of Marc's associates," she replied.

"Can I drop you anywhere?"

"I'll be picked up here," the woman said. "Nice swimsuit."

"Thanks, it's borrowed."

"See you later," she said, as a car pulled up. She got into it and was driven away.

Stone drove to Centurion, gave the guard at the gate a wave, and drove to the bungalow. He walked inside with his bags to be greeted by an astonished Betty Southard.

"Well, now," she said, "you've just topped Vance. He never walked in here in a bathing suit."

"It's a long story," Stone said.

"I'll bet, and I've got all day," she replied.

Chapter 21

STONE EXPLAINED HIS APPEARANCE, then he pointed at three large canvas bags on the floor near Betty's office door. "What are those?" he asked.

"Arrington's mail," she said.

"I'm sorry, I don't understand."

"After Vance's death, his fans kept writing. I've got two girls in the back room sorting it now. Those are the bags we haven't gotten to yet."

"I don't believe it."

"Well, believe this: Right now, opinion is running about sixty-forty in favor of Arrington being a murderess."

"'Murderess,' that has a quaint Victorian ring to it."

"I guess I'm just a quaint, Victorian girl," she replied.

Stone picked up his bags. "Where's the bedroom?" he asked. "Marc Blumberg wants me to move in here."

"Somewhere the *Inquisitor* can't find you?"

"I was just hugging her," he lied.

"Come on, I'll show you." She led the way down a hall and into a comfortably furnished bedroom with an adjacent bath and dressing room. "Want me to unpack for you?" she asked.

"Thanks, I can manage," he replied, laughing. "Go back to your mail; I want to get dressed." Betty left the room, and Stone got out of the swimsuit and into some clothes.

Betty appeared in the doorway. "Marc Blumberg's holding a press conference on TV." She switched on a set at the foot of the bed, and the two of them sat down to watch it as, on television, a secretary opened a set of double doors and the press poured into Blumberg's office, where he awaited them, seated behind an impressive desk.

"Thank you, ladies and gentlemen," Blumberg said, remaining seated. "I have a brief statement for you regarding the investigation into the death of Vance Calder. Can we hold the flash cameras until I've finished, please?"

When everything had quieted down, Blumberg began. "I have been retained by Vance Calder's widow, Arrington, to represent her during the investigation of her husband's death, not because she has anything to fear from the investigation, but because she wants to be sure that the Los Angeles Police Department is leaving no stone unturned in the pursuit of her husband's murderer."

"What about the photograph in today's *Inquisitor*?" somebody asked.

"I'll get to that in a minute," Blumberg replied. "Now, if I may continue?" He stared the room into silence. "Good. This is what we know so far: Last Saturday night, Mr. and Mrs. Calder were getting ready to go to a dinner party at the home of Lou Regenstein, chairman of Centurion Pictures. Mr. Calder was dressing, and Mrs. Calder was in the bathtub. A servant heard a loud noise, and when he investigated, found Mr. Calder lying in the central hallway of the house, near death, having received a gunshot wound to the head. The servant summoned the police and an ambulance, then sent a maid to let Mrs. Calder know what had happened.

"When Mrs. Calder saw her husband, she collapsed and had to be treated for shock by the paramedics when they arrived. Her personal physician was summoned; he sedated her and arranged for her to be moved immediately to a private clinic, where she remained until yesterday. She asked for a family friend, a New York attorney, Mr. Stone

Barrington, to come to Los Angeles to handle her affairs, and Mr. Barrington was summoned from Italy, where he was on vacation.

"When Mr. Barrington arrived, he spoke with Mrs. Calder's physician about her condition and learned that she was unable to remember anything that had happened between mid-afternoon last Friday and the time when she awoke in the clinic on Sunday morning. The moment Mrs. Calder was up to it, Mr. Barrington invited the police to interview her at the clinic, and yesterday, he picked her up there and took her to her Malibu home, where he hoped she might have some privacy to continue her recovery.

"Sadly, a tabloid photographer violated her privacy and photographed her with Mr. Barrington as she took the sun on a rear deck of the house. Mr. Barrington then left the house, giving her a hug before leaving, and that, ladies and gentlemen, was the photograph that was so outrageously misrepresented in the tabloid's pages.

"I am sorry to tell you that, as of this moment, the LAPD is treating Mrs. Calder as a suspect, and that later in the week, she will be interviewed by the district attorney's office. In anticipation of that meeting I arranged yesterday for her to receive a thorough polygraph examination from Mr. Harold Beame, formerly with the FBI, who is a renowned examiner. I am pleased to tell you that Mr. Beame has reported that, in his expert opinion, Mrs. Calder answered truthfully every question put to her. I can tell you that they were very tough questions; I know, because I wrote them myself."

This got a laugh from the group.

"However, when we meet with the district attorney, I intend to volunteer Mrs. Calder for another polygraph, administered by a qualified examiner of his choosing. Further, at that meeting, Mrs. Calder will answer every question put to her by members of the district attorney's office.

"Finally, Mrs. Calder has authorized me to offer a reward of $100,000 for any information leading to the arrest and conviction of her husband's killer." He held up a placard with a telephone number on it. "We ask that anyone with such information call both the police *and* this number. We wouldn't want anything to get lost in the shuffle at the LAPD."

Another laugh.

"That's all I have to tell you, at the moment, and I won't be answering any questions today. However, you may rest assured that I will be in contact with the media when there is anything of significance to report."

With that, Blumberg got up and marched out of his office, ignoring the questions shouted by the crowd.

Betty switched off the set. "Well, I guess that puts the ball in the D.A.'s court, doesn't it?"

"I believe it does," Stone agreed. "That was a very impressive performance."

"Did you approve the reward?"

"No, but I would have, if asked. I think it's a good idea. It might turn up something and, at the very least, it will keep the police busy with leads from people who want the money."

A phone on the bedside table rang, and Betty answered it. "It's Marc Blumberg," she said, handing Stone the phone.

"Hi, Marc; I saw your press conference. Very good, and you have my approval on the reward money."

"I thought I would have," Blumberg answered. "I want to meet with Arrington this afternoon; where shall we do it?"

"How about three o'clock at her house? You know where it is?"

"Yes, and that's fine."

"There's a utility entrance at the rear of the property. . . ."

"No," Blumberg interrupted, "I'll go in the front way; let the press see me."

"Whatever you think best."

"Just keep that phrase in mind, and we'll get along great, Stone. See you at three." He hung up.

The phone rang again immediately, and Betty answered it. "It's Arrington," she said, handing Stone the phone again.

"Hi."

"I just saw Marc Blumberg on TV; was that your idea?"

"No, it was his, but I wholeheartedly approve."

"I haven't seen this rag, but I take it the photographer I saw was responsible."

"Yes; that should give you some idea of how careful you have to be. Marc Blumberg is coming to the house at three this afternoon; be ready to meet him, and don't wear a bikini."

She laughed. "Touché. Will you be here?"

"Yes."

"See you then."

Stone hung up and turned to Betty. "Will you make some notes on the tenor of the mail you're receiving? I expect Blumberg will want to know about it."

"Sure; I'll go add it all up now." Betty left the room.

Stone finished dressing. For the first time, he was beginning to feel some optimism about the way things were going. Marc Blumberg was a considerable force, when aroused, and Stone was glad to have him on Arrington's side.

Chapter 22

HE HAD BEEN DREADING THIS CALL, but he couldn't put it off any longer. Stone dialed Eduardo Bianchi's private telephone number in New York. As usual, he got only the beep from an answering machine, no message.

"Eduardo, it's Stone Barrington. I would be grateful if you could call me sometime today; there's something important I have to talk to you about." He left the numbers of both the bungalow and the Calder house.

Then he called Dino. He could not remember when so much time had passed without a conversation with his friend, and he knew he had been putting off this one, because he knew what Dino would say.

"She's guilty," Dino said, after Stone had brought him up to date.

"No, she's not."

"You just don't want to believe it, because you think she killed him so she could have you."

Stone winced at the truth. "She passed a polygraph yesterday, aced it," he said lamely.

"Yeah, I saw Blumberg's press conference on CNN. I don't believe it; she must have been on drugs, or something."

"The examiner told me drugs couldn't fool him." It had occured to him that Arrington had seemed eerily calm since she had left the clinic.

"Look, Stone, I've been getting updates from Rick Grant, and while they may not have her cold, his people really believe she whacked her husband."

"I'm aware of their opinion," Stone said. "But don't judge her so soon. I'm here, on the spot, up to my ears in this, and my instincts tell me she's innocent."

"Stone, nobody's *innocent,* you know that. Everybody's guilty of *something.*"

"Not murder; not Arrington. She doesn't have it in her."

"Whatever you say, pal."

"There's something else."

"What?"

"I ended it with Dolce last night."

"Good news, at last! What made you see the light?"

"We had a transatlantic conversation that I didn't like the tone of, for one thing."

"And Arrington's free, for another thing?"

"There is that," Stone admitted sheepishly. "It was something I hadn't expected."

"Have you told Eduardo?"

"I have a call in to him now."

"That should be an interesting conversation."

"Any advice as to how I should handle it?"

"Oh, I don't know; how do you feel about South America?"

"Come on, Dino; how should I break it to him?"

"Right between the eyes, dead straight; he might respect that."

"I hope so."

"Then again, he might not. He dotes on that girl; if he thinks you've done her wrong, well . . ."

"Well, what?"

"You might not be well for very long."

"Dino, this isn't Sicily."

"To Eduardo, *everywhere* is Sicily."

"I see your point," Stone said.

"I think everything is going to depend on what Dolce says to

Eduardo," Dino said. "How pissed off was she when you broke it to her?"

"Pretty pissed off."

"Oh."

"Yeah."

"Maybe she'll cool off before she talks to the old man."

"Maybe."

"For your sake, I hope so."

"Thanks."

"You want me to take some time off, come out there?"

"I don't know what you could do, Dino, except keep me company. That, I wouldn't mind."

"You let me know if something comes up and you need me, okay?"

"Okay."

"I got a meeting; talk to you later."

Stone hung up. Why did everybody think Arrington was guilty, except him? Was he completely nuts? Blinded by how he felt about her? He made himself a sandwich in the bungalow's kitchen, then went into Betty's office. "How's the mail coming?"

Betty consulted a steno pad. "Nearly done," she said, "and opinion is running about two to one against Arrington."

"Swell," Stone said. He looked at his watch. "I've got to run; I'm meeting Marc Blumberg at the house."

Stone took the rear entrance, then watched through a front window as Marc Blumberg drove very slowly through the mob of press, through the gates, and up to the house. The lawyer certainly knew how to make an entrance.

Arrington appeared from the bedroom just as Blumberg entered the house. She gave Stone a peck on the cheek, then shook hands with Blumberg.

"How are you, Marc? It's been a long time."

"I'm teriffic, Arrington, and I hope you are, too."

"I'm all right, I guess. How is Arlene?"

"Very well."

"Tell her I miss my yoga class with her."

"I know she misses you, too."

Manolo stepped up. "May I get you anything, Mr. Blumberg?"

"No thanks," Blumberg replied. "Let's get down to work. Arrington, I want to talk with you alone at some length; where can we do that?"

"Vance's study would be a good place," she replied. "Can Stone be there?"

"Sorry, this is just you and me." He took a folder from his briefcase and handed it to Stone. "You might take a look at this while we're talking. We'll be a while."

Stone accepted the folder and watched as Arrington led Marc Blumberg into Vance's study and closed the door. He asked Manolo for some iced tea, then went out onto the rear terrace, took a seat, and opened the folder. Inside was the medical examiner's report on Vance Calder's autopsy.

Manolo brought the tea and left him alone. He began to read. Death as the result of a single gunshot to the right occipital region of the head. No news there. Subject a well-developed male of fifty-two years, seven months, six feet two, a hundred and ninety pounds. Stone's own height and weight. Drugs present in bloodstream: Zyrtec, an antihistamine; alcohol content: .03, a drink or two.

He was surprised at the number of scars found on Vance's body: two-inch scar over left collarbone—sutured; one-and-one-half-inch scar, inside of left wrist, unsutured, secondary tissue present; two-and-one-half-inch surgical scar, right shoulder; one-inch abdominal surgical scar; three-inch surgical scar, left knee, two-inch scar, sutured, right thigh; several small scars on both hands. X rays revealed some old broken bones—right femur, left tibia, and a broken nose. That, he reflected, had given Vance's face additional character, kept him from looking pretty. All in all, though, it sounded as though Vance had lead a rougher life than that of a pampered movie star. He noted the absence of any cosmetic surgical scars. Vance Calder had been the real thing.

. . .

More than an hour passed before Arrington and Marc Blumberg emerged from the study. Arrington looked decidedly pale and shaken, while Blumberg was his usual, cool, well-pressed self.

"I'm going to go lie down for a few minutes," Arrington said, and went into the bedroom.

"Well," Stone said, "do you think she's innocent?"

"She's my client," Blumberg replied, "so she's innocent."

"Come on, Marc, I want an opinion. So far, everybody I know except me thinks she did it."

"It doesn't matter," Blumberg said.

"It doesn't matter?"

"Not to me, Stone; but then I'm not in love with her."

Stone was surprised at this, but he said nothing.

"She's innocent until proven guilty, and I'm going to keep her that way."

"How are you going to handle the D.A. on Saturday?"

"I'm not going to handle him," Blumberg replied. "I'm going to stay out of his way, and let him at her."

"You really think that's a good idea?"

"Listen, the D.A.'s questioning is going to be nothing, compared with what I just put her through. I dragged her back and forth across the stones of her story for an hour, and she never budged from it. The woman is a rock, and the D.A. is not going to make a dent in her. She's a good actress, too."

"Actress?"

"She'll have a jury on her side from the moment she opens her mouth, and I don't have the slightest qualm about having her testify. O.J.'s team was smart to keep him off the stand—the prosecution would have gutted him, just as happened in the civil trial, but they won't lay a glove on Arrington, trust me."

"You think it'll go to trial?"

"Not unless they've got a lot more than I think they've got. We'll find out about that on Saturday morning. What did you think of the autopsy report?"

"Pretty straightforward. He sure had a lot of scars."

"I asked Arrington about that; he did most of his own stunt work. Over the years, it took its toll."

"That would explain it," Stone said. "God, I hope this doesn't go to trial."

"I wouldn't mind, if it did," Blumberg said with a small smile. "A trial would be a lot of fun."

Chapter 23

STONE GOT OUT OF THE BENTLEY and went around to the other side, where Manolo was holding the rear door open for Arrington and her son, Peter, and his grandmother, who had brought him back for the service, at the insistence of Marc Blumberg.

Stone took her left hand, tucked it under his arm while she held Peter's hand with her right, and led the little group through the open rear door of the sound stage, past a large truck with satellite dishes on top. The soft strains of a pipe organ wafted through the huge space. Schubert, he thought.

As he led them to a front pew, he took in the atmosphere, which was fragmented, and a little unreal. The cathedral set was not complete, being composed of only those parts necessary for the shooting of a scene. Everything at the rear—the choir loft, the organ and its pipes, the pulpit (or whatever it was called in a Catholic or Anglican church)—looked like the real thing, while other parts of the ceiling and stained glass windows were incomplete. A coffin of highly polished walnut rested in front of the pulpit. Stone wondered if Vance Calder's body was really inside, or if it was just a prop.

He deposited Arrington and Peter next to her mother on the front pew, then walked to the side of the seating area and stood. From there, he had an excellent view of the crowd. Perhaps twenty pews had been placed on the concrete floor, and they were packed with Hollywood aristocracy. Stone recognized several movie stars, and he was sure that the others were the crème de la crème of producers, writers, and directors. Two pews behind Arrington he was surprised to spot Charlene Joiner, the costar of Vance's last film, with whom he had, apparently, been sleeping. At the other end of the pew sat Dolce, accompanied by her father. Dolce pointedly ignored him, but Eduardo gave him a grave glance, and they exchanged somber nods. Eduardo had not returned his phone call.

Behind the twenty pews was a sea of folding chairs, occupied by the working folk of Centurion Studios—directors, carpenters, grips, bit players, script ladies, and all the other people who made movies happen. Stone counted four large television cameras—the studio kind, not the handheld news models, and he realized that they must be feeding to the big truck outside. A boy's choir began to sing, and Stone turned to find that the youngsters had filed into the choir loft while he had been looking at the crowd. It took him a moment to realize that their moving lips were not in synch with the music: That was recorded, and the boys were, apparently, child actors. The organist, too, was faking it; only the choir director seemed to truly understand the music. The whole scene was gorgeously lit.

As the strains of the choir died, and the boys stopped moving their lips, a richly costumed priest (or actor?) walked onto the set and began speaking in Latin. If he was an actor, Stone reflected, he certainly had his lines down pat. Stone was glad the coffin was not open, if indeed, Vance's body was inside, because this was the first funeral service he had ever attended where he was wearing the corpse's suit.

The clothes he had brought with him had been chosen for Venice, and Dolce had insisted on light colors. When he had confessed to Arrington that he had nothing suitable for a funeral, she had suggested he wear some of Vance's clothes, which had turned out to fit him very well indeed—so well, in fact, that Arrington was insisting that he have all of Vance's clothes, the thought of which made him uncomfortable.

"Look," she had said, "if you don't take all these perfectly beautiful suits, jackets, and shirts, they'll end up being sold at some ghastly celebrity auction. Please, Stone, you'd be doing me a great favor."

So now he stood staring at the coffin, wearing the deceased's dark blue Douglas Hayward chalk-stripe suit, his handmade, sweetly comfortable Lobb shoes, and his Turnbull & Asser silk shirt and necktie. The underwear and socks were, mercifully, his own.

The eulogies began, led by Lou Regenstein. They were kept short, and the speakers had, apparently, been chosen by ocupation: There was an actor, a director, a producer, and an entertainment lawyer. Each, of course, spoke of Vance's endearing personal qualities and gift for friendship, but his Oscars, New York Film Critics' Awards, and his business acumen were all covered at some length, as well.

When the service ended, the coffin was opened, and Vance's body was, indeed, inside. Those in the pews were directed past the coffin to Arrington, who stood alone, well to one side of the coffin, while those in the folding chairs to the rear were directed out the hangarlike doors at the front of the sound stage.

After speaking words of condolence, the mourners divided into two groups—some were directed toward the main doors, while the truly close friends and business associates were sent out the rear door, where their cars waited to take them to the cemetery.

Stone stood near the rear door and, shortly, Eduardo Bianchi drifted over, while Dolce remained in the line of mourners. Eduardo, dressed in a severly cut black silk suit, held out his hand and shook Stone's warmly. "Stone, I'm sorry not to have returned your call yesterday, but I was en route to Los Angeles and did not receive your message until this morning."

"That's quite all right, Eduardo," Stone replied. "It's good to see you."

"I expect that you called to tell me of yours and Dolce's . . . ah, difficulties. She had, of course, already told me."

"I'm sorry that I couldn't tell you, myself," Stone said. "This is not easy, of course, but I believe it is the best thing for Dolce. I'm not sure what it is for me."

"I understand that these things sometimes do not work out," Eduardo said. "People's lives are complicated, are they not?"

"They certainly are," Stone agreed.

"I understand that Dolce can be a difficult woman, and I know that Vance's death has, perhaps, meant a sudden change in your life. I want you to know that I remain fond of you, Stone, in spite of all that has happened. I had hoped to have you for a son, but I will be content, if I must, to have you for a friend."

"Thank you, Eduardo, for understanding. I will always be very pleased to be your friend and to have you as mine." To Stone's surprise, Eduardo embraced him, then turned and walked back to join Dolce in the receiving line.

The drive to Forest Lawn was quiet, except for Arrington's patiently answering Peter's questions about the service and who all the people were. Stone was glad he didn't have to answer the questions himself.

At the brief graveside service, Stone stood to one side again, and when it was over, he was surprised to be approached by Charlene Joiner, who held out her hand and introduced herself.

"I'd like to speak to you privately, if I may," she said.

Her accent was southern, and Stone remembered that she was from the same small Georgia town, Delano, as Betty Southard.

"This is probably not the best time," Stone replied. "I'm staying at Vance's bungalow at the studio," Stone replied. "You can reach me there."

"I'll call over the weekend," she said, then turned and went to her car.

After the service, Stone drove Arrington, Peter, and her mother home to Bel-Air. All the way, he wondered what Charlene Joiner could possibly have to say to him.

Later, he met Vance's accountant at the Calders' bank, where he signed a very large note on Arrington's behalf and drew a number of cashier's checks. Now he was ready for the district attorney.

Chapter 24

ON SATURDAY MORNING, Stone arrived at the Bel-Air house, entering through the utility entrance, as usual. Marc Blumberg arrived moments later, and since Arrington was not quite ready, they had a moment to talk.

"Where do we stand on bail?" Blumberg asked.

Stone took an envelope from his pocket. "First of all," he said, handing Blumberg a check, "here is your half-million-dollar retainer."

"Thank you very much," Blumberg said, pocketing the check.

Stone displayed the remaining contents of the envelope. "I also have a cashier's check for five million dollars, made out to the court, and five others for a million each, so we can handle any amount of bail up to ten million dollars immediately. If more is required, I can write checks on Arrington's account for another five million."

"I like a lawyer who comes prepared," Blumberg said. "Now, at this meeting, I don't want you to say anything at all."

Stone shrugged. "All right."

"It may get rough, and you may feel the need to come to Arrington's rescue, but allow me to make the decision as to when that becomes necessary. If we can get through this questioning without either of us having to speak, then we'll have won our point."

"I understand. If they arrest her, though, she's going to have to spend the weekend in jail. We're not going to get a judge for a bail hearing on a Saturday."

"Let me worry about that," Blumberg said. "And if, for any reason, we can't get bail, I'll arrange for her to be segregated at the county jail."

Arrington walked into the room, wearing a simple black suit and carrying a small suitcase. "Good morning, all," she said, and held up the bag. "I've brought a few things, in case I have to stay."

Stone was relieved that he had not had to suggest that to her.

"Let's go, then," Blumberg said. "I've hired a limo to take us all in comfort. We'll go out the back way, and we'll enter the courthouse through the basement parking lot."

The three of them joined Blumberg's associate, Liz Raymond, in the long black car and departed the property by way of the utility gate, unobserved. The ride to the courthouse was very quiet.

On reaching the courthouse, they drove into the underground garage and stopped at the elevators, where detectives Durkee and Bryant were waiting.

"Hello, Sam, Ted," Blumberg said, shaking their hands. Stone ignored them.

The group rode upstairs in the elevator, walked down a hallway, and entered a large conference room, where the district attorney and two of his assistants, a man and a woman, awaited, along with a stenographer. Blumberg introduced the D.A., Dan Reeves, and the two ADAs, Bill Marshall, who was black, and Helen Chu, who was Asian. No hands were shaken.

"Please be seated," Reeves said, and they all sat down around the table.

"As I understand it," Reeves said, "you are here to surrender Mrs. Calder."

Blumberg held up a hand. "Before any charge is made, I request that you question my client. It's my belief that, when you are done, you will see that an arrest is unnecessary."

"All right; do you have any objection to a stenographic record being made?"

"None whatsoever. I'd also like to volunteer my client for a polygraph; you choose the examiner."

"Yes, I saw your press conference," Reeves said dryly. "Shall we begin?"

"By all means."

Reeves dictated the names of those present and started to ask his first question, but Blumberg interrupted.

"I'd like the record to show that my client is here voluntarily and is willing to answer all questions."

"So noted," the D.A. said. "Mrs. Calder, you understand you are here because you are a suspect in the murder of your husband, Vance Calder?"

"I understand it, but I don't understand it," Arrington replied in a calm voice.

"Beg pardon?"

"I mean, I accept your characterization of my visit here, but I don't understand why I'm a suspect."

"That will become apparent as we proceed," Reeves said. "Mrs. Calder, please recount the events as you recall them on the evening of your husband's death."

"I have only one memory of that evening," Arrington said. "I remember being shown my husband's body as it lay on the floor of the central hallway of our house. Apart from that single image, I have no recollection of anything between midafternoon the previous day and the following morning, when I woke up at the Judson Clinic."

Blumberg spoke up. "For the record, Dr. James Judson, an eminent psychiatrist, is available to testify that Mrs. Calder is suffering from a kind of amnesia, brought on by the shock of her husband's violent death."

"So you have no recollection of shooting your husband?" Reeves asked.

"I would never have shot my husband," Arrington replied, "but I have no recollection of the events of that evening."

"So you don't know if you shot him?"

"I know that I would *never* do such a thing."

"But you don't *know*."

"Asked and answered," Blumberg said. "Perfectly clear."

"Mrs. Calder, is it possible that, while delusional, you might have shot your husband?"

"I have never been delusional," Arrington replied. "My doctor has explained to me that my amnesia has nothing to do with delusion."

"Have you ever threatened to kill your husband?"

"Certainly not."

Reeves took a small tape recorder from a credenza behind him and placed it on the table. "This is an excerpt from an interview with a friend of yours, Mrs. Beverly Walters."

"An acquaintance, not a friend," Arrington replied.

Reeves pressed a button.

"I told Arrington," Beverly Walters' voice said, "that I had it on good authority that Vance, during the filming of his last picture, was sleeping with his costar, Charlene Joiner, on a regular basis. She pooh-poohed this. I asked her if she would divorce Vance, if she found out that it was true. She replied, and these are her exact words, 'I wouldn't divorce him, I'd shoot him.' And this was two days before Vance was killed."

Reeves stopped the machine. "Do you recall this conversation with Mrs. Walters?"

"Yes, I do," Arrington replied.

"So you admit having said that you would not divorce your husband on learning of his adultery, but shoot him, instead?"

"I spoke those words in jest, and Mrs. Walters took them as such. We both had a good laugh about it."

"But you don't deny having said that you would shoot your husband?"

"Mr. Reeves, how many times have you said, in jest, that you would kill somebody, maybe even your wife? This is common parlance, and we all do it. I had no evidence of adultery on my husband's part. I regarded him at that time, and still do, as a faithful husband."

"But Mrs. Walters had just told you that she, quote, 'had it on good authority' unquote, that your husband was actually committing adultery with his costar, Ms. Joiner."

"Mr. Reeves, I would never accept Beverly Walters' word about such a thing. She is an inveterate and vicious gossip, who enjoys stirring up trouble, and that is why she is an acquaintance, and not a friend of mine. If her husband were not an occasional business associate of my husband, I would not see her at all."

"But she said she had it on good authority."

"'Good authority,' to Beverly Walters, is something she heard at the hairdresser's or read in a scandal sheet. Did you ask her to substantiate this rumor she was spreading?"

Reeves didn't reply.

"I assure you that if I were a murderous person, I would have been much more likely to shoot Beverly Walters than my husband."

Stone had to suppress a smile.

"Mrs. Calder, did you and your husband ever fight?"

"Occasionally—perhaps rarely would be a better choice of words."

"Physically fight?"

"No, never."

"I will reserve the right to present evidence to the contrary at a later date," Reeves said. "That concludes the questioning," he said to the stenographer. "Thank you; you may leave us now."

The stenographer took her machine and left the room.

Stone was surprised that Arrington's questioning had been so brief, and that no further evidence against her had been offered.

"Mrs. Calder," the district attorney said, "you are under arrest on a charge of second-degree murder. Please stand up."

Arrington stood, and the two police detectives began to handcuff her.

ON SUNDAY MORNING, Stone got up and went out for the papers. He'd have to arrange daily delivery, he thought. The studio, ordinarily a hive of activity, was dead on a Sunday. He drove through the empty streets, inquired of the guard at the gate where to get a paper, and for his trouble was rewarded with a *New York Times* and a *Los Angeles Times.*

"We get a few delivered for folks who are working over the weekend," the guard said.

Stone returned to the bungalow, and as he entered, the phone was ringing. He picked it up.

"Stone Barrington?"

"Yes."

"This is Charlene Joiner."

"Good morning."

"As I mentioned at the funeral, I'd like to get together with you; I have some information you might find interesting."

"Alright," Stone said.

"Why don't you come to lunch? There'll be some other people here, but we can find a moment to talk."

"Thank you, I will," Stone replied.

"Do you know the Malibu Colony?"

"Yes, I've been to the Calder House there."

"I'm six doors down," she said. She gave him the house number. "One o'clock, and California casual."

"See you then." He hung up, wondering what information she might have for him and what "California casual" meant.

Betty had left danish pastries in the fridge for him; he made himself some coffee and spent the morning reading the papers. The L.A. paper had a front-page story about Arrington's arrest, while the New York paper had a blurb on the front page and an inside story—this seemed to be the standard coverage. Marc Blumberg had issued a press release, detailing Arrington's willingness to answer all questions. "I don't expect this to go to trial," he said, "if the LAPD does its job, but should it do so, Mrs. Calder will testify without fear of any question."

Stone thought that was immoderate; things might change before the trial, and they might not want her to testify. Still, it sounded good now, and helped create the impression that Arrington had nothing to fear from a trial. He was troubled by the D.A.'s reluctance to disclose the evidence against her. Normally, they would use the press to reinforce the idea that they had a strong case.

He passed through the Malibu Colony gate a little after one, then drove to Charlene Joiner's house. A uniformed maid opened the door for him and took him out to a rear terrace. Charlene and another woman were sitting beside the pool, talking, both wearing swimsuits. Charlene stood up, wrapped a colorful sarong skirt around her lower body, and came to greet him, hand out.

"Hello, Stone," she said, taking his hand and leading him toward the other woman. "This is Ilsa Berends," she said.

Stone recognized the actress from her films. She was in her early forties, he thought, but in wonderful shape. "How do you do, Miss Berends," he said. "I've enjoyed your work in films." He turned to Charlene. "Yours, too. In fact I saw one on the airplane from Milan."

"You were in Milan recently?" Berends asked.

"Venice, really; I flew out of Milan."

"Vacation?" Charlene asked.

"Sort of," Stone replied. He turned to see another woman arriving, and she was another recognizable actress, though he could not remember her name. Five minutes later, two more arrived.

Charlene introduced everyone. "I'm afraid you're going to be in the middle of a hen party," she said. "You're our only man."

"The pleasure is mine," Stone replied. A houseman brought everyone mimosas, and half an hour later, they sat down to lunch.

The conversation was about L.A. matters—films, gossip, and shopping.

"I understand you're a friend of Arrington Calder," Ilsa Berends said to Stone.

It was the first question addressed to him by anyone. "That's right," Stone said.

"I also hear you used to live together," the actress said. This got everyone's attention.

"I think I'll stand on attorney-client privilege," Stone replied.

Everyone laughed.

"Were you there when Arrington was arrested?" another woman asked.

"I was at the meeting at the D.A.'s office, where Arrington had voluntarily appeared and answered questions."

"I think she did it," the youngest woman, who could only have been in her early twenties, said.

"Certainly not," Stone replied.

"The loyal attorney," Berends said.

"So far, the district attorney seems to have no evidence against her."

"Except Beverly Walters' statement," Charlene said.

Stone was astonished. "How did you know about that?" he asked.

Everybody laughed.

"Because Beverly has told everyone she knows about it," Charlene replied. "She would never be involved in anything like this without telling all of Beverly Hills."

"Well, I can tell you that her version of the conversation is different from Arrington's. It was an entirely innocent remark."

"Innocent, that she said she was going to kill her husband?" Berends asked.

"Haven't you ever said you were going to kill somebody?"

"No, not seriously."

"Neither has Arrington—seriously."

"You're sweet, standing up for her like that. You really think she's innocent?"

"I really do," Stone said. "Or I wouldn't say so."

"So, what's your strategy going to be at trial?" somebody asked.

"That will be for Marc Blumberg to decide; he's the lead attorney in the case. I'm just helping out when I can and handling Arrington's personal affairs."

"Oh, so Arrington had affairs, too?" someone asked.

"Her business affairs," Stone said, wagging a finger at her. "There's an estate to settle and a lot of other things to be taken care of."

"Didn't Vance have a lawyer?"

"Yes, but Arrington is entitled to her own representation."

"So, what have you handled for her?"

"Ladies, you'll have to forgive me; I've said about all I can."

"Oh, shoot," Berends said. "And there was *so* much I wanted to know."

"I'm sorry to disappoint you," Stone said.

The absence of further information seemed to cast a pall over the luncheon, and soon the women began leaving. Finally, Stone was left alone with Charlene Joiner.

"Thank you, Ramon," she said to the houseman, who was clearing the dishes. "Just put those things in the dishwasher, and you and Reba can go. Thank you for coming in today." She watched the man go into the kitchen, then turned to Stone. "Alone at last," she said, standing up and slipping out of the sarong. "I hope you don't mind if I get some sun."

"Not at all," Stone said. To his surprise, she didn't stop with the sarong; she unhooked her bra, freeing her breasts, and shucked off the bikini bottom. He noted that there were no sun lines on her body.

She stretched like a cat. She was tall and slender, and she obviously took very good care of herself. Her legs were long, her hips were narrow, and her breasts were impressive.

"They're original equipment," she said, catching Stone's glance.

Stone laughed. "I'm glad to hear it. You said you had some information for me." He tried to keep his tone light and his breathing regular.

She settled on the chaise beside his, turned her face to the sun and closed her eyes. "Yes, I do. It may not be important, but I thought you ought to know about it."

"I'm all ears."

"Vance and I use the same gardening service, which takes care of the grounds of both his Malibu and Bel-Air houses. The man, whose name is Felipe, was due here on Monday morning to cut the grass and do some gardening work, and he didn't show up. I called the service, and they sent somebody else that afternoon."

Stone waited for this to become relevant. "Go on."

"The man who came in the afternoon didn't do a very good job, so I called his boss and asked when Felipe would be back. He said he had called Felipe's house—he apparently lived with a sister—and was told that he had returned to Mexico over the weekend, and he didn't know when he'd be back."

"Did Felipe also work at the Calders' house?"

"Yes; he worked there last Friday and on Saturday, the day Vance was killed."

"And he suddenly went back to Mexico on the Sunday?"

"On the Saturday night, according to his boss."

"So he couldn't have been questioned by the police," Stone said. "That *is* interesting"

"I thought you might think so. The man did good work, but once I caught him in my house. He said he was looking for a drink of water, but he wasn't in the kitchen; he was in the living room."

"Did he know where the kitchen was?"

"Yes, he had been in there before. I think he fancied Reba, my maid."

"You think he might have stolen something?"

"I think he would have, left to his own devices. I told him not to come into the house again. If he wanted water, he was to ask Reba to bring it to him. There's a staff toilet off the kitchen he could use. His full name is Felipe Cordova; his boss says he's from Tijuana."

"Thank you for telling me this," Stone said. "There's something I'd like to ask you; it's a rude question, but I'd appreciate a straight answer."

"Was I fucking Vance Calder?" she asked.

"That's the question."

She laughed. "Sweetie, all of the women here today have fucked Vance, at one time or another."

"*All* of them?"

"Every one of them is a member of the I Fucked Vance Calder Club. The club is bigger than that, of course; we're only the tip of the nipple."

"Let's get back to my original question."

"You bet I was fucking him, and loving it." She smiled. "So was he."

"Where did these meetings take place?"

"You mean where did we fuck? I hate euphemisms. In his bungalow at the studio; in his trailer, when we were on location; in his Colony house just down the street; and here. Right up until the day before his death."

"How often did this happen?"

"Every day we could manage it; sometimes twice a day. Vance was always ready," she said, "and so was I." She turned toward him and placed a hand on his arm. "In fact," she said, "I'm ready, right now."

Stone patted her hand. "That's a kind thought," he said, "but it's very likely that you're going to be called as a witness for the prosecution at Arrington's trial, and . . ."

"I'll bet you could get me to say whatever you wanted me to," Charlene said, getting up and sitting on the edge of his chaise.

"That would be suborning perjury," Stone said, trying to keep his voice calm. "My advice to you is to tell the truth."

"I'll tell you the truth," she said, and her hand went smoothly to his crotch. "I want you right now, and," she squeezed gently, "I can tell you want me."

"I'm afraid . . ."

She squeezed harder. "Stone," she said, "you don't want to turn down the best piece of ass on the North American Continent, do you?"

Stone got to his feet, and his condition was something of an embarrassment. She got up, too. "Charlene," he said, "I don't doubt you for a moment, but, believe me, it could mean big trouble for both of us."

"It might be worth it," she said, rubbing her body against his.

Stone was backing away, but he could not bring himself to disagree. "I have to leave," he said, turning for the door.

"All right," she sighed, "but when this trial is over, you call me, you hear?"

Stone waved and walked quickly through the house and to his car. When he was finally behind the wheel, he noticed that he was breathing harder than the effort had required.

Chapter 26

STONE DROVE SLOWLY BACK to the studio, top down, trying to enjoy the California weather, instead of thinking about Charlene Joiner. He had read the newspaper accounts of her long-ago affair with the senator and presidential candidate Will Lee, and he had every sympathy for the senator. She was extraordinarily beautiful, all over, and, if Betty Southard's account of her prowess in bed was true, the senator was lucky to get out with his scalp.

He could not make the randiness go away. Just when he thought he had it under control, he passed the public beach area near Sunset, and a girl walking along the sand in a bikini got him going again. Stone sighed and tried to think pure thoughts.

As he walked into the studio bungalow, the phone was ringing, and Betty answered it.

"It's for you," she said.

Stone went into the study and picked up the phone. "Hello?"

"Stone, it's Rick Grant."

"Hi, Rick, what's up?"

"I just wanted to see how you're doing. I heard about the scene at the D.A.'s office. Blumberg pulled that one out of the fire."

"At least, temporarily."

"It was a shitty thing for the D.A. to do—try to make her spend the weekend in jail."

"Do I detect a sympathetic note?"

"Sort of."

"Rick, what have they got on her that they're not telling us?"

"I can't get into that," Rick replied, "but there is something I can tell you."

"Please do."

"They found a good footprint outside the French doors leading to the pool. A Nike, size twelve."

"That's interesting."

"The guy had walked through some sprinkler-dampened dirt, or something; there was only one good one, but they got a photograph of it."

"I learned something else," Stone said.

"Tell me."

"There was a Mexican gardener there, on both the Friday and Saturday, but he left the country Saturday night, went back to Tijuana, so he couldn't have been questioned by Durkee and Bryant."

"That's very interesting," Rick admitted.

"What's more, another customer of the same gardening service caught the guy in her living room, once. She thought he would have stolen something, left to his own devices."

"Pretty good; now you've got another suspect. That should take some of the heat off Arrington."

"It will, if Durkee and Bryant investigate—find the guy and bring him back."

"I wouldn't count on that," Rick said. "Getting somebody back from the Mexicans almost never happens. Unless he comes back across the border voluntarily, well, you're not going to see him. Do you know his name?"

"Felipe Cordova, and he's from Tijuana. Had you heard about this guy from your people?"

"No, and that's puzzling; I'll check into it. I'll pass this on to Durkee, and we'll see what happens."

"I'll tell you what I think, Rick: I think Durkee and Bryant, and now the D.A., have the hots for Arrington as a suspect, and they don't want to know anything that points to anybody else."

"Could be," Rick admitted. "Wouldn't be the first time that's happened."

"Happens all the time," Stone said. "In New York, and everywhere else. The path of least resistance, never mind who really did it; nail *somebody*."

"We've all seen that."

"And the high profile of this case has got them salivating for a high-profile perp."

"Could be."

"I think it's the O.J. thing," Stone said. "They lost that one, and now they want a big conviction to salvage their reputations."

"Possibly."

"Will you let me know what you hear about the Mexican gardener?"

"I'll do that."

"Talk to you later," Stone said into the phone, and hung up. He walked into Betty's office, but she was not at her desk. He felt the need for a shower and went into the bedroom. He undressed and stretched out on the bed, thinking to relax for a few minutes. Then Betty came out of the bathroom, and she was naked.

"Oh!" she said. "Sorry, I thought you'd be on the phone for a while."

"It's okay, Betty," he said, getting up. "It's not the first time we've seen each other in the buff."

She walked over and put her arms around him. "I just wanted to see if this feels as good as I remember. It does."

"It certainly does," Stone agreed. Then, before he could get into trouble, he held her off a few inches. "If I'm not careful, you'll seduce me," he said.

Betty laughed.

Then there was a blinding flash of light, followed by another. Stone and Betty both turned toward the door, astonished. The flash came again, then there was the sound of running feet leaving the cottage.

Stone blinked, trying to regain his vision.

"What the hell was that?" Betty cried.

"I don't know; what's the number for the main gate?"

Betty dialed the number and handed the phone to Stone.

"Main gate," the guard said.

"This is Stone Barrington; we've had an intruder in Mr. Calder's bungalow. Who's come in this morning?"

"In the last half-hour, only Mrs. Barrington," the man replied.

"There *is no Mrs. Barrington!*" Stone yelled. "Don't let her in here again!" He hung up and turned to Betty. "I'm sorry, it was Dolce; I didn't even know she was still in town."

"Well," Betty said, "ask her if I can have a set of prints."

"That would be funny, if I weren't so pissed off."

"Where were we?" Betty asked.

But Stone was already dressing.

"Where are you going?"

"I'm going to put a stop to this thing with Dolce."

"And how are you going to do that?"

"I'll talk to her."

"Lotsa luck," Betty said. "Looks to me as though you're past talking."

Chapter 27

STONE PARKED Vance Calder's Mercedes in the upper parking lot of the Bel-Air Hotel and walked quickly to Dolce's suite. He was going to have to have this out with her, once and for all. He rapped sharply on the door and waited.

A moment later the door was opened by a white-haired woman in her sixties, dressed in a hotel robe. "Yes?" she said, looking at him suspiciously.

"May I see Miss Bianchi, please?"

"I'm sorry, you have the wrong room," the woman replied, starting to close the door.

"May I ask, when did you check in?"

"About noon," she replied and firmly shut the door.

Stone walked down to the lobby and the front desk. "Yes, Mr. Barrington?" the young woman at the desk said. "Are you checking in again?"

"No, I'm looking for Miss Dolce Bianchi. Has she changed rooms?"

"Let me check," the woman said, tapping some computer keys. "I'm afraid I don't see a Miss Bianchi."

"Try Mrs. Stone Barrington," Stone said, through clenched teeth.

"Ah, yes. Mrs. Barrington checked out last night."

"And her forwarding address?"

She checked the computer screen and read off the address of Eduardo's house in Manhattan.

"Thank you," Stone said.

"Of course," she replied. "We're always happy to see you, Mr. Barrington."

"Thank you, and by the way, would you inform the management that there is *no* Mrs. Stone Barrington. The woman's name is Dolce Bianchi, and should she check in again, I would be grateful if you would not allow her to use my name in the hotel."

"I'll speak to the manager about it," the woman replied, looking baffled.

"Thank you very much," Stone said, managing a smile for the woman. He walked back to the parking lot, switched on the ignition, and called the Bianchi house in Manhattan. He got an answering machine for his trouble. Frustrated, he called Dino's number at home.

"Hello?" Mary Ann, Dino's wife, answered.

"Hi, Mary Ann, it's Stone."

"Hi, Stone," she said cheerfully, then her voice took on a sympathetic tone. "I'm sorry things didn't work out in Venice."

"Thank you, but I think it was for the best."

"Well, since you're not too broken up about it, I don't mind telling you, I think you're lucky to be out of that relationship. I mean, Dolce's my sister, and I love her, but you're far too nice a guy to have to put up with her."

"She registered at the Bel-Air as Mrs. Stone Barrington," he said.

"Oh, Jesus," Mary Ann breathed. "That's just like her."

"She checked out yesterday and said she was returning to New York, but there's no answer at the Manhattan house. Have you heard from her? I want to talk to her."

"Not a word; I knew she went to Vance Calder's funeral, and I thought she was still in L.A. Hang on, Dino wants to speak to you."

"So how's the bridegroom?" Dino asked.

"Don't start. She checked into the Bel-Air as Mrs. Stone Barrington. Are you sure that civil ceremony has no force in law?"

"That's my understanding, but I'm not an Italian lawyer," Dino replied. "Is Dolce giving you a hard time?"

"I'm staying at Vance Calder's cottage at Centurion Studios, and she barged in there this afternoon with a camera and caught me in bed with Betty Southard, Vance's secretary."

Dino began laughing.

Stone held the phone away from his ear for a moment. "It's not funny, Dino. I can't have her going around pretending to be Mrs. Barrington and behaving like a wronged wife."

"Listen, pal, you're talking to the guy who warned you off her, remember?"

"Don't rub it in. What am I going to do about her?"

"I guess you could talk to Eduardo; you two are such good buddies. Maybe he'll spank her, or something."

"Yeah, sure."

"I can't think of anybody else who could handle her."

"Neither can I."

"You got the Brooklyn number?"

"Yes."

"That's what I'd do, in your shoes—that, and talk to an Italian lawyer."

"Thanks, I'll talk to you later." Stone punched off, and it occurred to him that he knew an Italian lawyer. He dug out his wallet and found the cardinal's card. He looked at his watch; it would be early evening in Italy. He called the operator, got the dialing code for Rome, and punched in the number.

"Pronto," a deep voice said.

"Good evening," Stone said, "My name is Stone Barrington; may I speak with Cardinal Bellini, please?"

"Stone, how good to hear from you," Bellini said, switching to English.

"Thank you; I'm sorry to bother you, but I need some advice regarding Italian law, and I didn't know anyone else to call."

"Of course; how can I help you?"

"You'll recall that, before my sudden departure from Venice, Dolce and I went through some sort of civil ceremony at the mayor's office."

"I do."

"But I had to leave Venice before the ceremony at St. Mark's."

"Yes, yes."

"My question is, does the civil ceremony, without the church ceremony, have any legal force?"

"Not in the eyes of the church," Bellini replied.

"How about in the eyes of the Italian government?"

"Well, it is possible to be legally married in Italy in a civil ceremony."

Stone's heart sank.

"Can you tell me what this is about, Stone? Is something wrong?"

"I don't want to burden you with this, Your Eminence," Stone said.

"Not at all," the cardinal replied. "I have plenty of time."

Stone poured it all out—Arrington; Arrington and Vance Calder; Dolce; everything.

"Well," the cardinal said when he had finished, "it seems you've reconsidered your intentions toward Dolce."

"I'm afraid I've been forced to."

"Then it's fortunate that this occurred before you took vows in the church."

"Yes, it is. However, I'm concerned about my marital status under Italian law. Is it possible that I am legally married?"

"Yes, it is possible."

Stone groaned.

"I can see how, given the circumstances, this might concern you, Stone. Before I can give you any sort of definitive answer, I'd like to do a bit of research. I'm leaving Rome tomorrow morning for a meeting in Paris, and it may be a few days, perhaps longer, before I can look into this. Let's leave it that I'll phone you as soon as I have more information."

"Thank you, Your Eminence." Stone gave him the Centurion number, thanked him again, and hung up.

He started the car and drove slowly back to the studio. When he reached the cottage it was dark, except for a lamp in the window. Betty had gone.

Stone rarely drank alone, but he went to the bar and poured himself a stiff bourbon. What had he gotten himself into? Was he married? If so, the Italians didn't have divorce, did they? He had not wanted to question a cardinal of the Church about a divorce. He collapsed in a chair and pulled at the bourbon. For a while, he allowed himself a wallow in self-pity.

Chapter 28

STONE WAS SIGNING DOCUMENTS faxed to him from New York by his secretary when Betty buzzed him.

"Rick Grant on line one."

Stone picked up the phone. "Hi, Rick."

"Good morning, Stone. I had a chat with Durkee about this missing Mexican gardener, and I have to tell you that he and his partner don't seem to have the slightest interest in him."

"I suppose they're not interested in the footprint they found outside the house, either."

"Not much. It's a Nike athletic shoe, size twelve, right foot, with a cut across the heel. I got that much out of Durkee."

"Can you get me a copy of the photograph of the footprint?"

"I think you're better off asking for that in discovery."

Rick obviously didn't want to get more involved than he already was. "Maybe you're right."

"I thought of something, though."

"What's that?"

"I told you how tough it was to get suspects out of Mexico, but there might be something you can do."

"Tell me."

"I know a guy named Brandy Garcia. Brandy is a Latino hustler, does a little of everything to make a buck. He's been a coyote, running illegals across the border, he's run an employment agency for recently arrived Latinos, he may even have smuggled some drugs in his time, I don't know. But he's well connected below the border, especially in Tijuana, where he's from, and he might be able to find this guy, Felipe Cordova, for you."

"Sounds good."

"Trouble is, Cordova is not a suspect, so even if you found him and the Mexicans were willing to extradite him, nobody would arrest him."

"That's discouraging," Stone replied.

"I know. But you might try to talk to him, if Brandy can find him."

"How do I get hold of Brandy Garcia?"

"I left a message on an answering machine, giving him your number. He may or may not call; I don't know if he's even in the country."

"Okay, I'll wait to hear from him."

"Good luck."

"Thanks, Rick." Stone hung up.

Twenty minutes later Betty buzzed him. "There's somebody on the phone, who says his name is Brandy Garcia; says Rick Grant told him to call."

"Put him through," Stone said. There was a click. "Hello?"

"Mr. Barrington?"

"Yes."

"My name is Brandy Garcia; Rick Grant said I might be of some service to you." The accent was slight.

"Yes, I spoke to Rick. Can we meet someplace?"

"You free for lunch?"

"How about a drink?"

"Okay: the Polo Lounge at the Beverly Hills Hotel at twelve-thirty?"

"All right."

"See you then." Garcia hung up.

Stone opened his briefcase, found a bank envelope, and counted out some money.

Stone drove up to the portico of the Beverly Hills Hotel and turned his car over to the valet. Walking inside, he thought that the place looked very fresh and new. It was the first time he'd visited the hotel since its multimillion-dollar renovation by its owner, the Sultan of Brunei.

He walked into the Polo Lounge and looked around, seeing nobody who fit the name of Brandy Garcia. The headwaiter approached.

"May I help you, sir?"

"I'm to meet a Mr. Garcia here," Stone said.

"Mr. Barrington?"

"Yes."

"Come this way, please." He led Stone through the restaurant, out into the garden, and to a table in a shady spot near the rear hedge. A man stood up to greet him.

"Brandy Garcia," he said, extending a hand.

"Stone Barrington," Stone replied, shaking it. Garcia was slightly flashily dressed, in the California style, and perfectly barbered, with a well-trimmed moustache. He bore a striking resemblance to the old-time Mexican movie actor Gilbert Roland.

Garcia indicated a seat. "Please," he said.

"I don't think I'll have time for lunch," Stone said.

Garcia shrugged. "Have a drink, then; I'll have lunch."

They both sat down. There was a large snifter of cognac already before Garcia. "So you're a friend of Rick's?" Garcia asked.

"Yes."

"I've known Rick a long time; good guy. Rick was the first person to tell me I look like Gilbert Roland." He appeared to be cultivating the resemblance.

"Oh," Stone said.

"You think I look like him?"

"Yes, I think you do."

This seemed to please Garcia. The waiter brought them a menu. "Please. Order something. It would please me."

Stone suppressed a sigh. "All right. I'll have the lobster salad and a glass of the house Chardonnay."

"Same here," Garcia said, ogling two good-looking women as they were seated at the next table, "but I'll stick with brandy." "So," he said, finally, "Rick says you're looking for somebody."

"Yes, I am."

"What is his name?"

"Felipe Cordova."

Garcia shook his head slowly. "I don't know him," he said, as if this were surprising.

"I'm told he's from Tijuana," Stone said.

"My hometown!" Garcia said, looking pleased.

"He was working as a gardener in Los Angeles until recently." Stone tore a page from his notebook. "He was living with his sister; this is her name and address. He suddenly left L.A. on a Saturday night, the same night a murder was committed."

Garcia's eyebrows went up. "The Vance Calder murder?"

"Yes," Stone admitted. He had not wanted to share this information.

"I read the papers, I watch TV," Garcia said. "Your name was familiar to me."

"I want to find Cordova, talk to him."

"Not arrest him?"

Stone shook his head. "The police don't consider him a suspect. I just want to find out what he knows about that night."

Garcia nodded sagely. "There are some difficulties here," he said. The waiter arrived with their lunch.

"What difficulties?" Stone asked.

"Tijuana is a difficult place, even for someone with my connections. And maybe Señor Cordova doesn't want to talk to you. That would make him harder to find."

Stone read this as a nudge for more money. "Can you find him?"

"Probably, but it will take time and effort."

"I'm quite willing to pay for your time," Stone said.

Garcia pushed a huge forkful of lobster into his mouth and chewed reflectively. Finally, he swallowed. "And if I find him, then what?"

"Arrange a meeting," Stone said.

Garcia chuckled. "You mean a nice lunch, like this?" He waved a hand.

"I just want an hour with the man."

"How, ah, *hard* do you wish to talk to him?"

"I don't want to beat answers out of him, if that's what you mean."

"Are you willing to pay him to sit still for this, ah, conversation, then?"

"Yes, within reason."

"I am not reasonable," Garcia said. "I will require five thousand dollars for my services, half now and half when you see Cordova."

"I don't have twenty-five hundred dollars on me," Stone said. "I can give you a thousand now and the rest in cash when we meet Cordova."

Garcia nodded gravely. "For a friend of Rick's that is agreeable."

Stone took a stack of ten one-hundred-dollar bills from his pocket, folded them and slipped them under Garcia's napkin. "When?"

"Within a week or so, I think," Garcia replied, pocketing the money.

"You have my number."

Garcia suddenly looked at his wristwatch. "Oh, I have to run," he said, standing up. "I will be in touch." He turned and walked back into the hotel without another word.

Stone finished his lunch and paid the check.

Chapter 29

As Stone walked back into the Calder bungalow at Centurion, he could see Betty in her office, leaning back in her chair and waving the phone. "It's Joan Robertson, in New York," she called out.

Stone went to Vance's office, picked up the phone, and spoke to his secretary. "What's up?" He asked.

"Oh, Stone, I'm so glad I got you," Joan said breathlessly. "Water is coming down the stairs."

"What do you mean?"

"I mean that the main stairs of the house look like a tributary of the Hudson River. It's been raining hard here for three days."

"Oh, shit," Stone said. When he had inherited the house, the roof had seemed the one thing that didn't need renovating. It was old, but it was of slate, which could last a hundred years or more. Now it occurred to Stone that the house was over a hundred years old, and so was the roof. "Here's what you do," he said. "Call a guy named Billy Foote; he's in my phone book. Billy was my helper when I was renovating the house, and he can do almost anything. Tell him to buy a whole lot of plastic sheeting and to get up on the roof and tack it down everywhere. That'll stop the worst of it."

"Okay, then what?" Joan asked sensibly.

Stone realized he didn't know a roofer, let alone one qualified to tackle a slate roof. "Let me think for a minute," he said.

"Listen, Stone, I think you ought to get back here. There are clients you need to see, instead of just talking on the phone, and there's going to be damage to the house as a result of all the water coming in. Please come back."

Stone knew she was right. "I'll be home as soon as humanly possible," he said. "Call Billy, and tell him to hire whatever help he can and to start asking around about roofers who can deal with slate."

"All right," she said, then hung up.

Stone buzzed Betty.

"Yes?"

"Get me on the red-eye," he said. "I've got to go back to New York for a few days."

"Right; you want a car to meet you at the airport?"

"Good idea. I'm going over to Arrington's; you can reach me there, if you need me."

"Okay."

Stone packed his bags and loaded them into Vance's car.

Betty came out of the bungalow. "When are you coming back?" Betty asked.

"As soon as I can," Stone replied, giving her a kiss on the cheek.

"Stone, I think I'm going to be getting out of here pretty soon. Do you think you'll need me much longer?"

"I'd appreciate it if you'd hang around at least until I get back from New York.

"Don't worry, I'll clean up Vance's affairs for you, and I'll find somebody to do the job for Arrington when I'm gone. Now you get back to New York, and I'll see you when I see you." She gave him a sharp slap on the rump to send him on his way, and went back to her office.

All the way to Arrington's he thought about his house, how he loved it, and what must be happening to it. He called Joan on the car phone.

"Yes, Stone?"

"You'd better call Chubb Insurance and have them get somebody over there in a hurry. Tell them I need a recommendation for a roofer."

"Will do."

He entered the Calder property through the utility entrance, as had become his habit. Arrington heard the car pull up and met him at the back door.

She slipped her arms around his neck and kissed him. "I missed you," she said.

"How are you?"

"Bored rigid, as a matter of fact." She kissed him again. "And randy."

"Now, now, now, now . . ." Stone said, holding her away from him. "We can't allow ourselves to think that way, you know that."

"Come on in, and let me fix you a drink."

"I could use one," he replied. They settled in the little sitting room off the master suite. "I have to go back to New York for a little while," he said.

"Oh, no," she replied. "You're all I've got right now, Stone."

Stone explained about the roof and his impatient clients. "If there's as much water as Joan says there is, then it's going to take me some time to get things sorted out."

"But what will I do without you here?"

"Marc Blumberg is in charge of your case, anyway; I'm just an adviser."

"Marc is good, but he's no smarter than you are," she said.

"Thank you, but we're on his turf, and he knows it a lot better than I do. Who else could have gotten you bail on a Saturday?"

"I suppose you're right."

"I'll call every day," he said.

"You getting the red-eye?"

"Yes."

"Let's have some dinner before you go, then." She picked up a phone, buzzed Manolo, and ordered food. "And after dinner, will you please drive Mr. Barrington to the airport?" She thanked him and hung up. "I don't know what I would have done without Manolo," she said. "He's the most intensely loyal person I've ever met, besides you. Do you know that as soon as Vance was buried, he started getting offers from people, some of them my friends? And he turned down every one of them. He and Maria have just been wonderful."

"You're lucky to have them," Stone agreed. "On the subject of loyal help, Betty Southard told me this afternoon that she's going to leave as soon as Vance's affairs are settled, probably move to Hawaii."

"I don't blame her," Arrington said. "She's never liked me, particularly, so maybe it's best."

"She said she'd find somebody to work for you."

"Good."

"I'd like to wash up before dinner; will you excuse me?"

"Use Vance's bathroom, it's the closest," she said, pointing to the hallway.

Stone left her and found the bathroom. As he came back up the hallway, past Vance's dressing room, he thought something was odd, but he wasn't sure what. He walked back to the bathroom and looked at the wall backing up onto the dressing room, then he walked down the hallway and looked at the dressing room. There was something wrong with the proportions, but the bourbon he had just had on an empty stomach was keeping him from figuring it out. He went back and joined Arrington.

"How old is this house?" he asked.

"It was built during the twenties," she said, "but when Vance bought it in the seventies, he gutted it and started over."

"Did he make a lot of changes?"

"He changed everything; he might as well have torn it down and started over, but Vance was too keen on costs to waste the shell of a perfectly good house. After we were married, I redecorated the master suite, with his approval on fabrics and so forth."

"Did you tear down any walls then?"

"No, the space was already divided as you see it. Even though

Vance was a bachelor when he rebuilt the house, he provided for what he called 'the putative woman.'"

Stone laughed.

They had dinner in the small dining room and talked about old times, which weren't really that old, Stone reflected. A lot had happened in the few years they had known each other.

"I think I'd go back to Virginia, if I were allowed to leave town," Arrington said, "and just spend a few weeks or months. Do a lot of riding. I miss that."

"You've got room for horses here," Stone said.

"You're right; there's actually an old stable on the property, and there are still riding trails in the neighborhood. Did you know that the Bel-Air Hotel is built on property where Robert Young used to own a riding stable?"

"No, I didn't know that."

"Maybe when this is all over, I'll buy a couple of horses. Do you ride?"

"You're talking to a city kid, you know. I mean, I rode a little at summer camp as a boy, but that was about it."

"I'm going to redecorate this house, too," she said. "I don't want to sell it; it's unique, and I love it so. I didn't do a lot about the place, except for the master suite, when I moved in, and I'm tired of even that. You did such a good job on your house; will you consult?"

"I'll consult, when I get back," Stone said. He thought it was good that she was looking past the trial, instead of obsessing about it. He wanted her optimistic; otherwise, she'd come apart.

They talked on into the evening, easily, the way people do who know each other well. Then Manolo brought the Bentley around, with Stone's luggage already in the trunk.

"Don't stay any longer than you have to," Arrington said, kissing him lightly. "And by the way, it's time you sent me a bill. I can't have you devoting all your working time to me, and after all, I'm a rich woman."

"I'll probably overcharge you," Stone said.

"That would not be possible," she said, kissing him again, this time more longingly.

Stone allowed himself to enjoy it, and the drive to the airport passed in a haze of good wine and rekindled desire.

He checked his luggage, got to the gate, and boarded with only a couple of minutes to spare. The flight attendant was closing the door to the airplane, when she suddenly reopened it and stepped back.

Dolce got onto the airplane, and the flight attendant closed the door behind her.

Chapter 30

STONE WAS SITTING in the first-row window seat of the first-class section, and he watched like a trapped rabbit, as Dolce, cobralike, glided past, ignoring him, and took a seat somewhere behind him.

"Would you like a drink, Mr. Barrington?" the attendant asked.

"A Wild Turkey on the rocks," he replied without hesitation, "and make it a double." When the drink arrived, he drank it more quickly than he usually would have, and by the time the flight reached its cruising altitude, he had fallen asleep.

Some time in the night he awoke, needing the bathroom. On the way back to his seat, he looked toward the rear of the compartment and saw Dolce, sitting on the aisle three rows behind his seat, gazing unblinkingly at him. It was unnerving, he thought. He slept only fitfully for the rest of the flight.

When the door opened at the gate, Stone was the first off the airplane, nearly running up the ramp into the terminal. His bags were among the first to be seen in baggage claim, and a driver stood by with his name written on a shirt cardboard. He pointed at the bags and followed the driver to the waiting car.

He felt hungover from having the bourbon so close to bedtime, and the weather did not improve his mood. It was still raining heavily, the result of a close brush from a tropical storm off the coast, and even though the driver handled his bags, he got very wet between the car and his front door.

He tipped the driver generously, opened the door, and stepped inside his house, shoving his bags ahead of him. He tapped the security code into the keypad and looked around. The stairs had been stripped of their runner, which was piled on the living room floor, on top of a fine old oriental carpet that had come with the house, both of them sodden. A smell of dampness permeated the place.

He put his bags on the elevator and pressed the button, then he walked up the stairs slowly, surveying the damage, which, if not catastrophic, was still awful. Thank God for insurance, he thought. He walked into his upstairs sitting room, where there was more wet carpet, and watermarks on the wall next to the stairs, where the water from the breached roof had run down. At least it had stopped, he thought, though it was still raining hard outside. Billy Foote must have gotten the plastic cover over the roof. His beautiful house, nearly ruined. He thought about how hard he had worked to restore it. Now a few days' rain . . .

The security system beeped, signalling that Joan was arriving for work. He picked up a phone and buzzed her.

"Hi. Was your flight okay?"

"As okay as could be expected. Thanks for getting Billy over here."

"He did a good job. The insurance adjustor got here in a hurry, and he's sending a roofer to bid for the job as soon as it stops raining, if it ever does, and the carpet cleaners are coming this morning to take away all the wet rugs."

Stone looked around his bedroom. "Tell them to throw away the carpet up here," he said. "It's time to replace it, I think, and the stairway runner, too. I do want to save the oriental in the living room, though."

"Okay."

"Any calls?"

"None that can't wait until this afternoon," she said. "You probably need some sleep."

"That's true. I'll check with you later." He hung up, got undressed, went into a guest room, where the carpets were still dry, and got into bed.

He woke up around noon, showered, shaved and dressed, and went downstairs, where his housekeeper, Helene, had left a sandwich for him. He had just finished it when the front doorbell rang. That would be the carpet people, he thought, and instead of using the intercom, he went to the front door and opened it. Eduardo Bianchi stood on his doorstep, glumly holding an umbrealla. The Mercedes Maybach idled at the curb.

"Eduardo!" Stone said, surprised. He had almost never seen the man anywhere except on his own turf. "Come in."

"Thank you, Stone. I'm sorry to barge in, but I heard you were back from California, and I wonder if you could spare me a few minutes?"

"Of course," Stone said, taking the umbrella, and helping the older man off with his coat. "Come on back to my study. Would you like some coffee?"

"Thank you, yes," Eduardo replied, rubbing his hands together briskly. "It's terrible out there."

Stone settled him in a chair in his study, then made some espresso and brought in a pot and two cups on a tray.

"So, you're back in New York for a while, I hope?" Eduardo asked.

"I'm afraid not," Stone said. He explained the problem with the roof. "I have some clients to see, too, then I have to get back to L.A. I'm afraid Arrington still needs me there."

"Ah, Arrington," Eduardo said slowly. "A most unfortunate situation for her. Do you think she will be acquitted?"

"I think she's innocent, and I'll do everything I can to see that she is. Marc Blumberg, an L.A. lawyer, is her lead counsel; I'm just advising."

Eduardo nodded. "I know Marc; he's a good man, right for this."

Stone was not surprised, since Eduardo seemed to know everybody on both coasts. He waited for his near-father-in-law to come to the point of his visit.

"Dolce is back, too," he said.

"I know," Stone replied. "I caught a glimpse of her on the airplane, but we didn't talk."

Eduardo shook his head. "This is all very sad," he said. "I do not like seeing her so upset."

"I'm very sorry for upsetting her," Stone said, "but I could not do otherwise, in the circumstances."

"What are your intentions toward Arrington?" Eduardo asked, as if he had the right to.

"Quite frankly, I don't know," Stone said "She has some serious difficulties to overcome, and, if Blumberg and I are successful in defending her, I don't know what her plans are after that. I'm not sure she knows, either."

"And your plans?"

"I haven't made any. Every time I do, it all seems to come back to Arrington, one way or another."

"You are in love with her, then?"

Stone sighed. He had been avoiding the question. "I think I have to finally face the fact that I have been for a long time."

"Why did you not marry her when you had the opportunity?" Eduardo asked.

"I intended to," Stone replied. "We were going on a sailing holiday together in the islands. I had planned to pop the question down there. She was delayed in joining me, because she had been asked to write a magazine piece about Vance. The next thing I knew, they were married."

Eduardo nodded. "Vance could do that," he said. "He was a very powerful personality, difficult for a young woman to resist." Eduardo set down his coffee cup and crossed his legs. "Now we come to Dolce," he said. "My daughter is very unhappy. What are your intentions toward her?"

Stone took a deep breath. "Dolce and I have talked about this," he said. "I've told her that I think it would be a terrible mistake for both of us, should we marry."

"Why?" Eduardo asked, and his eyes had narrowed.

"This business with Arrington has taught me that I'm not free of her," Stone replied, "as I thought I was. Vance's sudden death was a great shock, and not just because I liked him."

"Arrington is once again available, then?"

"Well, she's no longer married."

"Has she expressed an interest in rekindling your relationship with her?"

"Yes," Stone said, surprising himself with his willingness to discuss this with Eduardo.

"And there is the child," Eduardo said.

"Yes; there was a time when we both thought he might be mine, but the blood tests . . ."

"And who conducted these tests?" Eduardo asked.

"Why do you want to know?"

"Indulge me, please."

Stone went to his desk and rummaged in a bottom drawer. The report was still there. He handed it to Eduardo.

Eduardo read the document carefully. "This would seem conclusive," he said.

"Yes."

"Who employed these 'Hemolab' people?" he asked, reading the name of the laboratory from the letterhead.

"Arrington, I suppose."

Eduardo nodded and handed back the document and stood up. "I am sorry to have taken your time, Stone," he said, "but I had to explore this with you in order to know what to do."

Stone wasn't sure what he meant by that. "You are always welcome here, Eduardo."

"Thank you," he replied.

Stone followed him to the door, helped him on with his coat, and handed him his umbrella.

"Dolce is ill, you know," Eduardo said suddenly.

"What? What's wrong with her?"

"Her heart is ill; it has always been so, I think. I had hoped you could make her well, but I see, now, that it will not happen."

"What can I do to help, Eduardo?"

"Nothing, I think, short of marrying her, and after what you have told me today, I think that would destroy both of you."

"Is there anything I can do?"

Eduardo turned and looked at Stone, and his eyes were ineffably sad. "You can only keep away from her," he said. "I think she may be . . . dangerous." Then, without another word, he turned and walked down the steps and back to his car.

Stone watched as the limousine moved off down the street, and the shiver that ran through him was not caused by the dampness.

Chapter 31

STONE MET with his anxious clients and soothed their nerves. He spoke to the insurance agent and got approval to begin repairs, then, because he could not bear to look at his damaged house, he went downtown to ABC Carpets and picked out new ones, arranging for their people to measure and install them. As he got in and out of taxi-cabs, he caught himself looking around to see if he had unwanted company, but he did not see Dolce.

At half past eight he was at Elaine's, giving her a kiss on arrival and being shown to his usual table.

Elaine sat down for a minute. "So," she said, "you're up to your ass in this Vance Calder thing."

"I'm afraid so."

"I always liked Arrington," she said. "I wouldn't have thought she could kill anybody."

"I don't think she did."

"Can you prove it?"

"I guess the only way I can prove that is by proving somebody else did it. Otherwise, even if she's tried and acquitted, too many people will believe she's guilty, and a smart lawyer got her off."

"I hear she's got a smart lawyer—besides you, I mean."

"That's right; he's doing a good job, so far."

"Stone." She looked at him sadly.

"Yes?"

"Sometimes people do things you wouldn't think they could do. People get stressed, you know, and the cork pops."

Stone nodded.

"If you want to get through this okay, you'd better get used to the idea that you may be wrong about her."

"I don't think I am."

"Protect yourself; don't tear out your guts hoping."

It was the first advice he'd ever had from her. "I'll try," he said. He looked up to see Dino and Mary Ann coming through the door. He especially wanted to see Mary Ann.

Everybody hugged, kissed, sat down, and ordered drinks.

"You got a little sun," Dino said, inspecting him.

"Out there, you get it just walking around."

Elaine got up to greet some customers, giving his shoulder a squeeze as she left.

"What was that?" Dino asked.

"Encouragement," Stone replied. "I think she thinks Arrington did it."

"Doesn't everybody?" Dino asked.

"Do you?"

"Let's put it this way: I think I'm probably more objective about it than you are."

"Oh."

"Let me ask you something, Stone: If you all of a sudden found out for sure that she did it, would you try to get her off, anyway?"

"That's my job."

"You're not her lawyer; Blumberg is."

Stone looked into his drink. "It's still my job."

"Oh," Dino said, "it's like that."

"Well!" Mary Ann interjected. "Isn't it nice to all be together again, and right here at home!"

"Don't try to cheer him up," Dino said to his wife. "It won't work."

Michael, the headwaiter, brought menus, and they studied them silently for a minute, then ordered. Stone ordered another drink, too.

"Two before dinner," Dino said.

"He's entitled," Mary Ann pointed out.

They chatted in a desultory manner until dinner arrived, then ate, mostly in silence.

"Mary Ann," Stone said, when the dishes had been taken away, "your father came to see me this afternoon."

"He did?" she asked, surprised. "Where?"

"At my house."

"That's interesting," she said. "He doesn't do much calling on people. What did he want?"

"To know my intentions toward Arrington and Dolce."

"Is that all? What did you tell him?"

"That I don't know what my intentions are toward Arrington, but that Dolce and I are not getting married."

"That wasn't what he wanted to hear, I'm sure."

"I know, but I had to be honest with him."

"That's always the best policy with Papa."

"When he left, he said something that scared me a little."

Dino spoke up. "That's what he does best."

"What did he say?" Mary Ann asked.

"He said Dolce is ill, and that she might be dangerous."

"Oh," Mary Ann said quietly.

"What did he mean by that?"

Mary Ann didn't seem to be able to look at him.

"I think Stone needs to know, Honey," Dino said. "Answer his question."

Mary Ann sighed. "When Dolce doesn't get what she wants, she . . . reacts badly."

"Now, *there's* news," Dino snorted.

"Exactly *how* does she react badly?" Stone asks.

"She, ah, breaks things," Mary Ann said slowly. "People, too."

"Go on."

"When she was, I guess, six, Papa gave her a puppy. She tried to train it, but it wouldn't do what she told it to. It was like she expected it to understand complete sentences, you know? Well, she . . . I don't want to say what she did."

"She broke the puppy?" Dino asked.

"Sort of," Mary Ann replied. Her face made it clear she wasn't going to say any more.

"I think she's been stalking me," Stone said.

"*What?*" Mary Ann said.

"She's shown up in a couple of places where I was. Unexpectedly, you might say. She registered at the Bel-Air as Mrs. Stone Barrington. She was on my flight home last night."

"Oh, shit," Dino breathed.

"I thought about trying to talk to her again, but I don't even want to be in the same room with her."

"That's a good policy," Dino said.

"I don't know what to do," Stone admitted.

"I'd watch my back, if I were you," Dino said. "Remember what happened to the husband . . ."

"Oh, shut up, Dino," Mary Ann spat. "She's my sister; don't talk that way about her."

"I'm sorry, Hon, but Stone's in a jam, here, and we've got to help him figure this out."

"Well, you're not helping by . . . what you're saying."

"Are you carrying?" Dino asked.

"Dino!" his wife nearly shouted.

"It wouldn't surprise me if Dolce is," Dino continued, ignoring her.

"No, I'm not," Stone said. "I don't think it's come to that."

"Listen, Stone," Dino said. "At the point when it comes to that, it's going to be too late to go home and get a piece."

Their waiter stepped up with a dessert tray.

"Nothing for me," Stone said.

"I'll have the cheesecake," Dino said.

"Nothing for him," Mary Ann said, pointing a thumb at her husband. "Especially not the cheesecake."

Dino sighed.

"Nothing for anybody," Mary Ann said to the waiter.

They got a check, and declined the offer of an after-dinner drink from Elaine. Dino grabbed the check and signed it, before Stone could react.

"That's completely out of character, Dino," Stone said, chuckling.

"Who knows how many more opportunities I'll have," Dino replied, getting an elbow in the ribs from Mary Ann for his trouble.

They made their farewells to Elaine and started out of the restaurant. As they shuffled toward the door, Stone felt Dino slip something fairly heavy into his coat pocket.

"Don't leave home without it," Dino whispered.

Chapter 32

STONE REACHED into his coat pocket, took out the pistol, and placed it on the bedside table. It was a little .32 automatic, not a service weapon, but the kind of small gun a cop might keep in an ankle holster, as a backup.

He undressed, got into bed, and tried to watch the late news, but finally turned it off. He was still loggy from the sleep upset of taking the redeye, and the conversation at dinner had depressed him.

He drifted off immediately and then was in a deep sleep. He dreamed, and something was out of place in his dream—a high-pitched squeal, as if from a great distance. Then the squeal stopped.

Stone sat straight up in bed, wide awake. The squeal was the sound the security system made to warn that it was about to go off; it stopped only when the proper four-digit code was entered, and it had stopped. Then he remembered that Dolce knew the code.

He got out of bed as silently as he could and rearranged the pillows under the duvet, to give the impression he was still in bed, then he picked up Dino's pistol, tiptoed to his dressing room, and stood just inside the door. There was enough light coming through the windows to let him see the bed.

He heard the light footsteps on the stairs, which were now bare of the carpet runner. They approached slowly, quietly, until they reached the bedroom, where they stopped. She was letting her eyes become accustomed to the nearly dark room. Then she began to move forward again, and she came into Stone's view.

She was wearing a black raincoat with the hood up, so her face was still in darkness, and Stone thought she looked like the angel of death; she carried a short, thick club in her right hand. She reached the bed and stopped, then, holding the club at her side, she reached out with her left hand and began to pull back the covers.

"Freeze!" Stone said. "There's a gun pointed at your head."

She turned slowly to face him, but the shadow of the hood still obscured her face.

"Drop what's in your hand," he said.

She released the club, and it fell to the bare wood floor with a soft thud.

"Now, reach behind you and turn on the lamp, and keep your hands where I can see them."

She turned away and switched on the lamp, then turned back toward him, brushing off the hood. Instead of the black, Sicilian coif Stone had expected, honey-colored hair fell around her shoulders.

"Why are you pointing a gun at me, Stone?" she asked.

Stone's mouth fell open. "Arrington! What the hell are you doing here?"

"Could you point the gun somewhere else before we continue this conversation?"

Stone put the pistol on the dressing room chest of drawers and turned back to her.

She looked down, amused. "You're still pointing something at me," she said, unbuckling her belt and shucking off the raincoat. She was wearing black slacks and a soft, gray cashmere sweater. At her feet, on the floor, was the folding umbrella she had dropped.

Stone grabbed a cotton robe from the dressing room and slipped into it.

"Aw," she said, disappointed, "I liked you as you were. Don't I get a kiss?"

Stone crossed the room and gave her a small kiss, then held her at arm's length. "I'll ask you again: What the hell are you doing here?"

"Aren't you glad to see me?"

"Of course not! You've jumped bail, for God's sake, don't you understand that? The judge confined you to your house!"

"Don't worry, he'll never miss me."

"Arrington, let me explain this to you. As of this moment, you've forfeited two million dollars in bail."

"It's worth it to see you," she said. "I missed you."

"You could be arrested at any moment, and if you are, you won't get bail again; you'll have to stay in jail until the trial."

"Nobody's going to arrest me," she said. "Nobody knows I'm out of the house, except Manolo and Isabel, and certainly nobody knows I'm in New York. Manolo has instructions to tell anyone who calls that I'm not feeling well, and to take a message. I can return any calls from here."

Stone sat down on the edge of the bed and put his face in his hands. "I'm an officer of the court," he moaned. "I'm supposed to call the police or arrest you myself."

"Oooooo, arrest me," she purred.

Stone heard the sound of a zipper and looked up. She was stepping out of her slacks, and she had already shucked off the sweater, leaving only her panties.

She looked around, hands on her hips. "Now where are those pesky handcuffs? You must have some around here somewhere, being an ex-cop, and all."

Stone put his face back in his hands, and a moment later he felt her slip into the bed. Her fingernails moved down his back, and he started to get up, but she grabbed the belt of his robe and pulled him back onto the bed.

"I know Marc Blumberg said we couldn't be alone together in my house, but now we're alone together in *your* house, aren't we? So we're playing by the rules." She reached around him and tugged the belt loose, then pulled the robe off his shoulders. She dug her fingers into his hair, pulled him back onto the bed, and ran a fingernail along his penis, which responded with a jerk. "I *knew* you'd be glad to see me!" she said, then she pulled his face to hers and kissed him softly.

"This wasn't supposed to happen," Stone said, when he could free his lips for a moment.

She pulled his body toward hers. "Well, if I'm going to be arrested and carted off to jail, it seems only fair that I should have a last meal." She bent over him and kissed the tip of his penis. "I believe I'm entitled to have anything I want to eat, isn't that the tradition?" Then she began to concentrate on her repast.

Stone stood it for as long as he could, which was a little while, then he pulled her up beside him. She curled a leg over his body, opening herself to him. He slid inside her and, lying face to face, they began to make love, slowly.

"It's been way, way too long," Arrington said, moving with him and kissing his face.

"You're right," Stone breathed, admitting it as much to himself as to her.

"Tell me you've missed me."

"I've missed you."

"Tell me you've missed *this*."

"I can't tell you how much I've missed this," he moaned. "There are no words."

"Then *show* me," she said.

And he did.

Chapter 33

STONE LAY, NAKED, on his back, drained and weirdly happy, for a lawyer whose client seemed to be trying to go to jail. It was a little after ten A.M., and they had made love twice since sunup. He heard the shower go on in his bathroom and the sound of the glass door closing. He wanted to enjoy the moment, but he couldn't; he was faced with the problem of how to get Arrington back into the Los Angeles jurisdiction without getting her arrested and himself into very deep trouble.

A moment later, she came back, wearing his robe and rubbing her wet hair with a towel. "Good morning!" she said, as happy as if she were a free woman.

"Good morning." He managed a smile.

She sat down on the bed, took his wilted penis in her hand, and kissed it. "Aw," she said. "Did it die?"

"For the moment," he admitted. "Tell me, how did you get here? Exactly, I mean; I want a blow-by-blow account."

"Well, let's see: First I called the airline and made a reservation, then I put a few things into that little bag over there," she said, pointing to the top of the stairs, where she had left it, "then I left a note for Manolo, got into my car, left the house by the utility gate, which you have come to know and love, and I drove to the airport. I parked the car, walked into the terminal, gave the young lady at the ticket counter my credit card—the one that's still in my maiden name—and she gave me a ticket. Then I got on the plane, and when I arrived in New York I took a cab here. Did I leave out anything?"

"Yes; your picture has been all over the L.A. and New York papers and *People* magazine, for Christ's sake; why didn't anyone recognize you?"

"I wore a disguise," she said. She went to her bag, unzipped it, and took out a silk Hermes scarf and a pair of dark glasses; she wrapped the scarf tightly around her head and put on the shades. "With this and no makeup, my own mother wouldn't recognize me."

"Why so few clothes?" he asked.

"I have a wardrobe in our apartment at the Carlyle," she said. "I was going to send you up there to get me a few things. I thought it would be foolish to dally in baggage claim, so I traveled light."

Stone sat up and put his feet on the floor. "Well, you were certainly right not to do anything foolish."

"Was that sarcasm I heard?"

"Irony."

"Oh. Shall I fix you some breakfast?"

"Oh, no; Helene will be downstairs by now; she can fix it. I don't want *anyone* to see you."

"Then I shall be served in bed," she said, sitting cross-legged among the pillows.

The phone rang, and Stone picked it up. "Hello?"

"Hi, it's Betty."

"Good morning; you're up early."

"Yep. When I got into the office, there was a message from someone named Brandy Garcia; ring a bell?"

"Yes; what was the message?"

"He said he'd found what you wanted, and he'd call again."

"If he does, tell him to call me at this number."

"Will do. How's New York?"

"It is as ever."

"Good; when are you coming back?"

"As soon as . . ." he stopped. The Centurion airplane, he thought. "Can you switch me to Lou Regenstein's office?"

"I could, but he wouldn't be in this early, and anyway, he's in New York."

"He is? Where?"

"I don't know, but I could ask his secretary when she gets in."

"Hang on." He covered the phone and turned to Arrington. "Do you have any idea where Lou Regenstein stays when he's in the city?"

"At the Carlyle," she said. "He has an apartment there, too."

"Never mind," he said to Betty. "I'll talk to you later." He hung up.

"You want to call Lou?"

"Yes; what's the number of the Carlyle?"

She found her handbag and her address book. "Here's the private line to his apartment." She read it to him as he dialed.

"Hello," Lou Regenstein's voice said.

"Lou, it's Stone."

"Hi, Stone, what's up?"

"How long are you in New York for?"

"About thirty seconds; I was on the way out the door to Teterboro Airport when you called."

"You going back to L.A.?"

"Yep. Where are you?"

"I'm in New York. Can you give, ah, a friend and me a lift?"

"Sure; how fast can you get to Teterboro?"

"Is an hour fast enough?"

"That's fine; see you there."

"Lou, will there be anyone else on the airplane?"

"Nope, just you and me—and your friend. Anybody I know?"

"I'll surprise you," Stone said. "See you in an hour." He hung up and turned to Arrington. "Get dressed," he said, "and put on your disguise."

"I'll have to dry my hair," she said.

"Then do it fast." He picked up the phone and buzzed Joan Robertson. "Morning."

"Good morning."

"I've got to leave for L.A. in half an hour; I want to drive, so will you come along and drive the car back?"

"Sure; I'll put the answering machine on."

"See you downstairs in a few minutes."

While Arrington dried her hair, Stone packed, put his bags in the elevator, and pressed the down button. Then he grabbed a quick shower and shave and threw on some casual clothes. "Ready?" he asked Arrington.

"Ready," she said, getting into her raincoat, wrapping the scarf around her head and slipping on her dark glasses.

They took the stairs to the ground floor. Stone led her through the door to the garage, put their bags into the trunk of the car, and opened a rear door for her. "You wait here, while I get Joan, and don't talk on the way to the airport; I don't want her to know who you are."

Arrington shrugged. "Whatever you say." She got into the car and closed the door.

Stone went to his office, signed a couple of letters, and brought Joan back to the car. "There's someone in the backseat," he said. "Please don't look, and please don't ask any questions."

"Okay," Joan replied.

He opened the passenger door. "You sit up here; I'll drive."

Stone pressed the remote button on the sun visor and started the car, all in one motion. He had visions of Dolce waiting for him in the street, and he wasn't going to give her time to react. He reversed out of the garage, across the sidewalk, and into the street, causing a cabby to slam on his brakes and blow his horn. He pressed the remote button again, put the car into gear and was off, checking his mirrors. He thought for a moment that he saw a dark-haired woman across the street from his house, but he wasn't sure it was Dolce. He made the light and crossed Third Avenue. He would take the tunnel.

The car was something special—a Mercedes E55, which was an E-Class sedan with a souped-up big V8, a special suspension, and the acceleration of an aircraft carrier catapult launcher. Something else for which he was grateful, at the moment: The car had been manufactured with a level of armor that would repel small-arms fire. He had been car shopping when it was delivered to the showroom and had bought it in five minutes, on a whim, at another time in his life when he feared that somebody might be shooting at him.

Rush hour was over, and he made it to the Atlantic Aviation terminal in twenty-five minutes, without getting arrested, all the while dictating a stream of instructions to Joan about what had to be done in the way of repairing the house.

At the chain-link gate to the ramp, he buzzed the intercom and gave the tail number of the Centurion jet. The gate slid open and he drove onto the ramp and to the big Gulfstream Four. He parked at the bottom of the airstair door, gave the bags to the second officer, who was waiting for them, and gave Joan a peck on the cheek. "Thanks for not asking any questions," he said. "One of these days, I'll explain."

Joan leaned forward and whispered, "She's just as beautiful as her pictures." Then she took the keys, got into the car, and headed for the gate.

Stone led Arrington up the stairs and into the airplane. Lou Regenstein was sitting on a couch, reading *The New York Times*. He looked up as Arrington took off her glasses and scarf. "Holy shit," he said. "What are you . . ."

Stone held up a hand. "Don't ask. You have not seen what you're seeing."

"Well," Lou said, standing up and hugging Arrington. "You're the nicest invisible lady I've ever seen."

The airplane began to move, and Stone began to breathe again.

Chapter 3 4

WITH THE TIME CHANGE in their favor, it was late afternoon when the G-IV touched down at Santa Monica airport. There was a short taxi to Supermarine, where Lou Regenstein's stretch Mercedes limousine was waiting at the bottom of the airstair when the engines stopped. It took a minute to load their luggage, then they were headed toward the freeway.

"May I use your phone, Lou?" Arrington asked. "I want to call home."

"Of course."

She dialed the number. "Hello, Manolo, I'm . . ." She stopped and held her hand over the phone. "Something's wrong," she said. "Manolo just called me, 'sir.'"

Stone took the phone. "Manolo, it's Mr. Barrington; is there someone there?"

"Yes, sir," Manolo said smoothly. "I'm afraid she's resting at the moment. Can I have her call you back? There are some gentlemen waiting to see her now."

"Gentlemen? The police?"

"Yes, sir," Manolo said, sounding relieved that Stone had caught on.

"Just arrived?"

"Yes, sir."

"Do this: Go and knock on Mrs. Calder's bedroom door and pretend to speak to her, then put the policemen in Mr. Calder's study, and tell them she's getting dressed, and she'll be a few minutes. Give them some coffee to keep them occupied."

"Yes, Mr. Regenstein, I'll tell her you called," Manolo said, then hung up.

Stone put the phone back in its cradle.

"Trouble?" Lou asked.

Stone nodded. "Tell your driver to get moving; the cops are at the house."

Lou picked up the phone and pressed the intercom button. "Get us to the Calder place pronto," he said.

Stone took the phone and told the driver how to find the utility gate.

Arrington looked out the window. She seemed finally to have grasped what a difficult position she had put herself in.

Ten hair-raising minutes later, the limousine pulled into the rear drive and stopped at the gate.

"We'll walk from here, Lou," Stone said. "Please ask your driver to leave our bags at Vance's bungalow." He shook hands with Lou, grabbed Arrington's hand and practically dragged her from the car.

"I don't have the remote control for the gate with me," he said. "Is there some other way to open it?"

"Not that I know of," Arrington said, jogging to keep up with him.

"We'll have to go over the fence, then." He hustled her into the woods beside the gate and made a stirrup with his hands, then practically threw her over the fence. She landed in a pile of leaves, and a moment later, he joined her. She was laughing.

"I'm sorry, this is so ridiculous," she said.

"We'll laugh about it later," Stone said, taking her hand and starting to run. They made it to the rear of the house, and Stone looked into the living room. "All clear," he said. "Now here's what you do: Go into your room, brush your hair, then go into Vance's study, looking ill. You don't feel well at all. Let me do the talking."

She nodded, then ran into the house and through the living room, toward the master suite.

Stone took a couple of deep breaths, made sure there were no leaves stuck to his clothes, then went into the study. Durkee and Bryant were drinking coffee and looking at Vance's Oscars, while Manolo stood, watching them.

"Afternoon, gentlemen, what can I do for you?"

"We're here to see Mrs. Calder," Durkee said.

Manolo spoke up. "I let Mrs. Calder know the gentlemen are here, Mr. Barrington. She'll be out shortly."

"Thank you, Manolo, that's all." He took a chair. "So, to what do we owe the honor of your visit?"

"We just want to see Mrs. Calder," Durkee said.

"She won't be answering any questions," Stone replied. "Surely, you knew that."

"We had a tip that she was in New York," Durkee said. "Show her to me; I'm getting tired of waiting."

Arrington chose that moment to enter the room. "Stone," she said drowsily, "what's this about? I was asleep."

"Sorry to wake you, Mrs. Calder," Durkee said.

"Are you satisfied?" Stone asked.

"I guess so."

Stone turned Arrington around and led her to the bedroom door. "You can go back to bed," he said. "Are you going to want dinner later, or do you want to just sleep?"

"I want to sleep," she said.

"Do you want Dr. Drake?"

"No, I think I'll be all right in the morning." She left the room, and Stone closed the door behind her.

He turned back to the two cops. "A tip? What kind of tip?"

"An anonymous call," Durkee said. "A woman. Said the lady had jumped bail."

Stone shook his head. "As long as you're here, tell me something."

"What's that?"

"Why haven't you interviewed the gardener, Cordova?"

"We have no reason to," Durkee said. "He's not a suspect."

"Do you think he might be connected to the footprint you found outside the back door to the house?"

Durkee and Bryant exchanged a glance. "Nah," Durkee said. "Anybody could have made it."

"A size-twelve Nike, and *anybody* could have made it?"

"Our investigation has not found the footprint or the gardener to be relevant," Durkee said. "Anyway, Cordova's in Mexico, and we'd never find him there."

"Have you made any effort?" Stone demanded.

"I told you, he's not relevant to our investigation. The murderer is in that bedroom."

Bryant spoke up. "Let's get out of here."

"By the way, Mr. Barrington, what are you doing here?" Durkee asked, with a smirk.

"I was working in the guest house," Stone replied. "I'm one of her lawyers."

"Nice work, if you can get it," Bryant said.

Stone opened the door to the study. "Manolo," he called, "show these officers the door, please." He turned to the two detectives. "And don't come back here again, without a warrant. You won't be let in."

The detectives left, and when Stone was sure they were off the property, he went into the bedroom and found Arrington at her dressing table, applying makeup. "Why are you putting on makeup?" he asked. "I hope you don't think you're going anywhere."

"Why don't we go to Spago for dinner?" she asked archly.

"Do you have any idea how lucky you just were?"

"Don't, Stone; I'm converted. I'm sorry I gave you a bad time." She smiled. "Not *very* sorry, though. I enjoyed my trip to New York."

"Give me your car keys," he said.

"Why?"

"Because I've got to get it back from the airport. Manolo can drive me."

She dug into her purse. "I took Vance's car," she said. "It's in short-term parking; the ticket is over the sun visor."

"I'll talk to you tomorrow," he said, kissing the top of her head.

"Won't you come back for dinner?" she asked, disappointed.

"I'm beat; I hardly got any sleep last night, remember?"

She smiled. "I remember." She stood up and kissed him. "I don't think I'll ever forget."

"Neither will I," he said, kissing her. Then he went to find Manolo, and they headed for LAX.

It was getting dark by the time he got back to the bungalow at Centurion. He checked the answering machine on Betty's desk, saw the red light blinking, and pressed the button.

"Mr. Barrington," Brandy Garcia's voice said, sounding exasperated. "I call here, and the lady says call New York; then I call New York, and the lady says to call here. I've got the item you want, and I'm going to call just one more time."

Then, as Stone stood there, the phone rang. "Hello?"

"Mr. Barrington?"

"Yes. Brandy?"

"Hey, Stone; I found your man."

"Where is he?"

"In Tijuana, of course."

"All right, you found him; now how do I find him?"

"You come to Tijuana."

"When?"

"Tomorrow afternoon; it's not a bad drive, three to four hours, depending on traffic. What kind of car you be in?"

"A Mercedes convertible, black."

"No, no, you don't want to be driving around Tijuana in that. You park your car at the border, and walk across; I'll have somebody meet you."

"All right, what time?"

"Say three o'clock?"

"I'll be there."

"Wear a red baseball cap, so my man will know you."

"All right."

"Cordova wants a thousand dollars to meet with you."

"For as long as I want?"

"How long do you want?"

"Maybe an hour, maybe more."

"He'll do that, and Stone?"

"Yes?"

"Don't forget the rest of *my* money, too."

"See you at three o'clock."

Chapter 35

STONE TOOK THE FREEWAY to San Diego and made it in three and a half hours. He had some lunch at a taco joint near the border, then put the money and his little dictating recorder into his pockets, put on the red baseball cap he'd bought at the Centurion Studios shop, parked the car, and walked to the border crossing. He was questioned by a uniformed officer.

"What's the purpose of your visit to Mexico?" the man asked.

"A business meeting."

"What kind of business?"

"I'm a lawyer," Stone replied. "I'm interviewing a witness."

"Let's see some ID."

Stone showed his U.S. passport.

"Are you carrying more than five thousand dollars in cash or negotiable instruments?"

Stone was not about to lie about this. "Yes."

"How much?"

"About seven thousand."

The man handed him a declaration. "What's the money for?"

"I have to pay the man who located the witness for me."

"Fill out the form."

Stone did as he was told, handed it over, and was waved across the border.

"You better be careful, carrying that much money," the officer said.

"Thanks, I will." Stone walked slowly down the busy street, waiting for somebody to recognize him. He saw no one, and no one seemed to take note of him. He had never been to Mexico before, and he was nervous. Everything he had read about the place in the newspapers had led him to believe that the country was a vast criminal enterprise, with drug dealers and kidnappers on every corner and a corrupt police force. So far, he didn't like it.

A block from the border, he sat down at one of two tables outside a little restaurant. A waiter appeared. *"Cerveza,"* Stone said, exhausting his Spanish. A moment later, he was drinking an icy Carta Blanca, the only thing he intended to allow past his lips on this trip. He had finished the beer and was wondering if he had come on a fool's errand when a small boy dressed in ragged jeans and sneakers ran up to him.

"Señor Stone?" the boy asked.

Stone nodded.

The boy beckoned him to come.

Stone left five dollars on the table and followed the boy. They turned a corner and came to a Lincoln Continental of a fifties vintage, a giant, four-door land yacht of an automobile. Brandy Garcia sat at the wheel and beckoned him to the passenger side.

"Give the boy something," Garcia said.

Stone gave the boy five dollars and stuck the red baseball cap on his head.

The boy turned the cap backward, grinned, and disappeared into the street crowd.

Stone got into the car and waited for Garcia to drive off, but he simply sat there. "Well?"

"I want the rest of my money, first," Garcia said.

Stone took a precounted thousand dollars from a pocket and handed it over. "The rest when I'm sitting down with Cordova."

"Fair enough," Brandy said, and put the car into gear. "Pretty nice buggy, eh?"

"Nicely restored," Stone admitted. "I haven't seen one of these in years."

Garcia turned a corner and sped down the street, oblivious of the pedestrians diving out of his way. "I got three more beauties at my house," he said. "I got a Stingray Corvette, a '57 Chevy Bel-Air coupe with the big V-8, and a '52 Caddy convertible, yellow. All mint."

"Well," Stone said, "I guess the Lincoln is the closest thing we're going to get to inconspicuous."

Garcia laughed and turned another corner. "Everybody knows me in Tijuana," he said. "Why be inconspicuous?"

Soon they were leaving the busy part of town and driving down a dirt street. The houses were getting farther apart, and after a while there were very few houses. Garcia slowed and turned down a dirt road; a mile later, he turned into a driveway and drove a hundred yards to a little stucco house in a grove of trees, with an oversized garage to one side.

"Here we are," Garcia said, parking next to a beat-up Volkswagen and getting out of the car. "Cordova is already here; that's his car," he said, jerking a thumb in the direction of the VW. Stone quickly memorized the license plate number before he followed Garcia into the house.

"How's Cordova's English?" Stone asked, as they walked through a tiled living room and out onto a patio.

"Ask him yourself," Garcia said, nodding toward a large man seated at a patio table next to a small swimming pool, hunched over a beer. "That's Felipe Cordova, and you owe me another three grand."

Stone handed him the money, then walked to the table and took a seat opposite the man, getting a look at his shoes on the way. He saw the swoosh logo. "Felipe Cordova?"

The man nodded.

Stone offered his hand. "My name is Barrington."

Cordova shook it limply, saying nothing.

"You have any problem with English, or you want Brandy to translate?"

Cordova looked at Garcia, who was stepping back into the house, and Stone took the opportunity to switch on the little recorder in his shirt pocket.

"English is okay," he said, but I got another problem—a thousand bucks."

Stone counted out five hundred and placed it on the table. "The rest when we're finished, and if you tell me the truth, there might be a bonus."

"What you want to know?" Cordova asked.

"You work for a gardening service in L.A.?"

"Yeah."

"You work sometimes for Charlene Joiner, in Malibu?"

Cordova smiled a little. "Oh, yeah."

"You work for Mr. and Mrs. Calder, in Bel-Air?"

"Yeah."

"You were at their house the day Mr. Calder was shot." It wasn't a question.

"I don't know nothing about that," Cordova said.

"Thanks for your time," Stone said. "You can leave."

Cordova didn't move. "What about my other five hundred?"

"If you want that, you'll have to start earning it," Stone said.

Cordova glared at him for a moment. "I didn't cut the grass that day."

"No, you were there to burgle the place."

Cordova chuckled. "Shit, man," he said.

"I'm not here to arrest you; I think you know the cops aren't going to find you here. They're not even looking for you."

"What makes you think I'm a burglar?" Cordova asked.

"Those Nikes you're wearing cost a hundred and eighty bucks," Stone said. "You didn't buy them cutting grass."

"Shit, man . . ."

Stone slammed his hand on the table. "Shit is right," he said. "That's all I'm getting from you."

"Okay, okay, so what do you want to know?"

"Did Calder catch you in the house?"

"I never got into the house," Cordova replied.

"You were right outside the door; you were seen," Stone lied.

"By who?"

"By Manolo's wife; you didn't see her."

"Then you know I didn't get in the house. I only got as far as the back door. I went in through a little gate where we take the equipment in."

"And what did you see at the back door?"

"First, I heard something."

"Like what?"

"Like a gun going off."

"How many times?"

"Once. I was almost to the back door when I heard it. I took a few more steps, and I looked through the door. It was a glass door, you know? With panes?"

"I know. What did you see?"

"I saw Mr. Calder lying on the floor in the hall, and blood was coming out of his head."

"What else did you see?"

"I saw the gun on the floor beside Mr. Calder."

"What kind of gun?"

"An automatic; I don't know what kind."

"What color?"

"Silver."

"What else did you see?"

"I saw a woman running down the hall."

Stone's stomach suddenly felt hollow, and he couldn't speak.

Cordova went on. "She was wearing one of them robes made out of that towel stuff." He rubbed his fingers together.

"Terrycloth?"

"Yeah. It had this . . ." He moved his hands around his head.

"Hood?"

"Yeah, a hood. She was barefoot; I don't think she had nothing on, except the robe."

"Could you see her body?"

"No, just her feet."

"Did you see her face?" Stone held his breath.

"No."

Stone let out the breath.

"But it was Mrs. Calder."

Stone's stomach flip-flopped. "If you didn't see her face, how do you know it was Mrs. Calder?"

"C'mon, man, who else would it be, naked and in a robe in the Calders' house?"

"But you didn't see her face."

"No, but it was her. Same size and everything; same ass, you know?"

"Which way was she running?"

"Away from me—that's all I know, man; I got the hell out of there, you know? I was over that fence and out of there in a big hurry."

Stone took him through it again, made him repeat every statement, but nothing changed. Finally, there was nothing else to ask. He shelled out another five hundred, and Cordova put it in his pocket.

"You want to make another three hundred?" Stone asked.

"Sure."

Stone put the money on the table. "Sell me your shoes."

"Huh?"

"I'll give you three hundred dollars for your shoes."

Cordova grinned. "Sure, man." He shucked off the Nikes and put them on the table. They were dirty, beat up, and huge. He put the money in his pocket, gave a little wave, and lumbered toward the house, padding along in his stocking feet.

Garcia came out of the house. "How'd it go?" he asked.

"Great," Stone said. "Just great. Get me back to the border."

"I see you got yourself some shoes." He held his nose.

"Just get me back, Brandy," Stone said, feeling sick.

Chapter 36

STONE DROVE BACK toward Los Angeles in a fog, torn between what he had believed had happened to Vance Calder and what Felipe Cordova had told him. He had thought Cordova had murdered Vance, but every instinct he had developed as a cop, interrogating witnesses, told him that Cordova had told him the truth in their interview.

"I've been fooled before," he said aloud to himself. Cordova still could have done it; maybe he was a better liar than Stone had thought. The only good thing about Cordova was that the LAPD had not questioned him, didn't want to. He would not like to see the Mexican on the stand, testifying against Arrington.

The car phone rang. Stone punched the send button, so he could talk hands free. "Hello?"

"Hi, it's Betty. Joan called from New York, said to tell you that everything was in hand with the house. The roofer is going to start in a couple of days, and it will take him a week to finish."

"Good news," Stone said.

"She also said that Dolce was waiting at the house when she got back from Teterboro, and that she told her that you'd returned to L.A. Does that mean we can expect more candid snaps?"

"I certainly hope not. I've already told the guard at the gate not to let her into the studio again, but maybe you'd better call and reinforce that."

"Will do."

"Any other calls?"

"Marc Blumberg called, said he just wanted to catch up with you. He's at his Palm Springs house; you want the number?"

Stone fished a pen and his notebook out of his pocket. "Shoot."

Betty dictated the number, and he jotted it down, careful to keep the car on track.

"Your bags are piled up in the entrance hall; want me to unpack for you?"

"Thanks, I'd appreciate that. I was too tired to bother last night."

"I'll send your laundry out, too."

"Thanks again."

"Stone you sound funny—depressed."

"I'm just tired," he replied. "The round-trip cross-country flight messed with my internal clock."

"Want to have dinner tonight?"

He knew what that meant. "Give me a rain check, if you will; I just want to get some rest."

"Okay, call if you need anything."

Stone punched the end button, then dialed Marc Blumberg's Palm Springs number and punched the send button again.

"Hello?"

"Marc, it's Stone."

"Hi, there, you in the car?"

"Yeah, I'm just north of San Diego."

"What are you doing down there?"

"I've been to Tijuana to meet with Felipe Cordova, of Nike footprint fame."

"What did he have to say for himself?"

"It's a long story; why don't we get together when you're back in L.A.?"

"Why don't you come here, instead? I'll give you some dinner and put you up for the night. You could be here in a couple of hours."

"Okay, why not?"

"You got a map?"

"Yes."

"Take I-15 to just short of Temecula, then cut east over the mountains."

"Okay, what's the address?"

Blumberg gave him the street and number and directions to the house.

"See you in a while." He hung up, then saw a sign for I-15 just in time to make the turn.

He found the turnoff for Palm Springs and followed the curving mountain road, enjoying the drive. His head began to clear, and almost without effort, things started to line up in his mind. First of all, he still believed Arrington was innocent; second, he felt that Cordova was the best suspect; third, he was going to do whatever it took to get Arrington out of this. He forced himself to consider the possibility that Arrington had shot Vance. If so, he rationalized, it must somehow have been self-defense. He could not let her be convicted, especially after what had happened in New York. He was in her thrall again, if he had ever been out of it, and all he wanted at the moment was a future with Arrington in it. By the time he had found Marc Blumberg's house, his ducks were all in a row.

The house was a large contemporary, sculpted of native stone and big timbers, on several acres of desert. Marc greeted him warmly and led him out to the pool. The sun was low in the sky, and the desert air was growing cool. A tall, very beautiful woman was stretched out on a chaise next to the outside bar.

"This is Vanessa Pike," Marc said. "Vanessa, meet Stone Barrington."

The two shook hands. It was difficult for Stone not to appreciate her beauty, especially since she was wearing only the bottom of her bikini.

"What'll you drink?" Marc asked them both.

"I'll have a gin and tonic," Vanessa replied.

"So will I," Stone echoed.

Marc motioned him to a chair opposite Vanessa, who showed no inclination to cover herself, soaking up the waning rays of afternoon sun.

"Aren't you getting chilly?" Stone asked.

"I'm rarely chilly," she replied, with a level gaze.

"I believe you," Stone said.

Marc came back with the drinks and joined them. "So, how'd you ever find Cordova?"

"A friend at the LAPD put me in touch with a guy named Brandy Garcia, who knows the territory down there."

"I've heard about him," Blumberg said. "A real hustler."

"Took him less than a week to find Cordova."

"Where'd you meet?"

"At Garcia's house. He seems to be doing very well for himself."

"I don't get it; why would Cordova talk to you?"

"Because I paid him a thousand dollars, plus another three hundred for his shoes."

"You got the Nikes?"

"I did."

"Was there a cut on the sole?"

"There was; they're in my car; they'll match the photograph the cops took."

"Now that is great! What did Cordova say?"

Stone took a deep breath and told the lie. "Denied everything; wasn't at the house that day, went to Mexico, because somebody in the family was sick."

"You couldn't shake his story?"

Stone shook his head. "No way to disprove it, without telling him about the footprint, and I didn't want to tip him off about that."

"You think there's any way of getting him back, so the cops can question him?"

"No, short of arranging another meeting and kidnapping him, and I don't think a judge would look kindly on that, not even a judge you play golf with."

"You're right about that."

"He's not coming back to L.A. anytime soon; he's gone to ground, and I doubt if we'll ever see him again."

"Well, we've got the shoes," Blumberg said.

"You think that's enough to win a motion to dismiss?"

"Maybe; I'd like to think about that. I'd really like to have more."

"Like a confession from Cordova?"

Marc grinned. "That would do it, I think."

Stone got serious. "We can't let this go to trial, Marc."

"Oh, I think I could win it," Marc replied cockily.

"Probably, but I don't want to take the chance, and I don't want Arrington to have to live with half the world thinking she murdered her husband."

"We'll go for the motion to dismiss, when I'm ready," Marc said, "and we'll play it big in the press, sow some doubt amongst the jury pool. Even if we lose, we can do ourselves some good."

"Let's don't lose," Stone said.

A Latino in a white jacket came out of the house. "Dinner is served, whenever you're ready, Mr. Blumberg."

"Thank you, Pedro," Marc said. "We'll be right in."

"May I use a phone?" Stone asked.

"Sure; go into my study, first door on your left." Marc pointed the way.

Stone went into the study, closed the door behind him, and picked up the phone on the desk. He checked his notebook and dialed the number for Brandy Garcia.

"Buenos dias," Garcia's voice said. "Leave me a message, okay?" There was a beep.

"Give your friend in Tijuana a message," Stone said. "Tell him there's a warrant out for him. Tell him to go where even *you* can't find him." He hung up the phone and went in to dinner.

Vanessa was sitting at a small table alone. She patted a chair next to her.

Stone was relieved that she had put on a sweater. He sat down. "Where's Marc?"

"He's down in the wine cellar, getting us something to drink."

Marc returned with a bottle of claret, opened it, tasted it, poured them each a glass, and sat down. He raised his glass. "To motions to dismiss," he said, "and to Vanessa."

"I'll drink to both," Stone said, raising his glass.

C h a p t e r   3 7

WHEN STONE CAME DOWN to breakfast, Marc was just finishing his coffee. Stone took a seat, and Pedro came and took his order for bacon and eggs.

"Sleep well?" Marc asked.

"Probably better than you did," Stone replied, trying not to smirk. "Where's Vanessa?"

"Still asleep. Tired." Marc smirked.

"I see."

"You should give Vanessa a call sometime," Marc said. "There's nothing serious between the two of us, and she's really a very nice girl."

"It's a thought," Stone said, noncommitally.

"I wouldn't like to see you all alone in L.A. Might affect your work on the case, that sort of frustration. And since Arrington is off limits . . ."

"You're too kind, Marc."

"I certainly am."

"Listen, Marc, I was thinking last night: Instead of making an announcement to the press about Cordova, why don't you just leak it a little at a time. Do you know a reporter you can trust not to reveal his sources?"

"You have a point: If the press gets wind of a suspect that the police have ignored, then the cops will look bad, and we won't appear to have had anything to do with it. I like it, and I know just the reporter at the *L.A. Times.*"

"Our judge, whoever he turns out to be, will probably hear about it, too, and when we demonstrate in court that the rumors of another suspect are true . . ."

"That is delightfully Machiavellian, Stone," Marc said. "You surprise me."

Stone didn't know how to reply to that. His breakfast arrived, and he enjoyed it, while Blumberg talked about golf in Palm Springs.

"You play? I'll give you a game this morning."

"I've hit a few balls; that's about it."

"You should take some lessons; that's how to get started."

"Golf in Manhattan is tough," Stone said. "I think you pretty much have to drive to Westchester, and that's if you can get into a club."

"Why do I have the feeling you aren't telling me the truth about Felipe Cordova?" Marc asked, suddenly changing the subject.

"I don't know, Marc," Stone replied, surprised. "Why do you feel that way?"

"You think Cordova didn't kill Vance, don't you?"

"He told a very convincing story."

"But you want the LAPD and the D.A. and a judge to think he did it."

"Just that he's a viable suspect, and the cops have ignored him. Shows a lack of good faith on their part."

"Let me ask you this: What happens if I get the charges against Arrington dismissed, then the cops find Cordova?"

"I don't think we'll ever see Cordova again; he's too scared."

"You said he denied everything, and you didn't contradict him by telling him about the shoeprint at Vance's house."

"That's right."

"So what happens to his story when the cops tell him about the shoeprint?"

"First, they have to find him; he's in Mexico, probably not in Tijuana any more. You know the problems with finding somebody down there, not to mention the difficulties of getting a suspect extradited."

"I'm talking worst case, here, Stone; I have to protect myself. If, by some miracle, the cops find Cordova in Mexico, or, more likely, he comes back to this country and gets arrested for speeding, or something. I have to know what he's going to say."

"My guess is, he'll try to implicate Arrington. He knows about the murder, knows she's been charged. He'll do everything he can to see that she takes the fall. That's my guess."

"I suppose that makes sense," Marc said. "You know, I've tried a lot of cases in my time, and a lot of them murders, too, but I don't think I've ever tried one where my second chair was in love with the defendant."

Stone kept eating his eggs.

"You're a bright guy, Stone, and I suspect a very good lawyer, so I'm going to rely on you not to do anything that will get *me* hung."

"I would never do anything like that," Stone replied truthfully.

"I can see how you might not want to tell me everything you know, to save Arrington's very beautiful ass, how you might even lie to me. That's okay, as long as it doesn't interfere with how I handle my case, and as long as it doesn't get me disbarred or damage my credibility with the D.A. and the judges in this town. That credibility is the most valuable asset I have in defending a client, and I don't want to lose it. I hope I make myself perfectly clear."

"Perfectly clear, Marc," Stone said, finishing his coffee. He looked at his watch. "Well, I think I'd better be getting back to L.A. Thanks for your hospitality."

Marc stood up and shook his hand. "And don't forget, if you get horny, call Vanessa; don't go sneaking into Arrington's bedroom. If that got out, it could screw us all." He handed Stone his card, with Vanessa's number scrawled on the back.

Stone nodded and put the card into his pocket. "I take your point." He left the house, got into the car, which smelled of Felipe Cordova's Nikes, and headed back toward L.A.

He was back at Centurion Studios by eleven-thirty, and Betty met him at the door of the bungalow, looking rattled.

"What's wrong?" he asked, tucking a finger under her chin and lifting her head.

"I've just had a very peculiar conversation with Dolce, if you can call it a conversation," she said. "Actually, it was more of a tirade."

"Oh, God; what did she say?"

"She went into some detail about what she would do to me if I ever, as she put it, 'touch him again.' She means you, I believe."

"I'm sorry about that, Betty; this has nothing to do with you, really."

"That's not the impression I got," Betty said. "Frankly, she sounded nuts to me. I'm scared."

"Tell you what," Stone said. "Why don't you take a trip to Hawaii, do some scouting for just the right place when you bail out of L.A."

Betty brightened. "You think you could get along without me for a while? Careful how you answer that."

Stone laughed. "It'll be tough, but I'll manage."

"Maybe that's not such a bad idea," Betty said. "I'll get you some help from the studio secretarial pool, then call the travel agent." She headed for her office.

"Any other calls?" he asked.

"Brandy Garcia called; said his friend has already got your message."

"I've no idea what *that* means," he replied, covering his ass.

"Oh, and I almost forgot: Dolce says you're to meet her at the Bel-Air for lunch at one o'clock."

"She's in L.A.?"

"Yep. And she said, 'tell him to be there without fail, or I'll get mad.'"

Stone gave a low moan.

Betty picked up her phone and dialed a number. "Try and keep her busy long enough for me to get out of town, okay?" she called to him.

"I wish I could reverse our roles," Stone replied.

Chapter 38

STONE ARRIVED AT THE BEL-AIR on time and with trepidations. What will I do if she starts shooting? he asked himself. What if she only makes a scene? What then? He liked to think he had had less than his share of arguments with women, and that he managed that by being easy to get along with. He had a dread of public disagreements, especially in the middle of places like the Bel-Air Hotel.

He wasn't sure where to meet her, so he wandered slowly through the lobby and outside again, toward the restaurant. Then he saw her, seated at a table in the middle of the garden café, wearing a silk print dress, her hair pinned to the top of her head, revealing her long, beautiful neck. Her chin rested on her interlocked fingers, and her mien was serene.

"Oh hello, Mr. Barrington," the headwaiter said as he approached. "Mrs. Barrington is waiting, and may I congratulate you?"

Stone leaned over and spoke quietly, but with conviction. "There is *no* Mrs. Barrington," he said. "The lady's name is Miss Bianchi."

"Yes, sir," the man said, a little flustered. "Whatever you say." He led Stone to the table and pulled out a chair for him.

Stone sat down and allowed her to lean over and brush his cheek with her lips.

"Hello, my darling," she purred.

"Good afternoon, Dolce."

"I hope you're enjoying your stay in Los Angeles."

"I can't say that I am," he replied, looking at the menu.

"Poor baby," she said, patting his cheek. "Maybe it's time to go back home to New York—yet again."

"Not for a while."

"But what's to keep us here?" she asked, all innocence.

"Business is keeping *me* here," he replied.

The waiter appeared. Dolce ordered a lobster salad and a glass of chardonnay, and Stone, the taco soup and iced tea.

"Why are you in L.A.?" he asked, hoping for a rational answer. She began rummaging in a large handbag for something, and Stone leaned away from her, fearing she might come up with a weapon.

She came up with a lipstick and began applying it. "I want to be with my husband," she said, consulting a compact mirror.

"Your husband is dead," Stone said through clenched teeth.

"You look perfectly well to me," she replied gazing levelly at him.

"Dolce . . ."

"And how is the murderess, Mrs. Calder?"

"Dolce . . ."

"I think I will be quite happy when they put her away."

"Dolce . . ."

"Vance was such a lovely man, and we were such good friends. I think it would be terribly unfair, if she got away with it."

"Dolce, stop it!"

"My goodness, Stone, keep your voice down. We don't want a public scene, do we?"

Stone decided to treat this as a negotiation. "Just tell me what you want," he said.

Her eyebrows shot up. "What *I* want? Why, I want whatever my darling husband wants. What do *you* want, dear?"

"I want to end this little charade of yours; I want us to go our separate ways in an amicable manner." He paused and decided to fire the last arrow in his quiver. "I want to be with Arrington."

Her eyebrows dropped, and her eyes narrowed. "Believe me when I tell you, my darling, that I will never, ever allow that to happen, and you had better get used to the idea now."

Stone felt his gorge rising, but the waiter appeared with their lunch, allowing him to cool down for a moment before continuing. "I don't understand," he said.

"You asked me to marry you, did you not?"

"Yes, but . . ."

"And I married you, in Venice, did I not?"

"That wasn't a legal marriage."

"Oh, Stone, now you're beginning to sound like a lawyer."

"I *am* a lawyer, and I know when I'm married and when I'm not."

"I'm afraid not, Sweetie," she said, attacking her lobster salad. "You seem unable to face reality; you're in complete denial."

Stone nearly choked on his soup.

"*I* am in denial?"

"A serious case of denial, I fear."

"Let's talk about denial, Dolce. I've explained to you, in the clearest possible terms, that I no longer wish to continue my relationship with you. I've explained why."

"I seem to remember your saying something about that, but I hardly took you seriously," she said.

This was maddening. "Dolce, I do not love you; I thought I did for a while, but now I realize I don't."

She laughed. "And I suppose you think you love Arrington?"

"Yes, I do." Funny, he hadn't said that to Arrington.

"But Stone, how can you love a woman who has murdered her husband? How do you know you won't be next?"

"That's a very strange thing for *you* to say," Stone said under his breath, trying to control his temper. "I seem to remember that you once had a husband who is now dead of extremely unnatural causes."

"That was the business he chose, if I may paraphrase Don Corleone, and he had to live with it." She speared a chunk of lobster. "Or die with it. You might remember that."

"I chose a different business, and I am choosing a different woman." My God, he thought, what do I have to say to get through to her?

Dolce shook her head. "No, Stone; you haven't yet come to the point where you have to make a real choice." She chewed her lobster. "But you will."

"Is that some sort of threat, Dolce?"

"Call it a prediction, but take it any way you like."

"Why would you want a man who doesn't want you?" he demanded. "Why do you demean yourself?"

She put down her fork, and her eyes narrowed again. "You do not know me as well as you will after a while," she said, "but when you do come to know me, you will look back on that remark as dangerous folly."

"That's it," Stone said, putting down his spoon, his soup still untouched. "One last time, for the record: I do not love you; I will not marry you; I *have not* married you. I love another woman, and I believe I always will. I want nothing more to do with you, ever. I cannot make it any clearer than that. He stood up. "Good-bye, Dolce."

"No, my darling," she replied smoothly, "merely *au revoir.*"

"Dolce," he said, "California has a very strong law against stalking; don't make me publicly humiliate you." He turned and walked out of the café.

All the way back to the studio he ran the conversation through his head, over and over. It had been like talking to a marble sculpture, except that a sculpture does not make threats. Or had she made threats? Was there anything in her words that could be used against her? He admitted there was not. What was he going to do? How could he get this woman off his back? More important, how could he get her off his back without grievously offending her father, whom he did not want for an enemy?

He parked in front of the bungalow and, finding it locked, used his key. On Betty's desk there was a note, stuck to a package.

"I've taken your advice, lover; I'm on a late afternoon plane. I'll call you in a couple of days to see how you're making out. A girl from the pool will be in tomorrow morning to do for you, although she probably won't do for you as I do. Take care of yourself."

He turned to the package, which was an overnight air envelope with a Rome return address. He opened it, and two sheets of paper fell out. The top one was a heavy sheet of cream-colored writing paper. Stone read the handwritten letter:

The Vatican
Rome

Dear Stone,

I have made the investigations I told you I would, speaking personally to the mayor of Venice. I have concluded that you and Dolce are legally married in Italy, and that the proper documents, which you both signed, have been duly registered. The marriage would be considered valid anywhere in the world.

I know this was not the news you wanted. I would offer advice on an annulment, but you are not a Catholic, and, you surely understand, I cannot offer advice on divorce.

You remain in my thoughts and prayers. If there is any other help I can give you, please let me know.

Warmly,
Bellini

Stone looked at the other piece of paper. It was printed in Italian, bore his and Dolce's names, and appeared to be a certificate of marriage.

"Oh, shit," he said.

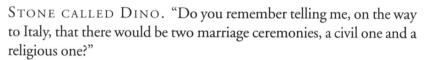

Chapter 39

STONE CALLED DINO. "Do you remember telling me, on the way to Italy, that there would be two marriage ceremonies, a civil one and a religious one?"

"Sure. Why do you ask?"

"You remember telling me that the civil ceremony wasn't legal until the religious ceremony had been performed?"

"Sure. Why do you ask?"

"Where did you get that information?"

"Which information?"

"The information that one ceremony didn't count without the other?"

"I said one wouldn't be legal, without the other. I didn't say it wouldn't *count*."

"Where did you get that information?"

"From Mary Ann."

"Is Mary Ann an authority on Italian marital law?"

"All women are authorities on marital law, in any country."

"Do you know where Mary Ann got that information?"

"No, why?"

"Because I want to strangle the person who gave it to her."

"My guess is, that would be Dolce. Good luck on strangling her without getting offed, yourself. What the fuck is this about, Stone?"

"I called Bellini to ask him about this. I just got a letter from him, along with a copy of my marriage certificate."

"You mean the ceremony is valid, legally?"

"Yes."

Dino began giggling. "Oh, Jesus!" he managed to get out.

"This isn't funny, Dino. I just had lunch with Dolce, where I made it as clear as possible that I was not married to her and didn't intend to be."

"Let me guess: She didn't buy that."

"You could put it that way. She as much as said she'd kill me or, maybe, Arrington if I continue to deny the marriage."

"Well, if I were you, I'd take the threat seriously."

"I *am* taking it seriously."

"What's your next move? I'm dying to hear."

"I haven't the faintest idea."

"Want a suggestion?"

"If it's a serious one."

"First, I'd see a divorce lawyer; then I'd watch my ass. Arrington's, too, which isn't too much of a chore, if I correctly recall her ass."

"Do you have any idea what it takes to get a divorce in Italy?"

"Nope; that's why I suggested a divorce lawyer. Listen, pal, be thankful you didn't get married in the Italian church. Then you'd *really* be in deep shit."

"Dino, I don't think I ever thanked you properly."

"Thank me for what?"

"For advising me to stay away from Dolce."

"You didn't take my advice; why are you thanking me?"

"It was good advice, even if I didn't take it."

"Well, I'm glad you remember; saves me from saying I told you so."

"I'm happy to save you the trouble."

"Listen, Stone, this isn't all bad, you know?"

"It isn't? What's not all bad about it?"

"You've got the perfect means of staying single now. Every time some broad presses you to marry her, all you've got to say is, that you're already married, and your wife won't give you a divorce." Dino suppressed a laugh, but not well. "And you'll be telling the truth. Millions of guys would envy you!"

"You don't happen to know an Italian divorce lawyer, do you?"

"Nope, and can you imagine what will happen if you get one, and then he finds out who you're trying to divorce?"

"What?"

"Come on, Stone, Eduardo is probably better known to Italian lawyers than to American ones."

"You really know how to make a guy's day, Dino."

"Always happy to spread a little cheer."

"See you around."

"Bye."

Stone hung up, looked at his watch, then called Marc Blumberg's office.

"Yeah, Stone?"

"Marc, I'm glad you're back from Palm Springs. Can I come and see you? I need some legal advice, on a subject not connected to our present case."

"Sure, come on over; I'll make time."

Stone was surprised to find Vanessa Pike in Marc's office, and relieved to see her fully dressed. "Hi, Vanessa," he said.

"I was going to run Vanessa home, as soon as I made a couple of calls," Marc said. "What can I do for you?" He looked at Stone, then at Vanessa. "Honey, can you go powder your nose?"

Vanessa got up, opened a door in the corner of Blumberg's large office and closed it behind her.

"What's up?" Marc asked.

"You do divorce work, don't you?"

"Who are we talking about, getting divorced?"

"Me."

"Sure, I do divorce work, but first the client has to be married."

Stone placed the letter from Bellini and the marriage certificate on Marc's desk.

Marc read the letter. "Wow," he said. "You're pals with Cardinal Bellini?"

"He was supposed to officiate at my wedding, in Venice. We had a civil ceremony on a Saturday, and it was my understanding that it wasn't valid until we had the religious ceremony. The call came about Vance's death before that could take place, and the next thing I knew, I was on a plane for L.A."

"This Bellini is a real heavyweight, you know," Marc said, and there was awe in his voice.

"Marc, focus, please! This is a marriage in name only; it wasn't even consummated—at least, *after* the ceremony."

"And who is . . ." he looked at the marriage certificate. ". . . Rosaria Bianchi?" His face fell. "She's not . . . she couldn't be . . ."

Stone nodded dumbly.

"Eduardo Bianchi's daughter?" His eyebrows went up. "Stone, I'm looking at you in a whole new light, here."

"I want out of this so-called marriage, Marc. How do I go about that?"

"Before we go into that, Stone, let me ask you something, something serious."

"What?"

"Are you looking to piss off Eduardo Bianchi? I assume you know exactly who he is."

"I know who he is, and I like him. He likes me, I think, or he did when he thought I was going to be his son-in-law."

"Have you told him about this?"

"He was at the ceremony, Marc."

"I mean, have you told him you want a divorce from his daughter?"

"I don't think he even knows the marriage is valid, but he knows that Dolce and I are no longer together. He was pretty understanding about it."

"Well, for your sake, I hope to hell he's going to be understanding about it. I wouldn't want to be in your shoes, if he decides *not* to be understanding."

"Marc, what am I going to do? How do I get out of this?"

"Well, assuming that you can find a way to stay alive, the situation shouldn't be all that bad. I once worked with an attorney in Milan on a divorce case." He looked at his watch. "It's too late there to call him now, but I'll call him in the morning, and we can see where we stand. I'm assuming Ms. Bianchi wants out, too."

"Don't assume that," Stone said.

"What should I assume?"

"Assume the worst."

Vanessa came out of the powder room. "May I reappear now?"

"Sure, honey," Marc said, "we're done, for the moment."

Stone got up to leave.

"Oh, Stone," Marc said, "would you mind giving Vanessa a lift home? I've still got some work here."

"Sure."

"If it's not out of your way," Vanessa said.

Stone shrugged. "I don't know where I'm going, anyway."

Chapter 40

STONE FOLLOWED VANESSA'S INSTRUCTIONS to a quiet street up in the Hollywood Hills, above Sunset Boulevard, where they turned into the driveway of a pretty, New England–style, shingled cottage. They had been quiet all the way.

"You all right?" she asked, when they had stopped.

"Yes, sure," Stone said.

"Tell you what: Why don't you come in, and I'll fix you some dinner?"

"I don't want to put you to any trouble, Vanessa."

"I gotta eat, you gotta eat," she replied.

"Okay." He got out of the car, followed her to the front door and waited while she unlocked it and entered the security system code. The house was larger than it had seemed from the outside, and prettily decorated and furnished.

"There's a wet bar over there," she said, pointing to a cabinet. "Fix us a drink; I'll have a Johnny Walker Black on the rocks."

Stone opened the cabinet, found the scotch, and found a bottle of Wild Turkey, too. He poured the drinks and followed her into the kitchen. There was a counter separating the cooking area from a sitting room, and he took a stool there. He wondered if she would now strip to the waist and walk around as she had in Palm Springs.

Vanessa turned out to be something of a mind reader. "Don't worry," she said, "I'm not going to take any clothes off. That was Marc's idea, in Palm Springs."

"Marc's idea? Why would he ask you to do that?"

"Oh, I was already fairly naked; he just asked me not to get dressed. Marc is concerned about you."

"Concerned how?"

"He thinks you need . . . companionship." She began rummaging in the refrigerator.

"Oh."

"Marc is a very kind man; I owe him a lot."

"Why?"

"I was in the middle of an awful divorce, and my lawyer was intimidated by my ex's lawyer. I ran into Marc at a cocktail party and complained about it, and he said he'd fix it. He did. He renegotiated my settlement, got me the Bel-Air house and a lot of money. I sold that house, bought this place, and invested the difference. If not for Marc, I'd probably be working as a secretary somewhere. As it is, I'm well fixed."

"Good for him," Stone said.

"He thinks that if you're fucking Arrington, it could hurt his case."

"He has made that point," Stone said.

"You two were an item before she married Vance, weren't you?"

"Yes, we were."

"Will you be again, assuming she doesn't go to prison?"

"Hard to say," Stone replied.

"Is that what you want?"

"Sometimes I do; other times, I don't know," he admitted.

Vanessa smiled. "I think it's what you want." She switched on the gas grill of the restaurant-style stove and put the steaks on, then started to make a salad.

Stone watched her move expertly around the kitchen. She was beautiful, smart, and, he did not doubt, affectionate. But Arrington was on his mind, and he could not get that out of the way.

. . .

They had finished dinner and were sipping a brandy before the living room fireplace.

"I'm having a tough time making a decision," Vanessa said.

"Anything I can do to help?"

"I'm in something of an ethical quandary. I've promised a friend to keep something in confidence, but to do that might harm someone else."

"That's a tough one," Stone said.

"The person who might be harmed is not a particular friend, though I have nothing against this person."

"Then why are you having so much trouble keeping your promise to your friend?"

"Because it might help Marc—and you—if I told you about it."

"Is there some way you can give me a hint without breaking your word to your friend?"

"I'm not sure. Perhaps if I tell you a little about it without revealing the friend's identity?"

"Sounds good to me."

"Marc says that he's worried that the police might have more on Arrington than he knows about."

"I've been worried about that, too."

"Well, you're both right to be worried."

Stone sucked in a breath. "Can you tell me any more?"

"I'm sorry," she said. "I don't think I can." She sipped her brandy. "It's just that there may very well have been a witness to what happened that night."

"You mean the Mexican gardener?"

"No, someone else. That's all I can say."

"Have you told Marc about this?"

"No, he'd just browbeat it out of me, and I'd feel terrible. I don't think you would try to do that."

Funny, Stone thought, he had been thinking about doing just that.

"Well," Stone said, "if you can ever see your way clear to tell me more, I'd like to hear it."

"I think that's unlikely," she replied.

Stone looked at his watch. "I'd better go; it's getting late."

She walked him to the door, and he gave her a peck on the cheek. "Thanks for dinner," he said, "and for the good company. I needed it."

"I'm sorry I can't be of more help," she said.

"You've at least confirmed our suspicions," Stone said, "and that's a help." He waved and started toward his car. She waited until he had backed out of the drive before closing the door.

The street was dark, and there were a few cars parked along the curb. As Stone put the car into gear and drove away, he noticed head-lights appear in his rearview mirror. Funny, he thought, he hadn't seen a car coming when he'd backed out. He watched the lights in the mirror until he reached Sunset, then lost them in the traffic.

Chapter 41

STONE WAS WAKENED by the sound of someone entering the bungalow. Since Betty was now in Hawaii, he wasn't expecting anybody, so he got into a robe and padded into the front room in his bare feet.

A young woman was seated at Betty's desk; she looked up, startled. "Oh," she said. "I didn't know you were here."

"I'm here," Stone said. "But why are you?"

"I'm Louise Bremen, from the secretarial pool; Betty wanted a temp while she's on vacation."

"Oh, of course; I'd forgotten. I'm Stone Barrington." He walked over and shook her hand.

"Anything special you want done?" she asked.

"Just sort the Calder mail and separate the bills. Betty uses a computer program to pay them."

"Quicken? I know that."

"Good; you can write the checks, and I'll sign them. I'm a signatory on the Calder accounts."

"Sure; can I make you some coffee?"

"I'll do it, as soon as I've had a shower," Stone said. He went back to his bedroom, showered, shaved, and returned to the kitchenette. He was having breakfast when the phone rang, and Louise called out, "Marc Blumberg for you."

Stone picked up the phone. "Marc?"

"Yes, I . . ."

"I'm glad you called. I had dinner with Vanessa last night, and she pretty much confirmed our suspicion that the police have something on Arrington they haven't disclosed. Seems there was another witness to what happened when Vance was shot."

"And who was that?"

"She wouldn't say; she said she had been told in confidence."

"And why didn't she tell *me* that? She certainly had plenty of opportunity."

"She said she was afraid you'd browbeat the name out of her. She seemed very serious about keeping the confidence. I think you ought to take her to lunch and press the point."

There was a long silence on the other end.

"Marc?"

"You haven't been watching television this morning, have you?"

"No; I guess I slept a little late. I'm having breakfast now."

"Vanessa is dead."

"What?"

"Her house burned to the ground last night. TV says the cops haven't ruled out arson."

"But I was with her; we had dinner."

"Must have been later than that. It's the husband, I know it is."

"She told me about the divorce; was he that angry?"

"As angry as I've seen a husband in thirty years of practice. I got her a terrific settlement, and I wouldn't have been surprised if he'd taken a shot at *me.*"

Stone found a kitchen stool and sat down. "I can't believe it," he said.

"Was she all right when you left her?"

"She was fine; she cooked dinner, and . . ."

"How late were you there?"

"I guess I left a little before eleven."

"You'd better talk to the cops, I guess."

"I suppose so, though I can't really tell them much."

"Did Vanessa give any hint at all about who her friend, the witness, might be?"

"No; in fact, she went to the trouble of avoiding mention of even the gender."

"It's bound to be a woman; Vanessa doesn't . . . didn't have men friends, except for me."

"Do you know who her female friends were?"

"She ran around with a group that hung around with Charlene Joiner. I don't know who the others were. You think you could look into that?"

"Sure, I'll be glad to."

"I've got to go; what with Vanessa's affairs to handle, I've got a lot on my desk this morning."

"Thanks, Marc; I'll get back to you if I find out anything." Stone hung up and wolfed down the rest of his muffin, while dialing Rick Grant.

"Captain Grant."

"Rick, it's Stone Barrington."

"Morning, Stone; what's up?"

"I've just heard from Marc Blumberg that a woman I was with last evening died in a fire last night."

"That thing in the Hollywood Hills?"

"Yes; Vanessa Pike was her name."

"Looks like a murder, from what I hear."

"I thought I should talk to the investigating officers."

"Yes, you should. Hang on a minute."

Stone waited on hold while he finished his coffee.

Rick came back on the line. "You know where the house is?"

"Yes."

"Meet me there in, say, forty-five minutes."

"All right."

They hung up, and Stone went to his desk and signed the checks Louise had printed out, then he got into his car and drove to Vanessa's house.

218

. . .

He smelled it before he saw it, the odor of burning wood, not at all unpleasant. He saw Rick Grant getting out of a car ahead of him and parked behind him.

The two men shook hands, and Rick lead Stone through the police tape. The house was nothing more than a smoking ruin. Rick went to two men in suits who were standing on the front lawn, talking to a fire department captain in uniform.

"Morning, Al, Bruce," Rick said. "Stone, these are detectives Alvino Rivera and Bruce Goldman. This is a former NYPD detective, Stone Barrington."

Stone shook hands and he and Rick were introduced to the fireman, whose name was Hinson.

"Stone, tell Al and Rick about last night."

Stone gave a brief account of his evening with Vanessa.

"Did she say anything about her husband?" Goldman asked, when Stone had finished.

"She told me about the divorce and her settlement. I gathered it wasn't an amiable thing. Her lawyer, Marc Blumberg, who introduced me to her, said the man was very angry about what he had to give her."

"She show any signs of stress or nervousness when talking about her husband?" Rivera asked.

"No, it seemed to be in the past, at least, to her."

"Does the husband look good for this?" Rick asked.

"Maybe. We questioned him this morning at his house. We still have to check out his alibi, but it sounds tight. If he's responsible, then he probably hired a pro."

The fireman spoke up. "The fire was started with gasoline near the master bedroom windows," he said. "We found a can, apparently from the victim's own garage. The perp had wheeled over a gas grill next to the house, and when the fire got going, the propane tank exploded. It must have been full, or nearly so, because it did a lot of damage. The explosion probably killed the woman."

"We haven't heard from the M.E. yet," Goldman said, "but that sounds right."

"You're a lawyer, right?" Rivera said to Stone.

"Right."

"You're in town about the Calder thing?"

"Right."

"When you left last night, did you notice anybody hanging around the street?"

"When I backed out of the driveway, there were no moving cars visible on the street, just parked ones, but as I drove down the block toward Sunset, I saw some headlights in my rearview mirror. My guess is, somebody was waiting in the street, then started up and followed me to Sunset. I lost the car after I turned."

"Any idea of what kind of car?"

"No, all I saw was headlights."

"So the guy was hanging around, waiting for you to leave and for her to go to sleep."

"Could be. I didn't notice anybody following when we drove *to* the house, but I wasn't watching my mirror especially."

"What was your relationship to Mrs. Pike?" Goldman asked.

"I met her the day before yesterday in Palm Springs, at Marc Blumberg's house. Late yesterday afternoon, I had a meeting with Blumberg in his office, right after he returned from the Springs, and she was there. He asked me to give her a lift home, and she invited me to stay for dinner. That was it."

"Did you have sex with her?" Rivera asked.

"No."

"Ever met the husband?"

"No; I don't even know his name."

"Daniel Pike; big-time producer/director."

"I've heard of him."

"You know any of her friends?"

"Blumberg says she's friendly with a group that hangs around with Charlene Joiner."

"Joiner, the movie star?"

"One and the same."

"We'll talk to her."

Rick spoke up. "Anything else you fellows require of Stone?"

"Not at the moment."

"You can reach me through the switchboard at Centurion Studios," Stone said. "I've got a temporary office there, and here's my New York number." He handed them his card.

"You here for long?"

"Until the Calder thing is done."

"Good luck on that one," Goldman said. "I hear the wife is toast."

"Don't believe everything you hear," Stone said.

He and Rick turned and walked back to their cars.

"Thanks for coming over here, Rick," Stone said. "They might not have been as nice, if you hadn't been here."

"Glad to do it. Stone, do you know something you didn't tell those guys?"

"No, that's everything."

"Good," Rick said, shaking hands. He got into his car and drove away.

Stone got back into his car. Well, almost everything, he thought. He had one other thought, but it was completely crazy, and he dismissed it.

Chapter 4 2

BACK AT THE STUDIO BUNGALOW, Stone called the Centurion switchboard. "Good morning, this is Stone Barrington, at the Vance Calder bungalow."

"Good morning, Mr. Barrington," a woman replied, "how can I help you?"

"Can you tell me if Charlene Joiner is working on the lot today?"

"Yes, she is; shall I connect you to her dressing room?"

"Thank you, yes."

The phone rang, and an answering machine picked up. Charlene's honeyed southern voice said, "Hey. I'm shooting, or something, at the moment, but I'll get back to you, if you're worth getting back to." A beep followed.

"Charlene, this is Stone Barrington. I'd like to see you sometime today, if you have a moment. You can reach me at Vance's bungalow. By the way, you should expect a call from the police, too, about Vanessa Pike's death." He hung up.

Louise Bremen came and knocked on the door. "Mrs. Barrington called," she said.

"Louise, there is no Mrs. Barrington," Stone replied, keeping his tone light. "Just a woman who claims to be that. Her name is Dolce Bianchi; what's her number?"

"She didn't leave a number," Louise said. "She just said you'd be hearing from her, and she kind of chuckled."

"Call the Bel-Air Hotel, and see if there's anybody registered under either name. If so, buzz me, and I'll talk to her."

"All right. Oh, and Mrs. Calder called, too."

"I'll return the call after I've spoken to Miss Bianchi."

A couple of minutes passed, and the phone buzzed. Stone picked it up. "Dolce?"

"No, Mr. Barrington," Louise said. "The Bel-Air says she's not registered there."

"Thanks, Louise. Try the Beverly Hills and the dozen best hotels after that, too. Ask about both names." He hung up the phone and thought for a minute. Actually, he admitted to himself, Dolce *did* have a right to call herself Mrs. Barrington, given the latest news from Italy, but it grated on him to hear her do it. Now he allowed himself to think about whether Dolce might have had anything to do with the torching of Vanessa's house and her death in the fire. Crazy, it certainly was, and he could not bring himself to believe that Dolce would have had anything to do with it, based simply on the fact of his visit there. He thought of mentioning it to the police, but dismissed the idea. He had no evidence whatsoever, and it might seem to the police like an attempt on his part to use them to rid himself of a troublesome woman. Still, he had to consider: If Dolce had been involved in Vanessa's death, might she try to harm Arrington? All the extra security he had arranged to guard the Calder estate was gone, since the press had lost some interest in her. Then he had a thought. He dialed Arrington's number.

"Hello?"

"Hi, it's Stone."

"Where are you? I've missed you."

"Same here, but I've been busy. I'm at the bungalow at the moment. Tell me, you're awfully alone there; how would you like some houseguests? The judge didn't bar that."

"I'd like *you* for a houseguest," she replied.

"I was thinking of Dino and Mary Ann, if I can get them out here."

"Oh, I'd love to see them! I've got cabin fever in a big way, and since you're being so standoffish, their company would be very welcome."

"I don't *feel* standoffish," Stone said. "Circumstances are keeping us apart."

"Would you visit me, if Dino and Mary Ann were here?"

"I think that would be perfectly kosher."

"Then, by all means, invite them!"

"I'll call you back." He hung up and dialed Dino's office.

"Lieutenant Bacchetti."

"Dino, it's Stone."

"How's sunny California?"

"You said you had some time off coming; why don't you come out here and see for yourself? And bring Mary Ann?"

"You in some kind of trouble, pal?"

"Maybe, I'm not sure."

"Dolce?"

"Possibly. A woman I had dinner with, somebody I'd met twice, died in a fire last night, not long after I left her house. It was arson, and they suspect her ex-husband, but . . ."

"And how can Mary Ann and I help?"

"You can come and stay at Arrington's."

"As extra security?"

"As houseguests. She says she'd love to see you both. She's been stuck alone in the house for too long, and cabin fever is setting in. There's a wonderful guest house, and some acreage; Mary Ann would love it."

"Hang on," Dino said, and put Stone on hold.

Stone tapped his fingers, waiting. He was beginning to feel a little cabin feverish, himself, even if he wasn't confined to quarters, and he missed his dinners with Dino at Elaine's.

"I'm back," Dino said. "Mary Ann's on board; we'll be out there tomorrow afternoon."

"That's great," Stone said. "I'll arrange for Arrington's butler to meet you at the airport, and we'll all have dinner together. The butler's name is Manolo; call Arrington's and leave your flight time with either him or her."

"Will do."

"Tell Mary Ann not to bring a lot of clothes; she can buy everything she needs on Rodeo Drive."

"Yeah, sure. If you mention that, I'll shoot you."

"Speaking of shooting, bring something, and will you stop by my house and bring me the Walther from my safe? Joan will open it for you; give her a call. And that little piece you loaned me is on my bedside table."

"Okay, see you tomorrow." Dino hung up.

Stone called Arrington and told her the news.

"I'll have Isabel plan something special for dinner," she said.

"Sounds great. Dino will let you know their flight time."

"Why don't you and I have dinner tonight?"

"Behave yourself."

"Oh, all right; just be here at seven tomorrow evening."

"I wouldn't miss it." Stone said good-bye and hung up. Almost immediately, the phone buzzed.

"Yes?"

"Charlene Joiner on line one."

He punched the button. "Hello, Charlene, how are you?"

"Terrible," she replied. "I'm very upset about Vanessa."

"It was a very bad thing."

"Did you know her, Stone?"

"I met her at Marc Blumberg's Palm Springs place a couple of days ago."

"You were right about the police; they're on their way over here now. Maybe you and I should talk before I meet them."

"No, you don't need a lawyer; just answer their questions truthfully. If we met first, it might make them think I'm involving myself in their case even more than I'm already involved."

"How are you already involved?"

"I had dinner at Vanessa's house last night; apparently, I was the last person to see her alive."

"Lucky Vanessa! At least she went with a smile on her face."

"It wasn't like that, Charlene," Stone said. "When can we get together?"

"Why don't you come over here for lunch? I'll be done with the police by then, say one o'clock, and I don't have to be back on the set until three."

"All right, where are you?"

"In the biggest fucking RV you ever saw," she said, "parked at the rear of sound stage six. It's got 'Georgia Peach' painted on the side."

"I'll find it. See you at one."

"I'll look forward."

Chapter 43

STONE FOUND THE RV at the back of the sound stage, and Charlene had not overstated its size. It looked as long as a Greyhound bus, and it, indeed, had "Georgia Peach" painted on the side. Stone was about to get out of his car when he saw the two policemen, Rivera and Goldman, leaving the big vehicle. He waited until they had driven away before getting out of his car.

He knocked on the RV door and, a moment later, it was opened by a plump middle-aged woman wearing horn-rimmed glasses, with a pencil stuck in her hair.

"You Barrington?" she asked.

"That's me."

"I'm Sheila, come on in." She sat down at a desk behind the driver's seat and pointed at a door a few feet away. "Charlene's expecting you."

Stone rapped on the door.

"Come on in, Stone," came the voice through the door.

Stone opened the door and stepped into a surprisingly well-furnished room. It contained a sofa, coffee table and a couple of comfortable chairs, a desk, a dressing table, and a king-size bed. Charlene's voice came from what Stone presumed to be the bathroom, the door of which was ajar. "Have a seat," she called. "I'm just getting undressed."

"What?"

"Sit down. You want a drink?"

"I'm okay at the moment."

Charlene stuck her head out the door. "You don't mind if I'm naked, do you?" It was a rhetorical question. Before Stone could reply, she stepped into the room, and, unlike the last time he had seen her, she was not even wearing her bikini bottom. "I hope you're not too, too shy," she said, "but I'm shooting a nude scene this afternoon, and I can't have any marks on my body from clothes or underwear."

Stone sat down on the sofa. "I won't complain," he said, but he felt like complaining. Why were women always walking around naked in front of him just when he was trying to be good? He was struck anew at how beautiful she was—tall, slender, with breasts that were original equipment, not options, and she was a lovely, tawny color. "Did you greet the cops this way?"

"For them, I put on a robe, but it left this little mark where I tied it around the waist, see?" She pointed at a slightly red spot.

"Can't have that, can we?" Stone said, lamely.

"The director would go nuts," she said. "Once I turned up with pantie marks and he shut down production until the next day, and I got a call from Lou Regenstein about it. You sure you don't want something to drink? Some iced tea, maybe?"

"All right, that would be nice."

She went to a small fridge, opened the door, and bent over, presenting a backside for the ages.

Stone took a deep breath and let it out slowly. There was not a hint of fat or cellulite anywhere. How did Hollywood do it?

She came back with a pitcher of iced tea and two glasses, then poured them both one and sat down on the sofa.

She pulled a leg under her, and Stone could not help but notice that she had recently experienced a clever bikini wax.

"The fuzz were very nice," she said.

"I'll bet."

She giggled. "I don't think they'd ever seen a movie star up close before. I mean, not *this* close, but close. You're by way of being an old acquaintance, so I don't mind."

"Neither do I," Stone said truthfully.

"Vanessa's death really shook me up," she said, but she didn't look shaken. "People my age are not supposed to die."

"You think the ex-husband did it?"

"I can't think of anybody else with a motive," she replied, shaking her head. "Vanessa was a sweet girl. You said you were with her last night?"

"Yes, I gave her a lift home from Marc Blumberg's office, and she asked me to stay to dinner."

"Oh, speaking of food, it should be here in a minute." As if on cue, there was a rap on the door, and Charlene got up and went into the bathroom. "You let them in, Sugar; I don't want to give the waiter a coronary."

"You don't seem to mind giving me one," Stone said, walking to the door. He heard a giggle from the bathroom.

Two waiters came in and, in a flash, had arranged two lobster salads and a bottle of chardonnay on the coffee table. They were gone just as quickly, and Charlene returned, just as naked.

"I'm starved!" she said, sitting down and attacking the lobster.

Stone poured them both a glass of wine. "Charlene, who were Vanessa's best friends?"

"You met most of them at my house," Charlene replied. "The ladies who lunch? The whole group was there, except for Vanessa and Beverly."

"Beverly Walters?"

"Yep. You know her?"

"I met her briefly in a restaurant once."

"Beverly's all right, I guess, but she wouldn't be in the group, if it hadn't been for Vanessa."

"What's Beverly's story?"

Charlene shrugged. "She's a Beverly Hills housewife, I guess. She came out here to be an actress and ended up giving blow jobs for walk-ons. Her husband saved her from that; now all she does is have lunch and shop."

Stone tried the lobster; it was perfect, tender, and sweet. "Where'd the food come from?" he asked.

"From the studio commissary; have you been there, yet?"

"No."

"You'll have to come with me, sometime, Sugar; that would do wonders for your reputation around here."

"You're not exactly shy, are you, Charlene?"

"You ever noticed *anything* shy about me, Sugar?"

"No, I haven't. Tell me, was this group of ladies with you on the day Vance was shot?"

"Was it a Saturday? Yes, it was, I remember, now. Sure, they were all there that day; we have a regular Saturday thing at my house."

"How late?"

"Later than usual, as I recall. Everybody's mostly gone by five or six, but a couple of people stayed right through dinner. I think it's *cleansing* to have dinner without a man occasionally."

"What time did Vanessa leave?"

"She didn't stay for dinner. I remember, they left, because Beverly had a dinner party to go to that night, and she had to get home and change. I don't know what Vanessa was doing."

"They left together?"

"Yes, they came and left in Vanessa's car."

"That's promising," Stone said, half to himself.

"Promising? How do you mean?"

"Sorry, I was thinking aloud."

Charlene, having eaten a third of her lunch, grabbed her wine glass and half reclined on the sofa, resting her feet in Stone's lap.

The view was transfixing, Stone thought, trying to concentrate on his lobster instead. "Are you and Beverly close at all?" he asked.

"Not very. Like I said, she's not my favorite person."

"I understand that Beverly is . . . talkative."

"Well, that's an understatement! We had to listen to every detail of every affair she had."

"Did she ever sleep with Vance?"

"Sugar, if Vance had ever had a social disease, half of Beverly Hills would have come down with it."

"I mean, did she ever talk about having an affair with him?"

"She tried, but she was late to the party; the rest of us had already had Vance."

"Vanessa, too?"

"Sure, and before she was divorced. Vance didn't discriminate against married women."

"Who is Beverly married to?"

"A producer on the lot, here: Gordon Walters. That's her entree around town; if she were ever divorced, she'd never get asked to dinner. Gordy's a sweetheart, but Beverly isn't all that popular. Everybody knows you can't tell her anything. It would be like putting it on a loudspeaker at Spago."

"Charlene, I wonder if you'd do a favor for me."

"Sugar," she said, poking him in the crotch with a toe. "I've been *trying*."

"Another kind of favor."

"Sure, if I can."

"Have lunch with Beverly Walters; see if you can find out what happened after she and Vanessa left your house that Saturday."

"Why do you want to know?"

"You can't share this with the ladies," Stone said.

She made a little cross with a long fingernail on her left breast.

"Beverly is a witness against Arrington, in this shooting thing. She's testified that Arrington told her she wanted to kill Vance. Arrington was joking, of course."

"Of course," Charlene said dryly.

"It's possible that Beverly might have been at Vance's house that evening, and that she might have seen something. I can't let Arrington go into court without knowing what Beverly saw. Do you think you could worm that out of her?"

"Shoot, Stone, I could worm Beverly's genetic code out of her, if she knew it."

"Vanessa said something about this to me, and I wouldn't like for Beverly to know that. Vanessa felt she was breaking a confidence, just by mentioning the possibility."

"That sounds like Vanessa," Charlene said, looking misty for a moment. "She'd be true blue, even to Beverly."

"When do you think you could see her?"

"She'll be over at the house on Saturday, with the others, I'm sure; we'll have some commiserating to do over Vanessa."

"I'd appreciate any help you could give me."

Charlene smiled a small smile. "How *much* would you appreciate it?"

"A lot," Stone said.

"I don't believe you," Charlene replied. "It's Arrington, isn't it? She's why I can't get you in the sack."

"We're old and good friends," Stone said.

Charlene laughed. "Well, at least you didn't say you were *just* good friends. I don't blame you, Stone; she's perfectly gorgeous. I'd hop into bed with her in a minute."

Stone laughed, put down his fork, and stood up. "I'll tell her you said so, if the occasion should ever arise. I've got to get going. Thanks for the lunch, and, especially, for your help."

Charlene put down her wine glass, arose, and came toward Stone. She snaked one arm around his neck, hooked one leg around his and kissed him, long and deep.

Stone enjoyed the moment.

"Just you remember," she said, "you owe me one."

Stone released himself and made his way out of the RV. On the short drive back to the bungalow, Stone made a concerted effort to forget how Charlene Joiner had looked naked and failed.

Chapter 44

STONE SPENT THE EVENING alone in Vance's bungalow, heating a frozen dinner and watching one of Vance's movies from a selection of videotapes in the study. It turned out to be one in which Charlene Joiner had costarred, and that didn't help him think pure thoughts. Her ability as an actress actually lived up to her beauty, which surprised him, though it was not the first of her movies he had seen.

He slept fitfully, then devoted the following day to a combination of Calder Estate business and correspondence FedEx'ed by Joan from New York, which kept his mind off naked women, living and dead. The noon news said that Daniel Pike was not a suspect in his ex-wife's death, but he didn't believe it. The police had probably leaked that information to make Pike think he was safe. He'd done the same thing, himself, in his time.

Arrington called early in the afternoon. "Dino and Mary Ann are arriving at three," she said, "and Manolo is meeting them. I can't wait to see them!"

"Same here," Stone said, and he meant it. Cut off from Arrington most of the time, he craved affectionate company.

"You be here at seven," she said.

"Can I bring anything?"

"Yes, but I don't think you'll share, in your present mood."

"When this is over, I'll share until you cry for mercy."

"Promises, promises! Bye." She hung up.

Stone left the studio at six-thirty, which would make him fashionably late to Arrington's. Then, after no more than a mile, the car's steering felt funny, and he pulled over. The front rear tire was flat. He thought of changing it himself, but there was a gas station a block away, and he didn't want to get his fresh clothes dirty, so he hiked down there and brought back a mechanic to do the work. As a result, he was half an hour late to dinner.

He entered through the front gate, for a change, and noted that there were no TV vans or reporters about. Manolo let him in and escorted him into the living room where Arrington, Dino, and Mary Ann sat on sofas before the fireplace. Another woman was there, too, but her back was to him.

He hugged Dino and Mary Ann, but when he made to embrace Arrington, she kept an elbow between them. "And look who else is here!" she cried, waving a hand toward the sofa. The other woman turned around.

"Dolce," Stone said weakly. "I've been trying to reach you."

"Well, you can reach me now," Dolce replied, patting the sofa next to her.

Stone started to take another seat, but Arrington took his arm tightly and guided him next to Dolce. "Dolce has told me your wonderful news!" Arrington said brightly, showing lots of teeth. "Let me congratulate you!"

Stone looked at Dino and Mary Ann, both of whom looked extremely uncomfortable. He sat down next to Dolce and submitted to a kiss on the cheek.

"My darling," she said, "how handsome you look tonight."

"I'm sorry I'm late," Stone said to Arrington, ignoring Dolce. "I had a flat tire on the way."

"Of course you did, Stone," she replied, as if he were lying.

Manolo brought him a Wild Turkey on the rocks, and Stone sipped it. This whole thing was insane; what was Dolce doing here? He discovered that he was sweating. "How was your flight?" he asked Dino and Mary Ann.

"Pretty much the same as being moved around the Chicago Stockyards with an electric cattle prod," Dino replied gamely, trying to hold up his end.

"Heh, heh," Stone said, taking a big swig of the bourbon. He stole a glance at Dolce, who was smiling broadly. He hoped she wasn't armed.

Across the coffee table, on the sofa opposite, Arrington was smiling just as broadly. She emptied a martini glass and motioned to Manolo for another. "Well, isn't this fun!" she said. "Old friends together again. How long has it been?"

"A long time," Mary Ann replied, as if it had not been long enough.

"Oh, Stone," Dino said, standing up. "I brought you something; come out to the guest house for a minute."

"Excuse me," Stone said to Arrington.

"Hurry back, now!" she replied.

Stone followed Dino out the back door and toward the guest house. "What the fuck is going on?" he demanded.

"How should I know?" Dino replied. "I didn't know Dolce was coming until she got here, ten minutes before you did. Mary Ann must have invited her, but she didn't say a goddamned thing to me about it." He opened the door to the guest house and led the way in.

"And she told Arrington we were married in Venice?"

"You bet she did, pal, and she laid it on thick. Arrington was smiling a lot, but she would have killed her, if there had been anything sharp lying around." Dino went to his suitcase and handed Stone his little Walther automatic, in its chamois shoulder holster.

"What am I going to do with this now?" Stone asked.

"I'd wear it if I were you," Dino replied. "You might need it before the evening is over."

Stone shucked off his jacket and slipped into the shoulder holster.

"My thirty-two automatic wasn't on your bedside table, where you said it would be, and it wasn't in your safe, either."

"That's weird," Stone said. "Helene wouldn't have touched it when she was cleaning; she hates guns, and Joan wouldn't have had any reason to be upstairs."

"I asked Joan about it, and she said she hadn't seen it."

Stone checked the Walther; it was loaded. He put the safety on and returned it to the holster.

"You're going to need a local permit for that, aren't you?" Dino asked.

"Rick Grant got me one last year when I was out here; it's in my pocket. Can you think of some way to get Dolce out of here? I've got to explain to Arrington what's going on."

"I should have thought you would have explained it to her a long time ago," Dino said. "That girl is *really* pissed off."

"I realize I should have," Stone said, "but I just didn't want to bring up Dolce while Arrington is in all this trouble."

"Well, *you're* the one who's in trouble, now, and we'd better get back in there, so you can face the music."

They went back into the house, and found Mary Ann struggling to keep some sort of conversation going.

Manolo came into the room. "Dinner is served, Mrs. Calder," he said.

Everyone rose and marched into the dining room.

"Now let's see," Arrington said, surveying the beautifully laid table. "We'll have Mr. and Mrs. Bacchetti to my left, and Mr. and Mrs. Barrington, here, to my right."

Stone winced as if lashed. Everybody sat down, and a cold soup was served.

"This is a beautiful house," Dino said.

"Thank you, Dino; Vance let me redo the place after we were married, so I can take full credit. Stone, where are you and Dolce going to make your home?"

Stone dropped his spoon into his soup bowl, splashing gazpacho over his jacket.

Dolce took up the slack. "Papa offered to give us his Manhattan place, but Stone has insisted that we live in his house," she said. "I'm *so* looking forward to redecorating the place. It's a little . . . *seedy* right now."

Stone could not suppress a groan. Dolce knew that Arrington had had a big hand in decorating his house. The soup was taken away, before Arrington could throw it at Dolce.

"And how is your father?" Arrington asked solicitously. "And all those *business* associates of his? The ones with the broken noses?"

Stone stood up. "Excuse me." He left the table.

Arrington caught up with him at the front door. "Running away, are you? You complete shit! You *married* that bitch?"

"I have a lot to explain to you," Stone said. "Can we have lunch tomorrow?"

"Lunch? I don't ever want to see you again! Not as long as I live!"

"Arrington, you're going to have to listen to me about this."

"The hell I do!" she hissed, then pushed him out the front door and slammed it behind him.

Stone was already in his car when he saw Dolce in his rearview mirror, coming out of the house. The gates opened for him, and he floored the accelerator.

He made a couple of quick turns, headed nowhere, just trying to be sure that Dolce wasn't following him. He made the freeway, then got off at Santa Monica Boulevard, so he could keep an eye on several blocks behind him. Sweat was pouring off him, and he was breathing rapidly. When he had to stop for a traffic light he took the opportunity to put the car's top down, and the breeze began to cool him. His breathing slowed, and he began to feel nearly normal, except that he was numb between the ears. He did his best to drive both Dolce and Arrington out of his head, tried to think of nothing. For a while he was in a nearly semiconscious state, driving by instinct, uncaring of his direction.

When his head cleared he found himself at a traffic light in

Malibu. He dug his notebook out of his pocket, looked up the number and dialed the hands-free phone.

"Hello?" she said, her voice low and inviting.

"It's Stone; I'm in Malibu. Are you alone?"

"I sure am," she replied.

"Not for long." He headed for the Colony.

Chapter 45

CHARLENE MET HIM AT THE DOOR, wearing nothing but a short silk robe. Neither of them said a word. He kissed her, then, without stopping, lifted her off her feet.

She climbed him like a tree and locked her legs around him. "Straight ahead," she said, removing her lips from his just long enough to speak. "Hang a right at the end of the hall."

He followed her directions and came into a large bedroom only steps from the sand. The sliding doors to the beach were open, and a breeze billowed the sheer curtains. She unlocked her legs and dropped to the floor, tearing at his clothes. Together they got him undressed and her robe disappeared. They dived at the bed.

Stone had been erect since she'd answered the phone, and Charlene wasn't interested in foreplay. He was inside her before they were fully on the bed, and she was already wet. They made love hungrily, rolling about on the king-size bed, he on top, then she. There were no words, only sounds—yells, bleats, cries, moans. The breeze from the Pacific blew over their bodies, drying their sweat, keeping them going. She came slowly to a climax, and Stone followed her more swiftly, penetrating her fully. More sounds, followed by gasps for breath, then they were both lying on their backs, sucking in wind.

"Good God!" she managed to say finally. "I've done a lot of fucking in my time, but I don't think I ever had a running start before."

"I was in a hurry," he panted.

"Oh, I'm not complaining, Sugar."

He turned and reached for her. "Again," he said.

She pushed him onto his back. "Now you take it easy," she said. "My call for tomorrow isn't until eleven, and you've got to last until then. I don't want you to leave in an ambulance."

Stone burst out laughing. "Oh, I feel wonderful," he laughed. "First time in days; I don't know how long."

"You've been wound a little tight, haven't you?"

"You wouldn't believe how tight."

"Well, I think I've just had a demonstration, and if it took you that long to start unwinding . . ."

"I think I may live now, if Dolce doesn't shoot me."

"Dolce? Is there somebody I don't know about?"

"My *wife*, God help me."

"Sugar, I believe we've skipped a part of your bio," she said, rising onto one elbow and tossing her hair over her shoulder.

"Paper marriage," he said. "Piece of paper, nothing more. Trouble is, it's an *Italian* piece of paper."

"Baby, you're not making any sense. Did you get drunk in Vegas, or something?"

"Happened in Venice," he panted. "The real one, not the Vegas one. Glorious place to get married."

"Did she Shanghai you?"

"I went voluntarily, I'm afraid. I don't know *what* I was thinking."

"So, what's the next level of that relationship?"

"The next level is divorce, and I have a feeling it's not going to be easy, since it has to happen in Italy."

"I don't understand how . . . wait a minute; you came out here just to help Arrington, didn't you?"

"Yes."

"Were you in Venice when you heard about Vance?"

"Yes. We'd had the civil ceremony; we were due for the big one, in

St. Mark's, the next day. When I heard about Vance, I dropped every-thing."

"Including Dolce?"

"Turned out that way."

"How did she take it?"

"Badly."

"And now you think she wants to shoot you?"

"Oh, no; she'd rather have me drawn and quartered and the pieces barbecued."

"What does she *want*?"

"Me, dead or alive."

"You mean she still wants to be married to you?"

"Apparently so. She's been introducing herself to the world as Mrs. Stone Barrington."

"Oops."

"Yeah, oops."

"Who is this girl?"

"Her last name is Bianchi."

"Wait a minute: at Vance's funeral I saw you talking to . . ."

"Her father."

"I've heard a little about him," she said. "Sounds like this could be tricky."

"Well put. Tricky."

She pushed his hair off his forehead with her fingers and kissed him. "I could hide you here for a few months," she said.

"I don't think I could survive that."

She giggled. "Probably not, but you'd last a while. What made you show up here tonight? Where were you earlier this evening?"

"I went to Arrington's house for dinner. Dolce was there."

"Well, that must have been a teensy bit awkward."

"You could say that. You could say I'm lucky I got out of there before the two of them tore me to pieces."

"And how did this little soiree come about?"

"I don't have the faintest idea. I arrived, and they were both there. I don't think I've ever been at such a complete loss."

"Poor baby," she said. "I suppose you need consoling."

"Oh, yes. Console me."

She swapped ends and began kissing him lightly, getting an instantaneous response.

He placed a hand on her buttocks and pulled her to his face, searching with his tongue.

She took him into her mouth.

He found her.

They remained in that position for a long time.

Chapter 46

STONE STOOD, his hands against the tile wall of the shower, his head under the heavy stream of water. His knees were trembling. He had no idea what time it was, except that the sun was up.

The bronzed glass door opened, and Charlene stepped in. She grabbed a bottle of something, sprayed it on his back, and began soaping his body. "How you doing, Sugar?"

"I'm shattered," he said. "I can hardly stand up."

"I can't imagine how that happened," she giggled. "All we did was make love."

"How many times?"

"Several," she replied. "Who's counting?"

He leaned back against the tile and let her soap him. "I have the strange but almost certain feeling that sometime early this morning I passed some sort of physical peak in my life, and that everything from here on is downhill."

"Sugar," she said, "that's the sort of peak that most men hit at eighteen. You should be pleased with yourself."

"I'm never going to be the same again; I can hardly stand up. You may have to carry me out of here."

She pulled him back under the shower and rinsed him, then turned off the shower. "Maybe if you hold my hand you can make it."

She led him out of the stall, dried him and herself with fat towels, and found robes for them both. "Come on, Hon; breakfast is on the table.

He followed her through the sliding doors and onto a terrace over-looking the beach. When they sat down a low wall cleverly blocked the view from the sand, but still allowed them a panorama of the sea. It was nicely private.

She removed the covers from two plates. His was eggs, home fries, sausages, and muffins; hers was a slice of melon.

"Why do I have so much and you so little?" he asked, digging in.

"Because you need your strength, and I need to keep my ass look-ing the way it does without surgery."

"It looks wonderful, especially up close."

"You should know; you were in and out of there a few times."

Stone sneezed.

"God bless you."

"I hope I'm not getting a cold."

"I don't think you can get a cold from anal sex."

"Good point; maybe I'm just allergic to something."

"For a while there, I thought you might be allergic to me."

Stone shook his head. "Not in the least."

"Then what took you so long to knock on my door?"

"Call it misplaced loyalties."

"That's it," she agreed. "Neither one of them deserves you." She smiled. "Only me. Tell me, do you always wear a gun to assignations?"

"What?"

"I seem to recall removing a shoulder holster from your body, along with everything else. Did you feel you needed a lot of protection from me?"

"A friend brought it out from New York for me. No offense."

"None taken."

Stone finished his eggs and poured them some coffee. "When are you going to see Beverly Walters?"

"Yesterday."

"You've already talked to her?"

"Well, you didn't give me a chance to tell you last night."

"What did she say?"

"She was coy, which is unlike Beverly. Normally, she spills every-thing, usually without being asked."

"But not yesterday?"

Charlene shook her head. "She had a secret, and she wasn't going to tell me. I couldn't worm it out of her."

"She was there, I think. She must have seen what happened."

"If I were you, I'd be worried."

"I am."

"What's your next move?"

"I don't know. We could depose her, get her under oath."

"Why?"

"The idea is to find out what the prosecution witness knows."

Charlene sighed. "The problem with that, Stone, is you don't *want* to know."

She had a point, he thought.

Stone got back to the studio bungalow a little before eleven. Louise Bremen, from the studio secretarial pool, was at Betty's desk. "Good morning," she said, handing him a phone message. It was from Dino, and the return number was at the Calder guest house.

"Good morning," he replied, pocketing the message.

"Oh, you've spilled something on your jacket," Louise said.

Stone had forgotten about the gazpacho from the night before.

"Take it off, and I'll send it over to wardrobe for you; they'll get the stain out."

"Thanks," Stone said. He went into the bedroom, took off the jacket, and put the Walther and its holster into a drawer, then he took the jacket back to Louise. "Have we heard anything from Dolce Bianchi?"

"Not a peep," she replied.

"Good." He went into the study and called Dino.

"Hello."

"Hi."

Dino spoke softly, as if he didn't want to be overheard. "Let's meet for lunch," he whispered.

"Okay, come over here, and we'll go to the studio commissary. Borrow a car from Manolo; he'll give you directions."

"In an hour?"

"Good." They both hung up. Stone buzzed Louise and asked her to arrange a studio pass for Dino.

Dino was introduced to Louise, then Stone showed him around the bungalow.

"These movie stars live pretty well, don't they?" he said.

"Better than cops and lawyers."

"Better than anybody. That guest house we're staying in is nicer than any home I've ever had."

"The pleasures of money."

"I'm hungry; let's eat. We can talk over lunch."

Stone drove him slowly through the studio streets, pointing out the exterior street set and the sound stages.

"It's like a city, isn't it?" Dino said.

"It has just about everything a city has, except crime."

"Yeah, that happens in Bel-Air and Beverly Hills."

Stone parked outside the commissary, which was a brick building with a walled garden. Stone showed the hostess his VIP studio pass, and they were given a table outside, surrounded by recognizable faces.

Dino took it all in, pointing out a movie star or two, then they ordered lunch.

"All right, what happened after I left last night?" Stone asked.

"Not much. What could compare to the scene just before you left?"

"What was Dolce doing there?"

"Mary Ann invited her, with Arrington's permission. It was an innocent thing on both their parts, I guess."

"How innocent could it be? Mary Ann was in Venice; she knew everything."

"She thought Arrington knew everything, too. You didn't tell her?"

"I hadn't found the right moment," Stone said.

"She was pretty upset after you left, even though she tried not to show it. I tried to smooth things over, but she wouldn't talk about you."

"I've never been double-teamed like that," Stone said.

"I felt sorry for you, but there was nothing I could do. You're going to have to find some way to square things with Arrington."

"As far as I'm concerned, the ball's in her court. I was ambushed, and I didn't like it."

"That wasn't her intention, Stone."

"Maybe not, but the result was the same."

"Fortunately, Dolce left when you did. Did you go together?"

"No, I outran her."

"You can't run forever."

"What else can I do? You can't talk to her like a normal human being. I've got Marc Blumberg working on an Italian divorce."

"I have a feeling this is not going to be as easy as divorce."

"Funny, I have the same feeling," Stone replied.

When they got back to the bungalow, Louise came into the study. "Lou Regenstein's secretary called. Lou would like you to come to an impromptu dinner party he's giving for some friends at his house tonight. He says to bring somebody, if you'd like. It's at seven-thirty." She laid the address on his desk.

"Let me make a call," Stone said. He found the number for Charlene's RV and dialed it.

"Hey, Sugar," she said. "How you feeling?"

"I think I've recovered my health. Would you like to go to a dinner party tonight?"

"Sure, but I won't be done here until six-thirty or seven."

"Have you got something that you could wear? We could leave from here."

"I've got just the thing," she said. "I wore it in a scene this morning."

"Pick you up at the RV about seven-fifteen?"

"Seven-fifteenish."

"See you then." He hung up. "Call Lou's secretary and tell her I'd love to come, and I'm bringing a date."

Louise went back to her desk to make the call.

"Who's the date?" Dino asked.

"Charlene Joiner."

Dino's eyebrows went up. "You kidding me?"

"Nope," Stone replied smugly. "She's a new friend."

"One of these days, you're going to screw yourself right into the ground," Dino said.

Chapter 47

CHARLENE KEPT STONE waiting for only fifteen minutes. When she emerged from her dressing room she was wearing flowing cream-colored silk pants and a filmy patterned blouse. Stone noticed in a nanosecond that the blouse was so sheer that nipples were readily in view.

"So *that's* what L.A. women wear to dinner parties." He laughed, kissing her.

"They do if they have the right equipment," Charlene replied, wrapping a light cashmere stole around her shoulders.

"You're going to be very popular tonight," Stone said.

"With the men, anyway. Whose house are we going to?"

"It's a surprise."

"I love a surprise," she said, settling into the car. "This is Vance's car, isn't it?"

"It is. I borrowed it."

"Such an incestuous town," she said.

With Charlene's help he found the house, or rather, estate, in Holmby Hills. Stone was beginning to believe that everybody in L.A.

lived on four or five acres. He stopped in the circular driveway, and a valet took the car. As they approached the house, the front door was opened by a butler, and they stepped into a large foyer. From across the living room beyond, Lou Regenstein headed toward them.

"Oh, my God," Charlene said under her breath.

"What's wrong?"

"I'll tell you later," she whispered.

"Stone!" Lou cried, his hand out. "And Charlene!" He looked a little panicky. "What a surprise!"

"For me too, Lou," she replied, accepting a peck on the cheek. She whipped off the stole, handed it to the butler, and swept into the room at Stone's side, her back arched, breasts held high.

Lou led them toward a tall, handsome woman of about fifty, who was talking to another couple. "Livia," he said. "You haven't met Stone."

"How do you do?" the woman said, taking Stone's hand. Then she turned toward Charlene, and her eyes narrowed.

"And of course, you know Charlene Joiner," Lou said.

"Of course," she replied icily, then turned and walked away.

There was something going on here, Stone thought, and he wasn't sure he wanted to know what it was.

Lou quickly turned to the couple Livia had been talking to. "And this is Lansing Drake and his wife, Christina."

Stone took the man's hand. "It's Dr. Drake, isn't it?"

"Yes, and your name?"

"I'm sorry," Lou said, "this is Stone Barrington, a friend of Vance's and Arrington's."

For a split second, the doctor looked as though he had been struck across the face, then he recovered. "Nice to meet you," he mumbled, then turned to Charlene. "And of course, I know you," he said, chuckling, his eyes pointing below her shoulders.

"Of course you do," Charlene said.

Lou's attention was drawn to the front door, where other guests were arriving. "The bar is over there," he said to Stone, pointing across the room. "Please excuse me."

Dr. Drake and his wife had suddenly engaged someone else in conversation, so Stone lead Charlene toward the bar.

"Pill pusher to the stars," Charlene said.

"Yes, I've heard of him; he's Arrington's doctor. What were you talking about at the front door?"

"If you hadn't been surprising me, I'd have warned you," she said.

"Warned me about what?"

"Livia; she hates me with a vengeance. Poor Lou is going to get it between the shoulder blades tonight."

"Who is she?"

"Lou's wife."

"I didn't know he even *had* a wife. Nobody's ever mentioned her to me."

"Nobody ever does, least of all Lou. They've had an arm's-length marriage for twenty years. Word has it they occupy different wings of this house. They're only seen together when he entertains here, or at industry events, like the Oscars."

"And why does she hate you?"

"You don't want to know."

"You're probably right." They reached the bar; Charlene had a San Pellegrino, and Stone had his usual bourbon.

"Did you see the look on the doctor's face when he met you?" Charlene asked.

"Yes; I thought he was going to break and run for a minute."

"This is going to be a very weird evening," Charlene said.

Stone looked toward the front door and nearly choked on his drink. "You don't know how weird," he said.

Charlene followed his gaze. "That, I suppose, is the fabled Dolce."

"It is," Stone replied, "and the man with her is her father, Eduardo."

Charlene linked her arm in Stone's. "Well, come on, then," she said. "I want to be introduced."

There was nothing else for it, Stone thought; may as well brazen it out. He walked toward the two, wishing to God he were on another continent. "Good evening, Eduardo," he said. "Hello, Dolce."

Eduardo took his hand, but not before a shocked glance at Charlene's highly visible breasts. "Stone," he managed to say.

Dolce said nothing, but shot a look at Charlene that would have set a lesser woman on fire.

"Eduardo, this is Charlene Joiner. Charlene, this is Eduardo Bianchi and his daughter, Dolce."

"I'm so pleased to meet you both," Charlene said, offering them a broad smile, in addition to everything else.

"Enchanted," Eduardo said stiffly.

"Oh, yes," Dolce said dryly, looking Charlene up and down. "Enchanted."

"Charlene is one of Lou's biggest stars," Stone said, because he could not think of anything else to say.

"I never go to the pictures," Eduardo said, "but I can certainly believe you are a star."

"Oh, Eduardo, you're sweet," Charlene giggled. She turned and snaked an arm through his. "Come on, and I'll get you a drink." She led him away, leaving Stone suddenly with Dolce, the very last place he wanted to be.

"Alone at last," Dolce said archly.

"Dolce, I . . ."

"Are you fucking her?"

"Now, listen. I . . ."

"Of course you are. That's what you do best, isn't it?"

"Will you listen . . ."

"I'm sure she's *very* good in the rack."

"Dolce . . ."

"Is she, Stone? Does she give good head?"

"For Christ's sake, keep your voice . . ."

"I'll bet she's spent more time on her knees than Esther Williams spent in the pool."

"Dolce, if you don't . . ."

"Oh, good, a martini," Dolce said, as a waiter approached with a tray. She took one, tossed it into Stone's face, returned the glass to the tray, and walked away.

The room was suddenly silent. Then Charlene's laugh cut through the quiet. "I don't *believe* you," she was saying to Eduardo, who, uncharacteristically, seemed to be laughing, too.

"Dinner is served!" the butler called out, and the guests began filtering toward the dining room.

Charlene came, took Stone by the arm, and turned him toward dinner.

"Let's get out of here," Stone said, dabbing at his face with a handkerchief.

"Are you kidding?" Charlene laughed, dragging him toward the dining room. "I wouldn't miss this dinner for anything!"

Chapter 48

THERE WERE SIXTEEN AT DINNER. Stone found himself near the center of the long, narrow table, on his hostess's left. Directly across from him was Dr. Lansing Drake, who had landed with Dolce on his right and Charlene on his left. Most men, Stone reflected, would have been delighted to find themselves bracketed by two such beautiful women, but Dr. Drake looked decidedly uncomfortable, and when Stone nodded to him, he looked at his plate, then up and down the table, as if seeking an escape route.

The woman to Stone's left seemed to be in her eighties and deaf, while the handsome and chilly Livia, to Stone's right, seemed disinclined to acknowledge his presence. Dolce, across the table, shot him long, hostile looks whenever his eyes wandered her way. Only Charlene seemed happy. She had drawn Eduardo, to her left, and between her large eyes and her beautiful breasts, she seemed to have him mesmerized.

"How long have you known that woman?" a deep, whiskey-scarred voice asked.

Stone jerked to attention. Livia had spoken to him. "Oh, we met only recently. This is the first time we've been out." That was, strictly speaking, the truth. They had done all sorts of things at home, but they had not been out.

"I would be careful, if I were you," Livia said. "She probably has a social disease."

"I beg your pardon?" Stone said, astonished that a hostess would say such a thing to her guest about his companion.

"More than likely, a *fatal* social disease," Livia said, ignoring his reaction.

"Mrs. Regenstein . . ."

"I detest that name; call me Livia."

"You detest your husband's name?"

"And my husband, as well."

"Then why are you married to him?"

"I find it convenient; I have for more than twenty years. But enough about me; let's talk about you. What did you do to little Miss Bianchi that would invite a drink in the face?"

"My private life," Stone said, "unlike yours, is private."

"You're going to be a bore, aren't you?" she asked.

"You will probably think so."

"Who are you, anyway?"

"My name is Stone Barrington."

"Ah, yes, Louis has mentioned you. You're that disreputable lawyer from New York who was screwing Arrington Calder just before she married Vance, aren't you?"

Stone looked across the table, caught Charlene's eye and jerked his head toward the door. Then he turned to Livia Regenstein. "Goodbye, you miserable bitch," he said quietly, then he got up and walked out of the dining room. He waited a moment for Charlene to catch up, then led her toward the front door.

While Charlene was waiting for her wrap, and the valet was bringing Stone's car, Lou Regenstein caught up with them. "What's wrong, Stone? Why are you leaving?"

"Lou, I must apologize; I'm afraid I don't have a scorecard for the games that are played in this town. I'm sorry if I made your wife and your guests uncomfortable."

"It's I who should apologize," Lou said. "Livia can be hard to take."

"I'll see you soon," Stone said. They shook hands, and he and Charlene left the house.

Stone put the top down. "I need some air," he said, turning down the street. "I hope it won't disturb your hair."

"Don't worry about it," Charlene replied. "Well, that was quite an evening. What were you and Livia talking about, dare I ask?"

"You, mostly," Stone said.

"Oh. I may as well tell you. For a short time Livia and I shared a lover."

"Not Lou, I hope."

"No, someone much younger. Shortly after I came into the picture, the man stopped seeing Livia. Livia has been livid ever since."

"This is my fault; I should have told you where we were having dinner."

"Listen, Sugar, don't worry about it; I didn't have half as bad a time as you."

"What were you and Eduardo talking about?"

"The movie business, mostly."

"He seemed fascinated."

"I'm sure he was. He spoke well of you, too."

"Did he?"

"He said you were a gentleman."

"And that was just before I caused a scene by walking out of an elegant dinner party."

"I'm sure his opinion of you hasn't changed."

"You know, until this week, I had never in my life walked out of any dinner party, and now, in the space of three days, I've walked out of two."

"Are you upset?"

"Not really; I must be getting used to it."

"I guess folks out here aren't working with quite the same social graces as their counterparts in New York."

Stone reached Sunset and turned toward the studio. "How'd you happen to come out here?"

"You want the fan magazine version, or the truth?"

"The truth will do nicely."

"Hang a left here," she said. "There's a nice little restaurant down the street, and we haven't had dinner."

Stone followed directions. "No, we haven't."

The restaurant was not all that small, but it was very elegant, and the headwaiter, spotting Charlene, had them at a special table in seconds. They ordered drinks and dinner.

"Okay, now tell me your story," he said.

"It's a strange one," she said. "I'm from Meriwether County, Georgia, near a little town called Delano."

"That's where Betty Southard, Vance's secretary, is from."

"True, but she was older than I, so we didn't really know each other. Anyway, I was pretty much a country girl, and I had this boyfriend who murdered a girl, in Greenville, the county seat. The court appointed a lawyer named Will Lee to defend my boyfriend."

"Wait a minute, is this the Senator from Georgia? The presidential candidate?"

"Yes, but not at that time. Old Senator Carr, who Will worked for, had a stroke, and Will ran for his seat, but the judge wouldn't let him out of defending Larry, my boyfriend, even though it was during the campaign. As you might imagine, the trial attracted a lot of press coverage."

"I think I remember this vaguely," Stone said, "but not the outcome."

"Larry was convicted and sentenced to death. A tabloid paid me for my story, and all of a sudden, Hollywood was sniffing around. Next thing I knew I was out here, with a part in a movie. Then there was another part and another, and the rest is pulp fiction."

"Amazing. Was the boyfriend executed?"

She shook her head. "I went to see the governor of Georgia and personally, ah, interceded on his behalf. His sentence was commuted to life without parole. We still correspond."

"Was he guilty?"

"Oh, yes."

"That's the damndest story I ever heard."

"There's more."

"Tell me."

"Will Lee and I had a little one-time encounter that became a side issue in the presidential race."

"That was you?"

"I'm afraid so. When I'm old and washed up, somebody's going to make a really bad TV movie about all this, and then I'm going to write my memoirs."

"I'm sure it will be a hot seller."

"You better believe it, Sugar."

After dinner, he drove her back to her car at Centurion, and they said good night.

"One thing," he said to her.

"What's that, Baby?" she asked, putting her arms around his neck.

"Dolce has taken this whole business hard. After tonight's events, I think you should be careful."

"You mean, watch my back?"

"Yes, that's what I mean."

She kissed him. "Sugar," she said, "Dolce doesn't want to mess with me."

"I hope you're right."

She kissed him again. "Should I go armed?"

"Do you own a gun?"

She nodded. "All legal-like, too."

"Try not to shoot at anybody; you might hit me."

"I shoot what I aim at, Sugar." She kissed him again, then got into her car. "By the way," she said, as she put the top down. "There's going to be a kind of memorial for Vanessa tomorrow at my house. Will you come?"

Stone nodded. "Sure."

"Just a few people. Six o'clock."

"I'll be there."

She gave a little wave and drove away.

Chapter 49

THE MEMORIAL for Vanessa Pike at Charlene's house seemed more of a memorial cocktail party, Stone reflected as he walked into the well-populated living room. Everyone had a drink, even if, in the California style, it was designer fizzy water, and there was a buffet at one end of the room laden with raw vegetables, melon, and other low-fat delicacies.

Charlene came and gave him a virtuous peck on the cheek. "I think you'll know a few people," she said. "Mingle while I greet."

Stone nodded, went to the bar, and waited while the barman ransacked the house for a bottle of bourbon. He would not bear his grief in sobriety, no matter what the West Coast convention. While he waited, he surveyed the room, picking out most of the women he had met on his first visit to the house, along with Dr. Lansing Drake and his wife and, somewhat to his relief, Marc Blumberg. At least, he'd have somebody to talk to. He collected his drink and joined Marc.

"What've you been up to?" Marc asked.

"Not much," Stone said.

"I think it's about time to go for a motion to dismiss," Marc said.

"I'm not so sure about that," Stone replied.

"Why not?"

"Because I think it's quite possible that Beverly Walters was there when Vance was shot, and she's the prosecution's prime witness."

"Are you sure she was there?"

"As sure as I can be without putting her under oath and asking her."

Marc mulled that over for a moment. "I wonder if she hates Arrington that much, that she'd testify?"

"She hates her enough to testify to a conversation in which Arrington, apparently in jest, says she'd kill Vance if she caught him with another woman."

"You have a point," Marc admitted.

"Have you heard anything new from the investigation into Vanessa's death?" Stone asked.

"They've cleared the husband," Marc replied, nodding toward two men across the room.

Stone followed his gaze and found the two cops he'd met after the fire at Vanessa's. "What are they doing here?"

"They must think the murderer is present," Marc said. "Such a person might call attention to himself by his absence."

"Have you caught them staring at anybody?" Stone asked, glancing out the big windows toward the beach.

"They're staring at you right now," Marc said.

Stone looked back toward the two detectives and found that Marc was not lying. Both men gazed gravely back at him. Stone raised his glass a little and nodded; both men nodded back. "You think I'm all they've got?"

"I guess so."

"What do you suppose they suppose my motive is?"

"Who knows?"

"I mean, I met her only twice, both times in your company. Did you notice any murderous intentions on my part?"

Marc shrugged. "Nothing obvious."

"I suppose they've questioned you about those meetings."

"In some depth."

"Do I need a lawyer?"

"*Everybody* needs a lawyer."

Stone laughed.

"But probably not you, not yet."

"That's a relief; I'm not sure I could afford you."

"Probably not."

"Excuse me; I need the powder room." Stone set down his glass. He left the lawyer and walked down a hallway to the first-floor half-bath. The door was ajar and he stepped inside and switched on the light. He reached behind him to close the door, but felt a pressure on it. Then he was pushed forward into the little room and someone stepped in behind him and closed the door. Stone turned to find Beverly Walters sharing the john with him.

"What the hell are you doing here?" he demanded.

She reached behind her and turned the lock. "Same as you; grieving for Vanessa."

"I mean in this toilet."

"I wanted to talk to you."

"We can't talk; you're a witness against my client. Surely you must understand that."

"Of course; that's why we're talking in here."

"We're not talking at all," Stone said. "There are two police officers here, and they work for the same department that's investigating Vance's murder. They would certainly report it if they saw us talking." He started around her, but she took hold of his lapels and stopped him.

"Listen to me," she said.

"I *can't* listen to you," he replied, trying to free himself.

She clung to him. "I'm going to testify against Arrington," she said.

"I believe I'm aware of that," Stone replied, taking hold of her wrists and trying to disengage.

"But you don't know what I'm going to say."

"I've already heard you testify once."

"But you didn't hear everything. I saw Vance murdered."

"Ms. Walters, please let me out of here."

"I can put Arrington in prison, don't you understand?"

"You can try," Stone said, "but I expect to have something to say about that, and so does Marc Blumberg. You're not going to get a free ride on the stand."

"I want you to tell Arrington that I'm sorry. That I'm fond of her. That I don't want to do it."

"Don't want to do it?" Stone asked, growing angry. "Then why did you talk to the police?"

"I felt I had to."

"We'll, you're an admirable citizen, Ms. Walters, but now I want you to get out of my way."

"Never mind," she said. "I'll leave." She turned, unlocked the door, opened it, and closed it behind her.

Stone locked the door. What the hell was wrong with the woman? He used the john, taking his time, then washed his hands and opened the door slowly. He peeked down the hall, saw no one, then left and went back to where Marc Blumberg was still standing.

"That took a long time," Marc said. "You all right?"

"I'm extremely pissed off," Stone said. He told Marc what had happened.

"Maybe she's crazy," Marc said. "Maybe that's our approach to questioning her. I'll put somebody on her and see if we can come up with some other erratic behavior."

"She said she saw Vance murdered, and she's going to testify to that."

"Well, at least we know what she's going to say on the stand."

There was a clinking of a knife on glass, and they turned toward the sound. Charlene was standing on the steps to the foyer; they made a little stage. She asked for everyone's attention, then a series of people came up and said a few words about Vanessa. They kept it light, but the crowd looked somber.

Finally, Charlene looked at Beverly Walters. "Beverly, I'm sure you'd like to say something; you and Vanessa were so close."

Walters looked down and shook her head, dabbing at her eyes with a tissue.

"Of course," Charlene said. "We all know how you feel. Everybody, please stay as long as you like. There'll be a light supper in a few minutes." She stepped down and made her way across the room toward Stone and Marc Blumberg.

"You handled that gracefully," Stone said.

"It's about all I can do for Vanessa," Charlene replied.

Marc spoke up. "Is Beverly Walters usually so reticent?"

Charlene snorted. "Beverly would normally not miss a chance to be the center of attention."

Marc nodded at the two police officers across the room. "I think she's getting quite a lot of attention," he said.

Stone looked at the two men, who had eyes for no one except Beverly Walters.

STONE AND CHARLENE sat on the patio overlooking the sea. The guests had all gone, and they were having a cold supper.

"Tell me everything you know about Beverly Walters," he said.

"Haven't I already?"

"I've heard bits and pieces, but I'd like to hear what you know about her."

Charlene took a deep breath, swelling her lovely breasts. "Well, she came out here as an actress. She'd had a nice part on Broadway, and somebody at Centurion saw her and brought her out to test her. She had a few small parts, but she didn't seem to be going anywhere, then she met Gordon, her husband, on a picture, and pretty soon they were married."

"Did she screw around after she was married?"

"Sugar, you have to remember where you are. It would have been a lot more noteworthy if she *hadn't* screwed around, and nobody took note of that."

"Did she ever sleep with Vance?"

"If she did she never talked about it, but I wouldn't be surprised. Quite apart from Vance's talents as a lover, lots of women would have slept with him just to be able to say they did. Beverly would have been one of those."

"But she never said she did?"

"Not to me, and I suppose, not to any woman I know, because I would have heard about it within minutes."

"Lots of people knew Vance slept around?"

"They did before he got married, but after that, he became a lot more discreet."

"He didn't stop sleeping around, he just became more discreet about it?"

"That's about right. As part of being more discreet, he might have slept with fewer women. I never discussed it with him."

"I don't mean to pry, but when you and Vance were sleeping together, it was after he was married?"

"Sure, you mean to pry, but I don't mind. Yes, it was afterward."

"Where did you meet?"

"My RV or his."

"Ever at his bungalow?"

"Once or twice, late, after Betty had gone for the day."

"He wouldn't have wanted Betty to know?"

"I guess not. Word was, they once had a thing going. Maybe he thought she might be jealous."

Stone picked at his salmon and sipped his wine.

"What are you thinking, Stone?"

"Sorry, I was just letting my mind wander. Sometimes that helps me sort things out."

"Have you sorted something out?"

"No."

Charlene laughed.

"Beverly did something strange tonight."

"What did she do?"

Stone told her about the incident in the powder room.

"She was probably hoping you'd ravish her on the spot."

"No, it wasn't like that."

Charlene shrugged. "Did you talk to Dr. Lansing Drake at all?"

"No," Stone replied.

"He seemed to get a little skittish when I mentioned you."

"He behaved oddly at dinner last night, too. Why might he feel uncomfortable around me?"

"Damned if I know."

"Tell me about Dr. Drake."

"He's the doctor of choice in Beverly Hills and Bel-Air," Charlene said.

"Why?"

"He's pretty easygoing; if somebody wants a Valium prescription, he's not going to give them a hard time about it. He knows how to keep his mouth shut, too. I'll bet he's cured more cases of the clap and gotten more people secretly into rehab than any doctor in town."

"Is he a decent doctor?"

"There are jokes about that, but I've never heard anybody say he really screwed up on something. I mean, he hasn't killed anybody that I know of. I think his principal talent is that he knows when to refer somebody to a specialist. That's his motto: When in doubt, refer. He can't get into too much trouble that way."

"I gather he's pretty social."

"Oh, he doesn't miss too many parties. He's not on everybody's A list, but he probably makes most B-plus lists. I think that's where he gets most of his business. People sidle up to him at a party and ask him about a rash, or something, and the next thing you know they're his patients. He's very charming."

"Did Vance go to him?"

"Oh, Vance thought he was Albert fucking Schweitzer. I've heard him talk about Lansing in the most glowing terms."

"So Vance trusted him."

"Implicitly."

"Is he your doctor?"

"For anything up to and including a skint knee. I've got a gynecologist who gets most of my business. I'm a healthy girl; I've never really been sick with anything worse than the flu."

"I'm glad to hear it."

"As a matter of fact, I'm feeling particularly healthy tonight. You don't have to be anywhere, do you?"

"I'm happy where I am," he replied.

She stood up, took him by the hand, and led him into the house and toward her bedroom. Once there, she unzipped her dress and let it fall to the floor.

"Promise you won't ruin *my* health," he said.

"Sugar," she replied, working on his buttons, "I'm not making any such promise."

"Be gentle," he said.

"Maybe," she replied, leading him toward the bed, and not by the hand.

Chapter 51

STONE MADE IT BACK to the Centurion bungalow, tired but happy, around ten A.M. Louise was at her desk, and she handed him a message from Brandy Garcia.

"He works from an answering machine," Stone said to the secretary. "Call and leave a message that he can reach me now."

"Dino Bacchetti called, too. He said you have the number."

"Right, I'll call him." Stone shaved and changed into fresh clothes, then went into the study. He was about to call Dino when Louise buzzed him.

"Brandy Garcia on line one."

Stone picked up the phone. "Hello?"

Garcia wasted no time on pleasantries. "I thought you should know that our mutual acquaintance from Tijuana is back in town."

"What?"

"Apparently, his sister—the one he lived with when he was here—is sick, and he's taking care of her kids."

"I thought you told him to lose himself."

"I did, my friend, but I can't follow him all over Mexico to make sure he stays down there."

"Do you have a number for his sister's house?"

"Got a pencil?"

"Shoot." Stone jotted down the number. "Call him and tell him to keep his head down."

"Will do, Chief." Garcia hung up.

Stone sighed. It was bad enough that Beverly Walters was going to testify, but if Cordova appeared in court, he might lend credence to her story. He called Marc Blumberg.

"Morning, Stone. Where'd you sleep last night?"

"None of your business," Stone replied.

Blumberg laughed. "You seemed to be hanging back when everybody else was leaving."

"We had dinner, and that's all you need to know."

"Okay, okay, what's up?"

"Our friend Cordova has turned up in L.A. again."

"That's bad," Blumberg replied. "I filed a motion to dismiss this morning. I hope we can get a hearing scheduled before the police find him."

"The one thing we've got going for us is that the police aren't looking for Cordova, although he doesn't know that."

"Do you know where to find him?"

"Yes. I can get a message to him if the police suddenly get interested."

"You want to prep Arrington, or shall I?"

"You'd better do it; she's not speaking to me at the moment."

"Oh? What went wrong?"

"It's too complicated to go into. Let's just say that she got angry about something she didn't have a good reason to be angry about."

"Stone, you are the only man I know whose relations with women are more complicated than mine."

"That's not how I planned it, believe me. Will you call Arrington?"

"Okay, whatever you say."

"How are you planning to handle Beverly Walters?"

"I'm planning to shred her on the stand."

"She may have been sleeping with Vance; I'm still working on find-ing out."

"Even if she wasn't, I think I'll ask her anyway. Several times, maybe. Anything we can do to damage her credibility puts us one step closer to getting Arrington out of this."

"I think you're right. Let me make another call to see if I can find out more."

"Let me know when you do."

"See you later." Stone hung up and buzzed Louise. "What time is it in Hawaii?" he asked.

"Three or four hours earlier than here, I think."

"You've got Betty Southard's hotel number, haven't you?"

"She's moved to a rented cottage, and I have the number."

"Go ahead and get her on the phone, and let's hope she's an early riser."

"I'll buzz you."

Stone sat thinking about Beverly Walters and Felipe Cordova and what they could mean to the charges against Arrington. The phone buzzed, and Stone picked it up. "Betty?"

"Aloha, stranger," she said.

"Hope I didn't get you up."

"You know I'm an early riser," she said. "Wish you were here to get my heart started in the morning."

"A pleasant thought, but I'm still needed here. You enjoying yourself?"

"So much that I'm thinking of making a permanent move here. Will you come see me?"

"When you least expect it."

"Why'd you call? Surely not just to wake me up."

"I wanted to ask you something."

"Go ahead."

"Beverly Walters. Did she and Vance ever have a thing?"

"Why do you ask?"

"Because she's the key prosecution witness against Arrington, and I need to know as much as possible about her."

"Vance didn't keep much from me, but he never mentioned Beverly in those terms. Anyway, he was pretty tight with her husband, Gordon."

"If he was sleeping with her, where do you think it might have happened?"

"In his RV, more than likely, but just about any place that was convenient."

"Did he ever bring her to the bungalow?"

"Not when I was around, but he didn't do that with his women, except maybe after hours. A few mornings there were signs in the bungalow that someone had been there."

"When was the last time you can remember?"

"No more than a day or two before he was shot."

"Did you ever find anything in the bungalow belonging to a woman?"

"Once or twice—a lipstick or a scarf. When I did, I just left it on Vance's desk and said nothing about it."

"Anything that you could identify as belonging to Walters?"

"Come to think of it, the lipstick I found was one I've seen her wear, but I suppose that's a pretty tenuous connection, isn't it?"

"Yes, it is. Nothing else?"

"Nothing I can think of. I'll call you if I think of anything else."

"Thanks, I'd appreciate that. It could be important."

"How's Arrington bearing up?"

"I don't know, to tell you the truth. She's not communicating with me at the moment."

"Uh, oh; I don't want to know about that."

"Good, because I'm not going to tell you about it. What do you have planned for the day?"

"The beach, of course. Can't you hear the surf over the phone?"

"You know, I think I can."

"That's all you need to know about my day."

"You take care, then."

"Bye-bye."

Stone hung up. That had been a disappointment. He called Dino.

"Yes?"

"It's me. How's it going?"

"I'm having a lovely time sitting around the pool, while Mary Ann and Arrington talk and giggle."

"Any thaw there?"

"A little, maybe; I'll have to pump Mary Ann. My guess is, though, if you want her to talk to you, you're going to have to make the first move."

"What did I do?"

"Nothing, nothing, just got married. That seems to have disappointed her."

"But . . ."

"Listen, Stone, you don't have to convince me. She's behaved badly and won't admit it. I'm just saying that you're going to have to make the move, whether it's logical or not. It's how women work."

"Tell me about it."

"I shouldn't have to. What's up with you? Anything happening?"

"Marc Blumberg has filed for a motion to dismiss the charges against Arrington, so he'll probably turn up over there pretty soon to prep her for her testimony."

"What are the chances of shutting this thing down early?"

"In my view? Two: slim and very slim."

"I guess you've got to make the effort."

"You bet. I don't want to hang around L.A. for another six months waiting for this to come to trial. I'm getting homesick for a little New York grit in my teeth, you know?"

"Yeah? Funny, I'm getting to like it here. Think the LAPD could use another detective?"

"You wouldn't last a month out here, Dino. It's all too easy; you're a New Yorker; you like things tough."

"Call Arrington and make nice, then maybe we can all have dinner together."

"Without Dolce?"

"Without Mrs. Barrington."

"Don't say that."

"Call her."

"Okay; see you later." Stone hung up and stared at the phone. He might as well get it over with.

Chapter 52

MANOLO ANSWERED THE PHONE. "Good morning, Manolo," Stone said. "It's Stone Barrington. May I speak with Mrs. Calder?"

"Good morning, Mr. Barrington; it's good to hear from you. I'll see if she's in."

She'd damned well better be in, Stone thought. Next time she decamps I'll let her wait out the trial in jail. "Thank you."

She kept him waiting for a long time. This wasn't going to be easy. "Yes?" she said finally, coldly.

"Good morning."

"What can I do for you?"

"You can be civil, for a start."

"I'm listening; what do you want?"

"I invited Dino and Mary Ann out here as much for me as for you. I'd like to see them. Shall we try dinner again?"

"Oh, I do hope Mrs. Barrington can make it."

"I hope not. And she's Mrs. Barrington only in her own mind, nowhere else."

"How did that happen, Stone? Did you get drunk and wake up married?"

"I could ask you the same question, but I think we should do our best to put our respective marriages behind us and get on with our lives."

Long silence. "You have a point," she admitted finally.

"If it makes any difference, I was on the rebound," he said.

There was another silence while she thought about that. "Come for dinner at seven," she said, then hung up.

Stone chose his clothes carefully—a tan tropical wool suit, brown alligator loafers, and a pale yellow silk shirt, open at the collar, as a concession to L.A. Arrington had always responded to well-dressed men, and he wanted very much for her to respond. He entered through the front gate, the TV crew having departed for more sordid pastures, and parked in front of the house.

Manolo greeted him, beaming. "Good evening, Mr. Barrington," he said. "It's good to see you back here." There was relief in his voice, as if he'd feared that Stone might never be allowed in the house again.

"Good evening, Manolo," Stone said.

"They're having drinks out by the pool; shall I pour you a Wild Turkey?"

"I feel like something breezier," Stone said. "How about a vodka gimlet, straight up?"

"Of course."

Stone followed Manolo down the broad central hallway, past the spot where Vance Calder had bled out his life on the tiles, and emerged into the garden, past the spot where Felipe Cordova had left his big shoeprint. Where had Beverly Walters stood? he wondered.

Dino waved from a seat near the pool bar, where he, Mary Ann, and Arrington sat in thickly cushioned bamboo chairs around a coffee table. He gave Dino a wave and pecked the two women on the cheek as if there had never been a scene at their last meeting. Manolo went behind the bar and expertly mixed Stone's drink, then brought it to him in a frosty glass on a silver tray.

"Thank you, Manolo," he said.

"That looks good," Arrington said. She pulled his hand toward her and sipped from his drink. "Oh, a vodka gimlet. Let's all have one,

Manolo." Manolo went back to work while, at the other end of the pool, Isabel set a table for dinner.

"I thought we'd dine outside," Arrington said. "Such a perfect California evening."

"It certainly is," Stone agreed. This was going well, and he was relieved.

"You know, before I married Vance I had always hated L.A., but evenings like this changed my mind. I mean, there's smog and traffic, and everybody talks about nothing but the business, but on evenings like this, you could almost forgive them."

"I think Dino has caught the L.A. bug, too," Stone said, smiling. "He was inquiring only today whether the LAPD would have him."

"*What?*" Mary Ann said. "Dino live out here? He wouldn't last a month."

"My very words to him."

"Maybe I wouldn't have to cop for a living," Dino said. "Maybe I'd become an actor. I could do all those parts Joe Pesci does, and better, too."

"You know, Dino, I believe you could," Arrington laughed. "Want me to call Lou Regenstein at Centurion and get you a screen test?"

"Nah, I don't test, and I don't audition," Dino said, waving a hand. "My agent would never let me do that . . . if I had an agent."

"That's it, Dino," Arrington said. "Play hard to get. Movie people want most the things they can't have. Your price would double."

Then, it seemed to Stone, the clock began to run backward, and they all became the people they had been before all this had happened. They were old friends, easy together, enjoying the evening and each other. The gimlets seemed to help, too. Soon they were laughing loudly at small jokes. Then Manolo called them to dinner.

No soup this time, Stone reflected; nothing to be dumped in his lap, and no Dolce to screw up their evening. They began with seared foie gras, crisp on the outside, melting inside, with a cold Château Coutet, a sweet, white Bordeaux. That was followed by a thick, perfect veal chop and a bottle of Beringer Reserve Cabernet Sauvignon. Dessert was an orange crème brûlée and more of the Coutet.

Coffee was served in Vance's study, before a fire, as the desert night had become chilly. The women excused themselves, and Stone and Dino declined Manolo's offer of Vance's cigars.

"Looks like the bloom is back on the rose," Dino said.

"The atmosphere is certainly warmer," Stone agreed.

"Arrington and Mary Ann spent the afternoon talking about you, I think. Mary Ann probably told her how lost you were without her, and how when Dolce came along, you were ripe for the picking."

"That's embarrassingly close to the truth," Stone said. "Have you heard anything from Dolce?"

"She and Mary Ann had breakfast together at the Bel-Air this morning."

"Is that where she's staying?"

"She's been cagey about where she's staying. I don't like it, frankly; I don't think this is over."

"Neither do I."

"Are you carrying?"

"No, and I don't know why I asked you to bring a weapon out here. A moment of paranoia, I guess."

"If Dolce is mad at you, it's not paranoid to go armed. If I were you, I wouldn't leave home without it."

"I'd feel a fool, wearing a gun these days," Stone said. "It took some getting used to when I was on the force, but now . . . well, it just seems, I don't know, belligerent."

"You've never liked guns, have you?"

"No, I guess not. I mean, I admire a well-made tool, and I guess that's what a gun is. Some of them are beautiful things, like the Walther, but I never liked the Glocks; they're ugly."

The women came back, and Manolo poured their coffee.

"Did Marc Blumberg see you today?" Stone asked Arrington.

"He came in time for lunch, and by the time he left, I was 'prepped,' as he put it. Sounds as though someone had shaved my pubic hair and painted my belly orange."

Dino made a face. "Such imagery! Only a woman could put it that way."

"Men are such babies," Mary Ann said. "So easily shocked. Dino, you couldn't make it as a woman for a single day."

"And I wouldn't want to try," Dino said.

They chatted for another hour, then Stone rose and announced his departure. Dino was stifling yawns by this time, too, and he and Mary Ann departed for the guest house.

Arrington walked Stone to the door. "I'm sorry about my behavior last time," she said. "I realize now that it wasn't your fault, that you were the victim."

"Hardly that," Stone said. "I knew what I was getting into."

"No, you didn't," She said at the door, resting her head on his shoulder. "You never do."

Stone put a finger under her chin, raised her head, and kissed her lightly. "I'm glad you and I are all right again."

"So am I."

"If it's any help, I'm already working on an Italian divorce."

"Any kind will do."

"I'd better go."

"Good night, sweet prince."

"And angels sing me to my rest? Not just yet, I hope."

He walked toward the car, then he stopped and turned. She was still standing in the doorway. "Arrington?"

"Yes?"

"I seem to recall that you never wore terrycloth robes."

"What a good memory you have. I always liked plain cotton or silk. What an odd thing to remember."

"Oh, I remember a lot more," he said, as he waved good night and got into the car.

All the way back to Centurion he thought about what she used to wear.

Chapter 53

THE FOLLOWING MORNING Marc Blumberg called and asked Stone to come to his office to discuss the motion to dismiss. Stone left Centurion and on his way passed the spot where he'd had the flat tire, reminding him that he had left the damaged tire at a service station for repair. He stopped to pick it up, and as he opened the trunk he saw Felipe Cordova's Nikes. He'd completely forgotten about them.

He arrived at Blumberg's office and was shown in and given coffee, while Marc finished a meeting in his conference room. Shortly, the lawyer came into his office and sat down at his desk.

"So," said Stone, "what's your plan? Who are we going to call?"

"Nobody," Marc replied. "That's my plan."

"Come again?"

"My plan is to cross-examine the prosecution's witnesses to within an inch of their lives. After all, it's they who have to make a case, not we."

"You don't think we ought to try?" Stone asked doubtfully.

"Let me ask you something, Stone: Can we prove Arrington *didn't* shoot Vance?"

"Maybe not."

"If we could prove she didn't do it, we'd be home free, but we can't. So we're going to have to cast so much doubt on the prosecution's case that the judge will throw it out."

"And how are we going to do that?" Stone asked.

"I know Beverly Walters better than you," Marc replied.

"How well, Marc?"

"Well enough, trust me."

"All right, I'll trust you."

"Have you got any other ideas about how we might proceed?"

Stone took a deep breath. "I think we ought to call Felipe Cordova."

"I thought he was lost in darkest Mexico."

"He was, but he's back in L.A. Brandy Garcia gave me a heads up."

"Doesn't it bother you that the prosecution would call Cordova, if they knew what we knew about his actions that night?"

"No."

"Stone, we're going to have Beverly Walters on the stand saying she saw Arrington shoot Vance, while Arrington doesn't remember *what* she did or didn't do. Cordova is just going to back up Beverly's story, isn't he?"

"I don't think so," Stone said.

"And why not?"

"A couple of reasons. First, Vanessa Pike told me she drove Beverly to the Calder house, and that Beverly saw what happened from the rear of the house, at the doors to the pool."

"Wait a minute. What Vanessa told you was that she drove *some-body* to Vance's; she didn't say who."

"But we know it was Beverly."

"How do we know that?"

"Because Charlene Joiner says that the two of them left her house together that evening, after a day lying around the pool."

"At what time?"

"At just about the time it would have taken for them to drive to the Calder house and arrive at the time Vance was being shot."

"Will Charlene testify to that?"

"Yes, to that and more."

"What else?"

"She'll testify that Beverly was wearing a terrycloth robe over a bathing suit when she left her house."

"So?"

"Cordova says he saw a woman next to Vance's body, and she was wearing a terrycloth robe."

"Did he see her face?"

"No."

"Then it could have been Arrington."

"Arrington doesn't wear terry robes. She likes plain cotton or silk."

"Can we prove that?"

"We can call her maid, who would know her wardrobe intimately, and who got her out of the tub and into a robe."

"I like it," Blumberg said. "But how are we going to put Beverly in the house?"

"I think she'll admit being outside, and it's a short step from the back door into the hallway where Vance died. And there's this, Marc: I'd be willing to bet that Cordova is not mentioned in Beverly's story, because she didn't see him."

"Yeah, but can Cordova prove he was there?"

"The police can; they've got a photograph of his shoeprint."

"Can he produce the shoe?"

"No, but I can; it's in the trunk of my car. I bought the shoes from Cordova in Mexico."

"Nikes, weren't they?"

"Right."

"There are millions of pairs of Nikes out there."

"There aren't millions of size twelves, and Cordova's have a cut across the heel of the sole that shows up in the photograph."

"You know, Stone, I think we're awfully close to being able to prove that Arrington didn't kill Vance."

"Close but not quite there. Cordova didn't see Beverly shoot him."

"And we don't have a motive."

"Or the weapon."

"Shit!" Blumberg said. "What could her motive be?"

"I think they were sleeping together. It could be that he told her to get lost, and she reacted badly."

"Could be, but how do we prove that?"

"I wish Vanessa were still alive; she could probably tell us."

"I'd give a million bucks for that gun with her prints on it."

"So would I," Stone agreed, "but it doesn't look as though we're ever going to find it."

"I'd give a lot for a witness who could put Beverly in the sack with Vance, too."

"Oddly enough, Beverly is known among her friends as a blabbermouth, but apparently, she never blabbed about a relationship with Vance."

"Except maybe to Vanessa."

"Maybe, but we'll never know."

Marc suddenly stood up. "Jesus," he said, "I just thought of something. Vanessa kept a diary."

"How do you know that?"

"She kept it in her handbag, and she'd write in it at odd moments. I tried to read it once, but it was one of those things like high school girls have, with a tiny lock on it."

"I know the kind you mean," Stone said.

Marc sat down again. "But it must have been in the house with her; it would have burned."

"I think I can find out about that," Stone said.

"How? From the investigating officer?"

"I have a friend in the department."

"Use my phone," Marc said, pointing across the room to a phone on a coffee table.

Stone went to the phone and dialed Rick Grant's direct line.

"Captain Grant."

"Rick, it's Stone Barrington. Can we meet somewhere?"

"I don't think that's a good idea, Stone."

"Why not?"

"You're defending Arrington Calder, and, I have to tell you, the investigators on the Vanessa Pike case are looking at you funny."

"All right, then will you do this for me? Call those officers and ask them if they found Vanessa's diary in their search of the premises after the fire."

"Why?"

"Because, if it still exists, it may have some information about Vance Calder's murder."

"If that's true, then it would have to go to Durkee and his partner, too."

"All I want is a copy. We could subpoena it, if we have to."

"All right, I'll check on it and get back to you."

"Thanks, Rick." He hung up and turned back to Marc. "If we hit paydirt in the diary, then we can demand that the cops get a search warrant for Beverly's house. Maybe the gun is there."

"Wouldn't that be nice?" Blumberg said.

Stone stood up suddenly.

"Where are you going?"

"To Vanessa's house. I don't think I feel comfortable with the cops seeing that diary before we do."

"Let me know what you find."

Stone headed for the door.

Chapter 54

STONE DROVE SLOWLY up Vanessa's street and down again, making sure that nobody from the police or fire departments was at the site. Satisfied, he parked across the street and got out of the car.

The house was a sad shell, with most of the roof gone and with large gaps in the walls. He ducked under the yellow police tape and stepped through one of the gaps into what had been the living room. The acrid smell of burned dwelling filled his nostrils, and with a shudder, he thought he detected a faint whiff of seared meat. A few charred sticks of what had been furniture remained in the room and the remains the sofa were recognizable. He recalled that he and Vanessa had sat there, sipping their drinks and talking, no more than an hour before she had died.

He walked on a runner of plastic sheeting that had been placed there like a sidewalk by the fire department investigators, to avoid disturbing evidence. As he moved through the rooms he noticed that the ash around him had a smooth surface, and telltale marks showed that the debris had been raked, in search of evidence. If anything were left of Vanessa's diary, which he doubted, then the investigators would surely have found it. His trip here had been for naught. Her purse and the diary had probably been in the kitchen, and there was no longer a kitchen.

Then he turned and saw something he hadn't seen before: the garage. He hadn't seen it, because on his last visit, the house had been in the way, but now he could look through a giant, charred hole and see the little building. It seemed older than the house, or maybe it had just not been updated over the years, the way the house had been. It looked like something out of the twenties, a meager, clapboard structure with two doors, the old-fashioned kind that featured a brass handle in the middle of the door. One turned the handle, lifted, and the door rose. Surely electric openers would have been added by this time.

He tried the doors. The first didn't move, but the second operated as it had been designed to. It took some effort, but he got the door halfway open and stepped under it. He tried a light switch on the wall, but nothing happened. The power had either been interrupted by the fire or turned off by the fire department.

A single car, a Mazda Miata, was in the garage. It was red, small, and cute, and he reflected that Vanessa would have looked good in it, her hair blowing in the wind. The top was up, and he tried the passenger door: locked. He walked around the car and tried the driver's door, with success. He found the trunk release and popped the lid. There was a spare, flat, and the jack, and an old pair of sneakers—nothing else.

He went back to the driver's door and tried to sit in the seat, but found himself jammed, until he could locate the release and move the seat backward. The courtesy lights illuminated the interior, and he looked around.

Women made a terrible mess of cars, he thought. The most fastidious woman seemed unable to avoid the buildup of used Kleenex, fast-food wrappers, and old paper cups in her automobile. He checked the tiny glove compartment, which held only a couple of parking tickets and a lipstick tube. There were some road maps in a door pocket, and nothing behind the sun visors. He got out of the car, and as he did moved the driver's seat forward and checked behind it. Nothing there. He reached across and felt behind the passenger seat, and he came in contact with something made of canvas.

He reached over, unlocked the passenger door from the inside, then walked around the car and opened the door. He moved the seat forward and extracted a beat-up canvas carryall bearing the logo of a bookstore chain. He set it on top of the car and checked its contents. Inside was a thick book on interior design, a wrinkled bikini, a bottle of suntan lotion, and a leather-covered book with a binding flap that ended in a brass tip secured by a tiny lock. Stamped on the front of the book, in gilded letters, was "My Diary." If the cops had thought to search the car, they had done a lousy job, Stone thought. He tried opening it, but the lock held.

He put the carryall back where he had found it, closed the car doors, returned the garage door to its original position, and walked back to his car. He was tempted to try to open the diary here, but he decided it might be best to do it elsewhere. He drove back to Marc Blumberg's building.

He walked into Marc's office, smiling, holding up the leather diary.

Marc took it and turned it over in his hands. "It's not burned at all," he said.

"It wasn't in the house," Stone replied. "I found it in her car, in the garage."

"Can you pick a lock, or shall I pry it open?" Marc asked.

"Hang on a minute; what's our legal position? I took this from her car with nobody's permission. Given that, do we want to break into it?"

"We can open it with the permission of her executor," Marc said.

"Do you know who he is?"

Marc grinned. "You're looking at him. Here's a paper clip."

Stone straightened the wire and began probing the lock. It was simple; one turn and it was open. He set the diary on Marc's desk and began flipping pages, while the two of them bent over it.

"Funny, I don't recognize any names," Marc said. "We knew a lot of the same people."

"Maybe she's giving people code names; if somebody got into the diary, it might save embarrassment."

"Let's start at the end and work backward," Marc said. They began reading; Vanessa had written in a small, but very legible, hand.

"Look, in the last entry she says she's going to Palm Springs to 'Herbert's' house. I wonder why she called me Herbert?"

"I guess you just look like a Herbert, Marc."

"Yeah." He flipped back further in the book. "There's mention here of a Hilda, quite often. Think that could be Beverly?"

"We need a context to figure this out," Stone said, turning pages. "Here, the pages are dated; this is the day Vance was shot. There's mention of Hilda, Magda, and Jake."

"Jake was Vance's character in one of his recent movies," Marc said. "*Fear Everything*, I think."

"She mentions lunch around the pool at Magda's. That must be Charlene Joiner. Here we go!" He began reading aloud. "'When we left Magda's, Hilda insisted on going to Jake's house, which I thought was nuts. She knew about this service entrance at the rear of the property. I wouldn't get out of the car, but Hilda, bold as brass, walked to the house. Hilda has admitted screwing Jake, but, Jesus, I never thought she'd have the guts to go to his house. She must have been gone ten minutes, then there was a noise, and a minute later, she came running back, breathless, and told me to get the hell out of there. She wouldn't say what happened but I'd be willing to bet that she ran into Mrs. Jake. God, that must have been embarrassing! She was still breathing hard when I dropped her off at her house. I've never seen her so discombobulated. I know I'll eventually hear about this from somebody else, even though she won't discuss it. Hilda can never keep her mouth shut for long—she'll either brag about this, or try for sympathy. Jesus, I'm so glad I didn't go with her!'"

"Well, *that's* pretty clear," Marc said, "but I'd feel a lot better if she had just said that she'd watched Beverly shoot Vance."

"All we've really got here is what Vanessa told me."

"Yeah, we've got to get Beverly to admit that she's Hilda, or get corroboration from Charlene on the stand that they were at her house that day."

Stone was flipping forward through the pages, looking at the dates after Vance's murder. "Look at this," he said. "'Hilda keeps trying to tell me something, but she can't get it out. She seems very guilty about something. Having seen the papers, it's not hard to figure out that Jake was hurt while we were at his house, but Hilda won't tell me what she saw there. I keep thinking maybe I should go to the police. I've got to ask Herbert about this, but how am I going to do that without betraying Hilda's confidence?'"

"I wish to God she had asked me," Marc said. "Maybe I could have done something to prevent her death."

"Wait a minute," Stone said, "are you thinking that Beverly set the fire at Vanessa's, because she knew too much?"

"It wouldn't be the first murder that was committed to cover up another murder," Marc said.

Stone sat down heavily, feeling enormously relieved.

"You look kind of funny, Stone," Marc commented. "Was it something I said?"

"Yes, it was," Stone replied. "I had never connected Beverly with Vanessa's death, but what you're saying makes perfectly good sense. I'm afraid that I thought someone else . . ." He stopped himself.

"That someone else murdered Vanessa?"

Stone nodded.

"Who?"

"I'd rather not say. If you're right, then it doesn't make any difference."

"I guess not." Marc picked up the phone.

"Who are you calling?"

"The D.A. I want him to see this diary. If we're lucky, maybe we won't need the motion hearing."

"Marc," Stone said, "we don't have anything we didn't before. Beverly has obviously already told the D.A. that she was at Vance's that night; otherwise, how else could she be a witness."

"You're right, but I have to turn this over to either the D.A. or the police, anyway, and it at least independently establishes that Beverly was there. She won't know what's in the diary, so maybe I can use it to rattle her at the hearing."

"Call the D.A.," Stone said.

Chapter 55

THE CAB CRAWLED UP THE STREET. From the rear seat Stone checked the house numbers, but most of them were missing, like a lot of other things in this neighborhood. Stone had taken a taxi, because he did not want to park a Mercedes SL600 in this block.

As it turned out, the house number was unnecessary, because Felipe Cordova was sitting on his sister's front porch, drinking from a large beer bottle, while two small children played on the patchy front lawn.

"Wait for me," Stone said to the driver.

"How long you going to be?" the driver asked. "I don't like it around here."

"A couple of minutes; I'll make it worth your while."

"Okay, mister, but hurry, okay?"

Stone got out of the cab, let himself through the chain-link front gate, and approached the house.

Cordova watched him come, curious at first, until he recognized Stone. "Hey, Mr. Lawyer," he said, raising the quart in salute. "You back to see me again?"

Stone pulled up a rickety porch chair and sat down. "Yes, Felipe, and I've brought good news."

"I always like good news," Felipe replied happily.

"The police are no longer looking for you," Stone said.

"Hey, that *is* good news."

"But you and I have a little official business."

"Cordova's eyes narrowed. Official?"

"Nothing to worry about," Stone said, taking the subpoena from his pocket and handing it to the man. "I just need you to testify in court."

Cordova examined the document. "The day after tomorrow?"

"That's right. Ten A.M.; the address is there." He pointed.

"What's this about?"

"I just want you to answer the same questions I asked you in Mexico. And I want the same answers."

"How much do I get paid?"

"That's the bad news, Felipe; I can't pay a witness. That could get us both put in jail."

Cordova frowned. "I'm going to have expenses, man."

"You can send a bill for your expenses, your *reasonable* expenses, like cab fare and lunch, to this lawyer." He handed Cordova Marc Blumberg's card. "See that it doesn't come to more than a hundred bucks."

"Suppose I don't want to testify?"

"Then, the police *will* be looking for you, and if you leave the country, you won't be able to come back. The border patrol will have you in their computer, and you don't want that, do you?"

Cordova shook his head.

"Relax, Felipe; there's nothing to this. When you get to the courthouse, you sit on a bench outside the courtroom until you're called, and then you take the stand, swear the oath on the bible, and you answer questions."

"Just like on *Perry Mason*?"

"Just like that, except on *Perry Mason,* the witness is always the murderer. We know you're not the murderer; we just want you to tell about the woman you saw in the house, the one in the terrycloth bathrobe."

"Oh, yeah."

Stone stood up. "Be sure you remember that word, Felipe: *terry-cloth*. I'll see you there at ten A.M. the day after tomorrow, and remember, that document means you *have* to testify or be arrested. You understand?"

Cordova nodded.

Stone patted him on the back and went back to his cab. "Okay," he said, "back to Centurion Studios." He took out his cellphone and called Marc Blumberg. "He's been served."

"You think he'll show, or should I send somebody out there?"

"He'll show."

When Stone arrived at the studio bungalow, Dino and Mary Ann were waiting for him.

"So this was Vance's cottage?" Mary Ann asked while being shown around.

"This was his office and dressing room," Stone replied. "Of course, he had an RV that served as a dressing room, too. All the stars seem to have them."

A young man pulled a golf cart to the front door and got out.

"Here's your tour guide," Stone said.

"Dino, don't you want to go?"

"I've already seen enough; I'll hang out with Stone," Dino replied.

"Then we'll get some dinner," Stone said. The phone rang, and Louise answered it.

"Stone, it's for you; the lady sounds upset."

Stone went into the study and picked up the phone. "Hello?"

"Stone, it's Charlene," she whispered.

"Why are you whispering?"

"Somebody just took a shot at me."

"Where are you?"

"At home. Somebody fired right through the sliding doors to the pool."

"Are you hurt?"

"No."

"Call nine-one-one. I'll be there as fast as I can."

"Hurry."

Stone hung up the phone. "Come on," he said to Dino. "I'll explain on the way. Louise, when Mrs. Bacchetti gets back, tell her we'll be back soon, all right?"

"Sure."

Stone grabbed the Walther automatic and its shoulder holster from a desk drawer, then ran for the car with Dino right behind him.

"What's this about?" Dino asked as they cleared the front gate and turned into the boulevard.

"You're about to meet a movie star," Stone said.

When they pulled up in front of the Malibu Colony house, there were no police cars in sight. Stone wondered about that, but he was relieved that there was no ambulance, either.

The front door was ajar, and Stone walked in cautiously, stopping to listen. He heard nothing. It was getting dark outside, and there were no lights on in the house. "Charlene?" he called out.

"Stone?" her voice came from somewhere at the back of the house.

Stone walked quickly down the hallway, followed by Dino. "In here," Charlene's voice said from somewhere to the right.

They turned into the sitting room of the master suite. Charlene was crouched behind the little bar, and she had a nine millimeter automatic pistol in her hand. She rushed to Stone and threw an arm around him. She was naked. "I'm so glad you're here," she said, the gun at her side.

"This is my friend Dino Bacchetti," Stone said.

"Nice to meet you," Dino said, looking her up and down. He reached out and took the pistol from her, removed the clip, and ejected a cartridge from the chamber.

"Why don't you get into some clothes," Stone said.

She ran into the bedroom.

Stone looked around. The big glass door to the pool side patio had shattered, and glass was everywhere.

Charlene returned, tying the sash on a dressing gown and wearing shoes.

"Where are the police?" Stone asked. "Surely they've had time to get here."

"I didn't call the police," she said.

"Why not?"

"I called you, instead."

"Start at the beginning, and tell me what happened."

"I was lying on the sofa there, reading a script, when I heard two shots. The glass door shattered, and I rolled off the sofa onto the floor and crawled over to the bar as fast as I could. My gun was in a drawer there."

"Dino, will you take a look around out back?"

"Sure."

"Wait a minute," Charlene said. She went to a wall switch and turned on the lights around the pool. "That'll help."

Dino slapped the clip back into Charlene's gun, worked the action, then went outside, the pistol hanging at his side.

"Do you think this was a serious attempt on your life?" Stone asked.

"Come here," Charlene replied, leading him around the sofa and pointing.

Stone looked at the two neat holes halfway down the back cushion.

"My head was right under the holes," Charlene said.

"You should have called the police immediately; they should be trying to find out who did this."

"I know who did it," Charlene said. "I saw her."

Stone's innards froze. "Her?"

"I believe these days she calls herself Mrs. Stone Barrington."

"Oh, Jesus," Stone said.

Chapter 56

STONE FOUND a paring knife behind the bar and cut into the sofa, just as Dino returned from the pool area.

"It's clear out there," he said. "The guy must have come up from the beach, since no traffic passed us on the way in here." He looked at what Stone was doing. "Whatcha got there?"

"Two slugs," Stone said, holding them up. "And it wasn't a guy."

Dino took the two lumps and looked closely at them. "Holy shit," he said.

"What?"

"These are mine." He held one up and pointed. "See? I made a mark there on each one, so if I ever got involved in a shootout, I'd know which slugs came from my weapon. These came from the thirty-two automatic I loaned you, Stone. How'd that happen?"

"It seems that Dolce took the gun from my house."

Dino groaned. "Are the cops coming?"

"I didn't call them," Charlene said.

"Why not?" Stone asked. "I told you to call nine-one-one."

"Two reasons: First, the tabloids would make my life hell if they found out that somebody shot up my house; second, I know who her father is."

Stone nodded. "All right."

"Also, once I had the Berretta in my hand, I figured I could handle her."

"Yeah, I thought I could handle her, too," Stone said. He turned to Dino. "Is Eduardo still in L.A.?"

Dino nodded. "At the Bel-Air."

Stone turned back to Charlene. "You want to come with us? Maybe you shouldn't stay here tonight."

"I'll come with you," she said. "I'll sleep at the studio in my RV; let me get some things." She disappeared into the bedroom again.

Stone picked up the phone, dialed the Bel-Air, and asked for Eduardo."

"Yes?"

"Eduardo, it's Stone Barrington."

"Good evening, Stone."

"It's important that I come and see you right away."

"Of course; I'll be here."

"I'll be there in an hour."

"Have you had dinner?"

"No."

"I'll order something."

"Thank you." He hung up as Charlene emerged from her bedroom, wearing jeans and a sweater and carrying a small duffel.

They drove into town, not talking much. Charlene wedged into the space behind the two front seats. Stone dropped Dino at the bungalow. "Tell Mary Ann I'm sorry I can't have dinner, but don't tell her what's happened."

"I'll send her back to Arrington's with the car," Dino said. "I'm coming with you."

"You don't have to, Dino."

"I'm coming."

"I'll be right back." He drove Charlene to her RV and got her settled there. "Will you be all right here?"

"Sure, I will. The fridge is full; I'll eat something and watch TV. Will you come back later?"

"Probably not," Stone said. "I have to take care of this."

"I understand."

"And thanks for not calling the police."

She gave him a little kiss. "Go safely." She held up the Berretta. "You want this?"

"Thanks, I have my own." He left her and drove back to the bungalow for Dino. Mary Ann was about to leave in Arrington's station wagon, and Stone traded cars with her.

"Don't hurt her, Stone," Mary Ann said.

"I don't intend to," Stone replied.

Stone drove to the upper end of the Bel-Air Hotel complex and parked the station wagon. Followed by Dino, he found the upstairs suite and rang the bell. Eduardo, wearing a cashmere dressing gown, opened the door and ushered them in.

"Good evening, Stone, Dino," he said.

"I'm sorry to disturb you, Eduardo," Stone replied.

"Not at all. Come and have an aperitif; dinner will be here soon." He pointed at the bar in the living room. "Please help yourselves; I'll have a Strega." He picked up the phone and told Room Service there would be three for dinner, then he joined Stone and Dino.

Stone poured three Stregas and handed two of them to Eduardo and Dino. They raised their glasses and sipped.

"Come, sit," Eduardo said, motioning them to a sofa. "Why have you come to see me?" he asked when they were settled.

"Eduardo," Stone said, "I'm sorry to have to tell you this, but about two hours ago, Dolce attempted to kill Charlene Joiner, the actress you met the other evening at the Regensteins'."

Eduardo winced, and his hand went to his forehead. His face showed no incredulity, simply painful resignation. "How did this occur?"

"Dolce apparently drove out to Malibu, parked her car, and approached Charlene's house from the beach. She fired two bullets through a sliding-glass door at Charlene, who was lying on a sofa, reading."

"Was Miss Joiner harmed?"

"No, only frightened."

"Do you think Dolce seriously tried to kill her?"

"I'm afraid I do, and she came very close."

"Where would Dolce have gotten a gun out here?" Eduardo asked. He seemed to be thinking quickly.

"Apparently, she took it from my house in New York without my knowledge. The gun belonged to Dino; he had loaned it to me."

"Does she still have the gun?"

Dino spoke up. "I saw no sign of it outside Miss Joiner's house, so I assume she does."

"Are the police involved?"

"No," Stone replied. "Charlene called me, instead of the police, and she has no intention of involving them."

"Thank God for that," Eduardo said. "This would have been so much more difficult."

"It's difficult enough," Stone said. "I feel responsible."

Eduardo shook his head. "No, no, Stone; something like this has been coming for a long time. If it hadn't been you, it would have been someone else."

"Why do you say that, Eduardo?" Dino asked. "Has she ever done anything like this before?"

Eduardo shrugged. "Since she was a little girl she always reacted violently if denied something she wanted."

The doorbell rang, and Dino jumped up. "I'll get it," he said.

"Dolce is all right most of the time," Eduardo said to Stone. "But she occasionally has these . . ." He didn't finish the sentence. "I had hoped that if she were happily married, she might be all right." He stopped talking while the waiter set the dining table, then he motioned for his guests to take seats.

He poured them some wine and waited until they had begun to eat their pasta before continuing. "She's seen a psychiatrist from time to time, but she always discontinued treatment after a few sessions. Her doctor advised me at one point to have her hospitalized for a while, but instead I took her to Sicily, and after some time there, she seemed better."

"What can I do to help?" Stone asked.

"I'll have to ask her doctor to recommend some place out here where she can be treated," Eduardo replied.

"I believe I know a good place," Stone said. He told Eduardo about the Judson Clinic and Arrington's stay there. "Would you like me to call Dr. Judson?"

"I would be very grateful if you would do so," Eduardo replied.

Stone left the table, called the clinic, and asked them to get in touch with Judson and have him telephone him at the Bel-Air. "I'm sure they'll be able to find him," he said when he had returned. "I was very impressed with Judson," he told Eduardo.

"Good," Eduardo said. "I'll get in touch with her own doctor and ask him to come out here and consult."

"I expect that, after treatment, she'll be all right," Stone said.

"I hope so," Eduardo replied, but he did not sound hopeful.

The phone rang and Stone answered it. "Hello?"

"May I speak with Stone Barrington, please?"

"Speaking."

"Stone, this is Jim Judson, returning your call."

Stone briefly explained the circumstances. "Do you think you could admit her to your clinic? Her father will be in touch with her doctor in New York and ask him to come out here."

"Of course," Judson replied. "When can you bring her to the clinic?"

"I'm not sure," Stone said. "We have to find her."

"Is she likely to be violent?"

"That's a possibility, but I don't really know."

"I'll have my people prepare, then. When you're ready to bring her here, just call the main number. I'll alert the front desk. If you need an ambulance or restraints, just let them know."

"Thank you, Jim; I'll be in touch." Stone hung up and returned to the table. "Dr. Judson will admit her," he said.

"But now we have to find her," Dino said. "Where do we look?"

Eduardo sighed. "I know where she is," he said sadly. "She's at the home of some friends of mine who are out of the country. We'll go there together."

Stone shook his head. "Dino and I can do this, Eduardo. Dolce is already angry with me; let's not make her angry with you, too."

Eduardo nodded. He found a pad, wrote down the address, and handed it to Stone. "I know I don't have to ask you to be gentle with her."

"Of course, I will be."

"But be careful," Eduardo said. "Don't allow her to endanger you or Dino."

Stone nodded and shook Eduardo's hand. "When this is done," Eduardo said, "there's something else I must talk with you about. Please call me."

"I'll call you as soon as we get Dolce to the clinic." He and Dino left before dessert arrived.

Chapter 5 7

WITH DINO NAVIGATING, Stone found the house. It was on Mulholland Drive, high above the city, a contemporary structure anchored to the mountainside by a cradle of steel beams. The front door was at street level, but the rear deck, Stone noticed, was high above the rocky hillside. The house was dark, but there was a sedan with a Hertz sticker on the bumper parked in the carport.

Stone parked on the roadside and headed for the front door, but Dino stopped him.

"Give me a couple of minutes to get around back," he said.

"Dino, the back of the house is at least fifty feet off the ground."

"Just give me a couple of minutes."

Stone stood at the roadside and looked out at what was nearly an aerial view of Los Angeles—a carpet of lights arranged in a neat grid, disappearing into a distant bank of smog, with a new moon hanging overhead. The air seemed clearer up here, he thought, taking a deep breath of mountain air. How had it come to this? he wondered. What had started as a passionate affair and had ripened into something even better was now broken into many pieces, ruined by Dolce's obsession with him and his own bond with Arrington. He didn't know where this would all end, but nothing looked promising. He glanced at his watch, then started up the driveway to the house.

The house's entry was dark, but as he approached, his feet crunching on gravel, he saw that the front door was ajar. He stopped and listened for a moment. Music was coming from somewhere in the interior of the house—a Mozart symphony, he thought, though he couldn't place it. Some instinct told him not to ring the doorbell. He pushed the door open a little and stepped inside into a foyer. He could hear the music better now. It seemed to be coming from the living room, beyond. He moved forward. A little moon and starlight came through the sliding glass doors to the deck, on the other side of the living room. He walked down a couple of steps. He could see the dim outlines of furniture. Then the silence was broken.

"I knew you'd come, Stone," Dolce said.

Stone jumped and looked around, but he couldn't find her. "Do you mind if we turn on a light?"

"I prefer the dark," she said. "It's better for what I have to do."

"You don't have to do anything, Dolce," he said. "Just relax; let's sit down and talk for a little while."

"Talking's over," she said. "We're way beyond talk, now."

"No, we can always talk."

The sound of two light pistol shots cracked the silence, and Stone dove for the floor, but not before the muzzle flash illuminated her, standing with her back to the fireplace, holding the pistol in both hands, combat-style.

"Stop it, Dolce!" he shouted. "Don't make things worse." He crawled behind a sofa, while wondering why his own gun was not in his hand.

She fired again, and he felt the thud against the sofa. "Things can always get worse," she said. Then he heard a sharp thud, and something large made of glass shattered against the stone floor.

"Stone?" It was Dino's voice. "Are you hit?"

"No," Stone replied. "Can I stand up?"

"Yes. She's out."

Stone stood up, found a lamp at the end of the sofa and switched it on. Dino stood before the fireplace, a short-barreled .38 in his hand, looking down. Stone came around the sofa and saw Dolce crumpled on the floor among the shards of the glass coffee table. Dino was standing on the hand that held the .32 automatic. Stone went to her and gently turned her over. "What did you hit her with?" he asked.

"The edge of my hand, across the back of the neck. I'm sure I didn't hurt her." He picked up the .32, removed the clip, worked the action, and slipped it into his jacket pocket. Stone picked up the ejected cartridge and handed it to Dino. "We'd better find the spent shells," he said. "Otherwise, when the owners return home they'll be calling the police."

Dino rummaged around the broken glass and recovered the shell casings. "I've got three," he said. "There was only one more, in the breech."

Stone found a phone and called the clinic. "This is Stone Barrington," he said to the woman who answered.

"Yes, Mr. Barrington, we've been expecting your call."

"We're on our way there."

"Will you require any sort of restraints?"

"I don't know," he replied. "Best be ready, though."

"We'll expect you shortly. Do you know how to get into the garage?"

"Yes."

"You'll be met there and brought up in the elevator."

"Good." Stone hung up, got his arms under Dolce, and picked her up. "Let's get her to the car," he said.

Dino closed the front door behind them, then got into the rear seat of the station wagon, helping Stone move Dolce's unconscious form into the car, then Stone went around to the driver's side.

"I hope to God we can get out of here before the cops show up," Dino said. "Some neighbor must have heard the shots."

Stone started the car and headed down Mulholland. "They'll find an empty house," he said.

"And a mess. Eduardo had better send somebody up there to clean up."

"I'll mention it to him."

They got as far as Sunset Boulevard before Dolce began to come to.

"Easy, Dolce," Stone said. "You just lie here and rest."

"Stone?" she said.

"I'm here, Dolce," he said from the front seat. "Just lie quietly. We'll have you home soon." He turned up Sunset and began making his way toward the Judson Clinic.

"Where's home?" she asked dreamily.

It was a good question, Stone thought, and he didn't have an answer.

There were two beefy men in orderlies' uniforms waiting in the garage with a gurney. Stone stopped the car, got out, and helped Dino remove Dolce.

"Where are we?" she asked. Her hand went to the back of her neck. "I've got a headache."

"We'll get you something for that," one of the orderlies said. "Why don't you hop up here and we'll get you upstairs and to bed."

"I don't want to go to bed," she said, looking around the garage. "It's early, and I'm a late person."

"We won't need the gurney," Stone said. "Come on, Dolce, let's go upstairs and get you something for your headache." He reached for her arm, but she stiffened and tried to pull away.

Dino stepped up and helped hold her as they got her onto the elevator.

An orderly pressed a button. "We've got a room ready," he said.

"What hotel is this?" Dolce asked

"The Judson," an orderly replied.

"Never heard of it. I want to go to the Bel-Air."

"The Bel-Air is full," Stone said.

"Never mind, Papa keeps a suite there; I want to go to the Bel-Air."

"Eduardo said to take you here," Stone said. "He'll come and see you in the morning."

The elevator stopped, and the party moved down the hallway, with Stone and Dino holding tightly onto Dolce. They got her into a room, where a nurse was waiting.

"Oh, no," Dolce said, struggling. "I know this place. I've been to a place like this."

The nurse came forward, a syringe in her hand.

Stone turned Dolce's face toward him. "It's going to be all right," he said.

She whirled, when she felt the needle in her arm, but Stone and Dino held her tightly.

"Oh, no," Dolce said again. "I don't want to . . ."

"Put her on the bed," the nurse said to the two orderlies, and in a moment they had her stretched out. She turned to Stone and Dino. "She'll be out in a minute, and she'll sleep for twelve hours."

Stone stood at the bedside and held her hand until her eyes had closed and she was breathing deeply.

A few minutes later Stone and Dino took the elevator back to the garage and got into the car.

"I don't ever want to have to do that again," Stone said.

"Then you'd better get a divorce," Dino replied.

Chapter 58

STONE LOOKED in the bathroom mirror; he did not much like himself this morning. Watching Dolce being sedated had shaken him badly, and later, explaining to Eduardo what had happened had not improved his state of mind. He had not slept much, and he was due at Marc Blumberg's office to prepare for tomorrow's hearing. He got into a hot shower and let the water run. The phone was buzzing when he got out.

It was Eduardo. "I saw her early this morning," he said.

"How was she?"

"Still sleeping; I just sat and looked at her. Her own doctor will be here today."

"Is there anything I can do, Eduardo?"

"Everything is being done that can be done. Later, if her doctor thinks you could be helpful, perhaps you could see her."

"Of course."

"I would like to take her to New York as soon as she is able to travel. Dr. Judson said he would consult with her doctor about that. If possible, I will take her home to Brooklyn and have her treated there."

"Perhaps she would be happier there," Stone said, not knowing what else to say.

"Stone, there is something else I must tell you about."

"What is it, Eduardo?"

"When I was at your house in New York we talked about the blood tests you took when Arrington's child was born."

"Yes, I remember."

"The tests were conducted by a laboratory here, in Los Angeles, called Hemolab."

"Yes, I think so."

"I think you should know that tests conducted by this company have, in the past, been known to be . . . manipulated. I cannot go into any detail about this, and I cannot discuss my reasons. Suffice it to say that this information is not just my opinion, but more substantial."

Again, Stone didn't know what to say.

"I don't know if, in your case, the results were accurate or not, and I have no way of investigating. You might wish to have the tests repeated by another laboratory."

"Thank you, Eduardo; I'll give that some thought." He would certainly do that.

"I must go now."

"I'll call you tonight to hear about Dolce."

"Thank you; I'll be in my suite all evening. Good-bye."

Stone hung up and sat on the bed, rattled by what Eduardo had said. He looked at the bedside clock: nearly eight; he was due at Marc Blumberg's office at nine to prepare for the hearing the following day. He shaved and dressed, then he called Dino.

"How you doing, pal?" Dino asked.

"I've been better."

"What do you need?" Dino could always read him.

"I'd appreciate it if you'd do something for me."

"Name it."

"Wait until midafternoon, then call the office of a Dr. Lansing Drake, in Beverly Hills. Tell him Arrington recommended him, that you're having abdominal pains, and that you'd like to see him late this afternoon. Then call me at Marc Blumberg's office and tell me what time he'll see you."

"You want me to go and fake it with this doctor?"

"No, no; I just want you to make the appointment, so that if he calls back to confirm who you are, he won't get me on the phone instead."

"Okay, I can do that. Dinner tonight?"

"Sure, if I don't have too much homework to do."

"Talk to you this afternoon, then."

"Bye." Stone was about to leave when the phone buzzed again. "Yes, Louise?"

"Brandy Garcia is on one."

Stone picked up the phone. "Yes, Brandy?"

"Stone, what's going on with Felipe Cordova? He called me last night, and he was upset."

"I subpoenaed him to testify at a hearing, that's all. He's at no risk by doing that."

"Yeah, but yesterday afternoon, he got *another* subpoena for the same time and place, this one from the D.A. And they searched his house, too. He didn't know what they were looking for."

Stone thought about that for a moment. "Somebody's got his wires crossed, that's all. There's nothing for him to worry about."

"He doesn't like this, Stone. I think he might bolt."

"Brandy, there's a thousand bucks in it for you if you can see that he shows up for that hearing."

"What am I going to tell him?"

"Tell him nobody's going to put him in jail; tell him anything you like, just have him there. Lead him by the hand."

"Okay, I'll do it for the grand. What are you going to give him?"

"I've already told him that I can't pay him to testify."

"I could give him a couple hundred, though?"

"Sorry, I didn't hear that; must be trouble on the line. Have him there, Brandy."

"You got it."

Stone sat in Marc Blumberg's office.

"I don't like this much," Marc was saying.

"What's the difference who he's testifying for? We know what he's going to say."

"Do we?"

"I think so. It might be more effective to let the D.A. get his story into the record, then bring out our points on cross."

"Okay, I buy that. Now, let's get started."

They worked through lunch, and at mid-afternoon, Dino called. "Hi."

"Hi. I've got an appointment."

"When?"

"As soon as I can get there."

"Thanks, Dino."

"Dinner?"

"Meet me at the studio at seven."

"See you then."

Stone hung up and turned to Marc. "Are we about done? There's somewhere I have to be."

"Go ahead; I'll see you at the courthouse tomorrow morning."

Stone looked up Drake's address in the phone book.

"My name is Bacchetti," Stone said to the receptionist.

"Oh, yes, Mr. Bacchetti," she replied. "Will you wait in examination room B, down the hall? And undress down to your shorts."

Stone found the room, which contained an examination table, a sink, and a cabinet for supplies. He did not undress; he sat down in the only chair and waited. A couple of minutes later, Dr. Lansing Drake entered the room, preoccupied with a clipboard in his hand.

"Mr. Bacchetti," he said, not looking up. "Just a moment, please." He went to the sink, washed his hands, then turned around. "Now, what seems to be . . ." His jaw dropped.

"I'm Stone Barrington, Dr. Drake; we met recently at Lou Regenstein's."

"I don't understand," Drake said nervously, looking toward the exit.

Stone got up and leaned on the door. "I won't keep you long, Doctor. My name will be familiar to you, because a while back, you submitted a sample of my blood, along with one from Vance Calder, to a company called Hemolab, for a paternity test."

"I don't recall," the doctor replied.

"Oh, I think you do," Stone said.

"Vance Calder was my patient," Drake said. "I have to respect his confidence."

"Vance is dead, Doctor, and now you have to deal with me. You can do it here, quietly, or you can do it in court. What's it going to be?"

Drake sagged against the examination table. "If Arrington should learn of this conversation . . ."

"I don't think that will be necessary. What I want to know, quite simply, is if the tests were run again by another laboratory, would the results be the same?"

Drake gazed out the window. "I honestly don't know."

"Do you deny altering the test results?"

Drake looked back at him. "I most certainly do." He looked away again. "That is, I don't know if the results were tampered with."

"And why don't you know?"

Drake sighed. "Vance came to me and said it was essential that the test prove that he was the father of the child. I conveyed that to someone at Hemolab."

"So I'm the child's father?"

"I said I don't know. I simply made Vance's wishes known. For all I know, he *was* the father. I suppose it could have gone either way, or there would have been no need for the test."

"Yes," Stone said, "it could have gone either way. I want to see the original test results."

"I'm afraid that will be impossible. At Vance's request, once the report was issued, the blood samples and the records were destroyed. The lab never knew who he was; the two subjects were simply labeled A and B."

"Then you knew when you saw the results."

"No, I didn't. I didn't care, really. I wrote a letter saying that Vance was the father, that's all. I don't know if he was or not."

"So, the test was just to have something to show Arrington?"

"I suppose. But if you ever tell her that, I'll deny even speaking to you."

"Thank you, Doctor," Stone said. He left the office and went back to his car.

Dino looked across the dinner table at Stone. "Are you sure you want to know?"

"Of course, I want to know; wouldn't you?"

"I'm not sure," Dino replied. "In the circumstances."

"What circumstances?"

Dino shrugged. "The present circumstances."

Stone thought about that. Arrington might still go to prison. In that case, he'd want to raise the boy—if he was the father. But if she were freed, then what? He and Arrington and their son would live happily ever after? That is, if the boy was, indeed, his son and not Vance's.

"If you've got to know, then here's what you have to do," Dino said. "You and Arrington and the boy have to go together to have blood drawn, two samples of both yours and the boy's. She sends one set to a lab, and you send them to another. Then you compare results, and you'll know."

"Yes, I suppose we would."

"But if the news of the test should get out, well, you'd have a tabloid shitstorm on your hands."

"Yes, we would."

"I think you need to do some more thinking."

"I think you're right.

Chapter 59

MANOLO DROVE Stone, Arrington, and Isabel to the courthouse, while Dino and Mary Ann followed in the station wagon. This time, they could not avoid the press, since the hearing had been placed on the court calendar, which was public. Even the underground garage was covered by the TV cameras, and it took both Stone and Manolo to keep them from following the group into the elevator.

There was another gauntlet to run, between the elevator and the courtroom, but Stone was relieved to see Felipe Cordova sitting outside the courtroom, with Brandy Garcia at his side. Brandy winked at him as they passed. Stone told Isabel to wait to be called, then he took Arrington into the courtroom, where Marc Blumberg met them at the defense table. Dino and Mary Ann found seats. Stone set down his briefcase and a shopping bag he had been carrying.

"Okay, we've been over this," Marc said to Arrington. "You'll testify as before, unless . . ."

"Unless what?" Arrington asked.

"Unless you've regained your memory."

She shook her head. "I don't remember anything after that Friday night, until I woke up in the clinic."

"Just checking," Marc said.

The judge entered, and the bailiff called the court to order.

"I'm hearing a motion to dismiss this morning, I believe," the judge said.

Marc Blumberg rose. "Yes, Your Honor. I would ask that the District Attorney's office present its witnesses, followed by defense witnesses."

The judge turned to the prosecution table. "Ms. Chu?"

The young woman rose. "The District Attorney calls Detective Sam Durkee."

Durkee took the stand, and under questioning, established that the murder had taken place.

When it was Marc Blumberg's turn, he rose. "Detective, you've testified that Mr. Calder was shot with a nine-millimeter semiautomatic pistol."

"Yes."

"Did you find the weapon?"

"No."

"Did you search the Calder house and grounds thoroughly?"

"Yes."

"How many times?"

"Three, over two days."

"And no weapon?"

"No."

"Did you search any other house for the weapon?"

"Yes, we searched the home of Felipe Cordova, the Calders' gardener."

"Oh? When?"

"Yesterday."

"I'm glad you got around to it. Did you find the weapon?"

"No."

"Did you search the house or grounds of Beverly Walters?"

"No."

"Why not?"

"Because she's not a suspect."

"I see. You say you searched the Calder house thoroughly. In your search, did you find a white terrycloth robe?"

"No, but I wasn't looking for one."

"When you arrived at the Calder house and first saw Mrs. Calder, what was she wearing?"

"A bathrobe, or a dressing gown, I guess you could call it."

"What was it made of?"

"I'm not sure; some sort of smooth fabric."

"Could it have been either cotton or silk?"

"Yes, I suppose it could have been."

"Could it have been terrycloth?"

"No, I'm sure it wasn't."

"What color was it?"

"It was some sort of floral pattern, brightly colored."

"No further questions."

The D.A. called the medical examiner and elicited testimony on the autopsy results, then, "Your Honor, the District Attorney calls Beverly Walters."

Beverly Walters appeared through a side door and was sworn. Chu began by taking her through her previous story of having heard Arrington threaten to kill her husband, then she continued. "Ms. Walters, where were you on the afternoon of the evening Vance Calder was murdered?"

"I was at the home of a friend, at a swimming party."

"And after you left the party, where did you go?"

"I went to Vance Calder's home."

"And how did you enter the grounds?"

"Through a rear entrance."

"Did you ring the doorbell?"

"No, I entered through the door to the pool and sneaked into Mr. Calder's dressing room."

"Was Mr. Calder present?"

"Yes."

"Where was Mrs. Calder?"

"She was taking a bath, I believe. That was what Mr. Calder told me when I spoke with him earlier."

"Having reached the dressing room, what did you do?"

"Mr. Calder and I made love."

"In his dressing room?"

"On a sofa in his dressing room."

"Was this the first time you and Mr. Calder had made love?"

"No, we had done so on a number of occasions."

"And where did these trysts take place?"

"In his trailer at Centurion Studios, in his bungalow there, and at his home, always in his dressing room."

"On the earlier occasions, when you made love in the dressing room, was Mrs. Calder present in the house?"

"Yes. We timed the meetings for when Arrington was in the tub. When they went out in the evenings, she was as regular as clockwork; she'd spend half an hour in the bath."

"Why did you take these risks?"

"Vance found it exciting, knowing that Arrington was in the house. He loved taking chances."

"After you had made love that evening, what did you do?"

"When we had finished, Vance began getting dressed and said I should leave, that Arrington—Mrs. Calder—would be getting out of her bath soon."

"And did you leave?"

"Yes, I left through the same door I had entered by."

"And after leaving, did you have occasion to return to the house?"

"Yes."

"Why?"

"I heard a gunshot."

"How did you know it was a gunshot?"

"I didn't, at first, but when I peeked back through the glass doors, I saw Mr. Calder lying on the floor of the hallway. Mrs. Calder was standing next to him, holding a gun in her hand."

"She was just standing there? Was she doing anything else?"

"She was screaming at him."

"What was she saying?"

"I don't know exactly; it was pretty garbled. I did hear her say 'son of a bitch.'"

"Was Mrs. Calder directing this abuse at Mr. Calder?"

"Yes. There was no one else there."

"What did you do then?"

"I ran back to the car. I didn't want Arrington to shoot me, too."

Stone glanced at Arrington. Her face had reddened.

Chapter 60

CHU TURNED TO THE DEFENSE TABLE. "Your witness, Mr. Blumberg."

Marc stood. "Mrs. Walters—it is *Mrs.* Walters, isn't it?"

"Yes," she replied, her mouth turning down.

"What were you wearing on this occasion?"

"I wasn't wearing anything," Walters replied. There was a titter among the reporters present.

"I mean when you arrived at the Calder residence. What were you wearing then?"

"I was wearing a robe. I had removed my swimsuit in the car."

"What sort of a robe?"

"A terrycloth robe."

"What color?"

"White."

"Did the robe have a hood?"

"Yes."

"When you left Mr. Calder's dressing room, you were wearing the white terrycloth robe with the hood?"

"Yes."

"Was the hood up?"

"Yes, my hair was still wet."

"You and Vance Calder argued on that occasion, didn't you?"

She looked startled. "I don't know what you mean."

"He was all finished with you, wasn't he? And he told you so?"

"No, *I* told *him* we were finished."

"And he didn't like that?"

"No, he didn't."

"So you did argue."

Walters flushed. "If you could call it that."

"No further questions," Marc said. "I ask that the witness be instructed to remain available; I may wish to recall her."

"The witness will remain available," the judge said.

Chu stood again. "The District Attorney calls Felipe Cordova."

The bailiff brought Cordova into the courtroom; he was sworn and took the stand.

"Mr. Cordova," Chu said, "you were gardener to the Calders?"

"I cut the grass every week."

"Were you present at the Calder residence on the evening Mr. Calder was murdered?"

"Yes."

"For what reason?"

"I was looking to steal something, if I could." He didn't appear to be embarrassed by this answer.

"Did you have occasion to approach the rear door of the house and look inside?"

"Yes."

"Why?"

"I heard a noise, like a gun."

"When you looked inside, what did you see?"

"I saw Mr. Calder, lying on the floor bleeding, and Mrs. Calder standing there, and a gun was on the floor."

"And what did you do?"

"I ran. I didn't want to be caught there."

"Your witness," Chu said to Blumberg.

Marc stood. "Mr. Cordova, you say you saw Mrs. Calder standing next to Mr. Calder's body?"

"Yes."

"How was she dressed?"

"In a bathrobe."

"What kind of bathrobe?"

"You know, the terry kind."

"Terrycloth?"

"Yes."

"What color?"

"White."

"Did the robe have a hood?"

"Yes, she was wearing the hood."

"Did you see her face?"

"Not exactly."

"Was she facing you?"

"Not exactly."

"Well, if you didn't see her face, how do you know it was Mrs. Calder?"

"I seen her before, you know, and I recognized her shape." He made a female shape with his hands, and the courtroom tittered again.

"Since you never saw her face, is it possible that the woman you saw was not Mrs. Calder, but another woman?"

Cordova shrugged. "Maybe."

Marc turned to the judge. "Your Honor, could we have Mrs. Walters back for a moment to try something?"

The judge waved both lawyers forward. "Just what do you want to try, Mr. Blumberg?"

"I'd like for Mrs. Walters to try on a robe for Mr. Cordova."

"I've no objection, Judge," Ms. Chu said.

"Go ahead. Bailiff, bring Mrs. Walters back to the courtroom."

Beverly Walters returned, looking wary.

"Mrs. Walters," the judge said, "I'd like you to put on a bathrobe for the court."

Walters nodded, and Stone handed Marc a white terry robe. He held it for the woman, and she put it on.

"Please put up the hood, step out of your shoes, and face the rear of the courtroom, Mrs. Walters," Marc said. She followed his instructions, and he turned to Cordova. "What about it, Mr. Cordova? Could this be the woman you saw?" He made the woman shape with his hands.

"Yeah, she could be," Cordova said.

"No further questions," Marc said.

Ms. Chu was on her feet. "Your Honor, now I'd like for Mrs. Calder to try on the robe for Mr. Cordova."

"Any objection, Mr. Blumberg?" the judge asked.

"None whatever, Judge."

The courtroom watched as Arrington slipped into the white robe and turned her back on Cordova.

"Mr. Cordova," Chu said, "could this be the woman you saw?"

Cordova nodded. "Yeah. I guess it could be either one of them; they look pretty much the same."

"No further questions, Your Honor. That concludes the District Attorney's presentation."

"Mr. Blumberg," the judge said, "do you have any witnesses?"

"Your Honor, we call Isabel Sanchez."

Isabel came into the courtroom, was sworn, and took the stand.

"Your Honor, my colleague, Mr. Stone Barrington of the New York Bar, will question this witness."

The judge nodded assent.

"Mrs. Sanchez," Stone began, "are you and your husband employed by Mrs. Arrington Calder?"

"Yes, we are," Isabel replied.

"How long have you worked for her?"

"Since she married Mr. Calder. We worked for fifteen years for him before they married."

"Do you, personally, perform the duties of a maid in the household?"

"Yes."

"Do your duties require you to deal with Mrs. Calder's wardrobe?"

"Yes, I do her laundry—her underthings and washables—and I gather things to be sent to the dry cleaners and an outside laundry."

"Would you say that you are familiar with Mrs. Calder's wardrobe?"

"Oh, yes, very familiar. I know her clothes as well as I know my own."

"Tell me, does Mrs. Calder own a terrycloth robe?"

"Yes, she does. She has terrycloth robes for the guest house, four of them, for the two bedrooms."

"What color are the guest house robes?"

"They are bright yellow."

Stone held up the white robe. "Is this Mrs. Calder's robe?"

"No."

"Of course not, since it was bought yesterday at the gift shop of the Beverly Hills Hotel. Does she own one like it?"

"No, she doesn't."

Stone went to the shopping bag and pulled out a bright yellow robe. "Is this the color of the guest house robes?"

"Yes."

He handed her the robe. "Take a look at it. Is this one of the guest house robes?"

Isabel examined the robe and its label. "Yes, it is."

He held up the two robes together. "These robes are very different colors, aren't they?"

"Yes, they are."

"Could you mistake one of these robes for the other?"

"No, they're different colors."

Stone held up the white robe. "Does Mrs. Calder own a robe this color?"

"No, she does not. Mrs. Calder never wears terrycloth, even around the pool."

"Do you know why?"

"She doesn't like it; she likes Sea Island cotton or silk. I've never once seen her wear a terrycloth robe."

"No further questions, Your Honor," Stone said. "And that concludes our presentation of witnesses.

"Ms. Chu, closing?"

Chu stood, looking chastened. "We have nothing further, Judge."

"Mr. Blumberg?"

"I believe the evidence speaks for itself, Your Honor. The District Attorney's own witnesses have exonerated my client."

"Mr. Blumberg, I believe you are correct. Your motion for dismissal of charges is granted, with prejudice." He turned to the D.A.'s table. "Ms. Chu, I believe you and the police may wish to speak further with Mrs. Walters." He rapped his gavel. "Mrs. Calder, you are free to go, with the court's apologies. Court is adjourned."

Arrington stood and turned to Marc and Stone. "What does 'with prejudice' mean?"

"It means the D.A. can't bring these charges against you again. You're a free woman."

"If it's all right," she said, "I'd like to leave by the front door."

"I'll tell Manolo to bring the car around front," Stone said.

She grabbed Stone's hand, and they made their way through the crowd of press. He passed Dino. "Follow Manolo in your car," he said. Dino nodded and, with Mary Ann, made his way from the courtroom.

"Mrs. Calder will have a statement on the front steps of the courthouse," Marc shouted over the din, and the press dutifully followed them outside. Microphones were set up on the steps, and Marc shouted for silence.

He faced the reporters, apparently relishing the moment. "Justice has been done," he said. "Arrington Calder is a free woman, and I only wish the police and the District Attorney's office had done their work earlier, instead of waiting for us to do it for them. Now Mrs. Calder would like to say a few words."

Arrington stepped up to the microphones. "I want to thank my attorneys, Marc Blumberg and Stone Barrington," she said. "But I have no thanks whatever for the media, who have made my life a living hell these past weeks. These are the last words I will ever speak to a camera or a reporter. *Good-bye!*" She stepped back.

Suddenly, a reporter in the front of the group held up a tabloid newspaper. "Mr. Barrington!" he shouted.

Stone, who had been about to lead Arrington away, turned and looked at the paper. What he saw was himself and Betty Southard quite naked, covering half the page. Both were looking at the camera, and black bars covered strategic areas of their bodies.

"Oh, shit," Stone said, involuntarily.

Chapter 61

ARRINGTON TOOK ONE LOOK at the paper and stalked off. Stone followed her as quickly as he could, with reporters shouting questions at him from both sides. He got Arrington into the rear seat of the Bentley, but before he could climb in, she slammed the door and hammered down the lock button. Stone was left on the sidewalk, surrounded by cameras and screaming reporters.

Marc Blumberg grabbed his arm and pulled him toward the curb as Dino and Mary Ann drove up in the Mercedes station wagon, and they both got into the rear seat. Dino drove away, while reporters scattered from his path.

"You can drop me at the garage entrance around the corner," Marc said.

Dino glanced back at him. "Congratulations; you sure nailed Beverly Walters. How did you know she and Vance had an argument?"

"I figured he dumped her. *Everybody* dumps Beverly, sooner or later, and I figured she didn't like it. At least, she admitted to an argument." Marc turned to Stone. "By the way, I had a call early this morning from my attorney friend in Milan, about the possibility of divorce."

"And?" Stone asked.

"The news isn't good. In order to get a civil divorce in Italy, the two of you have to appear before a magistrate and mutually request the action."

"Can't I sue?"

"Yes, but in a contested divorce, you'd have to subpoena her, and you can't do that in the United States. You'd have to serve her in Italy."

Stone winced. "Good God."

The car stopped at the entrance to the garage, and at that moment, there was a ringing noise.

Marc took a small cellphone from an inside pocket. "Yes?" He smiled broadly. "Sure, I'll see her. I'll go right now." He closed the phone and stuck it back into his pocket. "That was my office," he said. "Beverly Walters has been arrested for Vance's murder, and she wants me to represent her."

"Are you going to?" Stone asked.

"Sure, why not? Since the charges against Arrington were dismissed with prejudice, there's no conflict. Anyway, it's an easy acquittal."

Mary Ann turned around. "Acquittal? After what was said in court today?"

"Sure. My guess is that, since she wasn't a suspect, she was never Mirandized, so everything she told the police and everything she said in court is inadmissible. The only testimony against her is Cordova's, and he's already admitted that he couldn't distinguish between Beverly and Arrington in the robe."

"What about Vanessa Pike's murder?" Stone asked.

"There's no evidence against her," Marc replied, "or they would already have arrested her. Anyway, she may not have murdered Vanessa."

That was true, Stone thought, and the other possible suspect was in a mental hospital.

Marc opened the car door and offered Stone his hand. "Thanks for the fun," he said. "Now I've gotta go see my new client."

"And thank you, Marc. I'll get you a check tomorrow."

Dino drove away and pointed the car toward Bel-Air. "Hey, what was all that crowd of reporters after you about?"

Stone sighed and told them what had happened.

"Did Arrington see the paper?"
He nodded. "I'm afraid so."

They arrived back at the Calder house to find Manolo loading suitcases into the Bentley.

"Manolo," Stone asked, "is Mrs. Calder going somewhere?"

"Yes, sir," Manolo replied. "But you better ask her about that."

"She certainly packed fast," Stone said.

"Oh, she packed before we went to court," Manolo said. "And on the way home, she called Mr. Regenstein from the car. The Centurion airplane is waiting for her at Santa Monica."

Stone went into the house, followed by Dino and Mary Ann. Arrington was coming out of the bedroom. He stopped her. "Can we talk?" he asked.

"I don't think we have anything to talk about," she said. "I'm going to Virginia to be with Peter and my mother, and I don't know when I'm coming back. Why don't you join Betty Southard in Hawaii? The two of you were made for each other. Or, perhaps, you could move in with Charlene Joiner."

He took her arm, but she snatched it away.

"Good-bye, Dino, Mary Ann," she said, kissing them both. "I'm sorry your stay wasn't as pleasant as it might have been."

"Don't worry about it," Dino replied.

"Something I want to know," Stone said. "The amnesia: Was it real?"

"It was at first. After I came home from the clinic, everything gradually came back to me."

"So what happened that evening?"

"I don't think I'm going to tell you," she said. "You still think I might have killed Vance, don't you?"

"No, I don't."

"Sure you do, Stone. Anyway, you'll never know for sure, will you?" And with that she turned and walked out of the house. A moment later, the Bentley could be heard driving away.

Isabel came into the room. "Lunch is served out by the pool," she said.

Dino took Stone's arm. "Come on, pal. You could use some lunch, and probably a drink, too."

Stone followed him outside, and the three of them sat down. Isabel brought a large Caesar salad with chunks of chicken and served them.

"You did very well this morning, Isabel," Stone said. "Thank you very much."

"All I did was tell the truth," Isabel replied. She opened a bottle of chardonnay and left them to their lunch.

They chatted in a desultory way about the events of the past weeks, and Stone felt depressed. He finished his salad and tossed off the remainder of his wine. "Excuse me a minute," he said, getting up. "I have to make a phone call."

"There's a phone," Dino said, pointing at the pool bar.

"This one is private," Stone replied. "I'll go inside." He went into the living room and looked around for a phone, but didn't see one, so he went into Vance's study and sat at the desk. Someone had left the bookcase/door to the dressing room open. He got out his notebook and dialed.

"Hello?"

"Betty, it's Stone."

"Well, hello there. I heard about the court thing this morning on the news. Congratulations."

"Thanks, but Marc Blumberg carried most of the water. Listen, I called about something else, something you have to know about."

"Dolce's dirty pictures? I probably saw them before you did; it's earlier here, remember?"

"I'm so sorry about that, Betty."

"Don't worry about it; it's made me a lot more interesting to people here. I've already had three dinner invitations this morning."

Stone laughed. "You're amazing."

"I don't imagine the pictures went down quite as well for you. They must have caused problems."

"Well, what can I do about it?"

"Treasure the photographs, sweetie; I will. Bye, now."

Stone hung up laughing. Then he noticed that something seemed to have changed in the dressing room. He got up and walked through the doorway. The dressing room was empty of all Vance's clothes; only bare racks were left. The chesterfield sofa, where Vance's trysts with Beverly Walters had occurred, was all that was left in the room.

He was about to turn and go back outside to join Dino and Mary Ann, when he remembered something. He walked to Vance's bathroom, looked inside, then down the little hallway that separated it from the dressing room. He had noticed something odd here before and had forgotten about it.

He went into the bathroom and, with his outstretched arms, measured the distance to the door from the wall of the bathroom that backed onto the dressing room. Holding out his arms, he walked into the hallway and held his arms up to the wall of the little corridor. Then he measured the distance from the wall containing the dressing room safe to the door, and marked that off on the corridor wall. Most people wouldn't have noticed, he thought, but with his experience of remodeling his own house, he had. The wall containing the safe appeared to be about eighteen inches deep, instead of the usual four or six inches.

He went back into the dressing room, trying to remember the combination to the safe. "One-five-three-eight," he said aloud, then tapped the number into the keypad and opened the door. The safe was about four and a half inches deep; it was the kind meant to be installed in a standard depth wall between the studs. Or it appeared to be. He rapped on the sides of the safe, which made a shallow metallic noise, then he rapped on the rear wall of the safe, which made a deeper, hollower sound. Something was very odd here.

He rapped harder, and the rear wall of the safe seemed to move a little. Then, with his fingertips, he pressed hard on the rear wall. It gave an eighth of an inch. Then there was a click, and the seemingly fixed steel plate swung outward an inch. Stone hooked a finger around the plate and pulled it toward him, revealing a twelve-inch-deep second compartment in the safe. Inside, Stone saw two things: Vance Calder's jewelry box and a nine-millimeter semiautomatic pistol.

"My God!" he said aloud. "Arrington killed him." Then from behind him, a male voice spoke.

"I thought so, too."

Stone turned to find Manolo standing there. "What?"

"When I found Mr. Calder dead, I thought Mrs. Calder had shot him. They had had a big argument about something earlier; there was lots of shouting and screaming. It wasn't their first."

"What have you done, Manolo?"

"When I heard the shot and found Mr. Calder, the gun was on the floor beside him, where whoever shot him had dropped it. I thought Mrs. Calder had done it, and my immediate thought—I'm not sure why—was to protect her. So I took the gun and put it in the hidden compartment of the safe, and, so the police would think it was a robbery, I put his jewelry box in there, too, and closed it. They never figured it out."

Stone took a pen from his pocket, stuck it through the trigger guard of the pistol and lifted it from the safe. "Then it will have the fingerprints of the killer on it. Now we'll know for sure who killed Vance."

Manolo shook his head. "I'm afraid not, Mr. Barrington; I wiped the gun clean before I hid it. I was so sure that Mrs. Calder had done it. Of course, after this morning in court, I don't think so anymore."

"Does Arrington know you hid the pistol?"

"No. I never told her."

Stone put the pistol on top of the chest of drawers, then, weak at the knees, sat down one the sofa. "So we'll never know for sure."

"I know," Manolo said. "I'm a little surprised that you don't, Mr. Barrington." He picked up the pistol by the trigger guard, put it back in the safe's rear compartment, and closed it.

"I'll leave it there for a while, then I'll get rid of it and send the jewelry box to Mrs. Calder."

Stone was beyond arguing with him.

Chapter 62

STONE STAYED IN L.A. for a couple of more days, paying the last of the bills to come to the bungalow and seeing that Vance Calder's estate was released to Arrington.

After he had packed his bags and was ready to leave the bungalow, Lou Regenstein came into Vance's study.

"Good morning, Lou."

"You on your way home, Stone?"

"Yes, I'm done here. Louise can pack up Vance's things and send them to the house. Manolo and Isabel are still there."

"Have you talked to Arrington?"

"No, she isn't speaking to me."

"I should think she'd be grateful to you for everything you've done for her."

"Maybe, but there are other things she's not grateful to me for."

"The business in the tabloid?"

Stone nodded. "Among other things."

"Well, I want you to know that I am certainly grateful to you. Arrington is now the second-largest stockholder in Centurion, after me, and together, the two of us control the company. If she'd gone to prison, God knows what would have happened here."

"I'm glad it worked out all right."

"Is there anything I can do for you, Stone?"

"You can have someone drive Vance's car back to the house," he said, holding out the keys.

Lou accepted the keys. "I'll have my driver take you to the airport." Lou picked up the phone and gave the order. "He'll be here in a minute."

Stone looked around. "What will happen to Vance's bungalow?"

"Charlene Joiner is moving in, as soon as we've redecorated it to her specifications. She's Centurion's biggest star now."

"She deserves it."

They chatted for a few minutes, then Lou's chauffeur knocked at the door. "Shall I take your bags, Mr. Barrington?"

"Yes, thank you." He shook hands with Lou. "Thanks for all your help."

"Stone, you'll always have friends at Centurion. If there's ever anything, anything at all, we can do for you, just let me know."

"When you speak to Arrington, tell her I'm thinking of her."

"Of course."

Stone left the bungalow and was about to get into Lou's limousine, when Charlene drove up in a convertible.

"Leaving without saying good-bye?" she called out.

Stone walked over to the car. "It's been a weird couple of days; I was going to call you from New York."

"I get to New York once in a while. Shall I call you?"

He gave her his card. "I'd be hurt, if you didn't." He leaned over and kissed her, then she drove away. Before she turned the corner, she waved, without looking back.

Stone got into the limo and settled into the deep-cushioned seat. He'd be home by bedtime.

Back in Turtle Bay, he let himself into the house. Joan had left for the day, but there was a note on the table in the foyer.

"A shipment arrived for you yesterday," she wrote. "It's in the living room. And there was an envelope delivered by messenger this morning."

Stone saw the envelope on the table and tucked it under his arm. He picked up his suitcases and started for the elevator, then he looked into the living room and set down the cases. Standing in the center of the living room was a clothes rack, and on it hung at least twenty suits. He walked into the room and looked around. On the floor were half a dozen large boxes filled with Vance Calder's Turnbull & Asser shirts and ties. Then he noticed a note pinned to one of the suits.

You would do me a great favor by accepting these. Or you can just send them to the Goodwill.

I love you,
Arrington

His heart gave a little leap, but then he saw that the note was dated a week before their parting scene, and it sank again.

He'd think about this later. Right now, he was tired from the trip. He picked up the suitcases, got into the elevator, and rode up to the master suite. Once there, he unpacked, then undressed and got into a nightshirt. Then he remembered the envelope.

He sat down on the bed and opened it. There were some papers and a covering letter, in a neat hand, on Eduardo Bianchi's personal letterhead.

I thought you might like to have these. This ends the matter. I hope to see you soon.

Eduardo

Stone set the letter aside and looked at the papers. There were only two: One was the original of the marriage certificate he and Dolce had signed in Venice; the other was the page from the ledger they and their witnesses had signed in the mayor's office. These made up the whole record of his brief, disastrous marriage.

He took them to the fireplace, struck a match, and watched until they had been consumed. Then he got into bed, and with a profound sense of relief, tinged with sorrow, Stone fell asleep.

Acknowledgments

I AM GRATEFUL to my new editor, David Highfill, and my new publisher, Phyllis Grann, for their enthusiasm and hard work on this book. I look forward to working with them both in the future.

I must thank my agents, Morton Janklow and Anne Sibbald, and all the people at Janklow & Nesbit, for their continuing fine management of my career and their meticulous attention to every detail of my business affairs.

I must also thank my wife, Chris, who reads every manuscript, for her good judgment and acute insight, as well as for her love.

Author's Note

I AM HAPPY to hear from readers, but you should know that if you write to me in care of my publisher, three to six months will pass before I receive your letter, and when it finally arrives it will be one among many, and I will not be able to reply.

However, if you have access to the Internet, you may visit my website at www.stuartwoods.com, where there is a button for sending me e-mail. So far, I have been able to reply to all of my e-mail, and I will continue to try to do so.

If you send me an e-mail and do not receive a reply, it is because you are one among an alarming number of people who have entered their e-mail return address incorrectly in their mail software. I have many of my replies returned as undeliverable.

Remember: e-mail, reply; snail mail, no reply.

When you e-mail me, please do not send attachments, as I *never* open these. They can take twenty minutes to download, and they often contain viruses.

Please do not place me on your mailing list for funny stories, prayers, political causes, charitable fund-raising, petitions, or senti-mental claptrap. I get enough of that from people I already know. Generally speaking, when I get e-mail addressed to a large number of people, I immediately delete it without reading it.

Please do not send me your ideas for a book, as I have a policy of writing only what I myself invent. If you send me story ideas, I will immediately delete them without reading them. If you have a good idea for a book, write it yourself, but I will not be able to advise you on how to get it published. Buy a copy of *Writer's Market* at any bookstore; that will tell you how.

Anyone with a request concerning events or appearances may e-mail it to me or send it to: The Publicity Department, G. P. Putnam's Sons, 375 Hudson Street, New York, NY 10014.

Those ambitious fold who wish to buy film, dramatic, or television rights to my books should contact Matthew Snyder, Creative Artists Agency, 9830 Wilshire Boulevard, Beverly Hills, CA 90212-1825.

Those who wish to conduct business of a more literary nature should contact Anne Sibbald, Janklow & Nesbit, 445 Park Avenue, New York, NY 10022.

If you want to know if I will be signing books in your city, please visit my website, www.stuartwoods.com, where the tour schedule will be published a month or so in advance. If you wish me to do a book signing in your locality, ask your favorite bookseller to contact his Putnam representative or the G. P. Putnam's Sons Publicity Department with the request.

If you find typographical or editorial errors in my book and feel an irresistible urge to tell someone, please write to David Highfill at Putnam, address above. Do not e-mail your discoveries to me, as I will already have learned about them from others.

A list of all my published works appears in the front of this book. All the novels are still in print in paperback and can be found at or ordered from any bookstore. If you wish to obtain hardcover copies of earlier novels or of the two nonfiction books, a good used-book store or one of the on-line bookstores can help you find them. Otherwise, you will have to go to a great many garage sales.